THINGS PEO
THIS

It's exactly the right size to stick under the wobbly table leg of my office desk.

LONGTIME READER, FIRST-TIME BLURB WRITER

So many words!

SOMEONE TOTALLY NOT A FAMILY MEMBER

This story fills all its pages from margin to margin all the way through the book. It's like magic, only on paper.

A REAL READER

THE SHARP EDGE OF YESTERDAY

A ROUGH PASSAGES NOVEL

K. M. HERKES

DAWNRIGGER Publishing

THE SHARP EDGE OF YESTERDAY

Print ISBN: 978-1-945745-18-8

Electronic ISBN: 978-1-945745-17-1

BISAC Subject Data: 1. Fiction-Fantasy-Contemporary 2. Fiction-Dystopian 3.Fiction-Fantasy-Urban 4. Science Fiction-General

Cover artwork and design by R. J. Taylor

Published by Dawnrigger Publishing

dawnrigger.com

Printed in the USA

DEDICATIONS

For Paul, my beloved first reader. This book took more nurturing than most, and I would have given up on it a thousand times if not for your steadfast support.

All honor and respect to Tess, Emily, Berni, Jen, Mary, John, Shannon, Deb, Alice, Sharon, Megan, Rhiannon, Tina, Cheryl, Deirdre, and a host of others.
You cheered me on, listened to me read aloud and rant, re-read draft after draft, created new art for me, and in countless other ways fueled the creative fires where this novel was forged.
Thank you from the bottom of my heart.

THE SHARP EDGE OF YESTERDAY

1: THE WISE ACCEPT COMMAND

March 19, 2017, near Louisville, Kentucky

JACK SAW the billowing column of smoke the instant he materialized in Wilton Ridge, Kentucky—and that was all he saw before being blinded by the afternoon sun glaring down on the teleport pad. He moved to the edge of the raised concrete circle to clear the way for his partner's arrival, reaching into his suit jacket for his protective glasses as he went.

The dark lenses dimmed the light to bearable levels, and he took in the scene below the smoky sky: a narrow road full of moving cars and moving people.

Sirens wailed, adding high notes to a rumbling background hum of raised voices and revving engines. A crowd was gathering in front of a retail strip hugging the side of the road.

He bit back a curse. He'd hoped the emergency dispatcher from Intake was exaggerating when she delivered her sketchy mission brief, but no. He'd seen plenty of clouds and crowds like these during his hitch in the Marines. His current employer's record for disaster prevention was about to take a hard hit.

The Department of Public Safety called all spontaneous power onsets *hot* rollovers, but Jack would bet his upcoming hazard pay the person at the center of this evacuation was a new pyrokinetic talent. And when someone's rollover status unexpectedly shifted from *potential* to *active* in a fire-related ability, matters could get out of hand fast.

His partner Heather was going to be peeved. She grabbed every weekend shift she could because Intake reserved difficult cases for weekdays. Or as Heather put it, "The brass don't like missing tee times or brunch reservations, so they make sure the barn's closed up tight by end of business Friday."

As her trainee, Jack didn't have any choice about his assignments, but he'd had no complaints until now. They both had promotion exams coming up, and the hours between quick clean-up retrievals were great for studying. It was overtime with an automatic hazard bump too.

This time, though, collecting a citizen overdue for DPS reassignment wouldn't be fast or easy. Today they were going to earn every penny of that extra pay.

This will be like closing the barn door after the cow has burned down the barn and the rest of the farm too.

He couldn't go anywhere until Heather arrived, but he could get his bearings. Visualizing the map he'd been shown before transit, he checked the coordinates stenciled on the teleport pad. His temper flared as soon as he oriented himself in relation to the incident site.

"Seriously, you fuckers? Two miles out?"

The snarled words alarmed a nearby group of retreating civilians. They veered off the sidewalk, scattering across the parking lot to avoid him, and Jack kicked himself for losing control. This was no time to be scaring the nulls.

Still. Two *miles*? The DPS teleport crews never got him and Heather as close to assignments as he would've liked, but this was a new record. How could they *neutralize threats to the public in a timely fashion, with compassionate discretion and in accordance with relevant federal regulations* when they never arrived anywhere near their targets?

DPS regulations limited agent drops to official transit pads. That was why.

Jack knew that, but the knowledge didn't stop him from hating rules that got the way of doing the right thing. Any half-competent Marine Corps 'porter could've landed him within ten yards of the dispatch address. *And* they could've put him there with his sunglasses on his face, a detail the DPS 'porters seemed unable to master.

A Corps-style blind transit might've planted him partially underground or left him twenty feet in the air on arrival. But he'd be within sight of the poor P-series newbie accidentally incinerating their surroundings right now, and that was what mattered. Why couldn't the DPS make exceptions for people who could handle a bad drop?

Hell, he was *built* for rough landings.

When he rolled into his T-series power ten years ago, he'd ended up eight feet tall in his socks, strong enough to bench-press a car, and tough enough to stop bullets with his bare skin. His senses also extended well beyond null human norms, he regenerated fast enough to survive almost any imaginable injury—and that was in resting mode.

When his adrenaline got flowing—like, say, *now*—his body channeled energy into boosting his physical abilities. He tongued the tip of one elongating canine tooth and tasted blood, clenched fists until the thickening claws pricked his palms. *All pumped up and nowhere near the action. Stupid rules.*

He suppressed the urge to hit something. It wouldn't help, and he would have to face an Administrative Board for property damage. Besides, he wasn't being fair. The vast majority of

DPS employees were powerless nulls who couldn't survive being encased in something solid for a few minutes. The rules were designed to protect them.

But it also wasn't fair that Perry Franklin—age 52, asset manager, home address in Saint Louis, Missouri—was facing the worst day of his life and endangering everyone around him for an unknown range without support. Jack could be giving him that help right now if anyone on the civilian side understood the concept of ASAP.

It might be an institutional problem. The DPS was tasked with identifying and isolating at-risk citizens before their midlife superpowers arrived, and that was a long, slow process by design.

Diagnostics built in ample time for appeals, challenges, and re-testing between the date someone was classified a rollover risk and the date they began safety internment. No one liked sitting on a DPS camp bunk with their life on hold. The uncertainties of rollover made it necessary, but everyone wanted to be sure, first.

Current blood tests could not predict what *kind* of abilities someone would develop or exactly when rollover would arrive. But once someone's R-factor numbers began climbing, they gave an accurate picture of how *intense* their power would be.

The higher that level, the faster people ran out of appeals and challenges before Intake sent a collection team to their front doors. That skewed nearly all missed-rollover incidents to the lower end of the power spectrum.

Emergency Intake teams handled that deadly sliver between nearly and all.

How long since he'd arrived? How soon would Heather reach him?

Her talent for bystander-safe teleportation usually balanced out the conservative DPS transits. Her range was under a half-mile, and she could barely carry Jack one blink a day, but that was usually enough to get them straight to a dispatch address from the drop. Not today. And Jack couldn't do anything until the DPS 'porters got their asses in gear and sent her here.

They could've sent Heather *with* him, but no. Regulations prevented that, too. The rules were made by nulls for nulls, and they called for strictly-separated arrival times.

Never mind that Heather's kinesthetic senses protected her from arriving in an occupied space no matter who was 'porting her. One full minute between 'ports—that was the rule.

Jack ran the numbers in his head.

The incident clock would have started when the Wilton Ridge police called for Department of Public Safety backup. The message would've taken a minute to filter through channels to the regional office in Elgin, Illinois, where he and Heather were based. Figure another two minutes between the alert reaching the ready room and them getting to Transit. A minute for transit prep, and two minutes more to run through these absurd arrival protocols.

At best they were six minutes into the red zone. The chance of mass deaths was getting higher by the second. Casualties could rack up fast when someone's power came on hot.

He counted off seconds with impatience boiling up in his veins and brightening everything in his field of vision. "Come on, Heather, come on. Move it."

She popped into existence on the target pad, facing him, wings spread wide to correct her balance as her body solidified from thin air. The wings curved over her head once she folded them back. Her bright-yellow avian eyes, the golden-brown feathers covering her visible skin, and tufted plumage where most people had ears completed the impression of an eagle stretched into human form.

"Hi, Junior." She hopped off the two-foot drop from the pad

to the sidewalk, tugging at the hem of the specially-tailored gray blazer she wore over a blue blouse and gray trousers. "Why the big frown?"

He pointed to the sky above the trees behind her. "That."

And I hate it when you call me Junior. He didn't say that aloud. He couldn't deny the accuracy of the nickname. Heather was the senior agent, plus she was nearly thirty years older than he was. But he didn't appreciate the implication that he was immature and reckless.

When he was feeling brave enough to tease back, he called her Beakybird. It probably wasn't helping change her mind about the immaturity.

The pupils of Heather's eyes pulsed in and out as she took in the height of the smoke column. "Nuts. That looks like a literal hot rollover."

"Yeah, and we're here, not there."

Her wing feathers rustled as she planted her fists on her hips. "If you make one more complaint about Department 'port regs, I will leave Limburger in your locker."

That was a potent threat, and he knew from experience she would follow through. "You complain about the 'porters all the time."

"That's professional criticism. You're whining." Heather looked down her nose, which was a neat trick considering she was looking up a good two feet. "Apologize, or we go nowhere."

Senior agent. Training agent. Jack sighed. "Sorry. Now can we please go?"

"Sure. Hang on." Heather grabbed Jack by the arm and raised her wings, then grimaced and folded them back. "Rats. We're two miles out."

"I could've told you that. And I know you can't haul me there. I'd be sprinting already, but I had to wait 'til you got here safe. 'Port on ahead, I'll catch up."

"No. We stick together start to finish. Regulations." She pointed one taloned finger at him, "And do not say a word about it. Let's get moving."

She turned and started walking. The extra weight of her wings and the keel-like sternum anchoring their muscles made her gait awkward and slow. Jack clenched his teeth and passed her in four steps. His body density was too high to travel fast without putting a boot through the concrete, but long strides added up.

Heather made a rude noise at his back. Displaced air popped loud, and she reappeared ten yards ahead, at the corner onto a neighborhood street full of houses. Excess energy dissipated in a sunrise-colored flash, and a puff of cold, mint-and-rose scented air wafted back past Jack.

Every time, the scent was different. Heather had no idea why. Neither did anyone else, just like no one knew why some R-active people could see energy fields and others could not. Over half a century since First Night, mysteries still outnumbered the explanations.

When Jack passed her again, Heather said, "There's no point in rushing. If it's gone as critical as it looks, the Marines are there already."

"So what? You know what else is in those safety regs? 'The DPS is responsible for direction and support during Mercury Battalion deployments.'" Jack left her behind. "If we used Corps protocols, we would be on scene now."

"You're a civilian now," she called after him. "Get used to it."

"No." His temper bubbled, seething hot. He turned. "Look. I know I never got much schooling, and you have more life experience than I'll ever have, but you are wrong about this. I've been on the other side of it."

He'd rolled at a neighborhood baseball game, surrounded by family and friends, and he'd only been a kid. In the rare cases when powers came early, they always arrived without warning and manifested in destructive ways. Early-onset rollover also led to an early death, but that was a different problem.

The important part was that the DPS had arrived five minutes too late to save his father.

Collateral damage was the first military term Jack had learned, long before the DPS sent him from safety internment straight into the Marines. He'd never blamed the Mercury response team. He'd flattened three people before they arrived. If they hadn't acted, he might've mowed down dozens more in his pain and panic.

But if someone from the DPS had *been there*, maybe his dad wouldn't have tried to defend him from the Marines.

Heather stood there being silent and judgmental, so Jack asked, "What if it was your husband rolling up there, huh? What if it was your kid? Would you be yanking my chain then? Would you be *walking?*"

Power thumped in his blood, ached in his spine, begging to be released. More bad memories jabbed at him, and his vision went red at the edges. The R-powered Marines in Mercury Battalion were trained to protect the general public, not to help the unlucky souls caught in the throes of a power's untimely, uncontrolled arrival. They took fast, decisive action unless otherwise ordered.

While he and Heather were arguing, his old squad mates or soldiers like them might be acting as executioners because the DPS valued the lives of its agents above the lives of the people they swore to serve.

Safety first, my ass. He turned and started running, pavement be damned. He didn't have a family because the DPS put rules before people. He was never going to have a chance to get old, and he would rather lose his whole damned salary to fines than think about the past or the future.

Pop. An icy blast of fruity air blew into his face as Heather arrived in front of him. He wrapped his arms around her and skidded to a halt, carrying her forward. The tops of her wings tickled his face, and the sidewalk buckled underfoot.

Energy from her arrival streamed away like bright mist as Jack set her down. She glared up at him, and the feather-tufts that marked her ears slanted back. "Low blow, Junior."

"Truth hurts." He brushed a stray feather off his cheek. "Do you have any idea how many people die because Mercury is lousy at wait-and-see ?" *Too many.* "I don't want more deaths on my conscience, and the whole system is rigged against me, and it makes me want to scream."

"I know. I'm sorry. If it was up to me, I'd do things differently." She shrugged, wings and shoulders both. "But I can't change the rules any more than I can walk faster."

"I can go faster." Jack went to one knee. "If you won't blink ahead, then hitch a ride."

Her eyes went wide, and the pupils pulsed in and out. "Seriously?"

"Careful of the suit." Some Tees had mixed feelings about being ridden. Most of his dorm mates at Camp Butler had bitched nonstop during exercises where they had to carry other troops. He couldn't understand the fuss. Pretending he wasn't big enough to handle a rider or two wouldn't make him any smaller.

Heather put one foot on his belt and stretched to grab the shoulders of his suit jacket. Both taloned hands gripped tight. Once her feet were secure, Jack rose and took off at a flat sprint. Heather shouted in his ear over the crunch of his footsteps. "They're gonna charge you for that pavement if you're wrong about this."

"I'm not wrong." The incident clock was closing on nine minutes. Chances were good they were too late already. Block after block passed in a blur of people and cars moving the other direction until Heather shouted, "Get ready!"

Jack stopped moving. Heather tightened her grip on his shoulders and swept her wings up. Displaced air boomed when she snapped them down.

The world vanished. It was like falling through the night sky —plunging through endless, ice-cold, windy blackness.

Reality came back in a whoosh of icy brightness. The abrupt shift from dark to daylight made his eyes ache. His feet hit pavement, and a roar of sound assaulted his ears. The air tasted like ashes.

"Close enough for you?" asked Heather.

She'd brought them to the edge of the bullseye. Ahead, only a cluster of emergency vehicles and a narrow stretch of lawn separated them from the burning skeleton of a one-story brick building.

The Marjorie Miller Community Center—the name of the place according to a decorative brick sign by the sidewalk—was a total loss. A wide doorway and two rows of windows glowed like orange holes in the thick black smoke obscuring the building's remains. When the wind gusted, bits of melted metal beams poked out of the spinning cloud. Flames blazed high above the shell of the building and far out to the sides, lashing through the smoke. The top of the column was so high now that prevailing winds were flattening out the top like a thunderstorm.

The noise of it was deafening.

Fire sites were always loud. That detail never ceased to surprise Jack. They also stank in a particular way. The stench of burning plastic and concrete mixed with the odors of diesel fuel and fearful people: that was the signature smell of a pyrokinetic coming into power without warning.

No one was screaming. That was a good sign. So was the

unnatural nature of the blaze. The bushes and playground equipment beside the building were gray with falling ash but not seared. Sheets of colored paper skated over the ground, dancing in the wind created by the heat, not burned to cinders. None of the neighboring suburban tract homes or landscaping had been touched by flame.

Fire personnel shouted orders to one another, wrestling with hoses and directing water onto the closest roofs. They wouldn't be in full prevention mode unless they were confident about the main fire. That was another good sign. The fire department's talents weren't holding things in check, though. A few of the crew displayed the tell-tale auras of R-active power, but none wore a licensed active-practitioner's badge.

The Mercury response unit had to be doing the containment, but where were they? A pyro rollover rated at least a squad-level deployment, and this was Gateway Company's back yard. Gateway's roster ran heavily to Tees, and it was hard to hide a group of Tees in the open.

"Where are the Marines?" Heather asked, echoing Jack's thought as she slid off her perch on his back. "No liaison?"

"They must have their hands full, or they would've sent someone around." Jack looked up into the haze-clogged air. "Unless they're up top. We—*they* monitor crowded sites from the air if they have flyers or K-primes on the roster."

"And this is a crowd. No press, though. Can't hate that." Her crest flattened. "Oh, crap, press coverage. Somebody needs to call in a PR team."

"Not me." He didn't pretend disappointment. Trainee rank did have a few benefits.

She waved her hands. "I know. It can wait until we check in."

Police cruisers, doors blazoned with *Lafayette County Sheriff,* blocked the street at both ends. Deputies were wrangling a mob of spectators behind a tape line near the end of the block.

Nothing drew a crowd like a dramatic emergency, but this one was larger than average.

Some of the people carried signs that read, "God won't save you, Science will!" "Love Means Letting Go," and "Keep Families Safe!" They were being herded down the street away from the scene. Others were carrying placards that proclaimed "Prayer not Prisons," "Citizens For Choice," and "Freedom Not Fences." Most of them were being loaded into police vans.

"A camp protest?" Heather picked up one of the pieces of paper littering the sidewalk. "Yup. Flyers with today's date. Just what this situation needed."

Jack glanced at the hostile proclamations. The kind of person who objected to rollover quarantine was also the kind of person who would appeal their camp assignment to the fullest extent of the law, even if they endangered themselves, their families, and the general public.

"Probably what caused the situation," he pointed out.

"Good point. Oh, the delicious irony." Heather crumpled up the flyer. "That guy over there looks official. He might know what's up."

A tall, lean man wearing a suit and a sheriff's badge on a lanyard was approaching from the police line. His thinning black hair was lank with sweat, and he stank of fear. Jack couldn't blame him for that. He was clearly a null, with no hint of an energy aura. If the containment did fail, he would be dead before he knew it.

Dedicated, defenseless first responders like him surrounded every scene like this. They were the reason military response teams were authorized to end catastrophic rollovers if necessary, by any means necessary.

On paper, the Department was responsible for making those elimination calls. But as Jack was learning, the DPS gamed the system so that the Marines ended up with the burden of guilt.

It made him furious again when he thought about it, so he shut it out of his mind.

The sheriff introduced himself. Jack promptly forgot his name. Heather pulled her DPS badge from her jacket pocket and flashed it for him. After offering her name and Jack's, she said, "This site is under Public Safety jurisdiction as of now. Evacuation and containment are in progress?"

"We called a quarter-mile perimeter soon as we heard it was a pyro, and we'll keep pushing out until we get an all-clear. A buncha tro—" the sheriff's eyes flicked up at Jack, and he swallowed the word *troll* "—er, T-series Marines—dropped straight in a couple minutes back. The fire hasn't spread an inch since then, but the flames and smoke are getting thicker."

"That's not good," Jack said. It meant the pyro was pulling fuel from the air and the earth below the building. "That's really not good, Heather. Water table protection is a priority. If you don't veto lethal measures *right now,* we might not have anyone left to detain."

"Cool your jets, Junior. I've got this." Heather pulled her radio phone from its holster on the back of her belt. After collecting the local channel codes from the sheriff, she engaged the speaker function. "All receiving, DPS Intake Senior Agent Gardner assuming scene control. Op-four restrictions are now in force. Mercury, please confirm and identify."

A familiar voice came over the speaker. "DPS, Staff Sergeant Amy Goodall confirming for Mercury Response two-sixteen out of Gateway. Copy non-lethal measures, exceptions for imminent breach or direct attack. Any help for us from your side?"

Heather's wings flicked out and back. "I am too flammable for this event, but I have a reserve Mercury lieutenant I can detach to you. T5-Y Jack Coby?"

"Hell, yes, send him in! Any info on the firestarter will help too. He's communicating but combative."

Heather's ear tufts flattened. "Copy that, DPS out." She holstered the radio and nodded to the sheriff. "You heard her. We have his name. Diagnostics & Tracking got a facial recognition hit from a witness snapshot. Can you give us anything more?"

"Not much to tell, sorry." The sheriff ran a hand over his hair. "Most I can say about the guy is that he's not from around here. None of those no-good radicals will admit knowing him. Patio out back was ground zero. Local kids were doing a family support fundraiser. Protesters came from someplace over by Louisville. No casualties reported yet, but it's early."

"That's more than we had before. Thanks." Heather made a shooing motion at Jack. "Go on, help get him cooled off so we can get him away to a camp. If we're quick, we might even get in and out before any reporters arrive."

2: HATRED STIRS UP CONFLICT

March 19, 2017, somewhere near Louisville Kentucky

JACK TOOK OFF RUNNING. Heather was an optimist. They would never get this situation resolved fast enough to avoid the press. Reporters descended on scenes of blood and violence faster than flies got to dead bodies.

The firefighters waved him past without challenge. Looking like a storybook troll did come in handy at times. No one questioned his presence in places like this.

Given a choice between preserving his civilian clothes and getting around the building faster, he cut in close to save a precious minute or two. It would take a lot more than fire to destroy his Mercury-issue underlayer, boots, and protective glasses. Those covered the essentials, and that was what mattered now.

The putrid smoke obscured his sight, and he barreled through a wash of flame that charred his suit and shirt in seconds. The Department would cover the cost of replacement. He hoped.

His skin sizzled and popped too, but regeneration outpaced the damage well enough to keep the sensation to a tickle. It would take a much hotter fire than this one to penetrate his baseline armor, and he was already pushing rollover energy into his body as fast as he could to build it up. And with any luck, he would catch an energy boost from the Tees up ahead any second now.

Between one step and the next, the sizzling sensation in his lungs and skin vanished, replaced by a rush of exhilaration. *There they are.*

The Tees in the nearby Mercury squad were already pumped up to maximum power. The energy inside him recognized theirs and lifted him to their readiness level in a single heartbeat.

Null biologists called it a pheromone reaction. The physicists said it was energy transfer. Whichever it was, Jack had sorely missed sharing in it these last few months.

Smiling down at civilians and getting them safely through Intake was fulfilling, but action was easier than advocacy any day. It was also dangerous and sometimes excruciating, but at least when a crisis was over, it was done.

He should have argued harder when the brass suggested he leave the ranks and experience the world before his condition killed him. So far, he was not enjoying civilian life enough to make it worth the aggravation. Who would've guessed how much he would miss putting himself in harm's way?

A few more steps brought him around the back corner of the building. Smoke still obscured the view as he crossed a silvery line of melted fencing, but dots of rollover power appeared one by one ahead of him, too intense to be blocked by the haze. The spacing was a familiar pattern: seven tight points of energy bracketing one gushing fountain of it.

And then he was into the clear again where he could get a visual on them.

Off to his left was a rolling playfield big enough for multiple soccer games. Craters marred the grassy surface. Two of the Marines must have landed there on arrival.

Clusters of people watched from the far side of the field, where the park met a line of houses. Reflected firelight glinted off rows of camera lenses, and boom microphones waved above the heads of the crowd.

Journalists were defying the evac order as usual. Was it courage or insanity to sneak into an area that might be incinerated at any moment? Jack had seen reporters do it a hundred times, and he still wasn't sure. He also wondered how many news outlets would feature his image tomorrow. *Here's hoping it's on a happy story this time.*

The points of power in the thinning smoke ahead of him resolved into the visible forms of seven Marines in Mercury combat gear. They were bracketing a blob of fire shaped like a tall, pear-shaped human being. That would be Perry Franklin, probable conscientious objector, who ought to be questioning his life choices right about now.

The man's blazing pose radiated belligerence along with heat, and the shell of the building behind him blazed furnace-bright.

The four Marines on Franklin's far side were outwardly identical to nulls. Only the intense glow of their power signatures gave away how high their rankings must be. Their series designations weren't obvious either, but their uniform flashes gave Jack the essentials: W1-X, two H2-As, and an S2-J. The prime wildcat's X variant meant her exact power would be unique but useful. The importance of the two water callers was obvious. The presence of the strongman—strong woman, to be precise—was more of a puzzle.

An S2 might have the muscle power to wrestle Jack to a standstill, but strength didn't get someone into Mercury Battalion. The corporal's J variant must make her tougher than she looked. That wasn't too high a bar to clear. She looked like Jack's tiny, fierce foster mother, who was seventy-eight years old and frail with osteoporosis.

The three closest Marines had the usual Tee features—dorsal spines, horns, massive muscles protected by turtle-like subdermal armor plating, and skin colors never seen in a null human. The biggest one of them moved to intercept Jack.

Rampage energy had added a good two feet of height to Sergeant Amy Goodall's twelve-foot baseline, and the cranial spines jutting through her custom helmet rose well above that. The spines were painted with glittery polish as usual. Pink, today, which Jack would never tell her looked garish against her gold-toned skin.

Jack didn't recognize the two other Tees, but their badges provided him with their classifications, ranks, and names: T2-J PFC S. Bisbee and T3 PFC A. Creswell. And the puppy-like way they were watching Amy marked them as a pair of shiny new boots, not transfers into Gateway or detached from another unit for this operation.

Even the shorter of the two newbies was head and shoulders taller than Jack. That was weirdly comforting. There was nothing like being around other Tees to remind him that he wasn't nearly as scary as nulls thought he was. His power ranking was at the low end of the scale, and his Y variant slot muted many of the typical series characteristics.

Amy was grinning from ear to ear when she reached Jack. She punched his shoulder hard enough to rock him on his heels, better than a hug any day. "Jackass! Not dead yet, and rocking a sweet set of abs, too. Both those things make me happy."

Count on Amy to kick a painful topic to the curb straight off. Jack grinned back, flashing fangs without concern for the first time in weeks. "I'm gonna live forever unless this site goes critical while you drool over me."

The other two Tees shifted uncomfortably foot to foot. Not used to people dissing the goddess in charge of their world. Amy's smile fell away. "No worries. Janet—my wildcat, there—has him boxed six by six in a forcefield, and she still has eight-plus minutes of juice."

"That's impressive." Holding elementals in check took a lot of energy. Janet had a phenomenal talent. "I was afraid we would get here too late to veto a takedown."

"Thank the lab coat brigade. We take Bell readings on arrival, these days, and he was close to cracking the limit. Current doctrine says fall back and minimize interference. It works. He's still not stable, obviously, but if he burns out now, he'll only kill himself."

"Better than the alternative." Elemental powers had a nasty way of consuming their wielders during rollover. If Franklin had hit the Bell limit, he would've spontaneously combusted and made a big glassy crater out of this block in the process. The recently-identified Bell series of power signatures was saving a lot of lives. "The world owes Kris a big one."

"I call her with a big thank-you after every field trip," Amy assured him.

The limit was named after Grace Bell, the woman whose fatal transformation from human being to splatter of magma led to the breakthrough. But their squad mate Kris Stanislav was the Marine whose helmet camera provided the critical data. She'd recognized the significance of the recordings while recovering from injuries she sustained during the incident.

Jack's debt to Kris was a more personal one. He would be

dead if she hadn't taken his place on that mission. "How much time can you give me to talk him down?" he asked.

"Five minutes on the outside." Amy said, "But I don't like your odds. He keeps calling us murderers and homewreckers. What's his damage?"

Jack passed along what little they knew about Perry Franklin, including his opposition to internment. "I'm not hopeful," he admitted, "but I have to try."

"Go for it. Janet's forcefield will pass you in. It's a doozy. Variable and gas permeable. Even if she could choke him out, she wouldn't. It's too early to tell if he's a T-variant, and—"

"—no one wants another Tucson," Jack recited along with her. "Got it."

Until the late fifties, denying out-of-control pyrokinetics access to oxygen and combustibles was considered the ideal containment strategy. When they fell unconscious, they either stopped burning or burned up. Either way, problem solved.

Tucson changed all that. The response team had deployed their telekinetic forcefields as usual, and the target pyro had passed out and combusted to ash. Everything was going according to plan until the instant they released containment and let air re-enter the hot zone.

The resulting explosion fused four square miles of desert into glass.

Biologists and doctors added a new variant to their P-series charts, and Mercury units developed a series of field maneuvers using a similar flashover effect. The mechanics of it still stumped physicists, which was a sweet bonus.

Jack studied his target. A real martyr wouldn't still be standing there. He would've come at the Marines already. "What else has he been saying, specifically?"

"He's mostly been shouting bits of the Constitution and

daring us to shoot him." Amy snorted. "As if a bullet wouldn't melt."

Frightened, desperate bluster. Jack could work with that. "And if I can't talk him down?"

Amy walked forward with him. "We run over you. Or Command scrapes up an area-of-effect 'porter and takes the conservative option."

Jack was damage-resistant, not invulnerable. Being 'ported to the bottom of the ocean or into orbit would kill him along with Franklin. "Guess that's why I get the big bucks. Define run over."

"On Janet's final ten count, me and the boys will charge while Jim and Jam hose him down. If the dogpile doesn't put him out, then Bev—her J variant makes her heat and cold resistant, among other bennies—moves in to knock him cold. Ugly but workable."

She and the other Tees might end up in sickbay after direct contact with a pyro this powerful, but Franklin was unlikely to survive being pinned down by three Tees and clocked by an S-series.

Amy gave Jack a pat on the shoulder. "Go make us unnecessary, will you?"

"I'm on it." He squinted at the pyro's blinding-bright form and thought of one last detail. "Heather needs to know about the voyeurs across the field."

"You didn't hear? Oh, right. No clothes, no phone." Amy stepped back. "They're leashed. DPS Regional Ops gave site exclusive to WLGN's hardened news team—which currently includes your two favorite local celebrities. They'll be popping in any second. Wrap this up with a bow, and you can have a nice reunion."

Oh, no.

His favorite celebrity was Elena Moreno, a thousand pounds

of trouble in a perky, one-hundred-pound package. She was sweet sixteen, as photogenic as the day was long and twice as stubborn. And she had a talent for putting herself in harm's way on camera.

Fuck. The personal stakes had gone way up. Jack moved toward Franklin with both hands spread wide. Power and fear pulsed through his blood. When he was close enough for the heat to blister his arms, he sat down—no point in looming over a man wrapped in a firestorm of his own making.

The news also gave him an angle to play. "Listen up, Mr. Franklin. I'm DPS Agent Jack Coby, and I'm here to lend you a hand getting out of this. I gotta tell you, if you thought you were in trouble before, you are in *big* trouble now."

Franklin said, "I won't let the government drag me away to rot in a camp. If you're going to murder me, do it here in the open. I'm not afraid to die."

"I respect that." Jack swallowed hard to keep from chuckling. Why did he want to laugh? *Damned nerves*. "But how do you feel about a live television interview with a pretty teenaged girl? Because that'll be happening in about two minutes."

"What? No! Who would send a child into this?" Darkness rippled through the flames obscuring the man's body. "Not even the Department of Public Safety is that depraved."

"No, sir, they are not." Jack looked over his shoulder. Amy gave him a thumbs-up. Containment was holding. "No one *sends* Elena into trouble. The hard part is keeping her out of it. She's interning with Brian Grimm, which means you'll end up talking to them both."

"Brian Grimm from TV?" Franklin's face showed through the flames, forehead wrinkled, lips pursed. "The late-night guy? The one who got outed as R-poz?"

"That's the one."

Elena's null status had been exposed at the same time as

Grimm's, not that she'd ever been shy about admitting it. Their confidential R-test results were published by a major news outlet—along with those of several thousand other people with high public profiles—after a malicious data breach. That was how they'd met.

"Brian Grimm." Franklin sounded awe-struck. "Coming here for me?"

"Yes." *Gotcha.* Radicals loved nothing more than publicity. "If you power down and play nice, I can guarantee they will give you a chance to complain about the DPS to a national audience. Isn't that what you want?"

Even if Elena wasn't eager for a chance to talk to this jerk—which she would be—she owed Jack. There were some advantages to friendship with someone who had a knack for getting people to point cameras at her.

"Hey!" Fire crackled. A jabbing finger emerged from the smoky column. "I know you, too! You were at the Middle School Massacre! Is Elena the little girl who was in that photo with you? She's the one who makes speeches about poz rights and rollover accommodations."

"Maria Elena Moreno. That's her." *That damned picture.*

The image had won its photographer a Pulitzer. There were seven people in it. Why did people only remember him and Elena? *Because she's unforgettable and you're huge,* he reminded himself. "And she'll be here any minute. Come on, man. Let the firestorm go and come in quietly. I promise no one will hurt you, but you have to shut this down, for safety's sake."

"Don't tell me what to do!" Flame roared up, licked outward. Jack tensed, nerves singing. He was turning to dive aside and clear the way for Amy when Franklin's voice rang out again—anguished, not angry. "I can't. If I stop, you'll drag me away to die. I can't go to a camp. I *can't.*"

"Are you sure? Tell me, where else would you go? You sound

like an educated man—a smart one. You must see you'll be a deadly danger until your power settles. What's wrong with getting free room, board, and fire-safe personal essentials along with a crash course in pyrokinetic control? You don't *want* to hurt other people, do you?"

"No! I never thought this would happen." The last bit was soft, nearly lost in the furnace noise. Was the whirl of smoke slowing? "I don't—she's a null—she can't come here. You can't let her."

"Have you ever seen a tsunami, Mr. Franklin? It's only water rising, but it keeps coming and coming, pushing aside anything in its way. Unstoppable. That's Elena. Time's running out. You want her to be safe? Douse the fire and stand down. Otherwise, those Marines behind me will have to shut you down."

"No, no! This is a mistake. Go away, all of you. Just—go!"

"The Marines can't stand down until this gets resolved. You choose how that happens. You can have a TV interview in protective custody, or you can get your ass handed to you in a nasty, pointless fight. Think it over, Mr. Franklin. Think hard."

Distraction was the easiest way to break a newbie's connection with their erratic new energy reservoir. Asking Franklin to think was like throwing a bowling ball at a juggler already balancing five knives. Jack felt zero guilt over it.

One way or another, Elena, I am not letting you walk into this red zone. Silence fell. Seconds ticked away, marked by crackles and pops.

The roaring chimney of flame vanished first, leaving the smoke hanging empty like a ghost of itself. The charred remains of the building crashed down in a series of horrendous brittle crunches. In the quiet of the fire's absence, cheers could be heard from the front of the building and across the field.

Next, the massive flow of power around Perry Franklin evaporated as if it had never existed, leaving him unprotected by fire or anything else. The man blinked at Jack—pale, paunchy, bald, and as naked as the day he was born beneath a fine dusting of gray soot—and hastily covered himself. "Aw, heck. Where did it go?"

"Back wherever you got it the first time," Jack said cheerfully. "You'll learn. But not here, and not now. For the record, are you going to let the DPS help you now?"

"Yes. I—I'm sorry. I never—please." His voice hitched up tight, and his face and chest flushed red. "I can't be on television like this. This is so embarrassing."

Rollover was a complicated process. Franklin's talent could surge on its own again at any moment. Or he might call it deliberately if he put his mind to it. Jack didn't think he would, though, not when he'd been handed the prize of an audience.

And if he flared now, the Mercury water-callers could quickly and easily suppress him before he worked himself into another firestorm.

Things were looking up. Jack grinned. "You want to borrow a pair of pants?"

3: MAKE YOUR STAND WHERE PATHS MEET

March 19, 2017, still near Louisville, KY

ELENA SMILED the way her PR coaches had taught her to do, projecting empathetic friendliness with all her might. "This has been a great conversation, Mr. Franklin," she said. "Thanks for agreeing to come away from the incident site to this quiet spot."

It was quiet because it was a cemetery. Behind Franklin, ornamental trees with bud-heavy branches cast deep shadows over new grass, spring flowers, and polished headstones.

And past his left shoulder was the local First Night Memorial, offering its silent testimony to the dangers of uncontrolled rollover. Elena watched the marble columns when she wasn't looking straight at the camera over Franklin's right shoulder. Focusing past his face was best for everyone. He felt seen, and she didn't lose her temper.

She said, "You've explained why you were here protesting the Public Safety protocols, and shared what it was like to hit onset in the middle of it. Has your opinion of the Department changed, now that you're using its services yourself?"

"Nah. I mean, lookit this outfit." Mr. Franklin tugged at the collar of his papery baby-blue coverall. The silver emergency blanket covering his shoulders crinkled. "Who spends good tax money on crap like this? I only let them take me because I didn't want bystanders to get hurt, and I did want to say my piece on TV. Doesn't make them more competent or less evil."

The fabric of his coverall sleeves steamed gently, and pale trickles of smoke rose from darkening patches on the foil blanket. Elena squeezed her hands together until they ached and gritted her teeth to keep from saying, *Are you serious?* out loud.

The Department of Public Safety had given him a decent uniform. It had given him *three.*

First, he'd incinerated a set of fatigues rated for top-level Mercury Battalion elementals. Then he'd flamed one set of emergency coveralls—which were rated to Mercury standards, according to their prominent labeling—in the middle of Elena's first interview take.

The fault was not in the clothes. It was in Franklin.

If not for the DPS's intervention and containment protocols, he might've killed and injured uncountable innocents. And if not for Federal laws the DPS had drafted and pushed to pass, he would be facing criminal charges for property damage and endangerment.

But did the man feel a shred of gratitude? Nope. He complained about his free clothing and leered at her while he did it.

She stared past him and willed the coverall fabric to last a few minutes longer. That bare, pasty-white body was the last thing she wanted to see a second time. She looked at the pretty scenery behind Franklin while she searched her mind for an acceptable response to his ingratitude.

Golden sunshine slanted between deep blue lines of cloud low on the horizon, touching the hilly landscape and monument with spots of color, reflecting off the metal benches placed along the curving drive.

Elena liked cemeteries. Once she was done with this disaster, she would reward herself with a walk through this one. After she finished with Mr. Franklin. "I appreciate your honesty," she decided was the best angle to take. "And I agree there are ways the DPS could improve. I like to think I've been a pretty vocal advocate."

"You sure are pretty," Mr. Franklin said with a chuckle. "And yeah, you're like a dog with a bone about poz rights. Thought that whenever I saw you on TV. Pushy, but pretty."

She chose to ignore the choice of comparison. "So we both want change. What changes would you want to see? Better integration programs, assignments, and training programs more responsive to personal needs, things like that?"

"Nope. No point in any of it," Franklin said easily. "Government has no business interfering with nature. The DPS is a tumor on the body politic that must be cut out."

Don't nod. It will look like agreement, she told herself. *But don't frown!* "I think the First Night casualties buried around us might feel differently, don't you?" she said. "The DPS isn't perfect, but it does save lives."

Franklin's gaze briefly rose higher than her chest, and his smile was indulgent. "You keep thinking that, honey. You're young. You'll learn."

She frowned before she could hide the burst of resentment. Being patronized was nothing new, nor was being ogled by men who should know better, but age had nothing to do with her viewpoint. *Crap.* She hadn't been this off-balance during an interview in ages.

And Franklin smirked at her.

His odor was part of the problem. He stank of bitter smoke and burned hair. Maybe he couldn't help it, but the stench empowered a host of bad memories, flashes of the bloody bombing aftermath that she couldn't suppress. The longer they talked, the harder her heart thumped, and she was cold despite the hot lights bracketing their makeshift set on the cemetery parkway.

There were still questions on her script, but she needed to end this now. "I hope I'll always try to keep an open mind," she said, just to keep things moving, but her mind went blank there.

What was her transition line? Would she look like a total incompetent if she glanced at her notes?

The WLGN camera operator's hand came into view, one finger turning in a circle: *wrap it up.* Hands. Right. "Do you have any last remarks before I hand the show back to Brian?"

"Can't think of a thing."

Thank you, God. She pulled her smile back into place. "So let's—"

"No, wait," Franklin said. "I should thank you for letting me have my say. You're a sweet little cupcake. Not obnoxious or stuck-up at all."

He beamed at her, and his pale, sweaty face gleamed under the lights.

Did he expect Elena to thank him? *Ugh. He does.* She stood up and walked off-camera, brushing past Brian on the way. The broadcaster moved in, notes in one hand, microphone in the other.

Brian's earnest energy always made Elena think of a happy poodle. He was a slight man with long, expressive hands and a pouf of brown hair waving around his face, and he bounced enthusiastically when he got excited. He bounced into the tall director's chair Elena had vacated, eager to throw a few softball questions at Franklin before putting in a pitch for the weekly interview show where most of this material would appear.

That was assuming the station's legal department let it appear anywhere.

Elena grabbed her backpack and suit jacket from the rental van the crew had used to get here from the original incident site. Then she strode toward a nice, remote bench near the memorial to wait for things to wind down.

The rest of the television crew would be driving home soon, but she wouldn't be leaving with them. Brian had arranged for her to catch a DPS teleport home so she wouldn't get in trouble for working too many hours.

It would be faster in the end, but it meant a longer wait at this end of the journey. Regulations would keep the DPS team and the Marines on-site until Transit received a destination address for Mr. Franklin and sent him on his way to camp.

That was *clearly* nowhere near happening. The portable telepad was still in its transport pod.

Three DPS Transit specialists in blue-and-gray uniforms sat on top of the crate and chatted with Jack's feathery new partner-slash-boss. Elena wasn't sure of their relationship. Jack wouldn't give her a straight answer about it.

Everyone else was standing carefully out of camera range, alert but relaxed. It wasn't a lot of people, but it had felt like a crowd while she was with Franklin. Now she was glad they'd been there. If the material was as bad as she suspected, they might be the only audience the interview ever got. *No. I am not thinking about that now.*

Jack turned to watch her as she passed by. His brow ridge wrinkled in concern over his sunglasses.

Ugh, from bad to worse. She wanted space and silence, not an eight-foot overprotective escort tailing after her. Jack worried about everyone, but he especially fretted over her. It was a massive distraction sometimes. He would be better once things calmed down, but right now? No.

Thankfully, Sergeant Amy turned when Jack did. She made eye contact with Elena over Jack's head and nodded in a way that was also a smile.

The Marine's skull spines and bone structure made her face hard to read, but Elena had the knack of it. Jack had first introduced them way back when Elena was in middle school because —as he'd put it—he needed a teen girl translation service.

Relief zinged through Elena when she saw Amy distract Jack with a remark and pull him back into the conversation. *Saved!*

She was better off by herself. Jack was better off staying with the Marines, standing at ease on the lawn in a set of too-big fatigues that suited him better than the suits he'd been wearing since he joined the DPS full time. Amy knew how to deal with him.

Amy was the coolest. She was *so* good with people. An interview with Amy wouldn't have gone wrong. *Amy* was likable.

Elena's emotions boiled up again. She groaned. If the interview did get shelved, she would have to take the blame for the extra expense of doing it here at the First Night Memorial instead of staying at the burned-out community center. *Just great. Another failure to worry about.*

It should've been a great idea. She'd made her case to the news team while they waited in the queue for a cargo transit 'porter back in Elgin. Brian had pitched his producer over the phone once he finished gathering candids from witnesses, while WLGN's camera operator collected imagery of the primary site, and the prep team got Perry Franklin cleaned up and ready.

Gross Perry Franklin who had ruined everything.

The soft grass was silent underfoot. Elena stomped hard on it until she reached a nice bench near the top of the hill. There, she rubbed at her cheek where Mr. Franklin had pinched it early on, like she was a kid playing at grown-up. *Ick, ick, ick.*

The metal slats of the seat pressed cold against her legs and shoulders. She leaned back and focused on the peaceful view.

At the top of the closest rise, white stone angels bowed at either side of the First Night Memorial. Beds of yellow daffodils and a rainbow of tulips bobbed in the breeze. The light had gone flat as the sun sank into the approaching clouds, muting the pastel colors of the plantings.

Elena pulled out her journal and special journaling pen. Her thoughts flowed onto the paper in angry scratches of purple ink. *The problem,* she wrote, *is that Mr. Franklin is a slimy jerk.*

Her therapist said to write down everything and not keep it bottled inside, but the words were ugly and mean. She crossed out the statement with big looping strokes until glittery purple ink filled in the gaps, until nothing remained of her opinion but a damp lavender rectangle. Then she capped the pen with vicious energy.

The blot looked angry and frustrated, exactly how she felt. She wanted to feel sympathy for people in Mr. Franklin's position, but how could she be compassionate when she was disgusted?

She uncapped her pen again. *Why Why WHY can't he be a nice person? It's hard to make people like a conceited, selfish, paranoid, politically ignorant CREEP.*

A gust of cold wind ruffled the page, damp with the odors of new-turned soil and manure from the farms they'd passed on the drive here. She held down the paper and gazed across the rows of headstones and into the sky. Her spirits lifted, and the tightness in her chest and shoulders eased as the guilt blew away on the chill air. *Much better.*

Some people thought cemeteries were creepy, even modern ones like this, with polished slabs and fresh-mown lawns. Elena liked them all. New or old, tended or neglected, they reminded her that life could grow despite being surrounded by death.

Maybe there was a good side to showing how rollover affected imperfect and unlikable people too. Maybe that would help nulls understand rollovers were like everyone else: strong, weak, pretty, ugly, nice, not so nice. Everyone deserved kindness.

The way Franklin had smiled when she'd said the DPS saved lives, with mockery and something bleak in his eyes—she shivered. There was so much fear and hatred in the world.

The breeze brought her the murmur of Brian's measured voice reading the wrap-up script as the sun sank behind him. The lighting tech was a genius. The broadcaster's face was perfectly illuminated against a backdrop of clouds that blazed red and orange as the sinking sun broke through again. This part of the segment would look spectacular, at least.

Too bad Elena couldn't say the same for the interview's subject, who was waiting off-set and uphill from the camera operator now. He stood in the center of a hollow square formed by Jack and the Tees from the response team. The Marine who could cast force fields—Jan—was facing him in that space, with the two water callers keeping watch on either side and the last woman backing them up.

Mr. Franklin kept his chin up and his head turned so he wasn't looking at anyone. He frowned at nothing while he held tight to the waistband and collar of his coverall. His expression reminded Elena of her little brother, Marco.

When Marco was in one of his bad moods, he scrunched up his face in exactly the same kind of pout. The difference was, Marco was nine years old. Also, when Marco sulked, he got sent to his room. Everyone here was bending over backward to keep Franklin as comfortable as possible under the circumstances.

Not that he appreciated it.

Papa would call him an ass. Elena sighed. Papa would also

remind her to forgive others for their frailties and not cast stones. He was annoying that way.

The hair on her arms rose, the air crackled, and Heather appeared on a swirl of cold air scented like clove and crushed pepper. Elena blinked dust out of her eyes and sneezed.

The woman looked exactly like a bird crossed with a person, pretty gold feathers catching the sunset glow as she tucked her wings back. Street lights lit up along the cemetery drive as she approached, and her big, rounded eyes went reflective for a second, like a cat's.

She must be glad she didn't get stuck with an actual beak. Elena pulled her thoughts into order. Was she about to be 'ported home early for acting like a sulky baby? *Probably.* "Are you angry at me for running away?"

"What? No!" Heather cocked her head to the side. "Why would you think that?"

"Because it was unprofessional and childish? I figured you were either here to lecture me about that, or because Jack asked you to keep a closer eye on me."

Heather laughed. "Jack, take indirect action? No. He was two seconds from barging over here himself, but the big Marine with pink horns hit him with a clue stick. This needs a woman's touch, I think. I offered to make sure you're okay." Her voice gentled. "*Are* you okay, sweetie?"

Elena wanted to say she was fine, but she wasn't. "I needed some fresh air," she admitted, which was true enough.

Jack must respect Heather. He wasn't good about tolerating people he didn't respect. Still, she was a stranger. Her round, intense eyes might look kind, but Elena couldn't just admit how *dirty* she felt. Or how incompetent. So she said, "The smoke got to me. I've had a thing about smoke ever since the school explosion."

Also true. Just not the whole truth.

"Fresh air, huh?" Heather tilted her head to the side. The pupils of her eyes pulsed in and out. "Me, I'd want a hot shower with all the soap and shampoo in the world after dealing with that turd. And I'd follow up with a bag of potato chips and a pint of ice cream to settle my nerves. Between you, me, and the gravestones here, that man could use a swift kick in the balls."

Elena choked on a giggle, and then, to her horror, she burst into tears. She gulped for breath and covered her mouth. "I'm sorry. I'm so sorry."

"For what? Oh, drat. May I?" Heather gestured at the bench, sitting down once she got a nod of permission. A neat maneuver put her wings over the back of the bench so she could lean in and get one arm around Elena. "There, now. Let it out. You won't shock Auntie Heather. I've spilled my share of rage tears."

The woman's wings blocked the wind, creating a warm, comforting shelter. Elena's breathing settled to hiccups, and she wiped her face dry. Being allowed to *feel,* without being judged or told what to do differently—the kindness of it made her start crying again.

Neither of her best school friends really understood this part of her life. She'd found a confidant in her previous internship mentor, but Valerie lived in California, thousands of miles away. Letters and calls weren't the same as hugs. They hadn't talked in days, hadn't seen each other in person since the end of that exciting summer trip, and seeing was everything for Valerie.

Heather lifted her wings and her arms at once and produced a tissue from a pocket on her belt. "Here you go. I have more if you need them."

Having a new friend would be awfully nice.

"Why was he like that?" Elena said when she had control of

her voice again. "Mr. Franklin, I mean. His horrible opinions, and the way he looked at me, all of it!"

"Like I said, he's a turdface." Feathers rustled as Heather shrugged. "He doesn't read like a perv, for what it's worth. Which doesn't make it right or make you feel any better."

"No, not really." She'd lost count of the rude things she'd heard from men since her boobs came in big, but it never got easier. "I did everything wrong."

"Heck no, you were fabulous. You left without slapping him or playing into his flirts. That's a miracle, in my book."

"Are you sure?"

"Positive." Heather scooted away, giving Elena more space and stretching her wings at the same time. "Every denier I've ever met was a slimeball. Almost makes me wish the Department could phase out the Registered Objector option."

Elena protested, "But that would make things worse! Most people don't opt out because they're paranoid like Mr. Franklin. Some RO's have religious or cultural reasons. Or personal ones, family or health, and none of that is any of the government's business."

Heather blinked rapidly. "Uh. That was intense. I'm not arguing, you know. I said *almost*."

"And I didn't mean to bite your head off." Elena's face went hot, but she refused to squirm. At least Heather wasn't laughing at her. "I get worked up about it."

"I'm not upset. Startled." Heather stroked the feathers on her throat. "It's easy to get cynical in this job. You're like, the opposite of cynical. It's refreshing."

That was encouraging. Elena said, "It doesn't have to be this bad. The DPS creates some of its own problems. No one I've ever interviewed wanted to go through rollover without help once it started. Mr. Franklin didn't roll the way he did on purpose."

"Are you sure? He's a radical, and radicals do things for attention."

Light and shadows flickered across the shrubs before Elena could answer. She turned to check on the interview site. Heather shifted to provide a view between her wings and shoulders.

The red light on the camera was dark, and the big set lights had gone off. Smaller floods came to life, driving back a smaller circle of dusk. The crew bustled about, rolling up cables.

Brian set down his microphone, and his smile disappeared as if he'd dropped it too, which made Elena suspect he was as unhappy with Mr. Franklin as she was.

A production assistant came bustling up with two paper cups of coffee. Brian took them and walked into the ring of Marines, where he offered one cup to Mr. Franklin. By that time, Brian's face was once again a study in concentrated sincerity.

The way he could turn emotion on and off like a faucet was a trick Elena *really* wanted to learn. It wasn't on her official list of educational objectives—academic enrichment was the official excuse for the current arrangement—but it would be more practical than most of the technical knowledge she would need for the mastery tests.

No one was leaving yet. Elena sat back again and answered Heather. "Yes, I am sure it was an accident. He wasn't so weird and defensive before the cameras went on. He kept apologizing for the damage he did and the people he scared. If he'd wanted to hurt people, he could've, and he didn't. He's not evil."

"Mm." Heather sniffed. "I still don't like him."

"I don't either!" Elena took a deep breath. Sighed. "That's what bothers me most. Rude and angry people deserve kindness too, but it's so much easier to make R-factor issues relatable when people are nice."

"And isn't that the sad truth," Heather said. "You're fighting human nature there. It's hard for *me* to remember, and I should know better. The more troublemakers I deal with, the more they annoy me. I can't wait to rotate out of Intake into Outreach. Probably shouldn't say that, but it's true."

Someday, Elena would solve the mystery of why people blurted out confidences to her. Today she jumped on the opportunity. "Are you rotating soon? I do a door-to-door canvassing project for Outreach every summer, and insurance says I have to have a full-time security detail because of, you know."

"Because of people a thousand times worse than Mr. Franklin? Yeah, I get that. How big of a detail is it? Just me?"

"Usually two. Is Jack rotating with you? If he is, I would ask for him too. He helped me with the first canvass, back when he was a Mercury liaison. Would you mind?"

"We're partnered through the end of the year, so that works out perfectly. Why would I mind?"

"Because it's boring? All you do is wait nearby while I go through neighborhoods and ask people's opinions."

"Sounds like a cushy gig to me." Heather shrugged, wings and arms both. "Sure, why not?"

"Excellent. I'll put in the app at the end of the school year."

"Please do." Heather hesitated. "I hate to ask this, but what if Jack's gone before summer?"

"I'll still ask for you." Elena felt a pang of sadness. She hated thinking about that. "But I hope he's with us forever."

"Me, too. He's a likable grump." Heather stood up. "I should get back. The assignment must've come through."

The crew in Transit uniforms were unfolding a metal frame beneath one of the street lights, and the Marines stepped away from Mr. Franklin, clearing him a path. He didn't take it. He stood unmoving with both Brian and the gray-haired woman Marine—Jan—talking to the sides of his head.

He looked crumpled and unhappy, small and slump-shouldered. Elena was reminded of Marco and his tantrums again. Her brother was the meanest little boy in the world when he was tired, or hungry, or frightened. Or all three at once.

Fear.

Her chest went tight. *Of course*. She would've put two and two together earlier if Mr. Franklin hadn't flustered her so much. Fear was the reason he had bounced so hard between being whiny and defensive.

Well. Part of the reason. He was a creep.

But he wasn't wrong.

Elena had lost track of the single valid worry in his paranoid claims. If Mr. Franklin died after putting his life into the hands of the DPS, he wouldn't be the first or the last.

Every organization has a few bad apples, people said, and *Accidents happen.* They responded to tragedies with, *it isn't perfect, but look at the good parts,* and asked, *What can you do?*

Good people worked for Public Safety, people who saved lives and made the world a better place—but the Department also let bad things happen. Elena knew that better than most, and someday, somehow, she was going to make it work better for everyone. Even the paranoid, creepy jerks.

But all the good intentions in the world couldn't make her like awful Perry Franklin.

"Can I stay over here until he's gone?" Elena asked.

"Fine by me." Heather twitched, then tucked a hand behind her back. "Sorry, phone call."

She pulled the device out of a belt pouch, and a muttering voice emerged when she unfolded it. She half-turned away to listen.

Elena pinpointed what looked wrong about Heather's head.

She didn't have *ears*. She had tufted openings that went well with the fine, tiny feathers covering her face.

Heather pulled the phone away. "I was half-right. Mr. I'm-Not-Evil's camp assignment came through, but he's refusing to sign his Transit papers. I have to go be persuasive. No reason for you to rush back, though."

She raised the phone again and strode off. Her wings flared to show a gorgeous mottled pattern of light and dark feathers against the last of the failing light.

Elena gathered her journal and bag. She wanted to know what was going on more than she wanted to avoid Perry Franklin. Curiosity was a more powerful than disgust. And no one would think her weak if she got creeped out and retreated again.

Heather was three steps away when she stopped in her tracks. Her wings drooped. "You want—he *what*?"

Another listening pause followed. Elena caught up, nodding silently when Heather raised a taloned finger at her.

She could wait. She might die of curiosity, but she could be patient.

"Sure, I'll ask." Heather closed her wings tight. Then she snorted. "No, Jackass, I'm not taking that bet."

The phone went back in its pouch. Heather cocked her head at Elena. "Jack says to tell you Perry Franklin says he trusts you," she said.

Ew. She couldn't say that out loud. "Should that impress me?"

"Ew, no."

That reaction made Elena certain they *were* going to be friends, but it didn't satisfy her curiosity. "Then why should I care?"

"Because it's the reason I'm about to ask a huge favor."

4: HUMILITY COMES BEFORE HONOR

March 19, 2017, a cemetery outside Louisville, KY

THE TELEPORTER In Charge gave Elena a thumbs-up from his ready position beside the portable Departure pad. "Ready when you are, miss."

He was tall and thin, like a scarecrow with gray, thinning hair and wrinkles around his pale blue eyes. The ID on his bright blue DPS lanyard read *TIC Ace Khan*.

"Thank you, Agent Khan." Elena climbed up three metal steps to the green-painted target grid. The blue-tinted light from the street lamp washed colors into shades of gray, and the air had gone from chill to cold.

As soon as the interview ended, the news team had packed up everything but the single light stand and camera before they motored sedately away. The cemetery was dark and empty now. Out in the distance, frogs were peeping at one another in a loud chorus.

Elena could barely hear them over the sound of her pulse.

Her heart was thumping harder than if she was in the starting blocks for a sprint race.

She'd been teleporting for a year now, ever since she turned fifteen and got her state ID, but every trip was still exciting and slightly scary. And this one would be extra-special. Not because it was on video—all Transit jumps were recorded—but because it had to look perfect.

The viewscreen on the simple fixed camera confirmed the pad was centered in the frame. Behind the tripod, the Marine response team stood in a shadowy arc, anchored by Jack and Heather at opposite ends.

They wouldn't let anything bad happen to her.

She beckoned to the real star of this little improvised show. "Come right up, Mr. Franklin. Take a good look at the set-up. Check out the Arrival pad too. You'll see it's totally ordinary and safe."

"That's what you'd have to say, isn't it?" Mr. Franklin said.

He walked around the portable pad and across the drive to the red-painted Arrival grid under the lamp there. Trickles of smoke trailed after him like wispy ghosts. He had on another new coverall, creased and free of soot. Elena was glad she'd missed that change.

Mr. Franklin took his time coming back and stood looking up at her—pale, sweaty, and shrugging. "I dunno. Doesn't inspire confidence. The whole idea's unnatural. I read about so-called accidents all the time."

The 'porter rolled his eyes and stalked off to join his assistants by the Arrival pad they'd called in and set up. Mr. Franklin squinted after him. "What's his problem?"

Elena's training said she should find a soft way to explain, to spare his feelings, but she was done with that. Politeness and sympathy hadn't worked. Maybe bluntness would. It was easier, anyway.

"That was rude," she said. "Porters take client safety very seriously. The whole point of this demonstration is to show you a teleport is safe. Do you want me to prove it or not?"

"I do, but—" Fear shimmered in his watery, bloodshot eyes, obvious now Elena was looking for it. His throat worked as he swallowed. "But I don't see how it'll be proof for me. I'm nobody. Worse'n a nobody, after today. I'm trouble, and I don't matter to anyone. I've got no family. If no one ever hears from me again, it'll make things easier, won't it? Who would care if I just—disappeared?"

And there it was, out in the open. Elena glanced at the waiting faces in the dimness behind the camera, saw concern in Jack's scowl, impatience in Heather's stance, and annoyance on the faces of every Marine except Amy, who only looked sad.

One emotion fed all their different reactions. Shame. They knew Mr. Franklin's fear was a legitimate one, even if he was wrongheaded about the how of it.

She couldn't give him reassurance, but she could give him something else to clutch and hold. Connections were powerful things, and she could give him one.

She might've become nasty like him if people had pushed her away instead of reaching out to her, once upon a time. "I would care," she said, and she would, although she wished he wasn't so horrible. "I would."

She sat down on the Departure pad steps to put herself eye to eye with him. "You know what I swear to myself every time I hear about a hot rollover going wrong, or accidents at camps, or hate crimes?"

"Can't say I do," Mr. Franklin said. "I bet you're gonna tell me whether I want or not."

"I promise myself," she said, gritting her teeth on *you jerk*, "that I will find a better way. I think it just like that. *I will find a better way*. That means caring."

She'd written it as *there has to be a better way*, on the first page of her very first journal. She'd gotten it the summer she turned twelve, after her therapist recommended she start a feelings diary.

That was the summer Mama had handed baby Marco to Papa, kissed everyone good-bye, boarded her bus for camp, and changed the family forever. It was the summer Elena's father rolled into power too, screaming and convulsing on the living room floor in a squelchy puddle of blood and fluid that ruined the carpet.

It wasn't fair. A big complicated organization she didn't understand had turned her Mama and Papa into strangers and destroyed everything good in her life. She'd struggled for a year, hating the way things were, wishing the world was better—until the day a Humans First terrorist group targeted her school and nearly blew her up.

And that day, Public Safety agents and Mercury Battalion soldiers had died to save her life. They'd done that because it was *what they did*. Not because she deserved it or to make people like them more. They'd helped because helping mattered.

She'd thought hard about what to do with the life they'd given their lives to save.

Change didn't happen *to* people. People changed things. If she wanted a better world, she should be making it herself.

Her first chance to step up came a week later. Her R-test came back negative, and someone leaked it to the public. The reporters who came hunting for a follow-up story expected her to be relieved. As if she could ignore all the scary issues about power onset, internment, and discrimination just because she wouldn't face them herself.

She'd shocked them when she talked about making a better,

safer world for everyone, null or poz, latent and active. A bunch had laughed that first time. She'd repeated herself until they understood she was serious, and she'd worked to prove it ever since.

She hadn't lived up to her own promises today. This was her chance to make up for it. *Make the truth do as much work as possible.*

"You matter to me," she said to Mr. Franklin. "Not because I like you, because I don't, to be honest. But if anything bad happened to you while you're under DPS protection—which it won't, but I'm saying *if*—I would not rest until you got justice. I swear that, and I keep my promises. Ask anybody."

It was the kind of statement that made Mama roll her eyes and mutter about melodrama. But sometimes, drama was the only way to get people to listen. To believe.

Franklin didn't roll his eyes, but he did sigh in that aggravating way old people did when they were about to pat Elena on the arm and tell her she was sweet or cute or *so young*.

But he didn't do that. The sigh became a sniffle, and he wiped brusquely at his face. "That's all on the video, right? Can I get a copy?"

"Yes, of course." She had no idea how to make it happen, but she would find out.

"Heard and witnessed, too," Heather said from the sidelines, with a rumble of agreement from one or more of the others. "No one gets disappeared on our watch."

"Come on, people, enough with the insults." Agent Khan stalked back to the Departure pad. "Are we doing this or not?"

"Sorry, Agent Khan." Elena stood and took a deep breath. That was a mistake because Mr. Franklin's smoky body odor filled her lungs. "I'm ready."

Her voice squeaked despite her best intentions. She cleared

her throat. *Looking and sounding like a mouse won't convince Franklin this is safe.*

"Confirm client ready," Khan said, walking back a few steps to face her, arms folded. "Center of the pad, please."

Elena set her feet at the middle of the target circle painted on the metal grid. "Okay."

"Perfect. We'll skip the rest of the preliminaries, given how short a hop it is. Don't you worry about a thing, Miz Moreno."

"I'm not worried." Elena looked over his head, over Mr. Franklin, to the rest of the audience. Amy smiled back, unabashedly flashing fangs, and Heather waved cheerfully. Jack peered at her over the tops of his sunglasses, looking only mildly aggravated, which meant he was happier than usual. That was nice.

Khan's expression went vague, and he held up a hand with three fingers raised.

The world got hazy around the edges.

Elena relaxed as much as she could. Her stomach tried to glue itself to her spine.

Any other day, she would be starving by now. The WLGN team had collected her before lunchtime, and it was past six o'clock. Right now, she couldn't imagine being hungry.

Getting the stench out of her hair was going to take hours.

This literally stinks. The thought made her want to giggle, proof she wasn't in control of her emotions.

Khan only had two fingers up now. The cloudiness thickened.

Some teleports were nightmares of bodiless, pure nothingness that took far longer in memory than the few seconds recorded between departure and destination. Others were like falling *up* and through invisible holes in reality. The worst ones were the blinks that took no time but left behind visions that made no sense.

And to complicate matters, people could react differently to the same teleporter's ability. Her 'port in with the WLGN crew had been a breeze, but she wouldn't know how this one would affect her until too late.

One finger.

Blink.

Reality turned inside out.

Elena floated in a vast empty space full of floating lights. Her insides lurched into her ribcage, her heart beat four times, five, and then it was over. Snowy-bright afterimages cleared from her vision.

She was on the Arrival pad, standing wobbly-kneed with her shadow stretching long across the grass in front of her until it merged with the night. She turned to face the Departure pad, then spun in a circle, arms spread. "See, Mr. Franklin? Safe as can be."

Mr. Franklin had his face scrunched up in that anxious pout again, and his eyes were glued on Agent Khan back at the Departure pad. The 'porter was running down Elena's post-transit checklist, ticking off boxes. The Marines moved in closer and spread out, encircling the pad.

When Heather and Jack approached, Franklin sidled closer to Agent Khan, saying, "That was something. You do that every day for real?"

"Yessir. Singletons only, line-of-sight targeting, but I'm rated for twenty one-shots per day, any destination distance. Sign off and step up. I'll take good care of you."

"Huh."

Heather said, "Time to go, sir. We held up our end of the bargain."

"You sure did," Franklin said. "But it—the thing is—"

"Don't you dare back out now!" Elena hopped off the Arrival

pad and walked back to the Departure unit as fast as she could without running. "You promised!"

That got a bristling reaction from Mr. Franklin. His lip trembled, but his chin came up. "I did, and I'm a man of my word."

"Okay. Good." She took the clipboard with the Transit paperwork on it from Agent Khan and shoved it at Franklin. "Prove it."

He looked down his nose at her, and one corner of his mouth twitched up. "You sure are a *feisty* little thing," he said, but he took the release form and signed it.

Jack backed off and made space for Elena at his side, and Heather stepped back too. Her wing feathers brushed Elena's other shoulder. Elena hoped they got to work together again in the summer. The three of them would make a *good* team.

Mr. Franklin handed the forms back to the teleporter, then glanced at Jack. "You weren't joking about her."

Jack took off his sunglasses, looked long and hard at the man, then bared his teeth. "I don't joke."

Franklin's eyes got wide. Elena glared up at Jack. "What did you say about me?"

He tucked the sunglasses into his shirt pocket and tried the bared-teeth thing on her. Not that she would ever be scared of him. She bared her teeth right back before mouthing silently, "I'll get you back."

Jack's not-a-smile turned into a real one. It was just too bad he was so light-sensitive. He had nice melty-brown eyes hiding behind those dark lenses.

Transit Agent Khan put on a phone headset and spoke quietly to someone. Mr. Franklin went to the center of the Departure pad and stood splay-legged, arms folded. "I think I'm entitled to one last question," he said. "If it's so safe, why did the police drive us here from the community center? Why did the news crew drive home?"

Finally, reasonable questions. Elena searched for words to simplify the complicated way the news station handled regional events. Amy beat her to the answer with a laugh. "Budget, man, budget! 'Ports are expensive, especially for businesses. Vans and trucks are cheap. Speaking of expenses—"

She lifted a plastic-wrapped bundle. "Last extra coverall from the incident pack. You might as well take it. If you don't, it gets pitched into recycling with the other leftovers. Safety regs, y'know?"

Her height made it easy for her to pass it across to Franklin at his level. He turned up his nose at the offering. Smoke wisped from the top of his head. "Throw it out, for all I care. I don't need that garbage."

A tiny flame flickered to life on his shoulder. Jan, the W-series Marine, gestured to her squadmates. Water poured over both of Franklin's shoulders, extinguishing the flare and soaking his coverall.

"Aw, hell." His cheeks went pink with embarrassment, and he shook his arms to flick water drops off his fingertips.

Amy gave the packet a friendly, inviting shake. "Think of it as insurance. Hell, give it away if you want. You'll find plenty of takers in any camp. Yeah, they're one-size-fits-none like hospital gowns, but it's obscenely expensive to make cloth this durable."

Mr. Franklin opened his mouth, shut it, and sighed. "Dangit. You won't say I'm being a stubborn jackass, but you're thinking it, aren't you?" He took the packet, hugging it to his chest and tugging at his collar with the other hand. "Look, I'm not a bad guy. Today's been one big mess after another, and my life's upside down, and I'm not my best, though. So I gotta be fair, y'all have been more than kind. Thank you."

He set his feet and braced his shoulders back. "All righty, I guess I'm ready."

His stance was belligerent, but his chin was quivering again. Elena finally found it possible to dredge up a little sympathy for him. A very little. "You'll be fine," she told him. "Remember my promise to you."

"Believe me, I'm thinking of it," he said. "I'm not a coward, I swear I'm not, but this goes against the grain so hard, I can't even tell you."

Agent Khan raised his hand. "Client ready and centered. Counting down."

Static crackled through the hair sticking to the back of Elena's neck.

Mr. Franklin's pasty-pale skin got paler. He ducked his head, staring at his feet. Sweat dripped down the sides of his face. The air rippled with heat.

He was *terrified*, and that was too much for Elena. She put on her make-people-happy smile while she brushed at her prickling neck. "Mr. Franklin, did you ever hear why I walked out the door to face that Humans First group the day my school got bombed?"

"No." Mr. Franklin looked up, met her eyes. "Why?"

Three. A bright mist rose up the man's legs, swirling to surround his body as it climbed higher. Elena leaned forward like she was about to share a secret.

Two.

She said, "I'll tell you when I get the invite to your camp graduation. See you then!"

One.

Mr. Franklin's lips curved up, the thickening mist obscured his face, and he was gone.

All the emotions and doubts Elena had been pushing down came roaring up in a big, complicated rush.

Her knees went wobbly. She sat right on the dirty asphalt drive and swallowed back a lump that threatened to turn into tears. "I want to go home. "

Jack touched her head with a careful finger. "Hey, tiger. Don't fall apart on us now. You did great."

"I don't care. That isn't the point." Her chest ached, and her head spun. "I shouldn't have to do things like this. No one should. *That*'s the point. If people had more choices about rollover, if it wasn't internment or nothing, this wouldn't happen so much."

Rollovers like Mr. Franklin's were vanishingly rare these days, but for every showy, dangerous, public incident, there were uncounted private tragedies like her Papa's change. They mattered too. "Regulations shouldn't hurt and frighten people. People shouldn't feel so trapped by them. Laws should make life better, not harder."

Heather made a sharp half-sneezing noise before speaking to Jack over Elena's head. "She's worse than you, Jack. Do either of you know how to dial down the intensity?"

"Not that I've seen," Amy answered from the other side of the Departure pad. "Say, Agent Gardner, can I hitch a ride back with your team? No point in duplicating efforts when we live in the same town, is there? I'm thinking takeout food and collaborating on reports at the far end."

"That is superior thinking," said Heather. "But why don't we hit the Owl's Nest? Good food and plenty of space in the party room."

Food. Elena's stomach chose to wake up

"Can I come?" Elena asked. "I can do my homework while you work. Papa will have Teresa and Marco in bed by the time we get back, and I don't—"

She just didn't want to go home yet. And now that the smoke was gone, she was *starving*.

Heather exchanged a look with Amy before nodding. "Sure, as long as it's okay with your parents, but first things first. Let's make sure we're clear to wrap. Agent Khan?"

"I'm on hold—no, here we go." The teleporter put one finger to his headset, saying, "DPS Field Transit Nine-six-niner confirms Garfield Transit Arrival report, client safe and sound. Best of luck with him, Garfield. Nine-six-niner Out."

He turned to Heather. "Clean intake, Agent. We can jump you home in five minutes." He strode away to help his assistants pack away the Arrival pad they'd used for the demonstration.

"Fantabulous." Heather clapped her hands and addressed the Marines. "Time to put a bow on it. Sergeant Goodall, Mercury is released. Thank you, good work, let's never do this again."

Amy put three extra steps between herself and the next closest member of the squad. "You heard the nice agent, people. You're dismissed, return protocol Alpha-six. I'll see you for unit debrief at oh-nine-hundred."

The other Marines clumped up, Tees in a circle around their smaller squadmates. They promptly vanished.

Jack growled. Heather slapped him with a wing. "Not. One. Word."

"Aye-aye, ma'am, not a word about regulations." He nudged Elena gently and gave her a big smile when she looked up. His dark eyes twinkled, warm and shining in the dim light. "But I'm on Elena's team. We need to find better ways to do a lot of things."

"Listen to you young hotheads." Amy loomed over them. "Come the revolution, don't forget your old friend Amy, okay?"

"I wish I could tell when you people are joking." Heather tucked her wings tight to her body and edged back so she was clear of both Tees. Elena had seen that defensive reflex from a lot of people but never understood it. She felt safer in Amy's shadow than anywhere else on the planet.

Amy rubbed one of the horns that curved down along her face. "I'm not laughing. More like suggesting interagency cooperation. Once you have some solid plans."

A tight, bright sense of excitement filled Elena's heart. "I have plans right now!"

"Of course you do," said Heather, and Jack laughed, and for a moment, everything was all right in the world.

5. EARS THAT HEAR AND EYES THAT SEE

March 19, 2017, DPS CA Region 20 Offices, Riverside CA

VALERIE WADE SIGNED into her workstation, set her #1 MOM travel mug on its coaster, and wiped her sweaty hands on her skirt as alerts and messages scrolled up her screen. *Compliance Assessment, Joshua Anthony Moretti E9-E, 19:00* topped her schedule.

The cafeteria sandwich she'd grabbed on her dinner break turned to a hard lump in her stomach. Everyone said the first Administrative Board interview was the hardest. She hoped that was true. With an hour left before her first solo evaluation, she couldn't imagine anything being harder.

No, that wasn't true. She'd survived worse. Childbirth. Leaving her husband. Burying her mother. But in work terms, this would be the hardest thing she'd ever done.

The computer hummed to itself, the only sound in the little room. Silence encouraged quiet whispers of doubt.

This comfortable, private office couldn't belong to her. How could she do a job that required a big desk, upholstered visitors chairs, and a glass door with privacy blinds? Until five years ago, she'd spent her workdays in a polyester uniform that stank like old grease.

Who did she think she was fooling?

Nervous energy drove her to her feet. She maneuvered around the desk, past the cabinet full of recording electronics, to stand at the door. Gathering her courage, she tugged on the cord to open the blinds.

In her nightmares, the staff on the main office floor—nulls, every one—would stand up, point across the rows of gray cubicles, and shout, "Fraud! Fake! You incompetent loser! Go back to the gutter, you pathetic old riffie!"

In reality, no one pointed or sneered. The aisles of grime-darkened carpet were a-bustle with day staff packing up and leaving. The smaller crew of night-shift operators was filtering in, ready to cover emergency calls. People glanced Valerie's way and waved.

Her rollover talent revealed the uneasy curiosity they hid behind polite smiles. Their true emotions veiled their faces like fog—but she could also see their concerns were minor and understandable. She was a stranger to them, and they were nulls. Of course they were nervous.

She blinked away the impression, oddly comforted. Everyone had fears.

She inhaled, held the air, exhaled. Again. And again, breathing out anxiety the way she'd learned in the therapy sessions every new Adaptation & Placement agent had to attend.

She'd switched career tracks three times since rollover, collecting promotions and commendations along the way. Her counselors believed in her. The least she could do was believe in herself.

The brighter glow of a friendly face caught her attention—

one of the scheduling assistants was waving good-bye to her. Valerie waved back, then froze mid-gesture.

Two state police officers stood in the reception area, near the formed-plastic seating across from the vending machine and its bracketing pair of potted palms. Valerie's interviewee sat in one of the plastic chairs. His back was perfectly straight, and his hands were gripped on his thighs, holding the metal chain from his leg shackles.

Valerie slid her gaze past Joshua Moretti's distinctive profile and silvering dark hair with a practiced lack-of-focus. Seeing too much too soon was the biggest hazard of having a sight-based power. He deserved her full focus when it came time to judge him.

Holding him to the original appointment felt rude, like saying, *my time is more important than yours*. The police escort must have made record time through traffic from Camp Belvidere. An hour was an uncomfortably long wait. Maybe she should call them in now and be done with it.

No. That would send the wrong message. Public Safety had jurisdiction, and the DPS didn't bend its schedules for anyone.

Let the police sip their coffee and cool their heels. Let Mr. Moretti sit and pray for a reprieve. Valerie would clear her inbox, and if that didn't fill the time, she might sneak in a phone call to the boys. Getting home after their bedtime was the worst part of working the evening shift.

She smoothed down her skirt before sitting again. The security login box sat dead center on her screen, ready for her ID and password. The file headers for Moretti's DPS record and the arrest report peeked over the top, and the first screen of the assessment form sat open beneath it.

The hardcopy for this case had been on her desk when she arrived today, along with a scribbled note from her boss, Grant, that read, "Time to leave the nest, Wade. We've got a Judicial

Branch request. CBI called for a Board on a domestic, and the panel wants an expedited evaluation. There's a slot open at seven, but I'm out at five. This one's all yours."

The Judicial Branch was a DPS appendix to the federal circuit court system. The powerful civilian agents of the Special Directives Unit assisted null law enforcement, while the secure DPS-mediated Boards decided on cases that could not be tried safely or fairly in a public courtroom.

On paper, Evaluation provided recommendations and expert witness testimony to the judging panels. In practice, they dismissed as many complaints as they passed to the Judicial Boards, and their judgments were often quoted word for word in the final verdicts.

Moretti was charged with empathic spousal abuse. Valerie would be deciding his fate.

Her fingers shook so much she had to enter her credentials into the login box three times. She pressed her hands to the cool desk surface on either side of the keyboard to stop the shakes.

She was not a brave woman: that was a truth she'd seen in her mirror long before she rolled into her power. She'd had it literally beaten into her by a bully who showed the world a smiling face and became a monster behind closed doors.

Could she face an abuse suspect and be objective? Grant thought so. But what if he was wrong?

Stop thinking that way. You can do this. She touched the framed photos of Johnny and Gary next to her desk screen. She'd carried the weight of their lives for years, and she'd gotten less training for being a parent than she'd been given for this job.

If she wasn't ready now, she never would be. One long look would show her whether Joshua Anthony Moretti had criminally misused his powers. After that, she would be on the familiar ground of assigning codes to descriptions, filling out forms, and checking boxes.

Do the work. Let the rest take care of itself.

With that thought in mind, she straightened the paper forms she would need if the computer system went down—as it often did—and cleared her message queue. Then she gave both upholstered visitors' chairs a quick brush and removed a dead leaf from the spider plant atop the five-drawer filing cabinet that was nearly as tall as she was.

That took three minutes. The remaining forty-seven pressed against her fragile determination.

Calling the boys would be nice, but was it worth disrupting the bedtime routines their new home helper had established? Anna performed daily miracles with the boys, who now bragged about eating vegetables, taking baths, and brushing their teeth, but she got testy about making exceptions.

Scars never go away, Valerie reminded herself when she realized she was hesitating in fear of a confrontation. *But you can stretch them. Call.*

She paid the bills. If Anna got angry, they could discuss a change in schedule.

The desk phone rang as she was reaching for the receiver. She recoiled in blank shock when she saw the glowing red encryption button. The indicator buttons for audio and video lit up next, adding to the mystery.

A teleconference? Now?

Calls on that secure line were usually scheduled days in advance by people far up the rank ladder from her boss. The video technology was still classified, and the encrypted channel required special codes.

The phone rang again. Valerie shook off her paralysis and checked her hair before pressing the accept-call bar. A quick sweep of her headband smoothed the fine, blonde strands back into place.

The screen lit with the image of a smiling young woman's profile. Surprise wiped away Valerie's nervousness. "Elena? Where on Earth did you get an encrypted vidphone?"

Elena's eyebrows went up, and her smile broadened to a delighted grin. "Oh, goodie, it is like a TV. Hi, Val! Got a minute?"

"I can give you thirty," Valerie said, bemused and amused in equal measure. Here was a distraction indeed. Her ex-intern was in the habit of calling to ask for life advice, but not like *this*. "What's going on?"

"A lot! I won't keep you long." Elena's nose and cheeks were wind-chapped pink, her black hair was braided back but frizzing around her face, and her white blouse was wrinkled and blotched with gray and pink stains. Behind her on a knotty pine wall, steel road signs and framed photos reflected spots of glare from unseen lights. "But I'm so excited I can tell you face to face!"

"Speaking of faces." Valerie leaned back and crossed her arms. "The *phone*, Elena."

"It's Amy's," Elena said, which wasn't helpful. "Isn't it outrageous? I can't wait until they roll these out to the public, although I bet I'll never be able to afford one. Anyway, I had a weird day, but it got better over dinner, and now I have new ideas and a big project concept I want to run past you, and if you think it isn't a dream and impossible, then—"

"Elena. Please." Valerie appreciated the teen's boundless energy, but it was *exhausting*. "Can I get the condensed version?"

They'd come a long way from the day they'd met, staring warily at each other from opposing chairs in Graham's office. Valerie had barely started with Adaptation and Placement herself then, and she'd been too intimidated to ask what an intern was supposed to do.

She had met interns in her previous job with Salton Reservoir Control, though. She took that experience as her model, introducing Elena to the daily administrative routines and assigning her more as fast as the girl could master them.

Elena tackled filing and scripted calls with enthusiasm and dedication. Teaching procedures built Valerie's shaky mastery of them into solid confidence. Over their weeks together, they developed an easy camaraderie rooted in a shared desire to excel, and the summer flew by.

Shortly after the interns returned home, Valerie learned most of her A&P co-workers treated the internships like babysitting assignments. Later still, Elena confessed she'd expected to be stuck at a desk with textbooks to read and had been afraid to mention it in case Valerie changed her mind.

During that phone call, they'd shared a good laugh over the outcome of their misguided assumptions. But this wasn't a typical chat. Elena rarely struggled for words.

Valerie said, "Start at the beginning if you can't condense it."

"That would take *way* too long." Mischief danced in Elena's eyes. "Okay, basically I was talking big ideas with friends and realized you're in the perfect position to make the ideas work, especially now that you're in A&P. Hang on a sec. I should do introductions."

Her face blurred out of focus as she moved the phone. "Everybody, say hi to Valerie. I mean, Evaluation Agent Valerie Wade, DPS Adaptation and Placement."

The view settled to reveal a foreground checkered tablecloth and more wood paneling. One of the largest T-series rollovers Valerie had ever seen sat at Elena's left side. On her right was a woman whose face was covered in soft, downy feathers the same mellow gold color as the wings folded up behind her back. The Tee wore camouflage fatigues with Marine Corps badges. The bird woman wore a DPS-uniform-gray suit jacket over a blue blouse as dirty as Elena's was.

On the Marine's far side was another familiar face, this one in reflective sunglasses and a baseball cap. Jack Coby had on a tight gray tee shirt that strained over his armored muscles. This was the first time Valerie had seen him in anything but uniforms or suits—and there was something odd about his face, too.

Elena said, "Val, you know Jack, don't you? From when he picked me up for those Hollywood meetings?"

"I remember him." A based-on-a-true-story movie had been Elena's main reason for being in California the summer she'd interned. Valerie also remembered him having eyebrows, but that wasn't worth questioning now. "Did the sequel get green-lighted?"

"No, this is better! Meet my other friends. Sergeant Amy Goodall—"

The uniformed Marine waved a hand with impressive claws painted in a bright, cheerful pink that matched her dorsal spines. She smiled without showing any of the sharp teeth Valerie knew were behind those thin lips.

"—and DPS Senior Field Agent Heather Gardner."

"Just Heather," the feathered woman said.

The Marine nodded. "And I'm Amy."

Something about her reminded Val of Johnny's favorite teaching assistant. The Marine's voice was as deep as Jack's, but she used it in a quieter, lighter way. Her tone suggested patient self-assurance instead of annoyance.

Valerie said, "Then I'll be Val, and we can all be friends."

She checked the time once more. Still more than half an hour. "All right. It's a big idea, maybe impossible, better than a movie deal—Elena, are you plotting to take over the world again?"

"Of course she is." Jack's upper lip rose, revealing one fang. "Starting with the Department as usual."

From his tone, Valerie guessed he was rolling his eyes behind those dark glasses.

Elena protested, "I don't want to take it over. I only want to change it a little."

"Yeah? More like rebuild it from the ground up."

That remark earned him a visible eye-roll from Elena. "Okay, maybe, but not all at once. I thought of Val because she said if I wanted the Department to do anything, I needed to find a chink in the bureaucracy I could pry open."

"I said that?" Valerie suspected she'd mumbled something vague while not paying attention. "Wasn't that clever of me."

Elena had a way of dropping complex ideas into conversation that was both amusing and daunting. The few other teenagers Valerie knew were struggling to decide on a college major. Elena already had the life goal of a Senate seat firmly in mind. She exhaustively researched potential career paths and gushed about networking possibilities.

And Valerie excelled at making encouraging noises while other people talked. For many years, being a sounding board had been the best method available for avoiding the alternative role of punching bag.

Now she said, "So you found a bureaucratic chink?"

"Yes!" The teen bounced in place, oblivious to the indulgent looks she was getting from her tablemates. "We can prove it's possible to keep people out of camps by *doing* it."

"Babe, you're doing that thing where you give me a punchline and forget I haven't heard the rest of the joke."

Heather sat up straight, wings flaring slightly. "You feel that way too? That's wonderful. I mean, I thought I was dense."

"It isn't you," Jack assured Heather. "She does that to everyone."

"I do not—"

Amy said, "You do, kiddo, but it's okay." She rubbed at one of the horns that curved down along her cheekbones. "Why don't you let me bring her up to speed? I could use a dry run on this debrief."

Elena huffed and sat back. "Fine."

Amy adjusted the phone view to center on her, then tapped her long, colorful claws on the table, making the image wobble. "About the vidphone. It's a perk of my security clearance. I get detached for sensitive DPS ops on the regular. Most orders come face-to-face on a secure line, no paper trail. Personal use isn't a violation. It's encouraged. I checked. Now, about today."

The Marine provided a concise summary of a hot rollover incident with occasional contributions from Heather and Jack. Sidelong glances twice silenced Elena on the verge of speech. Amy finished up with, "And over French fries and beer, Elena got us chewing on what-ifs like, 'Was there any way to keep Franklin out of a camp?'"

"What if he had rolled as a P9, for example," Jack put in. "No firestorm, no Mercury scramble. Local firefighters suppress him, and the sheriff stows him in a jail cell on Failure to Appear charges while he calls Intake. Or say Franklin activated in a non-elemental series with no physical or visible component and didn't know he'd hit onset already."

"That last one describes most rollovers, high rank or low, elemental or otherwise, right?" Heather waved one taloned hand. "I grew up knowing I was poz, but I didn't know *if* I would activate until my R-factor spiked and I got my first Report For Assessment letter. Then the camp staff told me when I'd hit onset, but the feathers took *weeks* to come in."

Valerie remembered that fear of the unknown. "Can you

imagine how different our lives would be if we'd known for certain whether we would roll or not?"

"Boy, can I!" Heather flexed her wings. "While we're dreaming, why not wish the tests told us *which* power we'd get stuck with? I would've done a lot of things differently if I'd known I would end up with these."

Amy's chuckle was a bass rumble. "Same here. And talk about rebuilding the DPS! Most people in quarantine are wait-and-watch cases who get released within three months of onset. The DPS could close more than half the camps."

Jack spoke up. "We're getting off the topic. No matter how we worked Franklin's situation, there were only two scenarios where he didn't end up interned for the duration once he rolled. One outlier was a variation on the mess we cleaned up today." His sidelong glance at Amy was somber. "He might've flamed out and died."

"But there was a cheerful possibility too." Heather raised a finger capped by a delicate, pointed talon. "One get-out-of-camp-free card. Want to take a guess, Val?"

Where was this game going? Valerie wasn't sure, but she was willing to play. "If he was asymptomatic except for the rollover aura, his home DPS office might've let him cool his heels at home."

"No, but you're close. The aura is the key." Heather passed the conversation to Amy with a gesture.

The big Marine said, "He might've skated if he had an ice-cold onset into a cool, slow rollover between annual exams. He obviously didn't socialize with active poz, so he could've hidden a low-power energy field."

Valerie kicked herself for not thinking of that. "That's how I dodged camp. But it goes back to power series."

She had walked around with her new vision coming and going for months before anyone realized what was happening.

Once she was assessed, she was assigned a mentor instead of being shipped away. "The mentorship program is only open to minimally disruptive abilities like—oh." Understanding struck. "That's your chink, Elena?"

Elena nodded energetically. "Cross that with the Innovative Placements initiative. That's precedent for the DPS sponsoring —and then adopting—experimental private programs. If we submit a grant proposal for a home rollover program and get it approved, and if it works, maybe they'll enlarge the loophole."

Valerie bit her tongue. *Ifs and maybes.* "Elena, the IP program is about job retraining. Rollover is more complicated. And expensive. People in destructive series have to prove competence, which takes time—and resources. There are legal hurdles, too. The core regulations on rollover isolation haven't changed since 1943. To qualify for general release, individuals who have been assessed as R-active must establish to the satisfaction of a Public Safety representative that their rollover is complete, series is confirmed, *and* applicable safety criteria have been met."

Silence fell, so complete that only the on-screen affirmation of nods and wry smiles proved the call was still active. Anxiety heated Valerie's face with a blush and sent prickles of sweat down her back. "What did I say?"

Heather leaned close, her face looming on the screen. "Did you really just quote federal code word for word? Elena said you knew the regs inside and out, but wow."

Valerie's face went hot. "To be fair, it's the most commonly cited piece of DPS legislation in history, and I see it nearly every day."

She tugged nervously at her blouse. "Elena, I'm not trying to poke holes in your plan, but you'll have to collect signoffs from at least four different departments, then develop protocols, job descriptions, a procedures bible, and—and—org charts! And that's for the proposal. *If* you get approved, you'll—"

"I *knew* it!" Elena leaned past Heather to poke Amy's arm. "I told you she was the expert we needed."

"No, I'm no expert!" Valerie's heart sank. She was nothing but a diner waitress who'd barely graduated high school. She'd learned everything on the job and outside it, reading up and taking certification tests after hours and over lunch breaks. "It's obvious translating the Innovations program to Intake would be a huge challenge!"

"I said it was impossible," Heather said. "But I couldn't have listed specific objections off the top of my head like you did. Face it, woman, you have a skillset."

"A critical one," Amy said. "Jack and I can recruit people to help on the field side, but I didn't think we had a snowball's chance of getting through the grant process. Until now. You ready to join the revolution, Val?"

"If you want me," Valerie said, feeling faint. "But—are you sure?"

Jack leaned back, pushing his sunglasses down to gaze at her. "I do love seeing that Elena-ambush look on other people's faces," he said. "Ma'am, we damned sure can't do it without you. I'd give it maybe a fifty-fifty shot with you."

His aggressive slouch telegraphed his skepticism. Valerie wondered why he wanted to be involved if he felt that way—and then his first remark sank in, and she understood.

It was hard to say *no* to someone who believed in you the way Elena could, even if you didn't agree with her—and especially if you did. Cynicism and bitterness were emotional defenses against the pain of disappointment.

It looked like she and Jack had something in common.

"We need you." Elena made a sweeping gesture, including everyone on her end of the situation. "If you're willing to help."

No, I'll only fail you. She couldn't refuse. "I'll start on grant research after work tonight."

Tonight. *Oh, no.* Fear squeezed the air from her lungs. *The interview.*

The panic eased after a peek at the clock. "I only have a few minutes left. Can I make quick notes of your ideas?"

"We don't have much yet," Heather replied. "We identify people who object to internment, contact them when their bloodwork spikes, and monitor them until they hit onset and then guide them through rollover at home."

Elena made a face and fidgeted in her seat, waving her hands again. "Ugh, why is it so complicated? My abuela falling asleep with her candle lit is more dangerous than a P9 pyro. My papa lighting the grill is more dangerous."

Heather caught Elena's hand before it smacked her in the face. "You get hyper when you're tired, don't you, child? Professional translation, Val—we'll have to work up a ton of intersecting series and rank contingencies for deciding between home quarantine, short-term and long term, detention transfer options and so on."

Elena took a deep breath and blew it out. "Sorry. Anything would be better than full internment, right, Val? And I think people would adjust better to camp knowing someone *tried* to help."

Jack said, "You hope. I think they'll call it a bait and switch and be ten times harder to handle."

That had the sound of an ongoing argument—and it gave Valerie an easy out. "Either way, it's a start for me to build on. But now I do have to go."

After quick promises to coordinate another meeting through email with Elena, Valerie pressed *disconnect*. The screen went dark. The office felt small and empty.

Valerie's pulse sped up again, and a new, tight ache built

behind her rib cage. She was barely settled here. Was she really going to take on a time-consuming extra project when she should be concentrating her new job? Was she willing to risk everything on a potentially career-ending distraction?

Yes, she was.

This ache wasn't fear. It was hope, and she'd spent too many years living without it to turn her back on its return.

6: APPLY YOUR HEART TO UNDERSTANDING

March 19, 2017, DPS CA Region 20 Offices, Riverside CA

JOSHUA ANTHONY MORETTI was too handsome for his own good or anyone else's.

The impact caught her completely off-guard. She hadn't been affected by someone's outward appearance in a long time. She'd been prepared for pretty, given the man's Intake file and arrest photos, but up close, he was nothing short of stunning.

His looks were the type that improved with age. His lean body would have been gangling and clumsy for years after he reached his full height. The combination of black, wavy hair, sun-kissed skin, chiseled cheekbones, and glacier-blue eyes would've been *too* perfect before maturity added texture and character.

But at forty-nine—his age according to that Intake form on Valerie's desk screen—he was simply splendid. His eyes and mouth had collected laugh lines, his sideburns were a distinguished silver, and his broad shoulders testified to an active life spent doing things that built solid muscle.

His uniformed escorts prodded him through the open door into Valerie's office, where he stood, stiff-backed and imposing, in the narrow space behind the pair of visitor chairs. The lime-green prison jumpsuit was rumpled and unflattering, but that didn't matter in the least.

Valerie looked down, picking up a folder as an excuse, while her mind and body went numb. Moretti was gorgeous, and the most beautiful masks hid the worst evils. That was a life lesson she'd learned the hard way.

This was going to be even worse than she'd imagined. Moretti couldn't affect her mind, couldn't force her will—her talent protected her—but he was charged with using his empathic powers for illegal influence. When Valerie used her talent on him, she would have to *see* that inner ugliness.

The man's cuffs and shackles clanked. The sound jarred Valerie out of her contemplations. "Sit down, Mr. Moretti. Officers, please close the door on your way out."

"Ma'am, he's an E series. We have him in dampers, but are you sure—"

"—that DPS evaluation interviews are *private*? Quite sure." Without looking up, she did her best imitation of the firm tone Anna used on the boys. "This room isn't built for four. I'm equipped to handle this client. You may stand outside or go down to the lounge."

After a short pause, the door shut. A rustle and a glimpse of legs in green coveralls came into her view as Moretti chose the chair on the left side.

His hands appeared next, resting on his knees. The nails were chipped, the cuticles ragged. Those minor imperfections, like the band of paler skin on his ring finger and the oil stains in the folds of his knuckles, emphasized his rugged physicality.

The pre-rollover vocation on his Intake form was *rancher*. Given that profession, his physique, and the red box around his *religious denomination/spiritual preference* box, it was no surprise he wore a double set of dampers. Police took extra precautions with large, muscular men from groups known for flaunting federal laws.

Moretti's hometown church was on a Federal cult watchlist. There was a notation that he had left the community—the church rejected members who accepted government rollover training—but he'd been arrested on the property.

The lights on the wide metal bracelets and anklets blinked green, confirming what Valerie could see for herself; he wasn't projecting.

If the cuff sensors picked up any energy emission, those telltales would change color, and an alarm would sound. After a red-level warning, the devices delivered an electrical shock, increasing in intensity until the projection ceased—usually when the wearer was rendered unconscious.

In Valerie's experience, hurting people who were already upset left them less able to control themselves, not more, but control wasn't really the point. The devices were popular because they made nulls feel safer.

Their presence was a visual reminder that Moretti was no threat to her, but that didn't help. For once the emotion fighting with her sense of duty wasn't fear. It was revulsion.

She didn't *have* to use her vision. Most DPS evaluators were null. They did this job without her advantages. No one else would know if she based her conclusion on the case evidence alone.

The complaint file contained sworn testimony from multiple witnesses. The facts were clear. This big, handsome rancher had used his powers to bend his wife's mind to his will in front of their two children.

Valerie didn't even have to worry about how her decision would affect the family. The wife had applied to Family Safety

& Support the night of the incident. The FS&S report included a marriage dissolution form with the *rollover incompatibility* box checked, and *safety relocation approved: apply for clearance* in the contact information. They were safely out of the picture.

The temptation to condemn him was strong. No one would be shocked if she recommended permanent internment.

Her conscience wouldn't let her do it. She'd been given this assignment because she could see truths *beyond* the obvious. It would be wrong to pretend otherwise. The butterflies in her stomach were familiar enemies. Fear of seeing something horrible was still fear.

Fear could be defeated.

She lifted her chin and braced herself to see arrogance and self-absorption turned rotten, mean and dangerous, focusing her vision past the surface aesthetics to the core beneath.

And oh, what a surprising core it was.

The weight of the man's somber gaze shattered her dark fears and let clear, bright relief shine in. His physical form invited appreciation, but it didn't mask cruelty or calculating selfishness. It was a thin veneer over deep anxiety, exhaustion, and grieving heartache.

Joshua Moretti didn't have an abusive or manipulative bone in his entire body. He was one of the most compassionate, nurturing, fundamentally *kind* men Valerie had ever seen.

Also one of the most insecure.

The reality of him contradicted everything in his record. On paper, he was a clear and present danger.

E and F series powers were as dangerous as elemental talents. The social disruptions a projective empath or telepath could cause were potentially more destructive than unnatural disasters—and much easier to hide. Moretti was rated E9-E, the weakest rank in the series, but he'd struggled for a full year of internment before achieving safety certification. And he'd been reported for a violation the day after his camp graduation.

The system had reason to be worried about him. But *Valerie's* fears had been groundless. Moretti wasn't a vicious wolf in charming sheep's clothing. He was as harmless as a newborn lamb.

The revelation was dizzying. Shame put a bitter twist on her emotional rebound. Lines of pain ran through Moretti like invisible scars. She bore similar marks from psychic wounds inflicted with calculated cruelty.

This was a victim, not a victimizer, a survivor, not an offender. By getting caught up in his appearance and her expectations, she'd come *very* close to adding herself to a list of his unknown past abusers.

The silence was getting thick. "Well," she said. "You're a surprise."

Tears welled up in Moretti's eyes and spilled over before he could lift his cuffed hands to wipe them away. Metal jingled again as he bent forward.

"I'm a monster," he said. "I did everything they say. Lock me in a cell and throw away the key. It's no more than I deserve."

His quiet voice was as appealing as everything else about him. He even cried gracefully: his skin didn't blotch, he didn't snivel, and the tears clinging to his thick eyelashes and gave his sad expression a sweet touch of vulnerability.

But the bone-deep physical beauty was a shell over a dense mass of despair and remorse.

Self-loathing was a powerful indicator of guilt. That part of his essence fit the case evidence. Nothing else did. Valerie was as sure of his innocence as she was of her own name.

She squinted, which did nothing to resolve the visual conflict. *What a mess.*

With that thought, her churning confusion transformed into

something like excitement. She was good at cleaning up messes. Getting to the truths behind contradictory evidence, empathizing with the victimized—those challenges played to her strengths.

Time to be strong. "Don't say another word until I get the disclaimers out," she told Moretti. "Recorder on."

She recited her ID and the interview headers, then waited for confirmation chirps from the equipment. "Your turn. State your name and Social Service ID for the record, please."

He did so, then launched into a new round of self-recriminations.

Valerie lifted a hand. "Not yet. Next, I'm legally required to inform you I'm a B8-X, which is, in simple terms, a truth dowser. That's legally important."

She checked her notes to make sure she got the next piece exactly right. She knew phrases by heart, but the jargon sounded ridiculous coming out of her mouth. "I am authorized to deliver summary evaluations by means of my certified talent. These judgments may lead to criminal or civil charges. Your acknowledgment does not constitute agreement, and you may file a grievance as grounds for appeal of a Judicial Board verdict. Do you understand? Say yes or no aloud, please."

Moretti tipped his head to one side. "Yes? Yes, I understand, if that's what I need to say."

"Client acknowledgment received." Pity put a lump in Valerie's throat. He didn't really understand. He wanted to hear his sentence and end the uncertainty. He expected punishment and was resigned to it. No, he was *eager* for it.

The evaluation process was rigorous by design, but it was hardest on those who were gentle-natured. Moretti could not stand remembering the pain he'd caused or the possibility he might hurt someone else, and this was forcing him to think about both.

Valerie had a hard time understanding spiritual decisions, but she recognized the signs. She was glad she'd taken the extra time to look into Moretti's red-flagged church—she could see their doctrine at work in his remorse.

The Salvation Assembly Church of Christ In His Glory had broken off from a now-defunct doomsday cult out of Texas back in the forties, right after First Night changed the world. Its founder had pivoted effortlessly from preaching about the end of the world to warning about the damnation of the soul through R-factor contamination.

Moretti was primed to believe himself sinful, and his camp experience was still fresh in his memory. Certification required relentless, perfect control. After spending a week in a jail cell brooding over his mistake, it was no wonder he believed he deserved the worst imaginable penalty for an unauthorized projection.

His guilt sprang from faith, not fact. The outside world had to be more tolerant of minor slips than camp trainers. To err was human, after all.

Valerie fought off a case of highly inappropriate stress-related giggles. The E in Moretti's variant slot meant he didn't feel what others felt, only pushed his emotions onto them. He wouldn't understand laughter.

The sooner she relieved his fears, the better. "At this point, a null interviewer would ask questions to clarify points from the investigation and collect data to support their recommendation to the court. I'd rather deliver my evaluation first and do the Q&A after."

He hunched forward and bowed his head, staring at his clenched hands. Praying? "Sure, that makes sense. Get it over with."

Oh, this is far from over. Valerie could keep him out of prison, but mandatory relocation and probation were the minimum penalties for what he'd done. And if he skipped a single probation meeting without cause, he would go to prison for life. And he would most likely end up on Valerie's case roster unless there was an EF-resistant evaluator closer to the man's new home.

She filled out the proper form and read it twice before reciting the conclusion. "My evaluation is as follows. The incident under review constituted a minor infraction. No additional violations were logged during precautionary detention. The defendant will be released from detention and entered into a standard probation schedule, specifics TBD. This complaint is closed."

Moretti's confusion and disbelief came at Valerie like a pulse of pastel glitter. The dampers beeped, and the telltales flashed yellow. He tucked his feet under the chair and put his hands between his legs, hiding the lights.

"Sorry," he whispered. His voice quivered, and the emotional glitter melted away.

"No, that was a good recovery," Valerie assured him. "Under the circumstances."

Scolding him would be worse than pointless. It would be cruel. She'd known the verdict would surprise him, and dampers were sensitive by design. Projection didn't count as a violation unless the dampers delivered a shock.

She gave him a moment to compose himself. He was too good-looking for her comfort, but that essential goodness of his was something she had seen only once before. That relationship had ended in tragedy. Her heart ached to give Moretti's life story a happier outcome.

That didn't mean he needed coddling. There was more than one kind of support, and Valerie wasn't about to encourage the man's tendency toward self-pity. She said briskly, "I need a verbal confirmation, please."

"But—I—huh." He shook his head. His face flushed. "I don't get it. I'm not going back to jail?"

"No. You'll go to temporary lodging tonight, then back here tomorrow to work with Placement on residency and probationary employment."

He continued slowly shaking his head. "Now see, all that went right over my head. Look, ma'am, I'm not good with complicated. I'm not afraid to work hard, but Sarah was the one with the big brain and the education. She took care of—" He wavered into silence after mentioning his ex-wife, then rallied. "I'd appreciate you taking another shot at explaining."

"Of course!" Valerie let her face relax into a smile. "The legal language is awful, isn't it? Back when I rolled, I spent months crying over it."

"For real?"

"Oh, yes. I told myself I wanted to learn the jargon so I could explain it better, and now look at me slinging it around. Let me apologize by getting you out of those dampers."

The control program took a moment to load up. Valerie typed her authorization and Moretti's ID into the release fields, and three heartbeats later, four latches popped open.

Shadows against the blinds hinted that the police escort had taken her up on the idea of waiting right outside. She might as well tell them the verdict, release them from their wait, and give them back their equipment.

Moretti bent to remove the shackles, then cradled the devices in both hands as he heaved a sigh. "I felt safer with them on."

"You're stronger than you think." She finished printing releases the officers would need, collected them in a folder and stood.

Moretti rose to his feet when she did. Her nerves jumped, but she accepted the dampers and walked past without flinching. It was a sign of respect, and her reflexes would eventually calm down. She hoped.

When she opened the door, a wave of cleaner-scented air wafted in from the office floor. The state police officers stepped away and apart, turning to face her. The one on the left, a young, pale man who was a few hours past needing a shave, put his palm on the butt of his pistol. Valerie waited, pulse thumping in her throat, until they relaxed slightly.

"We heard the dampers beep, ma'am." said the man's partner, a strong, older woman with full lips and narrowed eyes. "Is everything all right?"

"Everything is fine," Valerie handed over the dampers. "I've recommended against proceeding. That closes out the complaint. You'll want these clearances for your reports."

She was able to satisfy their remaining suspicions and get them on their way with minimum fuss. It was surprisingly easy to put on the mask of a confident professional. Maybe—just maybe—she did have skills.

Once they left, Valerie shut the door and returned to her chair. "There. That's settled. Things will get easier from now on, I promise."

"Funny thing is, I believe you." Moretti's smile was brief and directed at the pictures on Valerie's desk. "I should've known you were a mother. You have the voice. Both yours?"

"Johnny takes after their father." Oh, why had she said that? "But let's focus on you right now."

Valerie had three Transition Housing complexes on speed-dial. The night desk manager at the first one answered with heartening speed. She requested an escort, and once the arrangements were made, she walked Moretti through what he could expect when he arrived.

He nodded earnestly during the explanation. "I'm grateful,

honestly, but I still don't understand why I'm not going to prison."

"That's simple: burying people alive doesn't fix anything they break when they screw up. The DPS will clean up this mess and give you a chance to prove you can do better. But you only get *one* chance. Don't waste it. Clear?"

"Clear."

There were the tears again. It was unfair that he could look that good while tears ran down his face. It was astonishing how easily he cried. Most men she knew were not so comfortable with their own emotions.

"That was the easy part," Valerie warned him. "We still have to go over the case complaint and the conditions of your release."

He wiped his cheeks dry. "Tell me what I have to do. I want to redeem myself, I swear."

"First, the bad news. You can't go home again. Ever. Relocation is part of the probationary release."

She was prepared for objections. Moretti had been born in the county where he'd lived until rollover, and people who had only ever known one home didn't uproot well. She'd learned that when her mother moved in with her and got a refresher course when Mom returned to the hospital during her final illness.

Moretti took in the news with an uncomprehending frown, so Valerie gave him more details. "When you meet with the Transition agent tomorrow, you'll arrange for personal effects —clothes, furniture and so on—to come to you. They'll pick up anything you signed over to the jail for safekeeping, too."

At the mention of jail, Moretti rubbed his hands on his legs. The rough fabric of the coveralls rustled. "I was carrying everything I owned in a knapsack the night I was arrested," he said, "so that part's easy. Everything else went to Sarah when I left for camp and got expelled from the church."

"Everything? I saw that, but I didn't realize it was so—thorough." Valerie ran a finger over the relevant section in her research notes. The Salvation Assembly believed rollover should be handled with faith and prayer alone. "The church leaders changed their minds about you, then?"

Moretti licked his lips. "They said it was Sarah's doing. They bent the rules for her. Her grandpa founded The Ranch. Am I going to have to talk about them?"

"Will that be a problem?"

The Salvation Assembly Church owned substantial acreage near Sacramento and operated as an independent community. The Ranch—always printed using capitals—looked like a comfortable, prosperous settlement in their online recruitment materials. And according to the closest DPS office, the Salvation Assembly congregation kept to itself, to the point of trucking in materials they couldn't supply for themselves.

"I swore vows," Moretti said, which was an evasion, but a truthful one. "But I guess there's plenty that isn't secret."

"I'll try to be sensitive," Valerie assured him. "But I do have questions."

The Assembly Church dutifully registered their children and complied with annual testing. Their DPS district had the lowest per capita rollover rate in the state, which was convenient since they also had the state's highest camp exemption stats.

Few church members had ever rolled into a non-exempt talent like Moretti's, however, and none of the others had been allowed back. The explanation for his homecoming might shine a light on the reasons it had gone wrong.

Moretti was looking pale and uncomfortable. Valerie eased

off the topic. "Before we dig into that, is there anything else you want to ask me?"

He shrugged. She waited. The office was so quiet the recording unit's whirring was audible. The air conditioning clicked on, and a cool draft swirled through the small room.

Moretti's eyes narrowed. He'd thought of something. "When you said home, you meant the whole ranch, didn't you? Not just the house."

"Sorry, yes. Normally you would only need to avoid a neighborhood, not a whole town, but it's a single property, so it's all off-limits." she hesitated, by the pain radiating off Moretti. "I know this must be a hard pill to swallow."

He waved off the sympathy. "The elders won't welcome back their prodigal son back twice. The police said Sarah and the girls—" He stopped there, aura glittering slightly, face full of sadness and bitter anger. "I blew my chance with them."

He stood and paced from wall to wall and back. "I wouldn't go now if they begged me. She was right to run away, you know? Not from me, but from—" He stopped mid-sentence again. The air glittered. "I lose my grip if I talk about it, but I can't hold it in."

"You'll learn how," Valerie assured him. "You'll work with someone every week for the year of your probation. It might even be me. For now, sit. Breathe deep. We're almost done, and then you can get some rest."

He sat. Back straight, jaw clenched, hands clenched, he inhaled, exhaled. Nodded. "Go on."

"I need you to talk me through what happened that night. I know—" she added before he could voice the objection she saw in his eyes. "It'll be hard, and I know you've been over it a dozen times for the police. That will go under court seal. This is for your probationary report. It's more personal, and it will only be shared with other evaluators. Do your best. I won't push."

"So it's like a confession?"

"Maybe? I'm not religious. Does that make you uncomfortable? I can make a note for your weekly check-ins. We try to accommodate clients with compatible agents."

"This is fine. It's easy to talk to you, and I found out at camp there's more ways to God than I ever dreamed, like Sarah and I used to talk—" The air glittered briefly, and he swallowed hard. "I'd better not use her name. Where do you want me to start the story? When Elder Smith called me?"

"That's fine. I won't interrupt unless I get confused."

For the next half-hour, she compared his recollections of the incident to the witness testimonies. The work supported her initial conclusion: Joshua Moretti was guilty of bad communication and ignorance, but he was innocent of the charges.

Her opinion of the church, on the other hand, went downhill from indifferent to suspicious. Something about the church's secret workings shamed and worried Moretti. Valerie didn't need a truth sense to know that. The man was as transparent as glass.

He was also glass that would crack if she pressed it hard. He was exhausted and emotionally wrung out. She wasn't in much better shape. Whatever this secret was, it could wait.

She led Moretti through the official phrases that ended the interview recording. She was typing a brief summary to complete the written evaluation when Moretti spoke up with a quiet and unexpected ferocity.

"She was right to forsake me," he said. "I never meant to push, but I did. But I gotta say it hurts that I can't say I'm sorry to my own wife."

He wrapped his arms around himself and stared at a point on the wall over Valerie's head, radiating pure anguish. But *not* projecting it. The emotions around him were red and bright like fresh blood, but he held them in.

She couldn't let his words stand unchallenged. These hard words would not be a blow to break him—this was a cleansing best done before that wound scabbed over. "She is your ex-wife, Mr. Moretti. The sooner you get used to thinking of her that way, the better."

"I can't say *ex*. It isn't respectful." He sniffled. "They're just gone. Cops said I would never find them."

"Don't try. They've been issued new IDs and accepted relocation assistance. You must not look for them. It's a stalking felony to try. You did what you did. Your ex did what she did. You have to move on."

"It feels more like cutting out my heart than moving on." Moretti blinked away more tears, then unexpectedly smiled. It was a rueful expression. "Huh. 'We all bleed when our lives meet the sharp edge of our yesterdays.' Figures I get it now that it's too late to matter."

Valerie stared at him in bafflement. *What a strange remark.* "Was that a quotation?"

"Yes. No." A heavy sigh.

Light dawned. "It's something she said. Your *ex*-wife." It couldn't hurt to underscore that point. Sarah Moretti sounded like someone Valerie would have liked. *Unless she intimidated me to death.*

Moretti said, "She was always moving, thinking things, *doing* things. She would get a thought, write it down and stick it up somewhere, to remember for later. Notes all over. Poems. Prayers. That saying about sharp edges got taped to our fridge after she—when her father died. I saw it there when I went home. She never could explain it in a way that made sense to me. We quarreled over things like that."

Who calls it quarreling? "I see," Valerie said, but what she saw were hints of a secret Moretti wasn't ready to share.

"I am glad she ran," he said again, with that gut-wrenching

vehemence Valerie couldn't explain. "She's safe, and she gets a new start. I guess I'll hold onto that part. Maybe I should have a new name too. For my new life."

He did a lot of guessing. Was he ever sure of anything? Valerie noted that point in her evaluation. "If you're serious, I can set it up. First name, last, or both?"

"First name, I think," he said. "I'm not a Joshua. I never was. My dorm mates at Twin Oaks called me Sal, from Salvation Assembly. I might like that. It would be like keeping a piece of the faith even though I'm dead to the church."

"When you're sure, you'll need forms." Valerie pulled up the documents from the central database and printed off copies for him to review. "And if helps, rollover incompatibility is the second most common cause for divorces, right after adultery. When the children are eighteen, they can choose to waive confidentiality separately if they want."

Spouses rarely opened their files after the mandatory one-year cooldown period. But children old enough to remember the non-custodial parent sometimes did.

His hope was a bright glory to see. "Well, then. That's something to keep me going."

Valerie considered warning him about the odds, but if a small dream helped him cope with his other losses, then let him dream. She said, "My mother used to say, 'Take comfort where you find it.'"

He smiled. "Wise woman."

Not really. "I miss her." Most of her mother's ideas had been thoroughly wrongheaded, but fighting with her had rarely been worth the consequences.

A message flashed on her screen: the escort from the temporary housing unit had arrived.

He was a short skinny man with a limp who claimed an F5-C telepathic talent and whose hair and wrinkled skin were coordinating shades of eye-watering fuchsia. Valerie invited him inside and made introductions, then watched until the two men turned the corner in the elevator lobby.

Someone on night shift had made popcorn. Her stomach growled.

She had survived—and more than that. She might have done good. It was time to go home and take comfort in hugging her children—and to work on Elena's dream of a better future.

Before shutting down for the night, she bookmarked reference materials on her laptop to read before bed. Designing a grant application and project outline would be a monumental undertaking. Part of her already regretted agreeing to make the attempt. The success of Elena's vision would rest on a foundation Valerie designed. That was a terrifying thought.

But if it worked, it would be magnificent.

She was in the elevator, staring at her frizzy-haired, rumpled reflection before she recognized the second new emotion bouncing around her rib cage. Once she identified hope's new companion as excitement, she smiled the rest of the way to the lobby.

7: TWO HANDFULS OF VEXATION

August 17, 2019, 414 Elm Drive, Elgin, IL

WHEN DESTINY KNOCKED on Grace Reed's front door, she was in the back yard trimming the herbs in her summer planters. The rap of knuckles on wood interrupted her happy thoughts of potting and harvesting and launched her straight into a panic attack.

Common sense whispered *it's the pizza driver*, but a mental short-circuit connected the idea of a stranger at the front door to the unbearable conclusion: *they've found us!*

Terror ripped through nerves wound tight from other worries, obliterating reason, which insisted no one from her past would ever knock politely and wait.

If Joshua Moretti wanted to reclaim his daughters and his runaway wife, he could walk inside and make Grace believe she wanted him there. And if the elders had discovered her refuge here, they would insist the police break down the door and pin her to the floor to teach her proper humility.

But what if? cried her worn and weary conscience.

Fear-soaked memories rippled down the long months to drown the present, becoming as real as the hot air she struggled to inhale. Golden late-afternoon sun dimmed to night, the syrupy humid air went dry and metallic, and the hum of busy cicadas became a mellow voice she had never thought to hear again. "Hi, my love. No, don't be scared. Let me in."

Josh stood at the door to the house they'd built together and wielded the accursed power he'd accepted damnation to obtain. The church elders waited behind him in the dusty rock garden out front, smiling as they stood aside and let a cursed man succeed where they'd failed. She bowed her head, obedient to his will, and was lost.

Her sweat turned cold and clammy against her skin as she struggled against the remembered sensation of eerie, unnatural acceptance. Her muscles went rubbery, too weak to hold her up, and her pulse raced so fast it sent flashes of light across her vision.

She fell to her knees, fighting for breath, and prayed, *God give me strength.*

Her broken, aching heart thudded against her breastbone. Her empty lungs would not fill. She wrung her hands until the honest callouses on her palms scraped the soft flesh of her wrists, smearing dirt and sweat across her skin like claw marks.

She had no right to ask God's help. She was already damned. To protect her daughters, she'd committed heinous crimes. But if she was taken now, what would be the point of her sacrifices?

Another knock traveled through the house, from the locked screen door at the front, down the center hall, and out the open patio slider. The sound thrust her from the bleak past into the bright, hot afternoon. She clutched at the lifeline of her senses: a stripe of glare beyond the shade of the patio awning, the taste of salt on her lips, the scent of a sage leaf crushed under her knee. Those were real.

Fear made lies of her memories. She had *not* bowed her head and let Josh bend her mind the way a gardener trained vines onto a trellis. After one frozen, eternal second, she had slammed the door shut on her heart. She'd grabbed keys, purse and children on her way out the back door. And in their pride, the elders hadn't thought to block the garage.

She was flinching from shadows, fighting the demons of her shame. Such waking dreams came less often than they had in the first weeks after her escape, but they sometimes ambushed her on the heels of surprise.

The phantoms born from shattered faith and bloody guilt were persistent, and everyday worries left chinks in her emotional defenses, leaving gaps for the bigger fears to slip through.

And so many worries were competing for her attention now. She thought of the red-bordered envelope sitting unread in the drawer of the hall table, and her chest went tight all over again. *I'm not ready, Lord. I need more time.*

A cracking male voice carried through the house. "Hello? Anybody home? Jake's Pizza. I got two large pies here for a Maggie Reed?"

See? Pizza. Grace took a deep breath of warm, herb-fragrant air, then another, easing them past the tightness in her chest. *Not your second-worst nightmare coming true.*

She called out, "Yes, sorry, just a moment!"

No one would ever look for her here. Sarah Moretti, raised a devoted daughter of the Salvation Assembly Church of Christ In His Glory, never would have sought refuge in Elgin, Illinois, a stronghold of the church's most powerful enemies. Grace Reed, licensed preservation specialist and single mother of two, was gratefully putting down roots here.

The past could not touch her. The records were sealed. The Public Safety laws she had once despised now protected her from the husband who had betrayed her—and from the church she had betrayed in turn. The girls were safe from the perils of Grace's misdeeds. They had documents and savings. They had been here more than two years without trouble.

The soothing recitation of facts beat back the whirl of panic. Her heartbeat steadied, and tight muscles unknotted. This was only a delivery, and pizza was not her problem.

Her daughters were the ones throwing an impromptu party. She wiped her hands on her faded-blue cotton work dress and picked up the garden hose.

The stream of water hit the wall below the air conditioner for the upstairs bedroom—purchased with the girls' collected chore earnings and installed with Grace's help—then splattered loud against glass as she trained the spray around the unit and across the second window.

The sash slid open, and thumping drumbeats blasted outside, chased by screaming waves of guitar and warbling electronic noises.

Maggie stuck her head outside. The so-called music drowned out her voice, but her mouth made a familiar shape: the word "What?" drawn into a long wail of irritation. Memory supplied Grace with the proper aggrieved tone.

The volume of the complaint doubled to audible levels when Lauren came up beside her sister. They shouted all three syllables of "M-o-om" at her in perfect unison as someone else muted the music.

The twins both had their black curls piled high on their heads in complicated braids, and the makeup on their faces did nothing to hide their sulky expressions. They looked most like their father when they were annoyed, a detail that bothered Grace more than she liked to admit.

Their pale eyes, blue and violet, made a striking combination with their dark hair and bronzed skin. Rude strangers asked if they were adopted after comparing them to Grace, with her dark eyes, freckled skin, and sun-bleached mousy hair. Polite people remarked they would be beauties when they grew up.

Josh had always said the girls inherited their mother's sweet smile and sharp brains. A fresh pang of loss sliced into Grace's heart at that memory, the way grief often did after fear's retreat.

"Your supper's here." She kept her voice steady, hiding her pain to spare them. "You'd best hurry. They've knocked twice already. I left money in the key tray. Bring the food and the friends out here, please. I'll set out plates and napkins for you."

"Fine!" The window slammed down.

The music stopped, and a shout bounced through the house and back to Grace out the patio door. "Stay there, pizza guy! We're coming as fast as we can!"

She should discuss indoor voices and respect with them again, but she hated ruining their time together with lectures. Every happy day of this summer was a victory in defense of their remaining innocence.

The girls had taken their first R-factor screening test at the end of the school year, and the results killed any hope their two years of peace would stretch out forever. Both girls carried the potential for damnation in their blood.

The same mark of evil lived in Grace's body, but it wasn't a trait like blue eyes or brown hair. It lay dormant through generations and skipped whole branches of family trees. Despite knowing Josh's fate, despite the nights when she lay paralyzed with terror over her own future, she had clung to the possibility that the girls would be passed over.

There was hope, of course. The curse afflicted a third of humanity, but less than ten percent fell beneath its full weight. Maggie and Lauren might never face the choice their father had. They might never be tempted to accept the same fate.

Positive tests still meant they faced new worldly responsibilities. Starting in the fall, their weekends and school breaks would be spent fulfilling government service obligations and attending supplemental classes about R-factor biology and the details of rolling into power.

Grace couldn't argue against the importance of doing good works. She did wish Lauren and Maggie could skip the extra classes. The public schools draped their explanations in the language of science, but the material they covered was nothing new to her children.

They'd been baptized into the congregation at the age of six. They had been learning about the perils and possibilities of rollover since their first year of lessons. Schooling them twice would waste time and continue the erosion of their religious commitment.

She did her best to ignore the part of her mind that whispered, "But would that be a bad thing?" Her faith had always been an anxious, brittle thing that clung to rigid observance because it rested on a wobbly foundation of doubts and questions. These days, she was questioning everything.

Would she be strong enough to take the path of faith if God led her to the crossroads? Would it be damnation if she made the same choice Joshua had? What if her children faced the test? What would she choose for them?

At the root of those doubts lay the most painful question of all: why had Josh's sin consumed him?

He hadn't been the first of their community to take the government's thirty pieces of silver, but no one had expected it. He was a loving husband and a doting father. Why hadn't his goodness been enough to see him through his test?

God didn't make mistakes.

Maybe it was *her* fault. Maybe she was the unnatural creature her father had called her at the end of his life. Maybe she'd chosen wrong at every turn. Maybe she had damned Josh first and was leading the girls down a different path to hell's fires.

Beneath her tangled emotions lay a yawning pit of loneliness. Had she done the right thing, cutting him out of her life as surely as if she'd wielded a knife? She might have been able to make her peace with his return if he'd been cursed with a physical power, or if only he'd let her *choose—*

No, no, no.

So many teachings had turned out to be lies or dark shadings of larger truths. She wanted to believe the elders were as fallible about their stance on damnation as they'd proved to be in so much else—but was that a desire for truth or temptation? How would she know?

If ignorance was bliss, uncertainty was agony.

Laughter, thumps, and slams from indoors served as a warning that the girls upstairs were setting aside whatever they'd been doing. Her struggle had to be set aside for another time. Yesterday's wounds were beyond repair. Tomorrow might never come. *Sufficient unto the day…*

Any minute now, she would have half a dozen girls whining at her about sweat, mosquitoes, and ants. That was enough trouble for now.

She loved the feel of late summer here, where life ripened slow and sleepy, wrapped in soft heat by day and night as if the earth was relaxing after the frenzied growth of May and June.

The twins had been raised in California's dry inland climate and had no interest in the land, only in its bounty. They never stopped complaining about the humidity.

They had grumbled and whined through their morning yard chores about the nasty, sticky, frizzy-hair-making weather. And when their usual friend-gaggle had showed up, they'd packed themselves into the air-conditioned bedroom to paint their nails, argue about celebrities, do absurd things to their hair, and act their age.

And that was fine. The freedom to be young and silly was the greatest gift Grace had to give them.

Gifts. The thought reminded her she ought to say a meal blessing before Lauren and Maggie brought the food and their friends outside.

The girls had embraced their new lives with enthusiasm, easily shrugging aside the church routines Grace had enforced diligently until their move here. Most things she did embarrassed them these days, but shows of piety caused the most groaning and rolling of eyes.

She wanted her children to choose their own paths to God, not be forced onto the road she'd taken, but she could not shake off the comforts of a lifetime. Rituals were her rocks of comfort when she felt adrift in the world.

Discretion was the compromise. She bowed her head now and murmured a hasty, "Thank you, Lord, for what we receive from your bounty, now and every day. Amen."

Footsteps thundered down the stairs, followed by shrieks of laughter, a sound to warm the heart of any mother raising two angsty teens. Grace gathered that bubble of happiness around herself as she put away her garden tools and brushed the picnic table clean. In the front hall, the girls shouted out shrill comments, and the hinges on the cheap screen door squealed open.

Silence fell, followed by a loud declaration of disgust. "Mo-o-om!"

Grace prayed for patience. "Lauren, honey, I told you, the money's in the tray. And don't yell."

"She *knows*, Mom." Stomping footsteps punctuated Maggie's yelling voice, getting louder with each step. "We. Heard. You. This. Is. Something. Else."

Then she was opening the patio screen. Her dark braids bounced with indignation. "Lauren's paying him, and everyone's flirting because he's on the varsity baseball team. But there's someone here for you, too. From the DPS."

The news smashed through Grace's fragile calm and scoured it away. Her vision went snowy, and horror made a sound like roaring wind in her ears. She sank onto the bench of the picnic table on knees too watery to hold her up.

Not now, was all she could think. *Not like this.*

Small, damp hands clasped hers, and Maggie's voice whispered low and fast, "Oh, Mommy, no, D-P-S, not D-addy. I'm so, so sorry. I should have said Public Safety. If it was anyone from Salvation, Lauren and I would've shouted and run back to you like we practice. I didn't mean to send you into one of your spells. Please come back. Please say something."

No, please, I'm not ready. Grace's heart formed the objection her mouth was too dry to shape. She forced her lungs to work, and her vision returned, hazy gray and blurry. Her lips closed over truths Maggie didn't need to hear.

This wasn't a betrayal of traumatized nerves. This was a legitimate terror. A visit from DPS Intake agents was the one nightmare worse than her ex-husband or the elders coming after her, and it was one whose arrival was already overdue.

Three official notices had arrived since her annual blood test in June. The last one had been delivered by a messenger who demanded a signature. She hadn't read them. She remembered the ones Josh had received, and she wasn't ready to learn she was about to lose the future she gave up everything to make.

Those letters meant the taint in her blood was growing stronger, that rollover was on the horizon. God would be putting her to the test. Worse, the envelopes had been bordered in red, which meant her religious exemption had been refused.

Denial kept her from drowning in resentment and bitterness. She could not face the thought of being imprisoned as Josh had been. She would never hold to the teachings surrounded by unbelievers. Only by ignoring the Assessment summons could she pretend she stood a chance against temptation.

The DPS didn't *know* anything. Their tests didn't tell them which Devil's curse she carried in her tainted blood. They only knew the strength of it exceeded their precious thresholds, or its profile didn't fit in the right box in their endless tables of predictions and possibilities.

Those guesses gave them the authority to strip away her rights, but they were wrong just as often as they were right. She'd done her research. Most people forced to sit for weeks or months inside camps gained powers so harmless they were released immediately after they accepted their curse.

The Devil used science to collect sinners. Despair joined fear and swept it away, leaving frozen numbness in its wake. Deep inside, she had always known agents would come to take her away. The unfeeling bureaucracy she had used to escape her old life was about to destroy the new one.

Lauren knelt beside her sister. "What did you do, Maggie?"

"Nothing! It wasn't my fault! I told her about Elena and her weird DPS project, and she had one of her spells."

Their beloved squabbling voices were as good as a lifeline: the girls were still here. This couldn't be a raid. The DPS used police and military units to arrest conscientious objectors. They didn't let children run ahead to warn their parents. They didn't endanger innocents.

Had there been a change in her status?

No, that didn't track either. They would have called or sent another letter. Or sent agents. Nothing made sense.

Lauren—grumpy, impatient Lauren—gently rubbed Grace's

back in slow, steady strokes. "It's okay, Mom. Breathe in, breathe out. It's nothing. Really nothing. Maggie shouldn't have shot off her stupid mouth like that."

Maggie's arms tightened, and she whimpered.

Grace squeezed, sending reassurance with the contact. "Lauren, don't call your sister stupid. Say you're sorry." It was reflex, that correction, and overseeing the ensuing mundane ritual of sibling reconciliation helped her collect the rest of her wits.

After a sullen apology was made and accepted, Lauren said, "Anyway, Elena is at the door. She graduated last year, but she's working for some DPS scholarship. Surveys or polls or something. Should I tell her to go away?"

"No, don't do that." That might result in exactly the kind of attention Grace was trying to avoid. If nothing else good came of this day, it had proved she couldn't go on like this. She would accept this false alarm as the blessing it was.

Tomorrow, she promised God and herself. *Tomorrow, I will call.*

She sat up straight, releasing Maggie's hands so she could reach out and stop Lauren from nervously picking at her cuticles. "If it's nothing, don't fuss over nothing. Who is Elena? Should I know her?"

The name rang no bells. The girls were supposed to introduce their friends, but they weren't as diligent about it as they could be.

Lauren backed away and flapped her hands. "Everybody knows Elena. She gives speeches and stuff. I could ask her to come back tomorrow, and Maggie and I could clean up the downstairs."

"I'm fine. Invite her in, please." Volunteering to clean meant impressing this girl must be important to Lauren. The old house was a handyman special, and the renovations were taking longer than Grace had expected. Most of the rooms on the first floor had ducts, wiring, and plumbing exposed, and her tools and supplies were stacked everywhere. "Don't be ashamed. A little honest dirt never hurt anyone."

Lauren smiled. "That's what she said. I'll talk with her until you're ready."

She skipped back indoors, past the rest of the girls who had collected in the kitchen with the pizza boxes. They were pretending to hand out plates and choose slices, but they were mainly watching Grace through the patio door.

They pretended politeness, some smiling while others whispered and snickered. Grace's chest hurt, and her heart fluttered, but she would not show weakness, not facing those predatory stares. She brushed her hands together and rose to her feet. "Thank you, Maggie. I'm sorry I scared you."

Maggie raised sad, vivid blue eyes to search her face. "Are you sure you're all right? You looked so—I don't know. Please don't be mad at me?"

"I'm not angry, baby." She was too embarrassed to be angry. Maggie was the family's sensitive one, with a big heart that was quick to forgive and easily bruised.

Grace gave her vulnerable girl a reassuring hug, then walked through the kitchen as if she didn't care what a bunch of teenagers thought of her.

They sidled out of Grace's way and murmured greetings as if they hadn't been laughing at her thirty seconds earlier. Once she passed, they dismissed her entirely and began chattering about soda flavors.

Grace ducked through the plastic tarp separating the house's finished areas from the work zone. There, she paused to correct her assumptions about the girl waiting in the foyer off the cluttered living room.

The mention of high school projects had given Grace the

wrong idea. She'd been expecting a leggy adolescent like her daughters and their friends. Elena was shorter than Lauren, and small-boned, but she had birthing hips and heavy breasts. She carried herself with a remarkable poise. *Not a girl. All grown up.*

Elena's long, black hair was pulled back in a tidy ponytail, sleeked tight against her head, and her briefcase and a linen blazer gave an impression of maturity. Her outfit also included flip-flop sandals and walking shorts, but the choices made her seem practical rather than unprofessional.

Lauren looked ungainly and childish beside her.

Grace was fiercely glad to see those differences. Lauren and Maggie would grow into poise and moderation soon enough. No need to rush the process. By the time she was Elena's age, she had already carried and lost her firstborn. God willing, her daughters would be spared the pain of growing up too fast, too early.

She was borrowing trouble again.

Young or not, mature or not, Elena was working with the DPS and should be treated with discretion as well as courtesy. Grace wiped her hands clean on her dress—*too late to do anything about the grass stains*—and smoothed back her hair. "Lauren, would you please introduce us?"

"Sure!" Lauren smiled with eyes that said, *please don't humiliate me.* "Mom, this is Elena Moreno. Elena, this is my Mom."

Elena offered her hand. "Hello, Ms. Reed."

A sense of almost-recognition scratched at the back of Grace's mind. Elena's face was round, and her skin was bronzy brown, rose-tinted on the high cheekbones. Her wide-set eyes were deep brown. Her long, straight hair was much darker than Lauren or Maggie's brunette curls. Her smile reminded Grace of the Virgin Mary painting in the family's Bible.

Her fingers were warm and calloused. Grace released them

after a firm, quick shake. "Nice to meet you. Or—I'm sorry, but have we met before?"

The color in Elena's cheeks deepened. "No, but I hear that a lot. Is this a bad time? I can come back later or on another day."

"You are a welcome distraction," Grace assured her. "Please, sit down."

Elena hesitated, and Lauren said, "Um. Mom. I can clear our drawings and stuff off the dining room table if you want."

She sounded desperate, and Grace glanced around, trying to see it with fresh eyes.

Their home had good, elegant bones and would be lovely once it was freshened up, but the place was a hundred years old and had been neglected for decades.

The parlor was their testing and staging area. Old paint flaked off the walls everywhere they hadn't cut holes or experimented with paint colors, and the vile brown carpet was dusted with plaster and full off holes where they'd tested stains on the underlying wood. The shabby secondhand furniture fought for space with toolboxes, power tools, extension cords, stacks of supplies, and bags of debris.

The rest of the house was messy, but this room was the worst. It looked like a dump. The dining room wasn't much better. And the kitchen—

A shout went up from the kitchen, something fragile crashed and broke, and gales of laughter followed. "It's FINE," Maggie yelled. "Diane dropped her iced tea. We're going outside, I promise."

Grace considered the impending storm of complaints about bugs, germs, and other exaggerated outdoor threats, then she raised her voice. "Maggie, honey, I've changed my mind. Go ahead and take your food upstairs." She gave Lauren a quick nod. "Help her with the spill, please. Be sure to get all the glass and grab extra napkins for upstairs."

Lauren took off. Grace dredged up a smile for her guest. "The girls say you're doing a survey? I hope you don't mind talking outside. It's stuffy indoors without the fans and dusty with them."

"I have questionnaires, yes. Among other things." Elena eyed the sagging couch. "Outside sounds great."

"Let's give them a moment to get out of the way."

The main stairs were in the front of the house, off the parlor, and further conversation had to wait until the enthusiastic, noisy girl parade marched through. Grace refrained from issuing any reminders to wash out cups and separate the compost materials from trash. *Not today.*

As the chattering horde passed, girls greeted Elena by name and waved. Elena shook her head as she waved back, then combed her hair behind one ear with two fingers.

The gesture jogged Grace's memory. Recognition tingled through her. She had seen that nervous gesture before. *On television.*

"I remember now," she said. "I've seen you on channel 2, on the news! You're the troll charmer from the school bombing back in '14."

"That's me." Elena bent her head and touched the DPS logo on her jacket. "I do guest commentary for WLGN, and I did a whole year of work-study with them, too. I hate the phrase *troll-charmer,* by the way. It's almost as bad as calling someone a troll instead of using their proper series type. Or his name. Jack's rollover designation is T5-Y, by the way. Not *troll.*"

The sharp, unexpected hostility was quite a mood swing. Grace had accidentally triggered those in her daughters over the years, but this one shocked her nonetheless.

The intensity of the girl's gaze sent shivers up Grace's spine. If Elena gave a bad report to some DPS supervisor, someone might check Grace's name and see those overdue notices. *And also,* her conscience whispered, *troll may be accurate, but it's also unkind.* Surprise was no excuse for cruelty.

She said hurriedly, "You're right. That was a thoughtless remark and a rude one too. I apologize."

Elena's expression softened on a blink, and a rosy blush spread across her whole face. "And wow, I was rude right back, wasn't I? Val says—people say I get too defensive too easily. Oh, boy. I'm sorry."

"Defending a friend is nothing to be ashamed of." Grace gestured to the hall. It was easier to smile than she'd expected. "Please, why don't we go outside and start over?"

"I don't know. Are you sure? I mean—I don't know."

Her discomfort sent a wave of sympathy through Grace. This was no seasoned professional, despite her polished appearance. This young woman wore the costume of adulthood well, but the fit wasn't comfortable yet.

"I was rude first," Grace reminded her. "I don't get to meet a local celebrity every day, and my mouth ran off before my good sense could catch up. I can let it go if you can. Come out back and relax. I am curious about this project of yours." That was stretching the truth, but surely God would forgive a little white lie in a good cause.

After a moment's hesitation and a stiff nod, Elena said, "Sure, that's fair."

Tension had locked up Grace's shoulder muscles. She discreetly stretched them as she escorted Elena through the house and onto the patio. Once seated at the picnic table in the shade of the awning, Elena shrugged out of the linen blazer, smoothing down her sleeveless blouse with a sigh of relief. "That is much better. It's nice in the shade. Pretty yard."

She craned her head around, eyes bright on the raised vegetable beds and planters, skimming past the pre-fab shed in one back corner. The girls had painted it in rainbow stripes, with a lilac-colored door, and it looked like a miniature cottage with the flowers around it.

Grace said, "It's even nicer when the evening breeze comes up. May I offer you some iced tea along with the apology? Or lemonade, or water? We don't have soda."

"Lemonade, thank you. Do you mind if I get myself organized here?"

"Make yourself at home. I'll be right back."

Grace washed the only two glasses left in the kitchen—sitting dirty in the dish drainer, of course—then glanced outside after dodging around the mess of wet paper towels between the kitchen island and the refrigerator. The girls would have work to do later.

Outside, Elena set her briefcase on the table. The clips released with cheerful clicks. Out came an official-looking metal clipboard, the kind with extra storage inside for papers and pens. Next came a large yellow envelope thick with contents and stamped with multiple labels. That was followed by a smaller clipboard with several pages already folded over, showing a form with columns of text and check boxes.

Last, she brought out a thick, rainbow-striped pen with a big purple pouf on the top.

Grace poured out two glasses of lemonade with renewed hope for the day.

8: THEY WHO WAIT SHALL RENEW THEIR STRENGTH

August 17, 2019, 600 block of McHenry St, Elgin, IL

JACK COBY SAT on the crunchy dry grass in Patton Park and pondered the unfairness of ice cream. The cold treat would arrive soon, but he was hot now—sticky, uncomfortable, *I-should-move-to-the-Arctic* hot—and having to beg a friend to buy ice cream for him was putting a hell of a damper on his mood.

In a better world, he would be able to buy his own damned ice cream. In a perfect world, he wouldn't be craving ice cream in the first place. In that ideal reality, he and Heather would be sipping the same cold drink Elena's survey participant had offered her.

In this reality, no one wanted to *participate in a frank and friendly exchange of ideas* in front of the people they had opinions about—and that wasn't counting the residents who were too spooked by Jack's size or Heather's feathers to answer their doors.

They'd learned early on that Elena got better results if they stayed out of sight. And pacifying the subjects of her studies was more critical now that she was leaving behind recruiting materials for the Camp Liberty Program.

Valerie had included provisions for participation by off-duty and detached-duty agents in the grant proposal. That allowed Jack and Heather to take CLP contracts and continue as Elena's security detail—and they got paid better for the few weeks the detached assignments lasted, so he wasn't complaining there.

But Elena still couldn't drag along an eight-foot-tall T-series bruiser like him or an exotic like Heather when she went door-to-door. Camp Liberty's prospective clients often had a beef with the DPS. Working solo gave Elena more room to dodge around their hostility.

So Jack and Heather did their guarding from up to three blocks away. They hung out in the neighborhoods, played cards in office lobbies, or sat in libraries and did CLP case research. Elena had always worn a mic on her survey work, and she knew a long list of *I need you* and *rescue-me* code phrases. Now that she had her own radiophone as well as a wire, she had a panic button too.

Eavesdropping and providing color commentary were Jack's favorite parts of the exercise. He keyed up his mic as soon as Elena stopped talking. "Aren't you supposed to ask for a cookie to go with your lemonade?" he asked. "And then a straw?"

Elena mashed random phone buttons and filled his earpiece with loud beeps, her non-verbal version of "Stop distracting me." Then she said under her breath, "I am not a mouse. I am a tiger."

"Yes, you are." He smiled. He'd known she would recognize the picture book reference. It was his favorite read-to-kids choice for Outreach storytimes, right after the pigeon books.

One of the fringe benefits of this detached duty was the two-week break from department routines like library and school visits. The pay was good too, plus it was an enjoyable catch-up reunion with Heather, who kept rotating, while Outreach wouldn't let Jack go. On the good days, this gig was almost as satisfying as a return to the Corps would be.

This was not a good day.

The best spot inside Heather's range was a park across from a quaint retail strip of converted historic houses, and it was a miserable excuse for *best* on a sunny August afternoon. The shadows were lengthening, but the forecast said the heat and humidity wouldn't break until midnight, if then.

Jack didn't have to worry about sweating through his tee shirt and cargo shorts—his body hadn't shed heat that way since his rollover. He did have to deal with being cooked alive inside his skin. Even if he could sweat, it wouldn't keep his insides cool. His body density was too high for that. The physical damage wasn't an issue long-term, not when he could continually regenerate, but that didn't make the cycle comfortable.

The shade didn't help much, either. The block of unprotected grass was soaking up sun on all sides. At this point in the afternoon, the heat coming up from below was almost as bad as the sun beating down from above.

Heather got relief by taking regular trips into the air-conditioned shops, but that wasn't an option for Jack. This area didn't cater to the needs of humanity's more extreme members.

The shops were converted houses as old as the ones on the street Elena was visiting. Those had been old a century ago, according to Elena. She acted like her father had been around when they were constructed.

Civil rights legislation required businesses to provide equitable accommodation, but historic buildings got code exemptions. Most stopped at widening a doorway or two, maybe reinforcing their floors, and offering curbside service to everyone those measures didn't help.

That group included Jack.

The flashing neon sign in the ice cream shop window taunted him with its cheery declarations. *Ice Cream—Fresh Fudge —Kettle Corn. Watch Us Make It Here!*

That would never happen. If he tucked in his shoulders, he could get through the door easily enough. But he might destroy something fragile while maneuvering around the narrow interior full of glass cases and trinket displays and tiny chairs. He would definitely be in everyone else's way the whole time. On the most fundamental level, he didn't fit in.

It wasn't fair, but life rarely was. Those buildings had been around longer than the existence of rollovers. There was no justice in destroying big chunks of history for the crime of failing to meet every current need.

Heather got to chill her wings under an icy ventilator blast and eat a sundae. Jack got to swelter in the inadequate shade of a tree and listen to Elena discuss drink choices with her interview candidate. That was just the way things were.

Iced tea or lemonade? That was what Elena was deciding. Jack would've gladly taken either. Instead he would sit here and wait until Elena needed a ride or a consult.

Waiting, he reflected, was the root of all his frustrations.

Early-onset rollovers like him died young. Everyone knew it. Only he kept on not-dying. He'd expected to die in the Corps. That had been his refuge for a decade. Now he was stuck waiting in this civilian life he still didn't much like.

He'd mastered the day-to-day aspects, and recently he'd started enjoying his work again, so there were good parts.

But it was mostly a pain in the ass.

His landlord was a greedy jerk who scammed residential zoning permits for a bunch of crappy refitted storage units. He only had a car because Camp Liberty was leasing him a military surplus vehicle that could handle his weight. He'd done a lot of walking and worn through a lot of expensive boots before that happened.

And as for friends, the last of his original support group had died nine years ago, and the current crop of early-onsets got on his nerves. They were all so damned young, always whining and posing, except for the ghouls who were running a death pool.

They were stuck in a waiting game, like him.

That raw truth made getting angry about other hassles feel pointless.

And he did have friends. Most talked too much about their aches and pains, low-sugar diets, cancer scares, or blood pressure meds, and one wouldn't shut up about politics and colleges and history, but they were good people.

He just didn't have much to add to most conversations.

The ground quivered hard enough to shake the branches overhead. A rumble of sound followed a second later. Distant gunfire chattered next, punctuated by deeper booms. Those would be mortars or more fancy earthmover work. The distinctive roar of wind-driven flame drowned out everything else for a moment, and then quiet fell.

A whiff of sulfur tainted the shifting breeze, and grit crunched between his teeth.

Someone was having a *very* bad day on Camp Butler's practice range. Every military-grade wind rider was expected to prevent off-range drift during exercises, both as a matter of pride and to keep the peace with the base's neighbors. They needed to step up their seismic mitigation too.

Nobody liked having their windows rattled, and nothing alarmed civilians like a hint of brimstone in the air. The phone in Camp Butler's Community Relations office would be lighting up with complaints any second now.

Over his earbug, he heard a murmur followed by Elena saying, "Worried? No, startled. I knew Gateway was hosting joint exercises with fire and air from Lone Star and Choteau Companies. Their field discipline is usually better than that."

Jack chuckled to himself. Elena was a treat. Great minds did think alike.

A pause, another murmur, then from Elena, "I hang out with a retired Marine, remember? Also, my papa prints off the Camp Butler public information sheet on Sundays after church. We live on the northwest side, so it's mostly dust for us. It's really loud this close. That can't be fun with night exercises."

Mercury Battalion's power-wielding forces provided the nation with critical defensive troops. People liked that part. They didn't like the effects of the dirty, noisy, violent business of maintaining combat skills. Training exercises were a regular source of community friction.

Grace Reed's house was barely three blocks from the razor-wire topped fence at the practice range's northeastern edge. That explained how an unemployed single woman with two teenaged daughters had ended up with a big, rambling home on a fenced, half-acre corner lot.

He'd been questioned that point during the planning phase for today's route. The finances didn't make sense at first glance. And things that didn't make sense usually came back to bite security on the ass.

Elena had promptly pointed out the whole block was a patchwork of rundown pre-World War Two homes and glossy rebuilds, and informed him that Grace had outbid the Elgin Historical Society for it in a foreclosure auction after it sat unsold for years.

She was full of trivia like that, courtesy of her architect father. He worked with the Society's preservation specialists. Heather had helpfully pointed out it probably hadn't sold because it looked like something out of a horror movie. And she'd laughed when Jack warned her not to curse their luck.

Was Heather going to spend the rest of the afternoon in that shop? The more Jack thought about ice cream, the more he wanted it.

The next explosion rattled his tree so hard that little green things fell off the branches and pelted him. Two slips that close together meant this was a great week to be on a detached assignment for CLP. When Gateway got too many complaint calls to handle, they requested DPS Outreach support. *No, thank you.*

Jack couldn't blame people for being upset when exercises disrupted their lives. That didn't mean he enjoyed working the phone bank. The outrage got tedious fast.

It wasn't the Corps' fault Elgin had expanded right up to Camp Butler's perimeter, even if this subdivision had been here first.

It wasn't as if outsiders had to look at the range—the fences sat atop thirty-foot berms planted with unfriendly hedges—but the area was ripped to pieces once a month at minimum. After fifty-odd years of fires, floods, artificial earthquakes, gas attacks, and impacts from every kind of ordnance known to humanity, the zone was an ugly mess of blasted bare ground, piles of rubble, and foul wastewater ponds, and preventing spillover was a baseline expectation baked into the exercise plans. Containment was one-third of Mercury Battalion's motto after all.

Yes, this was a good day to be working the civvie side. Jack was uncomfortable sitting here, but at least he wouldn't be facing an epic ass-chewing *after* running around a blasted moonscape while pyros tried to fry him and earth-movers pelted him with rubble.

He was hot, though. And craving ice cream.

Heather came outside with a paper sack clutched in one clawed hand and a plastic bag of ice the size of a sea bag in the other. She wore a flower-print sleeveless sundress with a wide belt since they weren't representing the DPS today, and the sunshine raised gold highlights from the feathers covering most of her skin. Heat shimmered from the sidewalk underfoot, and her crest flattened in distaste as the steamy afternoon air enveloped her.

She moved aside to adjust the headset that gave her hands-free access to the radiophone in her belt pouch, and another woman exited the building, pushing a stroller out the door. Heather brought her wings up and out. The feathery barrier spanned several feet to either side and stretched over her head.

The toddler inside the stroller waved a gold-brown feather at her and howled with laughter.

Heather charmed a remarkable number of children with the molted primaries she kept in her belt pouch. With a sweep of wings, she blinked the short distance to Jack's side.

Dust and fluff drifted through the air she'd left empty. The giggling toddler made grasping motions as his mother pushed him down the sidewalk. The look she aimed across the street wasn't a frown, so Jack raised a hand and wiggled his fingers. "I see you made another friend."

"He said 'please,' and his mom invited me to sit at her table. We got talking." Heather set the ice on Jack's lap and handed over the paper bag. "There y'go, hot stuff. Best I could do."

"Much appreciated." The dusty scent of her teleport wafted over Jack, smelling of roses and pepper. He relocated the ice to the small of his back, leaning gratefully into the wet chill.

The paper bag held two pints of mint chip and a wooden spoon too tiny to bother using. He sucked the ice cream straight from containers, and it was as delicious as he'd hoped. Creamy pinpoints of dark chocolate added a spicy tingle to every melting swallow. He savored the rich, aromatic sweetness, but it didn't last long.

"Thanks, that hit the spot," he said as he licked his fingers.

"Man, I wish I could eat ice cream by the tub." Heather folded in her wings and sat carefully to avoid pinning her feathers under her butt. She adjusted the belt that held her phone, pocketbook, and other essentials, then slanted her head at Jack. Her pupils contracted and expanded rapidly, inspecting more than the visible spectrum. "You are still baking hot."

"I can keep ahead of the damage." He could regenerate any injury that didn't obliterate him outright. "This is Elena's last interview, and I'll hit the icebox at the office once we're done."

"It could be a while. I have a hunch the CLP pitch will win over this one, and that means we'll have to do a meet and greet."

"Want to bet a steak dinner on it?" The religious objectors rarely gave Elena a chance to sell them on Camp Liberty. The ones who did listen rarely fit the eligibility profile. He'd been hoping Grace Reed would refuse Elena at the door, but no luck. They were chatting away like old friends.

"Do you ever bet anything *except* a steak dinner?"

An indignant beeping erupted in Jack's earpiece—Elena sending her official "stop bugging me" signal this time. He checked his mic button, then the screen of the unit clipped to his belt. "I'm muted. Must be you, Heather."

"Crap." She pulled out her handset and punched at it. "Yeah. I accidentally hit the mic. I hate these new picture phones."

"You are a crabby old lady."

Heather prodded his arm with a sharp talon. "And you're a grumpy old man."

They both paused to listen to an exchange between Elena and her hostess about the legal disclosure paperwork. Then Heather said, "I'll take that bet. She named herself Grace, Jack.

That tells me she'll be willing to do anything to stay out of a camp."

"It tells me she's not rational." The memory of Grace Bell's desperate voice screaming for help rose up to haunt Jack. "I bet she wants nothing to do with anything DPS-related."

A man could hope. He didn't understand fanatics, and he had yet to meet a one who would have a rational conversation.

Heather said, "Get ready to lose, Junior. And are you *sure* you can hold out another hour or two? You're as red as a boiled lobster."

Working with mothers could be a major aggravation. "I'm sure, but just in case—" He popped the empty ice cream containers into his mouth and ground them to mush between his back teeth. "That should be enough boost to tide me over."

T-series biology didn't follow the rules. Most creatures Jack's size had daily energy requirements in the tens of thousands of calories. Under normal circumstances, he barely took in what an average null human did. Only when he reached his limit for converting rollover energy did he need to refuel. Nothing about his digestive tract worked the way doctors said it should.

The mysteries frustrated the medical community, but Jack didn't much care. He didn't go bankrupt buying groceries: that was the important point. Clothes were expensive enough.

He mainly ate to enjoy flavors. If he needed extra energy, he could process anything he could get into his stomach—and with diamond-hard teeth, there wasn't much he couldn't chew. All calories were good calories

Heather watched the paper bag and the plastic spoon follow the empty pint cylinders. "I can grab you something more substantial if you want," she said, sweetly helpful. "Maybe some bricks or a concrete block?"

One particularly bad morning—the day after a taxing Intake

retrieval—Heather had caught him gnawing on rebar to get his energy reserves back up. To make matters worse, she'd seen him turn down the offer of a cheese pastry a few minutes earlier.

It made perfect sense to him. Fuel was fuel. Cheese was disgusting. Heather was never going to let him forget it.

"Nah," he said. "I'm good." He picked up a handful of gravel and crunched it down more for the satisfaction of seeing Heather's eyes go big and round than because he needed it. Then he pulled down the brim of his ball cap to cut the glare of the lowering sun and relaxed against the bumpy ice bag.

Long, boring, uncomfortable waits were a damned sight better than the alternative, which would involve getting between Elena and assassins, stalkers, terrorists, or garden-variety muggers.

"Mind if I check in with Donyel?" Heather asked. "He left a message. Talia had a bad day at camp."

Heather's daughter was attending a day camp, and both parents fretted about things like social skills and reading levels. Jack thought they worried too much, but he didn't have kids. "Go right ahead. Say hi from me. I'll keep an ear on Elena."

Heather walked off, tapped at the radiophone earpiece on the headset and spoke softly into her throat mic. Her crest drooped under the assault of direct sunlight, and she lifted her wings to shade herself as much as to give herself privacy.

With luck, the weather and the family drama would be the worst things they faced today. Jack was mentally selecting side dishes for his future steak when his earpiece beeped again, followed by Valerie's call-tune.

He sat up straight and waved to Heather. She ended her call and returned, tapping her cheek to confirm she had Elena's surveillance covered.

There wasn't much to surveil. Elena was alone, waiting while Grace dealt with a towel crisis elsewhere in the house.

Jack nodded thanks and took a firm grip on his temper before he tapped accept-call. This wasn't unexpected, but it wasn't a welcome interruption either. "Hi, Valerie. What's up?"

"Nothing, really." Her voice was soft and hesitant. "Just wondering, how is our girl's day going?"

Jack swallowed several variations on *liar, liar, pants on fire.* They both knew she wanted to know something specific, but there was no point in pushing her on the point. Pushing Valerie was like pushing water.

If she was going to be vague, he was free to interpret the question any way he wanted. "It's going well. She's collected half a dozen Camp Liberty interest forms today. Word must be getting around. People come at her with questions as soon as she gets private with them."

And if that didn't satisfy Valerie's curiosity, she could damned well ask a direct question. One of these days, she would have to stop being afraid of him. It wasn't like he would bite her.

"That's great news," she said, then went silent long enough to make Jack wonder if he'd lost her. Then she said diffidently, "Any good candidates for testing the prime-level protocols?"

That was a more obvious hint, but Jack wasn't giving up that easily.

"Two so far." Part of their collaboration with the DPS included limited access to the R-factor status of everyone in the areas Elena canvassed. The confidentiality agreement had clocked in at a boggling eighty-seven pages. For all he knew, he'd signed away his essential freedoms for the privilege. "Both in pre-rollover with high spike assessments, likely to make rank three or better. We're ready."

Word was getting out because Camp Liberty had guided

eleven happy Elgin residents through home rollovers in the past eighteen months. Nothing succeeded like success.

They'd tested their basic procedures on low-factor cases who might have escaped internment. So far, the system had worked equally well for their high-factor candidates. The last three clients had been potential primes who rolled lower than predicted.

Valerie was using the readiness question to push a personal agenda. *That* was the point she didn't want to bring up for Jack to shoot down again.

His objection was the minority report. Everyone else loved Valerie's idea, even Amy, who he'd expected to know better. If there was one lesson Jack had learned in the Corps, it was to never base command decisions on emotion.

"I hope you're right. We're bound to get a prime soon." Valerie paused again. "Um. I don't suppose you remember which homes Elena's seen already?"

She would tiptoe around it all day. Jack lost patience with the game. "Quit it, Val. You want to know if Elena's gotten an answer from Grace Reed. The answer is not yet. She's at the house right now. And Grace Reed is upstairs cleaning up after her kids, so Elena's alone if you want me to patch her into the call so you can bug her instead of me."

"No, don't disturb her. I didn't mean to make you angry. It is not a bad idea, it's—"

"It's over and done, Valerie. Drop it." Jack clenched his teeth hard. "I have my opinion, you have yours, I was outvoted, and that's that. We're giving Reed the next slot if she wants it, and she'll get every bit of support I can give her as leader of her transition team. Are we clear?"

Some people would not take yes for an answer. They wanted to talk about it. And talk and talk and talk. It wasn't enough to say you would do your job to the best of your ability, oh, no. You had to say you were *happy* about it.

Civilians, Jack thought. He didn't say it, not even under his breath. If Heather heard, she might leave a hunk of Limburger in his car. Again. "Are we clear?" he repeated.

Valerie cleared her throat and sniffed. "Clear."

"Okay, then. Good." He switched to Elena's channel for a moment. "Hey, tiger. Call Val as soon as you have a go/no-go on Reed, will you? So she stops hassling me? Thanks."

Heather cocked her head to the side and frowned at him. He shrugged.

"Thank you," Valerie whispered, and the earpiece clicked as she disconnected.

9: EAT AND DRINK AND BE GLAD

414 Elm Drive, Elgin IL

ELENA WAS SCOWLING at her briefcase on the picnic table when Grace returned from upstairs. The striped canvas patio awning rippled in the breeze, casting tinted shadows across her face.

Grace sat across from her and picked up the forms she'd been filling out. "Extra towels located, flooding averted. Sorry about the delay."

"No problem. I was thinking." She made circles in the condensation under the pitcher in the center of the table before picking up her glass to take a sip. Her frown melted away. "This is delicious, by the way."

"Thank you. It's fresh." Grace smiled back, pleased that their social chat earlier had smoothed over the initial friction. She nodded to the two dwarf lemon trees in their planters at the edge of the patio. "Straight from these babies. They come indoors in the winter and keep the house smelling like summer."

"Neat. They're pretty." Elena gestured around the yard with her drink. "The whole yard is outrageous. Beautiful, I mean. Like a little patch of country. It looks bigger than I know it is."

"The girls call it our secret garden because of the privacy fence." Grace completed the last line of check boxes and glanced over the papers one last time before handing them over. "I think I covered everything."

There had been no place for name or address, but they were otherwise similar to census and R-Factor registry forms she'd filled out dozens of times over the years. *Render under Caesar,* she thought wryly, and said, "I would imagine the DPS has this information for me already."

Her R-factor status was conspicuously absent from the forms. Legally only the DPS could ask for that information, although other people did all the time.

"Oh, but I work *with* the DPS, not for the DPS," Elena said with earnest concern. "That's why I have to give out those disclosures." She set aside Grace's forms and pulled a stapled document from the large yellow envelope. "The data is anonymous, and each part is optional. Here's the legal stuff for the next part."

"I hope you don't mind." The first page displayed a government infobase portal address to visit if she wanted electronic copies. Grace took her time over the dense language, looking for loopholes or traps. The disclaimers outlined standard confidentiality limits on anonymous information. "I don't mean to seem paranoid," she remarked when she finished, "but I've been burned before. These are impressive protections."

"That's what the lawyers said." Elena took another sip of lemonade. "I like people being cautious. It's why I do this like an interview. I'll skip past sections you aren't comfortable talking about. Incomplete written surveys, we wouldn't know if the questions were skipped by accident."

"And what *are* we going to be talking about?"

"Your opinions about the R-factor population and the DPS. I've been tracking this since middle school. I'm using the same data for some political position papers. And a friend is doing a sociology project for college credit. That's why everything is on paper. In case it's challenged, like with ballot signatures."

"You're very ambitious, aren't you?"

"You mean, 'aren't you a little young for this?'" Elena didn't roll her eyes, but Grace saw the impulse in the way she blinked.

"Maybe." Grace suppressed her smile, not wanting her sympathy misinterpreted as mockery. Being young and female meant a constant fight to be taken seriously. "You did say you started in middle school."

"After the bombing. I said if I was old enough for people to shoot at me, I was old enough to ask why. The PR people thought I would get bored or grow out of it. But I won't. I never will." Her tight scowl fell away, replaced by a wrinkled nose and a half-shrug. "I'm getting too intense, aren't I? It's only—I can't stand that there's so much hate in the world."

"Don't apologize for knowing that true evil exists. Oh, dear." Grace raised her glass to hide her dismay. Why had she mentioned evil? "I don't mean to preach. I only meant you know about hate more than most people because of the school attack."

And *that* sounded patronizing.

Elena wasn't laughing at her, but Grace wanted to dissolve from embarrassment. "I admired your courage," she said firmly. "That's all I meant."

"Well, thank you." The girl's mood brightened. "I'm actually glad you see it the same way I do. Some people think the Marines who saved my life are the evil ones, which is why I get defensive. That day changed my life."

"Understandably." Grace agreed, ashamed of her earlier slip again.

In a roundabout way, the school bombing and its aftermath had changed her life too.

She had spent hours scouring the news articles and struggling with questions she dared share with no one. How had good people, with reasonable fears, committed such horrific actions? Was unwavering hatred of authority any better than unquestioning trust? If the Devil could wear a beautiful face, might the opposite be true as well?

Such questions had made her review her own life in painful, awful ways, and that had made leaving the church easier when the time came. Not easy, but easier.

"Life is so strange," she said. "I'm enjoying this—more than I expected, to be honest—but it took a terrible thing in your past to bring you here to meet me."

"See, I was thinking exactly the same thing, so we have that in common too." Elena grinned and raised her glass. "One more thing before I get started with real questions. I have to say you have a beautiful home."

The unlikely compliment tickled Grace's sense of humor. "Thank you, but it's hardly beautiful yet. We had to do the foundation work first to get an occupancy permit. The interior is taking longer than I hoped. It should be tidied up by Christmas."

If she was still alive at Christmas. *No.* She shoved that thought deep into the abyss. *Not. Now.*

Elena shook her head. "I'm not being polite. My papa does architectural design, so mess is my normal. Our last house was tarps, power tools, and plaster dust for two whole years. He taught me to see the bones, the woodwork, and detailing. Edwardian, right?"

"Yes!" Warmth touched Grace deep inside. The unexpected

joy of encountering a kindred soul took root and twined through her. "These homes went up in the late nineteenth century, early twentieth. I don't meet many people who know that."

"You should meet Papa. He *gushes*. When he found out I was canvassing around here, he insisted I keep my eyes open for potential fixer-uppers. He gives addresses to our realtor so he can offer on them before they hit the market."

"That's smart. Things go fast. The property values collapsed after the All-Equality riots in the sixties, but investors are swarming now. A tax break went through last year. The training range is the only reason the prices aren't sky-high."

"Mrs. Fletcher down the block pretended the noise was thunder through our whole talk. It was kind of funny."

Mrs. Fletcher was a bossy gossip who stuck her nose in everything and stirred up trouble with lies and half-truths. Grace stuck with the more diplomatic observation, "It's more polite to say nothing than to get into arguments."

Elena squirmed in her seat. "It isn't like they do maneuvers for fun. They're practicing to save lives. But I suppose that's no comfort when they're making your windows shake."

I suppose was a teen's version of an olive branch. Grace accepted it in the spirit given. "It was worse when we had to buy bottled water for a week after they accidentally poisoned the reservoir. I count my blessings. They do warn us, and they reimbursed us for the water. Besides, if they trained elsewhere, I wouldn't have this place, and I love it."

"I can tell by the work you're doing. Are you going to keep the tin ceiling? If not, can my papa buy it from you? One of the ladies on the 400 block bragged about pitching the ugly metal into the landfill when she moved in, and when I told Papa, his heart broke."

"That would be Mrs. Williston. You can tell your father I

salvaged most of her tin and the crown moldings. And assure him I am keeping my vintage elements."

"Oh, good." Elena fiddled with her pen. "I'm way off-topic."

The fidget and awkward remark forcefully reminded Grace of the difference in their ages. "You aren't here to chat about home renovation. I'm sure I am gushing as badly as your father does."

"I enjoy it," Elena assured her. "Really. But okay. Here we go."

She pulled the metal clipboard closer and opened it with a squeak of hinges to reveal blank printed forms. "In case anything sounds familiar, I based the main part on an official survey the DPS did ages ago, before the Cape Horn Incident."

"Cape Horn? Do you mean the Gulf Uprising? The camp that declared independence and got away with it?"

Elena wiggled the pen. It looked embarrassed. "Sorry, yes. I have to use the official name. DPS Media Relations says the other name is embarrassing and inaccurate."

"They should be embarrassed by what caused it, not by what people call it."

"Nice point. Wait. There's a spot later for comments like that." Elena copied the long number from the envelope label onto an underlying sheet. She flipped back one page. "Here's a good spot to start. What were your first impressions when you heard about Cape Horn?"

"I wasn't shocked. I was raised knowing internment camps were horrible places."

Retrospectives made the broadcast rounds every year on the anniversary of the event. And each year, more internees from Camp Horn Island came forward to relate the appalling abuses they had survived.

The Ranch congregation had come together to view those shows the same way they watched First Night documentaries and coverage of events like bombings. The elders disliked media, but they loved reminders of the violence inherent in the system.

Grace remembered her father being bitterly disappointed that the "Uprising" was bloodless and abrupt. It had begun and ended one fine evening when a cluster of bewildered, disoriented DPS camp staffers and a few of the internees showed up on the mainland.

And Horn Island itself disappeared.

It was visible from orbit but vanished from view if approached by air or sea, and sightings of spirits and disturbances in the area were common. Anyone who sailed too close to its map coordinates was teleported to shore without warning. The mystery was television ratings gold.

Grace said, "Mainly I remember pitying the poor souls who stayed behind."

"Huh. The follow-up is, why do you feel that way?"

"They're trapped there forever." They had used their powers to create a tropical paradise, judging from the satellite photos, but at what cost? "They overthrew their captors, but they still can't escape."

"Interesting perspective." Elena made a note.

Grace also pitied the rebels for winning their earthly refuge at the cost of their souls, but that wasn't something to explain to a non-believer.

And a tiny doubting whisper asked, *And do* you *still believe it?* The thought festered in the back of her mind. Were the powers that came with rollover sinful, or was her understanding faulty? Were her doubts a temptation leading her off the path of righteousness?

"I get caught up in unimportant details," she said to get things moving again. "My teachers always said so." *And the elders.*

"There's no such thing as an unimportant detail," Elena said with all the confidence of her youth. She flipped back to the first page. "I use this as my template because the outrage and calls for reform died down. I wanted to know why. I compare answers over time and across age, income, and other variables."

"Variables like R-factor status?"

"If you're comfortable sharing it, yes. But it's specifically illegal to ask, which is why it wasn't on the personal information form, and totally not necessary."

Her sincerity was sympathetic, pleasant, and calm. Grace's next thought came tumbling out. "Do *you* mind saying?"

"No, but I'm null, so I don't have much to lose. And when my test results went public without my permission, it felt awful. Also, I can only imagine what it's like to live with the fears poz do. I try to be sensitive."

That earnestness made it easy to share. Besides, it would hardly be a secret much longer. "I'm poz. High factor, due to roll within the year, if there's a box for that."

"The DPS has a box for everything," Elena said with a wry half-smile as she wrote the information on the first page. "Okay. Actual first question."

The survey focused on opinions about various R-factor activities, from annual testing and the necessity of internment, to commercial use of the national registry and the unfair advantages rollovers had in certain employment fields. The same ideas were raised in different phrasings and encouraged nuanced responses. Long minutes went by in conversation.

The shadows were lengthening by the time they reached the end of the last page. A breeze gifted them with a swirl of cool air. The scent of roses and drying prairie grasses passed across the patio, and the awning flapped.

While Elena put everything in the yellow envelope, Grace

refilled both their glasses, rattling the ice in the empty pitcher. "Do you get different answers to the same questions over time?"

"Yes and no. Public confidence in the DPS is down across the board. Not only with poz respondents and unspecified, but also with nulls. Support for internment is dropping fast."

"Not fast enough." Bitterness swept through Grace, and righteous anger rose, unexpected but too forceful to stop. "As long as camps exist, tragedies will pile up. Look what happened to my name-twin."

"Your what?" Elena's face clouded, then cleared. "Oh, right. Is it weird having the same name as someone famous who died?"

"It can be uncomfortable." Some things were more important than comfort. When the DPS had built her new identity, they'd encouraged her and the girls to choose names with personal meaning.

She'd thought long and hard about how far she would go to keep faith with her vows and protect her children, and she'd chosen a name that would remind her of the choices she would face if God put her to the test.

And that test was coming. Nervous tension pulled the muscles along Grace's spine so tight they felt like metal rods. Grace Bell's case was used by politicians to justify camps, which was ironic since the woman might have lived a long and happy life with her family if internment hadn't torn her from her home.

Grace couldn't stop herself from finishing that thought aloud. "Grace Bell deserved better," she said. "The camp system is wrong, and opposing it is a moral and civic duty. There was no place in your survey to say it like that, pure and simple. There should be."

An instant later, she regretted her outburst. She'd agreed to cooperate today to prevent trouble, not to cause it. Worry shivered under her skin, itched in her fingers and toes, and her breath caught in her throat. *What have I done?*

Elena might not be a DPS employee, but she worked with them, and she was staring, those wide dark eyes solemn. Then her smile broke out again. "Wow. You sound exactly like a friend of mine. She's totally laid-back most of the time, but sometimes she makes these big, dramatic proclamations. She sounds right even when I don't agree. Which I do. Agree with you, I mean."

"You do?" Grace clasped her hands in her lap, trying to squeeze the anxiety away.

"Of course! I advocate for reform every time I'm on TV. I thought you said you'd seen me. No, sorry." Elena shook her head. "That isn't fair. Anyway, I didn't start because of the school bombing by itself. I have opinions because my papa nearly killed me and my sibs. You haven't heard that part?"

"If I did, I've forgotten. What happened?"

"Mama rolled first, so Papa skipped his tests and stalled with appeals because if he got interned too, the DPS would've placed me, my little brother, and my sister in different foster homes for the year and maybe forever."

"And he rolled hot." Grace's stomach clenched. Of course he had rolled badly. The man hadn't prepared himself for his trial, hadn't raised his children to understand the battles their elders faced. They hadn't been ready to help him make the hard choices. "I'm so sorry."

"Me, too. One minute he was reading a book, then he's screaming and bloody and has poison fangs and claws. It wasn't fair that he went through that in front of us. It was wrong." Elena's passion made her voice crack. She ducked her head, combed her hair behind one ear again. "Anyway. I'm on your side. The system has to change."

The fumbling confession was a balm to Grace's overworked nerves. "I hope those beliefs won't get me—or you—in trouble."

Elena shook her head. "This talk is confidential, and don't worry about *me*. I'm not shy about saying it in public. But there's another thing you might want to hear about."

"Another survey?"

"No, it's a non-profit some friends of mine started." Elena ran her fingers along the edge of the open briefcase. "Setting it up was how I spent my gov service year after high school, and I'll work for them full time after I graduate college if things keep going as well as they have been, but that isn't the point."

She paused for breath and grinned. "Sorry, but it's really exciting. The *point* is, I'm allowed to distribute information and collect interest forms and applications. The organization is an official DPS partner."

By the time she ran out of words, her cheeks were flushed, her eyes bright, and she was bouncing slightly. Grace's curiosity warred with amusement. "That certainly sounds exciting. What does this organization *do*, exactly?"

"Oh, geez." Elena's laugh was self-conscious. "It's an at-home rollover assistance program. For everyone—everyone so far, anyway—it's been an honest-to-goodness legal alternative to internment. We call it Camp Liberty."

An alternative to internment. This was literally the answer to Grace's prayers. Hope rose up in her heart, so bright and intense it dazzled her for a moment. Tears stung her eyes. *Thank you, God, oh, thank you.*

"I want to apply," she said once she could see again. "I'll take the information, but I already know I want in."

Elena beamed as she handed over a white folder with a glossy red and blue shield on the front. "In that case, here's the packet."

10: PATIENCE IS BETTER THAN PRIDE

414 Elm Drive, Elgin IL

GRACE READ and signed the top sheet, a standard declaration of interest and documents release, detached her copy, and turned to the first page of the application.

Elena made a small, surprised sound. "You don't have to finish it today. The interest form is all Camp Liberty needs to verify you have a qualifying condition—which you do, from what you said. There's an online app at the AmeriNet address on the header. I don't want to overwhelm you."

Was that concern or a polite escape attempt? Grace would sleep better knowing she'd done what she could, but they had been sitting here over an hour. "And I don't want to keep you, but the sooner I finish, the—"

The squeak of the sliding glass door interrupted her. Lauren stopped tugging on the handle with the door half-open and spoke through the screen. "Hi, Mom, can we—oh, hey, Elena. You're still here."

"Hi, Lauren. What's up?"

"Not much." Lauren fidgeted with the insulation on the door track. Maggie came up beside her, waving through the glass, and their friends came huddling up behind them. Grace recognized the unmistakable signs of permission about to be asked for something the girls were afraid she would refuse.

Lauren pulled out the extra-bright smile she only used when she was hiding something. "We cleaned up everything and put the crusts in the compost bin, Mom, and the leftovers are covered on a plate in the refrigerator in case you want them later."

Oh, yes, they wanted a favor. Cleaning up from a meal without a single reminder—that was a dead giveaway. So was false generosity. They knew Grace didn't like pizza.

She looked to Elena. "Are you hungry? I'm sure Lauren would be happy to heat up a slice for you."

Lauren bristled, and Maggie blushed. Grace gave them both a warning look. They were clever, her girls, but she was their mother, and they would do well to remember that.

"No, thank you," Elena said. "My Mama is home on leave, and she's teaching my little sister how to make empanadas. Teresa will cry if I don't eat at least as many as I do when Mama makes them. It does smell good. Where was it from?"

Lauren's frown melted back to a smile. "Jake's? On Forest Avenue?"

"Oh, sure. Have you ever tried Giuseppe's? They have the best cheese sticks."

One of the other girls squealed and clapped. "I love Giuseppe's! Coach Davies takes us there after meets."

"Yes, that's when I first went." Elena cocked her head to one side. "I'm sorry, I don't know your name, but didn't you run track on Coach's middle school team last year?"

"I'm Sue Pesche. This fall, I'll be doing freshman cross-country. You know my brother Simon, I think. He did hurdles? He's at U of I now?"

"Yes! He graduated a year ahead of me. The year we went to state. He was great!"

Grace cut in before things got out of hand. "Lauren, did you need something?"

Elena's interest in people's lives obviously wasn't limited to surveys. As amusing as it was to see her acting her age for the first time, discussions about food and boys could go on for hours.

Lauren waved both hands as if gathering her thoughts. "Adele's mom says we can do a sleepover there tonight if all our parents say yes. So we called, and everybody has said yes, so we're asking if it's okay to spend the night there?"

Maggie piped up. "We packed toothbrushes, pajamas, sleeping rolls, footie socks, clean clothes, and a thank you card for Mrs. Wahlberg for the morning. We remembered everything."

Everything except asking first. Grace held her temper. They'd come a long way from the girls' first adventure, which she had nearly ruined with frantic calls to the other mothers in the neighborhood.

They'd "forgotten" to tell her about the party to avoid being told they couldn't go. The hosting parents hadn't checked to see that everyone had permission to be there because the group of friends was in and out of each others' houses all the time. She'd panicked when they didn't come home before dark.

A long, tear-drenched family meeting had resulted in a strict rule: they were only allowed to attend sleepovers whose hosts had proof of *prior* informed consent from every attendee. Earlier this year, one of the other mothers had thanked Grace privately for enforcing the higher standard.

Lauren jumped into the silence. "Please, Mom. It's the last

time when we can do a big summer party. Kirsten and Brittany both have to go on family vacation next week, and then school starts."

Maggie, never as eloquent nor as manipulative as her twin, said, "Please-please-pu-leeeeese?"

"That isn't helping your case," Grace told her, but a night without them would be a rare treat.

Maybe she could work up the courage to pull out those DPS letters and read them. If she had an option beyond internment, she should find out how much time she had left to plan.

No amount of hope, however bright, could banish every fear. Avoiding internment would not guarantee surviving rollover.

Leave the future's worries in the future, she told herself. *Give them happiness now.* She forced a smile for their sake. "Of course you can go."

The girls shrieked and danced in a collective show of happiness. Grace shooed them off, and her heart swelled with bittersweet guilt. Her daughters were precious to her, but sometimes she dreamed of a clean home free from unpredictable drama, random shrieks, or pouting.

She called after them, "Take money from my purse and get ice cream. Harwood Dairy is having a sale."

A retreating chorus of cheers met the suggestion. Grace got up to close the door the girls had left open in their excitement. "Some days, they make me proud," she said when she returned. "Some days, not."

Elena's expression was rueful. "I finally understand why Mama threatened to sell me to the circus so many times. I'd like to think I'm better now, but she's threatening to rent out my room the day after I leave for college."

Grace wasn't sure if she should laugh or not. Silence fell. She settled into her chair, tugging at her sundress to cover her dirt-speckled knees. "I was saying the sooner I know if I qualify, the happier I'll be. You certainly don't have to wait."

"Oh, I don't mind. You can meet two of the transition team members today if you're up for it. They happen to help me with these surveys, so it's easy to arrange."

"A job interview?" She glanced at her dirty nails and legs and resisted the urge to touch her hair. Humility was a virtue, but there were limits. "I don't think so."

"No, it's so *you* can interview *them*. They like to thank everyone who fills out an interest form, and you'll be a step past that."

"Let's see how I feel when I'm done."

Meeting the adults involved might be a relief. If they weren't people she could work with, false hope would have less time to put down roots. Another benefit of the girls being gone: she wouldn't have to worry about them eavesdropping.

The personal data section of the Camp Liberty application was comprehensive, with questions covering a wide range of health and habit information. No alcohol, yes, a religious restriction, meat several times a week, number of blood relatives who died of this or that—the distillation of her life into columns of check boxes could have been depressing, but she found the exercise oddly soothing.

Once she checked off the last one and turned the page to the next section, she found a block of questions asking for more details about her objections to DPS rollover protocols. Her spirits sank at the thin lines provided for the answers. "I guess I will have to wait after all. My handwriting is unreadable. I'll do it on my computer later."

"Or—I could write them down for you." Elena bit her lip. "If that isn't weird."

"I'd be grateful."

Elena took the form and secured it to her clipboard. "The

first question is: have you already filed for an opt-out? If so, what kind? Explain."

"Yes, I've filed for religious exemption." Grace did not snarl the jargon phrase, but some of the old, bitter anger escaped. "Not that it means a thing."

The opt-out clause was smoke and mirrors designed to lull a gullible public into complacency.

Elena nodded. "And your denomination? I'm Catholic, in the interests of full sharing."

"I was raised in a small, independent congregation out on the West Coast. It's an offshoot of the Brothers and Sisters of Freedom if you're familiar with them."

Elena gave the garden another look, nodding. "I know a little. It's one of the Denial cul—uh, groups. Everyone lives off-grid and home-schools. They call government aid illegal interference but stay out of trouble. And they consider rollover to be a curse from God."

"No, it's a curse from the Devil. We allow his worldly servants to test us for the mark of sin, we respect our neighbors, and we pray for redemption. If the taint consumes one of us, we take care of our own, within the community,"

The recitation came straight from the holy writings, rising from memory without effort. So she had always been taught and tried to believe. And she'd continued to act on those beliefs despite cutting the worldly ties to her past.

Hadn't she continued to say her prayers and follow the guidance in the holy teachings? Hadn't she prepared a refuge, should the worst of evils befall her or her children?

She had, and yet the words of the litany tasted bitter in her mouth. "I should say, we try to live that way. The government would declare the church a threat and dissolve it if members refused camp orders, but accepting internment means leaving the church and everyone you love forever. The elders call it the Devil's tithe."

"Ugh." Elena glanced up and down quickly as she wrote. "Sorry. That was a sympathy ugh, not a judgmental one."

"It's always a tragedy."

The memory of those red-bordered summons burned in Grace's mind. She could *not* go to a camp. Surrounded by strangers, she would surely be lost to her curse.

Or would it be losing? Had Josh been weak, or had he been brave enough to reject a flawed interpretation of God's will? Had she misjudged him when he accepted rollover?

What if she had misjudged him *after*? Maybe running away from him had been the wrong decision.

No. That doubt was easy to reject. The other uncertainties were harder to shove aside. The conflict tied her stomach in tight, hot knots.

The swirling breeze carried the scents of sun-warmed herbs, smoke from a neighbor's barbecue. Elena had stopped writing and fiddled with her pen, watching her with a worried air.

Grace shook her head. "That's enough, I think."

"Would you say your objections to internment are more religious or more personal?"

Grace's head throbbed. She rubbed her temples. "I object for both reasons equally? I've left the church, but I still believe internment tears people away from everything we hold dear right when we need support most. When our futures and our souls hang in the balance, why isolate us and throw more change and uncertainty at us?"

"Hang on, let me get that." Elena scribbled. "Okay, should religious groups be allowed to oversee rollovers in private facilities instead? Licensed and inspected, of course. Elaborate."

"No." Five years ago, she would have said *yes* without hesitation. "Maybe. I don't know."

Elena looked up, face carefully neutral. "Elaborate?"

The quiet way she waited for clarification was eerie in someone so young. *An old soul perhaps, but too innocent to burden with my secrets.* Grace thought through several answers before saying, "The Salvation Assembly would never agree to government oversight of any kind."

And for good reason. Her grandfather had left the Brothers and Sisters of Life because they were too lenient with the cursed in their congregation. "Some rituals must be done in secret to be sacred."

Elena didn't look up this time, but she nodded. "And the government certainly doesn't like anyone having secrets except them."

They went through the multi-page document together. Elena handed it back so Grace could complete a final sheet with legal, medical, and emergency contact information.

When she finished, her hands ached. She unclenched them then folded them together in her lap again. "Now what?"

Elena checked over the pages. "Now you're officially an applicant, and I invite my friends to meet you. We'll be in the area again tomorrow and the next day too, if you'd rather set a time."

"No." She might as well get it done. "There's a telephone in the kitchen."

"Thank you, I have one." Elena swung her legs over the bench and took a radiophone from the inner pocket of the blazer she'd taken off earlier. "I'll be right back."

She walked out between two flower beds, dark ponytail swinging over her back, free hand touching the bobbing yellow heads of tickseed and sunflower as she spoke quietly with her friends.

Soon she was walking quickly back. "They're waiting on someone right now," she said. "Is a half-hour too long to wait?"

The hesitancy left Grace suspicious about the vague reason, but her resolve hadn't weakened. "That's fine. My evening is free, and it gives me time to wash up. If it wouldn't be rude to leave you out here."

"I don't want to be in your way. I can wait out front."

"You'll do no such thing. Make yourself at home. There's more lemonade in the refrigerator, and the bathroom is the door next to the stairs. The tile is torn up, but everything is clean and works."

Ten minutes was ample time for a quick wash. She brushed her hair and put on an unstained dress. Finding clean socks that matched took an extra minute. When she returned to the patio and slipped on her boots, Elena was out among the vegetable beds, peering at the tomato plants.

Spots of red peeked out between the drooping green leaves. Grace itched to grab a harvest basket, but she'd already washed up.

She joined Elena in the hazy, slanting sunshine. Humid heat kissed her clean skin, tickling the damp hairs at the back of her neck. The air over the garden beds hummed with busy insects zooming back and forth from bloom to bloom.

Elena said, "This is amazing. Please say you'll tell me how you do it."

"Gardening isn't complicated." Grace adjusted the salvaged lumber edging with her boot. Should she put on fancier shoes? No. If they couldn't accept her for who she was, their program wouldn't work for her. "Dig holes, plant seeds, pull weeds, and water when it doesn't rain."

"That can't be all." Elena waved a hand at the last of the bolted lettuces. "What are these? Does anything need to be picked? Could I do it?"

She radiated sincerity with every cheerful question. Grace eyed the girl's dressy shorts and light-colored top. "There's no need for you to work. I'm always looking for new people to take extra tomatoes and zucchini this time of year."

Elena tilted her head, and a dimple formed in one cheek. "I could pretend that's why I'm asking, but that's a lie, and lying is a sin. I did mention I'm Catholic, right? Anyway, I'm genuinely interested. Don't you ever meet someone, and right away you think, *I like this person. I want to be friends?"*

"No."

"Never? That's funny. I do it all the time. Look, no one in my house can keep plants alive. If you're willing to show me around, I think that'd be a fun way to spend the wait."

Her self-assurance was infinitely astonishing. "Are you *sure* you're only eighteen?" Grace asked.

Elena's eyes sparkled. "Very sure. My mentor Valerie says my insides are older than my outsides. She *sees* things, you know? I used to think I wouldn't mind rolling into a power like hers. Small, invisible, helpful. I used to pray for that before I found out I was null."

Here was another of those marvelous ideological differences. Elena's acceptance of her friend's curse was more than personal. When she talked about it, she sounded *wistful.* She saw no contradiction between praying for salvation and hoping for rollover. Surely those ideas were incompatible?

The truth came to Grace like a soft whisper on the breeze. She could march obediently down the familiar road she no longer trusted—or she could step aside, into the fearful wilderness, and open her eyes to new wonders.

If ever she had felt the hand of God moving in her life, it was now. She had prayed for guidance so many times, and here was living proof that real faith did not follow a single, narrow path. That had to mean something.

"Please." Elena put a hand on Grace's arm. "It's beautiful, and I would love to know more."

Grace put her hand over Elena's. "In that case, I'd love to introduce you to my garden."

"Magnificent!" Elena pulled away and bounced on her toes. "Tell me if you get tired of questions."

11: WHATEVER YOUR HAND FINDS TO DO, DO IT WITH ALL YOUR MIGHT

August 17, 2019, DPS CA Region 20 Offices, Riverside CA

VALERIE CHECKED HER DESK CLOCK, did the simple time zone calculation, and debated whether to call Jack and Heather for another update.

Best to leave them be. No one liked being nagged. They were competent and motivated, and Elena often ran over the allotted time with interviews when she met someone interesting. Valerie caught herself chewing on a strand of her hair and folded her hands so she wouldn't start chewing her nails.

Logic didn't stop her anxiety. The stakes were too high this time for her to relax. She pulled Grace's DPS file to her main screen one more time. There was no such thing as being too informed.

Her sight talent didn't work on images, but she didn't need to be psychic to draw conclusions from Grace Reed's photo. The haphazardly-trimmed hair and bloodshot eyes told a story Valerie knew by heart: too tired and too busy for proper haircuts or skincare, too worried to sleep well, resigned to wearing old clothes and not eating enough because growing children came first.

Valerie wore suits and skirts over lacy blouses and shiny pumps these days, but she would never forget the headaches a hairnet could cause. She knew desperation when she saw it. She'd steeped in despair for years before rolling into her new sight.

Grace's weary determination all but leaped off the screen. What abilities were slowly maturing behind that careworn face? The attached medical report predicted a major power would crash over her like a rogue wave. Her spike results were at the top of the range. The DPS had to weigh risks against rights. Internment was a foregone conclusion despite the exemption request and appeals on file. Her voluntary-appearance time window would close in four days.

This situation was exactly the kind of problem they'd designed Camp Liberty to solve—*if* Grace would let them help. Elena had enthusiasm and earnestness on her side. Maybe the delay was a good sign.

Valerie put her hand on the stacks of approved dispensations, exceptions, and talent requisitions she'd put in motion earlier today. Transportation. Diagnostics. Communications. Perimeter protection. The departmental permissions had been filed, and the necessary exceptions were lined up. Camp Liberty was ready to make a free-range rollover happen for another presumptive prime-level client.

The wait would be less stressful if the logistics weren't so unpredictable. High-potential positives were more likely to roll hot, and a hot prime rollover could turn into an emergency at the drop of a hat.

If their first prime client was any kind of success, they could use the leverage to apply for expansion. But if their good intentions went up in flames—or drowned in a literal sinkhole, dissolved in acid, or putrefied with rot, to name a few of Valerie's nightmare scenarios—rebuilding public—and governmental—trust could take years.

This had to work. They were as ready as they ever would be, and Grace was as close to a perfect test case as they would ever find—which raised another unhappy possibility. Was Grace *too* perfect?

When it came to power, coincidences were never to be trusted. *If this is a go, I could ask for an F-series consult.* She should also check the general precognitive postings to see if any of them might apply.

The long interview meant Elena was doing her persuasive best. Once Grace signed the interest form, and if meeting Heather and Jack didn't put her off, Valerie could move the case forward, and everything would work out fine.

A soft, calm voice cut into her contemplations. "Looks like you're having second thoughts about something, Agent Wade."

"What?" Valerie corralled her wandering thoughts. She'd been staring across the desk at Joshua call-me-Sal Moretti. "You can use my name, Sal. I'm not your counselor anymore."

"All right, then, what are you worrying over, *Valerie*? Is it me?"

"No."

He took a long pull on his iced latte, twin to the one dripping condensation onto a coaster on Valerie's desk, and the last bit of liquid in his cup gurgled up through the straw. He didn't *say* Valerie was lying. Not out loud. She could read the message in his cool, blue eyes, and he knew it. He raised one dark eyebrow.

She was having third and fourth thoughts, not second ones, and she was afraid she'd failed to think of a fifth or a sixth one that would come back to haunt them. But none of her worries centered on the man who was sitting in her visitor's chair and making a brown coverall look stylish.

"I'm fretting over the Camp Liberty case I'm hoping you can help with," she admitted. "I appreciate your patience over the delay. I expected to be either briefing you or apologizing for wasting your time by now. It can't be easy to sit there wondering if there's a job for you or not."

"Yeah, it's a tough choice. Chat with my old counselor over fancy coffee, or load bottles onto pallets in a hot, dirty warehouse." Sal set down his cup and spread his arms wide as if physically embracing the office. "No complaints here, Agent Wade—Valerie. I just had a two *year* job anniversary thanks to you. If I can help, great. If not, no harm done."

Sal worked inventory control for an anti-freeze manufacturing firm. He'd taken the job as part of his probation and held it ever since. It was a solitary, tedious occupation, but the list of legal job options for people with his talent was short and notably lacking in human contact.

Valerie was pleased to see him showing the social confidence he'd worked so hard to learn in their sessions together. There were more lines on his face and more gray hairs on his head, but he had gained a steady, emotional serenity to match that vigorous physical presence.

He leaned forward in the visitor's chair and braced his hands on his knees. "Not sure what I can do for your start-up, though. Can I get a hint? I'm good with secrets. Raised in a cult, remember?"

"I remember." His concern was sincere, and his control was good. Valerie told him, "I can say your background is what makes you perfect for the job."

He raised both eyebrows at that. "You need a mostly harmless E-series loser who knows about cults? Awesome."

Self-deprecation *and* slang? He'd come such a long way since rollover. "You have been spending too much time in the mall, Sal Moretti."

The Camp Liberty phone next to the stack of papers beeped cheerfully. When she saw the call code on its screen, her pulse thudded loud in her ears. No video, thankfully. Jack's reflective sunglasses made his face a blank she couldn't help interpreting as hostile.

She hit *accept* and put the handset to her ear. "Hi, Jack, what's the word?"

"We're on for the meet and greet," Jack replied. "In fact, if you can swing a 'port out here, we're a go for the contract. Reed took the bait, hook, line, and sinker. Application's signed and witnessed. Happy now?"

His deep voice made the device buzz. Valerie pictured him in her mind, eight feet of armored muscle, sharp fangs, bristling protectiveness—and reminded herself that intimidating body was wrapped around a heart full of kindness that didn't transmit in his voice. "I'm thrilled. That's wonderful news. I'll arrange two 'ports with Transit and meet you at the address."

"Two? Oh, him." He had answered his own question without missing a beat. "Okay, that's a waste of time and money, but money's your worry. Mine's field safety, so keep him out of sight unless she signs a waiver. I don't want a domestic case to blow up in our faces because you want warm fuzzies and happy endings."

Valerie clenched her hands and swallowed her nerves. *Don't appease him. Don't apologize. Pretend he's Johnny or Gary and be firm*. "I didn't push it to a vote because I'm sentimental, Jack." And if she had, Amy would've voted against her. The Marine didn't have a sentimental bone in her large body. "I did it because she fits our criteria perfectly, except for the religious complications. And guess who knows about those things?"

Sal sat up straight, his tanned face turning a shocked, muddy gray. Surprise, curiosity, and fear blazed up. Valerie raised a finger to him—*wait*—while Jack said, "I've said it before, and I'll say it again. Never met a knowledge expert who was worth the trouble."

The line went dead. He never said good-bye. Valerie found herself smiling as she set down the phone. Jack was short-tempered and stubborn, but he was a team player. He would come around. She hoped.

"Who were you talking about?" Sal asked. His hands were tightly clenched together, but his emotional overload was still under control. "You're setting up a Camp Liberty for someone from the Ranch, aren't you? That's why you want me."

Valerie flipped open Grace's hardcopy file and pulled the photo. She hoped she was right about Sal, tried to trust what training and talent told her about him. Her fingers still trembled as she laid the photo on the desk. "I can't tell you more. Not yet. Maybe never."

"Oh, God." He stood and paced the small room in a tight circle, stopping on every pass to stare at the image with a hunger so intense it made Valerie's eyes water. The yearning was free of obsessive heat, dipped in misty shades of grief and sadness.

So that's what a broken heart looks like, she thought.

Sal dropped into the chair again, averting his eyes and tucking his hands under his arms in the grounding technique he used when he was on the verge of projecting. "But how can I —" His voice wavered. "I thought she—I can't. Can I?"

"Can you see her? I don't know. You understand what she's facing better than anyone else in the world. Are you willing to help her transition team with cultural issues? If she agrees to a limited ID release, it'll mean traveling to work locally. If she doesn't waive confidentiality, you'll help through phone conferencing and talking hypotheticals."

"Yes. Whatever that means. Whatever you need. Poor Sarah shouldn't face rollover alone." He looked up, hope bright in his face now. "Where is she?"

"I can't tell you anything unless she signs that release." Valerie tossed her laptop, extra pens, and printed copies of the CLP Intake documents into her shoulder bag. "But she'll hardly be alone. She and Jack will interview compatible assistants together, and once she hits onset, a team moves in. But you? You may never be directly involved."

"Direct, indirect, I'm all in." He hesitated. "How did you find her?"

"We didn't *find* her. We pull DPS files for background research on potential clients, and I saw your name. Once I put two and two together, I put in a clearance request for the sealed relocation files to confirm it wasn't a coincidence."

Reading through the partially-redacted details of Grace's life had been enough to make Valerie think a cultural consultation was a good idea. And while reconciliation wasn't her main motive, she could hope for one. Grace had listed Sal as an alternate emergency contact for her children in the event of her death. That had to mean something.

Valerie said, "I almost skimmed right past your name in her new file. I never knew what she looked like; the criminal complaint didn't include any photos."

"Photography steals pieces of your soul," Sal said. "No filming allowed on the Ranch, and we were taught to avoid cameras as much as possible when we went into the world for work and school. State IDs and RFI cards were the only photos most of us had."

That was the kind of information the team needed. "See? That's why I want your input. Details like that can turn into conflicts. Worst case, you get a consultation contract with an hourly rate. Best case, you're there for your family through the rollover process. Placing children with relatives is always the preferred solution."

He rose to his feet. "No—Valerie, no. You can't send them to Sarah's family or mine. You can't."

She glimpsed something dark in his concern, but it was gone before she could interpret it. "Again, not Sarah, and not your choice. Please don't make me regret this."

"You won't, but if my knowledge is what's important, then I'm telling you, they wouldn't be safe at the Ranch."

Secrets flitted like wraiths around him, and the bleakness in his eyes was guilt. "I hear you," Valerie said. "If it comes to that, tell Jack, the team leader."

She collected the pre-programmed radiophone and charging unit from the bottom drawer and set them on the desktop. "This is for your Camp Liberty communications. Can you wait in the Transit ready room? I'll know in an hour or two whether you'll be on-site or not. Other team members may want to talk to you before then."

He inspected the device, checking its screen before pocketing it. "I'll wait. I'll pray."

Of course he would. "It can't hurt. Maybe keep your fingers crossed too?"

"That, too." His lips curved, a twitch of a smile that bared those bleak and aching regrets inside. "I wish I could go back in time and change it, but I can't. This time I'll do better, with God's help."

He was silent the whole way to Transit, which occupied a big concrete block of a building at the far end of a hot, sandy breezeway from the building where Valerie worked. Inside, the dispatcher directed Sal to one of the standby rooms and dropped Valerie's name into the Departure queue with an ETD of ten minutes.

She was hurrying down the long, echoing hall to her

assigned Departure cubicle when the one detail she'd forgotten popped into mind.

Her home helper Anna needed to know about the schedule change.

The realization left her lightheaded. She'd covered this unlikely possibility with Anna before leaving in the morning, and they had agreed on contingency plans, but that didn't help. She only felt secure when she could do everything she was supposed to do when she was expected to do it.

Asking for help was still hard. If she'd remembered earlier, she could've sent an email. Notes were always easier. Best to get it out of the way before she forgot again.

To Valerie's relief, the call went straight to the message recorder as she'd hoped. Anna would be collecting the boys from school at this hour, and she wouldn't check her phone if she was on the road.

"Hi, Anna. The latest CLP project is moving fast, and I'm needed on site. Let the boys pick a consolation supper and warn them I won't be there for bedtime. I'm so sorry for the short notice. I promise I won't keep asking for extra nights and evenings forever." She couldn't afford it. "We can talk when I get in. A million thanks. You're a lifesaver."

She left messages on the boy's accounts since their phones stayed at home during school hours. For Gary, eight going on eighty, she kept it simple. "Hi, sweetie. I'm stuck at work. Anna will take care of you tonight, and I will give you ten hugs when I get home."

Ten-year-old Johnny needed boundaries more than comfort these days. "Hi, Johnny. I can't come home, and I know it isn't fair. Remember you promised to be polite and do what Anna says, including homework and chores. Ask first if you need to break something. Don't hit Gary. I love you even when you're mad at me. Bye, now."

She exhaled heavily as she disconnected.

Camp Liberty was an exhilarating project to be involved in, and she was proud of everything they were accomplishing. Her heart still ached when she didn't get to tuck her boys into bed at night.

And that, she reminded herself, was why they were doing this work.

12: GARDENS AND PARKS AND ALL KINDS OF FRUIT TREES

414 Elm Drive, Elgin IL

GRACE WAS DELIGHTED to see her hard work given the admiration it deserved for once. Elena clearly enjoyed the short tour. Her questions came dressed in praise and arose from observations so concentrated it seemed she soaked in the experience through every pore.

They meandered between the rows of vegetable beds and around the herb circle, through the wildflowers to the back corner of the yard opposite the one where she'd built a red wooden toolshed.

"I love how everything around the edges looks wild and natural but also cozy and secure," Elena said. "Was it like this when you moved in?"

"The privacy fence and the foundation plantings, yes, but everything was neglected and overgrown. This is my favorite spot."

Grace ducked beneath spreading branches heavy-laden with fruit and straightened, patting the dappled gray trunk of her apple tree. "Here's my pride and joy. Come up close. It's the only way to get the full effect."

"You have apples already!" Elena picked her way through the windfalls underfoot without a single complaint. Flies and bees hummed irritably, but none rose from their feasting. Her hair swept over her shoulder in a dark fall as she bent to avoid reaching twigs, and she lifted her face to peer at the fluttering green leaves overhead. "Oh! So many! Like little gold ornaments against the sky. What kind are they?"

"I'm not sure yet. It's an heirloom variety, sweet but small, and they brown fast. It was nearly gone when we moved in. Now that it's recovered, I should get it ID'd."

Decades of neglect had reduced the tree to a gnarled tangle of rot and suckers. The first summer here, Grace had devoted many afternoons to pruning out dead branches and treating disease, but the raggedy remnants hadn't inspired hope. When her efforts produced only sparse growth, she'd resigned herself to the tree's eventual demise.

Instead, to her surprise and pleasure, an exuberance of new leaves and blossoms had arrived with spring. A little rest and love had given the tree enough strength to shake off the injuries of its past.

There was probably a lesson in that. God offered a lot of lessons people overlooked.

"So neat. Is this ripe?" Elena touched a fuzzy green-yellow fruit with one gentle finger. "May I try one?"

Grace picked out two ripe ones and bit into her own, watching leaf-shadows flicker over Elena's face as the girl enjoyed her first crunchy bite. The quiet moment was a precious gift. Grace finished first and tossed the core to join the windfalls. "I know what you meant now," she said.

"About what?" Elena finished her apple, retreated to the grassy path away from the bees, and licked her fingers clean.

Grace joined her, and they made their way back toward the house together. "When you asked earlier if I'd ever met someone and right away and thought, *I like this person.* I said, 'no.' Now, I have. Thank you for letting me see the beauty of my garden through your eyes."

"It was my pleasure!" Elena's smile came up brighter than ever. "Thank you for letting me gush over it. People say I'm too much for them. Too much what, they'll never say, but there it is."

"And here we are." They were back in the shade of the patio awning, with the ripe air cooling around them. Grace drove back the shadows of fear with renewed hopes for her future. "If you want more hands-on experience, you're welcome to drop by and play in the dirt any time."

"I'll take you up on that, don't think I won't." Elena bent over a yarrow plant in the bed closest to the patio, then jerked upright. Yellow pollen dusted her nose.

"Bees?"

"No, my phone." Elena rubbed her nose and checked the device. "Heather says they're here. They rang the bell."

Grace's stomach rolled over, and she fought a ridiculous, futile urge to say she'd changed her mind. That was fear tempting her into error. When God opened a door, only a fool turned away. If she refused this unlooked-for offer, then tomorrow or next week or next month, DPS agents *would* come for her.

"I should get my things and go meet them," Elena said.

Looking down, Grace noticed the bits of dead grass, flecks of apple, and dirt on her work boots. "Why don't we go out the side gate together?"

"Perfect." Elena typed a quick note on the phone and quickly packed away her things while Grace collected her completed application and information folder.

Elena hugged her briefcase to her chest like a shield when she was done. "I hope you like Heather and Jack," she said. "It might be hard to see at first, but they're good people."

Hard to see? Grace put two and two together. "You're reminding me that Jack is a—T-series. Is Heather another rollover with physical changes?"

Elena nodded, her face solemn. "She has wings and feathers. And she teleports. They make some people uncomfortable. We've had applicants back out after meeting them. I hope it won't make you change your mind."

The sour fear in Grace's stomach rose into her throat. She'd thought she was learning tolerance, she was *trying,* but her heart quailed at the thought of accepting help from anyone so visibly damned.

What happened to your resolve? she asked herself. She licked her lips. In doubtful times she reverted to a sheep whose first and last instincts were to freeze or bolt for safety, but rollover was not a threat she could escape.

Besides, if ever a child could walk safely with a lamb among lions, here she stood in front of Grace, with flecks of purple glitter on her cheek and worry putting a line between her brows.

The taste of bitter salt and acceptance kissed Grace's tongue, and a strange, quiet peace washed away the queasy fear. God had come to Saul on the road to Damascus to show him the way. He'd brought this hope to Grace in her own home, a salve to smooth over the wounds of her bloody past.

No matter how much her soul dreaded the journey ahead, she could not—*would* not—turn back. "Thank you for the warning." She led the way toward the gate. "I don't think I would've handled the shock well."

The relief in Elena's face was ample reward for her courage. Grace tucked the application under her arm and spun open the combination lock on the side entrance. The tall wooden gate swung wide.

Elena hurried through so fast Grace expected her to take off running. Instead, she stopped after a few steps and turned on her heel. The tall viburnums beside the garage arched overhead, framing her in living green.

"This is going to work out fine," she proclaimed with the confidence of a prophet. "Wait and see."

13: THE KEEPERS OF THE HOUSE TREMBLE AND STRONG MEN STOOP

Near 428 Elm Drive, Elgin IL

"SHE'S ON HER WAY OUT," Heather came down the stairs from the front door and rejoined Jack on the sidewalk. She moved her wings, sending a cool breeze past him. "Guess you don't have to test the porch yet."

"Fine by me." Jack stayed on the nice, solid concrete. The house was one of those wide, old, pointy-roofed places with a wood porch across the whole front. Breaking someone's home made for awkward introductions. "Never a good sign when they don't invite us inside. Don't hold your breath for a contract."

"Don't be a sore loser. You want to go double or nothing on it?"

"No." He would rather lose that bet.

Elena came strolling out of the side yard between the garage and the house like an innocent little puppy—a puppy with a smile on her face, a blush coloring her cheeks, and Grace Reed walking beside her.

Jack couldn't see what made this woman so special. She looked like a thousand other middle-aged women he'd met: tallish and skinny, with long, knobby fingers, sun-wrinkled skin, and frizzy brown hair. She wore a faded blue floral dress over work boots, and she plodded along like someone marching to their own execution.

Her face had a stiff look Jack could recognize a mile away, typical of someone Elena had blindsided with charisma.

When Grace spotted him, she stopped and made a small noise so soft Jack doubted else anyone else heard it. The fear rolling off her overpowered the underlying scents of dirt and soap.

This was not going to work, and everyone would blame him.

He tipped back his ball cap. *Time to play goofy and harmless.* "Hey, tiger, you look happy. Want to introduce us to your new friend?" *Before she bolts like a rabbit or the neighbors get nosy?*

They'd been lucky so far. Aside from one gaggle of teen girls on bicycles, the street was quiet. That wouldn't last. Most of the houses nestled up close to the sidewalk, protected by ranks of bushes trimmed to precise right angles, with one tall tree standing proud in each parkway strip.

This was the kind of neighborhood where everyone got into everyone else's business, and early evening was dog-walking time. Soon there would be families and couples out and about.

Grace Reed's house was on the highest part of the street, lording it over the rest with extra-tall bushes against the porch and sides and a black metal fence guarding an overgrown lawn along the front. It looked like the kind of place kids dared each other to visit on Halloween.

If they didn't get off the sidewalk, they were going to attract attention.

Elena turned up the wattage on her smile. "Jack, Heather,

this is Grace Reed. Grace, meet Jack Coby and Heather Gardner. They watch over me to keep me safe when I canvass, and Jack's also the transition team coordinator for Camp Liberty. I took her through the application, Jack, so it's all in order. Here you go." She took papers from Grace and handed them over. "Wait 'til you see her amazing yard. Is Valerie coming?"

"She should be here any minute." He hoped.

He exchanged a look with Heather, and she stepped up. It was always a toss-up, which one of them should speak first. Heather had a better instinct for making a good impression.

Grace's eyes went wide, but she tentatively offered her hand instead of running away. That was promising. "Nice to meet you," she said in a voice that implied the opposite.

Heather lifted sharp-taloned fingers, demonstrating why she preferred to avoid handshakes. "Pleased to meet *you*, Ms. Reed. Is there somewhere we can sit down to talk while we wait? I'm sure you have questions."

Her wings flexed as she lowered her hand. Feathers rustled.

"Do those work?" Grace blurted out, then turned red and clapped both hands over her mouth. "I can't believe I said that out loud," she said through her fingers.

Heather's laugh was genuine. "I can. The first thing I said when I saw them was, 'Are those mine?'" She combed her fingers through her top feathers, then spread her arms and wings wide for full effect. "They are pretty, but they're mostly useless."

Jack knew a straight line when one was tossed at him. "Now me, I'm not pretty, but I'm also not useless." He came forward a step, using his best Outreach slow-and-easy body language. "And any friend of Elena's is a friend of mine."

He put out his hand, blunted claws on display. Grace's gaze moved from Heather to him, and she hesitated before extending her hand, but she did make the effort.

"That's a kind thing to say," she said. "Thank you."

Their fingers touched, and Jack's nerves jumped hard as energy jolted into him. It came out of nowhere, disastrously uncontrolled, pulsing through his blood. His vision went red around the edges. *Challenge. Protect. Destroy—*

No! He yanked his hand away and smashed down his body's reaction with trained willpower and one overriding thought: *NO.*

Pumping up to battle readiness was the last thing this situation needed. A stride put him behind Heather again, and he clamped iron discipline over the rampage reaction as he moved, dumping energy as fast as he could shed it.

Excess power bled into the air and lit up every feather on Heather's body in golden light. Her crest fluttered in an intangible breeze. She snapped her wings open, curving them protectively forward. Sparks danced in the air.

Grace turned paler than pale and closed her eyes. Her lips moved silently—praying, maybe. Jack could sympathize. If thinking *what the fuck* counted as a prayer, then he was praying too, and he stared at the faint energy rippling around Grace.

There hadn't been the slightest sign of an aura a second earlier. He had never seen the precise moment of onset outside of training films, but there was no mistaking that glow.

This case just kept getting better and better, where better meant FUBAR.

With an onset surge this strong, Grace would be topping the rating scale of whatever power series she ended up in. And if she was about to roll *hot* with that energy, they were in big trouble.

Elena put a hand on Grace's arm and gaped at the visible part of the show. "Wow, that's beautiful. You look like an angel, Heather. Where did that light come from?"

And that was pure Elena. Too busy being curious to know

when she should be frightened. As usual, he would have to worry enough for both of them. Until they got a handle on Grace's rollover profile, this was not a safe zone.

Heather was rubbing at her eyes with the backs of her hands. Dazzled, from the looks of it, which meant she hadn't seen that aura. "Code Red, Heather," he said. "We've got a Dice-Roll here. No joke. Get her gone."

Heather's crest went flat, and she didn't waste time on questions. She swept forward and caught up Elena in a loose embrace, turning to tug her clear and grunting as she brought her wings sweeping down. Elena said, "What? No! I want—"

A gust of sage-scented chill hit Jack's face, displaced air popped, and they were gone. That was one problem solved. Heather would see Elena safely home and check back as soon as she could.

That left the potential crisis in his hands.

He popped the cover off the panic pager on his belt. Camp Liberty had been granted a Mercury scramble code for emergency aborts, and there was also a DPS Transit pad at the other end of this block. If something went wrong, he could have a tactical unit here in two minutes, and an Intake crew would arrive on their heels.

He didn't want to break Elena's heart by dumping this case, but he also did not want to go down in history as the man who let a hot rollover level a chunk of Elgin. If that aura kept building, if Grace *kept* rolling, he would have no choice. He could live with his friends being pissed off. There would be other clients.

The glow dimmed and flickered out. Jack moved his finger off the abort button.

Good. He wouldn't have to face someone rolling in a single, massive eruption of power. And Grace wouldn't have to live through it like he had.

She opened her eyes and ran her hands over her face and

arms before hugging herself. She looked embarrassed, not panicked, which was a good sign. It meant she hadn't felt anything yet. "What was that?" she asked. "Where did the light come from? Are you all right? You looked—frightened. Are you —bigger? How did that happen?"

Jack shrugged, stalling for time. She wasn't going to like his answers, and he'd gained more than body mass from the shocking energy surge. His teeth had dropped when his skin hardened, and rampage fangs alarmed people. He concentrated hard and dumped enough power to get his mouth in order.

The effort made his jaw ache.

"I'm fine," he said. "And yes, I'm bigger. It was you. You didn't do it on purpose, but it was a pulse of R-factor—rollover —energy."

"Me? Rollover? Oh, no." It was a horrified whisper. Then Grace's chin came up. For a flashing moment, she reminded him of Heather—all brown, bird-like gestures, angular limbs, and anger. "Does this mean it's too late for your program? Because I am not going to a DPS camp. I can't."

She had fight in her, that was certain. Her eyes never got higher than his chest, but her desperation was the ferocious kind, not the lie-down-and die kind.

He ought to advise the woman to call the DPS for a pickup, but the rest of Camp Liberty's founders would never speak to him again if he did. *No, be honest.* He wouldn't be able to live with himself if he did that.

This time, he didn't have to be the bad guy. "No, ma'am, it isn't too late. I'm holding your app right here." He put it behind his back before she got a good look at the three-inch claws he currently sported. "Elena said everything's in order, and we prioritize based on need, among other things."

That was true, although no one had imagined anything this immediate. On the bright side, if he said yes, no one would ever have to defend why Grace was chosen over any other candidate. *Val owes me for this.* "As long as there's no major disqualification, we can take you. If that's what you want."

"God help me, what choice do I have? Yes. I want it."

"Okay. They tell me that's called a verbal contract. Valerie will go over the real one with you when she gets here."

His part would be organizing a transition on the fly. The challenge appealed to his pride.

The timing was FUBAR, but if he took the shortest preparation schedule in the book and cut half of it, he could make it work. Assuming Grace didn't go hot. If that happened, all bets were off.

This wasn't a secure location. "Ma'am, can we go inside to wait? If any of your neighbors are active rollovers, they might report on you."

She said uncertainly, "There's Ben Miller, down the block. He might—oh! What if the DPS is already on the way?"

Hints weren't going to work. Jack spelled it out. "If we're on private property and you're in Camp Liberty, I have the authority to turn Intake away. They could force the issue outdoors, but once you're inside, the law's clear. "

"Fine." She stepped onto the long grass. When Jack followed her off the driveway, she warded him away with upraised palms. "That's far enough.."

"No, it isn't." Valerie could not get here soon enough. Making nice with nervous clients and walking them through the red tape was her job. "Inside would be better."

"I won't let you into my home where no one can see us." Grace looked up far enough to meet his eyes. "I trusted Elena, but you disappeared her. Your partner looks like an angel, but she might be a fallen one. I don't know if you're here to save me or lead me into my damnation."

"Okay." Jack waited. Some days he wished he'd never left the Corps. Civilians made no sense. "Do you want me to leave?"

"No. Maybe. No. I need to pray for guidance."

"Here?"

She shrugged. "It's private property."

He was never going to understand religious people. Never. "It's your party."

To kill time, he pretended to look at her application, nodding at intervals. Then he pulled up his contact lists and prepped a priority message to send for everyone on the CLP alert list. He would be damned if this failed because *he* dropped the ball.

Getting a team here on zero notice would be the easy part. Flexible availability was one of the advantages of a personnel roster heavy on people retired from their first careers. He wouldn't have the usual time to orient them, prep the site, or pre-order supplies, but beggars couldn't be choosers.

Cars honked on a nearby street. Cicadas hummed, loud-soft-loud, high up in the parkway trees. Grace ran her hands up and down her arms and paced back and forth along the edge of the lawn.

Jack was distracted and didn't notice she was getting closer until her aura flickered to life again. Energy licked out in streamers, dancing along his nerves. He backed off fast, bracing for another surge, but this was an ebb tide, pulling at his bones and flesh as it went, taking the remaining augmentation with it.

He ran his tongue over his fully retracted fangs and worked the ache out of his knuckles. Not even another Tee ramping up or crashing nearby had ever caused such a swift response.

Where the *hell* was Valerie? "Don't do that," he said as calmly as he could.

"I was trying to make myself less scared of you." Grace

swayed, and Jack wondered what he could do if she passed out. "Why did you move away? You changed again."

"That was you again, and it's why *stay at arm's length* is Camp Liberty ground rule. Don't take it personally."

"I—won't." She looked at her hands then up at him. "Are you sure it's me? I don't feel different. I'm not ready for this."

"No one ever is." Jack shoved down a flash of painful memory. He wouldn't wish his rollover on his worst enemy. "This is perfectly normal."

That was a big bouncer of a lie, but honesty was not always the best policy.

Light flashed at the end of the block, six houses past the Reed home. A spinning dome of mist nearly as tall as Jack glowed on the concrete circle, fading to reveal a roundish blonde woman in a gray suit.

Finally. Let Valerie deal with this mess. "And here's the answer to your prayers," he said to Grace.

She replied, "Oh, thank God," proving she'd missed the sarcasm.

Valerie was frowning long before she reached them. Her eyes glimmered—the telltale that she was *looking*—and when Jack handed over the application, she raised eyebrows at its crumpled condition.

"This is unexpected," she said, which had to be the understatement of the year.

"Val, this is Grace Reed. I already told her we'd take her on," Jack said before Valerie could ask anything else. "I hope I didn't overstep, but we didn't have anyone else scheduled, and onset makes her a priority, right?"

Val got points for being quick on her feet. She slanted a look at him, narrow-eyed. "We never want to turn away anyone who needs help. Thank you, Jack."

Then she nodded to Grace. "Hello, I'm Valerie Wade. My day

job's in DPS Adaptation and Placement, but tonight I'm here as the Camp Liberty Administrative Director. How are you feeling?"

She was speaking in her calm, almost-confident office voice, the one Jack wished she would use more often. It had its usual effect.

Grace stopped hunching her shoulders, and color came back to her face. Tears spilled down her cheeks. She wiped them brusquely away. "I'm embarrassed and scared. And I can't shake your hand because I don't know what will happen."

"I know how frustrating that is." Valerie made a gesture like a long-distance pat on the arm. "Given your condition, the faster we get you settled in, the better. We need to go over a bunch of long, complicated forms."

"More forms?"

"I'm afraid so. I know you just did the application, but there's a reason people call the DPS the Department of Paper Shuffling," Valerie said. "Where would you like to do this?"

"Inside. This way." Grace walked up the path to the front door.

Valerie followed after a glance over her shoulder at Jack. "Grace, is there a place for a transition team to set up their equipment? You do understand you're about to be inviting several strangers into your space for however long it takes? I'm sorry to pester you with questions, but—"

Grace looked back. Her mouth turned up at the corners, and the skin around her eyes crinkled. "But there's usually more time?"

"Yes, exactly." Valerie's smile wobbled with her relief. "They can use the garage if that's easier."

"No, it's full of paint cans and wire spools." After an assessing look at Jack, Grace frowned. "I have two small rooms upstairs, plus the basement. It isn't finished, but it's wide open, and there's a door to the outside."

"That's generous, thank you."

Jack growled. He couldn't help it. He got paranoid refusals. Valerie made jokes and got instant cooperation.

Grace flinched back. "Please don't think badly of me. I am struggling with this, and it's easier—oh." And like that, she was back hugging herself again. "I have so many questions. How does this work? What are my girls going to do?"

Valerie stopped short of Grace's position. "Those are good questions. There's a lot to discuss, but the important part is that we are here to take care of you. Focus on that."

"You meant that? Really, truly?" Grace's eyes teared up again, and she sniffled. When Val nodded, she began sobbing in earnest.

That made no sense to Jack, but from the look on Valerie's face, it was the response she'd expected. She waved him toward the house.

Jack went carefully up the steps and opened the front door.

14: AS EVERYONE COMES, SO THEY DEPART

Somewhere unexpected

"—TO STAY HERE!" Elena was saying when Heather jumped them into a black, still nowhere outside of reality.

Elena's stomach lurched. The sensation of flying through pure darkness was familiar, but the instinctive fear of falling still made her pulse race. At least it didn't hurt. She could sense her body and Heather's arms around her, strong, solid, and real.

The glide through nowhere didn't last long. Heather returned them to reality a little above the ground as always, and she mantled her wings over Elena on landing.

"Fff—augh! Let me go!" Elena tossed her head against the primary feathers tickling her face. Her heart was beating fast. Anger flared up. "I am going to kick that overprotective, stubborn jerk of a Marine. He had no right. You have no right. Take me back!"

"What? No!" Heather turned Elena around with effortless strength and held her carefully in both taloned hands. Her facial feathers made her face hard to read, but fear made her voice crack high. "DiceRoll, honey. Hot rollover in the area. Maybe you don't care if you die, but do you want the DPS to pull the plug on Camp Liberty? Because defying onset sequestering is how that happens. You're a null, Elena, and there are *laws*."

Shame and horror cooled her temper. She knew the panic codes. She knew the laws. She'd helped design the yard signs Camp Liberty posted. How could she have been so *selfish*? "I don't want that," she said, and she didn't care if her voice was wobbly. "I'm sorry. I was caught up and forgot. Will Grace will be all right?"

Heather sighed. "I don't know. After I see you home, I'll go back to—"

She froze, wings half-furled, staring past Elena. Her pupils dilated and pulsed. Elena pulled away, scratching her own arm in the process, and turned to see what had startled her.

And then she froze too.

They weren't at the Shoppes on Elm where she'd left her little car parked behind Jack's huge vehicle that morning. They stood on an open hillside near a single spreading tree, overlooking a rolling vista of pastures and green-gold rows of corn. A tall blue silo rose above rooftops not far away, and puffy, gray clouds floated in a hazy sky. The warm, damp air was still, heavy with the scent of manure and dry grass.

Elena looked back, past Heather's wings. The view didn't change. Giggles bubbled up through the odd calm that always came over her when impossible things happened. "I don't think we're in Kansas anymore, Toto."

"How can you joke about this? We're in western Iowa." Heather flapped into the air briefly, landing with a thud. "I think? It looks like it, and my geo-sense agrees with my eyes, so I think it's working fine, unlike my 'port ability. This is bad. How did we get here?"

"You teleported us here, obviously." Elena turned in a circle. "We're both safe and sound. That's good, isn't it?"

"Not when I didn't plan it, no. And we left Jack with a crisis on his hands. I have to call in." Heather tapped her headset. Then again. "Or not. Is your phone working?"

It wouldn't turn on. "No."

Heather shook her head. "Maybe whatever fried me fried them too. I would swear in court I did everything I usually do to go from here to as far as that farm right there."

She pointed to the silo and spread her wings, but she didn't disappear. Elena waited a polite interval before asking, "Is it not working now?"

"I don't know, and I don't plan to test it. I was checking to see if the power pull felt any different." Heather shook herself. "Nope. It feels normal, but here we are. This is awful."

"I hope you're okay." Worry spread other tendrils through Elena's thoughts. "I hope Grace is okay. Jack will take care of her, won't he?"

"I'm sure he'll do his best." Heather tucked in her wings and gave Elena a wan smile. "At least there's people close by. Let's ask to borrow their phone."

They walked. And walked. The distance hadn't seemed so far from the hilltop, but a muddy stream and a herd of cows led to a long detour into a cornfield and out again. If Elena had been alone, she would've gotten lost twice over. And Heather was *slow*. Long shadows stretched across the landscape by the time they reached the farm.

Elena took heart from the number of vehicles parked near the barns, but those hopes were dashed the instant they reached the house.

The woman who answered the front door refused to let them inside. The first man who joined her gave directions to the closest town while holding a kitchen knife in one hand. The second one, who came around the house from the back with a shotgun resting on his shoulder, suggested they move along fast because the area wasn't safe at night.

Elena kept her temper under control until they got down the long driveway to the road, but she only stopped fuming when Heather told her the noise was scaring the cows. She *hated* knowing people would be cruel if they could get away with it.

The driver of a passing truck restored a little of her faith in humanity. He gave them a ride to his place, let them borrow his telephone, and offered a ride into town where they could catch the eastbound night bus.

First, Heather called her husband. Next, Elena called her parents, reaching her father just in time to forestall a worried call to the Elgin DPS office. Then came a scary few minutes between leaving a message on Jack's voicemail and Valerie picking up her phone.

The news that the situation at Grace's house was under control made Heather cheer, but the updates left Elena floundering in mixed feelings.

Grace wasn't rolling hot, which was a relief, and she *was* coming onboard as a Camp Liberty client, which was exciting. Jack had put a transition team together in no time, so once the legal papers were filed and precautions were in place, Elena would be allowed back on site.

That was all good news, but it left her with nowhere to aim her frustration and leftover fear. It wasn't right to blame Jack for everything, but she couldn't help herself. If he hadn't overreacted and sent them away, then maybe Heather's power wouldn't have gone wrong and stranded them hundreds of miles from home.

Heather reported the 'port malfunction next, and her boss promptly put her on unpaid leave until she recertified. That was bad news-good news too. She wouldn't have to report to a camp like a misfiring elemental, but recertification might take weeks. Initial safety tests took priority and appointment slots could get bumped over and over. Heather could still work with Camp Liberty while she waited, but Elena would have to either postpone the rest of the summer canvass or request a new security team.

Both options sucked. She still wanted to scream at the unfairness of it.

She kept that inside because tantrums were childish, but she couldn't stop the shakes. Heather took charge of thanking their host, getting his contact information on the ride into town.

There wasn't much to the place. Two stop signs, one traffic light, a post office, and a few stores made up the main street. Its highlights were an entrance onto the interstate highway and an all-night diner where the regional busses stopped around midnight.

The diner food wasn't bad, but Elena wasn't hungry. She must have looked pathetic. When Heather asked for a box to pack up Elena's uneaten half-sandwich, the server added a bag of chips and a cookie for free.

They spent the evening waiting in their squeaky vinyl booth, with Heather saying she felt like a mother hen with one tired, cranky chick and making worried noises when Elena didn't laugh.

Finally they were on the bus, in the accommodations section. Heather sat between Elena and the other passengers on a wing-friendly bench. The air was stuffy, the engine was loud, and someone in one of the regular seats was eating tuna. Everything smelled gross, and the bench cushion sagged.

Elena wiped the window with a napkin from her restaurant bag, leaned her forehead against the clean paper, and watched the white line of the highway shoulder rushing past, meeting thin reflections of her face and the reading lights above the bus seats.

"You want to talk about it yet?" Heather asked.

"No." That wasn't true, and it wasn't fair. "I told her everything would be fine. And now I'm not there. I've failed her. I've failed everyone."

"Oh, no, sweetheart. You need a hug. " Heather slid an arm around her and bent her wing over them. "I know how you feel, but it isn't true. You aren't a failure, and neither am I. I refuse to believe it."

"You mean the teleport going wrong? That wasn't your fault." Here she was wallowing in self-pity when Heather was facing the loss of her ability. "I'm sorry. You must be so worried, and now I'm being a burden."

"Never." The hug was a fierce squeeze, and Heather kissed her on the forehead. "You give me hope. It *will* be fine. We'll get through it together."

Elena fell asleep like that, tucked under her friend's wing, comforted and comforting.

15: PITY THOSE WHO FALL AND HAVE NO ONE TO HELP

August 17, 414 Elm Drive, Elgin, IL

GRACE FELT comfortable with Valerie from the instant they met, but that easy, instant rapport created an equally powerful desire to *not* like the woman. Warm first impressions had burned her enough times to leave her suspicious of them.

Elena had slipped past her usual defenses with relative ease, but Elena had worn charisma and innocence like wings and a halo. Valerie Wade did not inspire the same kind of trust.

By the time the woman was ready to present the CLP contract, everything about her was grating on Grace's nerves.

The Camp Liberty Administrative Director was too soft, harmless, and friendly to believe. She had an intent but timid way of watching things, like a worried mouse. Her eyes were remarkable, vivid green in color and large in her wide, square face. Her dark blonde hair was as fine as cornsilk and tucked neatly beneath a hairband.

They were much alike in height, but Valerie was cushioned and curvy everywhere Grace was narrow and knobby. The flowy material of Valerie's suit and its DPS-standard dove gray color flattered her in ways Grace's clothes never did.

Everything about Valerie was soft, even her voice. They sat on a diagonal at the breakfast bar, separated by a safe expanse of countertop, and Grace caught herself leaning forward a dozen times to catch low-voiced words.

After that packet of papers was signed and whisked away into the shoulder bag, Valerie placed a red disk the size of her thumbnail on the counter and slid it across. "And here's your first bit of official Camp Liberty equipment."

Grace clenched her fists in her lap. "What do I do with it?"

"You wear it. Like this." Valerie tugged her collar aside to show a similar disk, this one blue, above her collarbone. "One of our team regulars, Shelly, specializes in distance 'ports using tokens. It's a safety precaution."

"A precaution for who?" The disk was cool and damp against Grace's fingers. It felt like plastic and had a paper backing. The church had called teleportation a forbidden fruit, and it was one she'd never been tempted to try. Apparation was a power for devils and angels, not humanity. "Safety for me? Or against me? And when do I get to meet this team?"

"Soon, I think." Valerie drummed her fingers on the countertop. "The best precautions never get used. Those are for everyone's safety. You can refuse yours, but the quarantine rules are much stricter, and the risks are much higher."

She looked at the refrigerator, at the calendars and the chalkboard with Maggie's drawings and Lauren's loopy handwriting. The message couldn't be clearer.

Grace peeled the backing and pressed the token to the skin between her throat and shoulder. She slipped a fingernail along the edge. The seal felt tight. "You keep saying my team like you aren't part of it."

Valerie gave a surprised laugh. "I'm not, really. Transition crews need, um, defensive skills and talents. All I do is see unseeable things. I do most of the documentation and filings. The client set-up part is usually finished well before onset. The team's 'porter will send me home to my kids in California when we're done here."

"Nice for you." Grace quelled a shudder. "What's left to do?"

"That depends on you. Are there any legal loose ends you'd like to tidy up?"

There were many, and she had been wondering how to bring up the topic. Suspicion had a familiar, sour flavor. "Why do you ask?"

"Lots of people put off planning, so there are special allowances for rollover filings. If you want, I can do simple wills, set up trusts, and assign beneficiaries for things—you name it, the DPS has a form for it," Valerie offered. "I can arrange witnessing and notarizing too."

Ever since Grace had heard Jack say the word *onset*, she'd been thinking about the bad decisions she'd made when she built this new life. Desperation had led her horribly astray.

If this opportunity hadn't come along, if she had been interned, her daughters would be in a financial mess at the mercy of strangers. Or worse, they might have unsealed their old identities and reached out to their relatives.

Being fostered to strangers would be traumatic, and if they went back to the Ranch, they would not be welcomed as lost lambs but as sheep to be fleeced and slaughtered.

What was I thinking?

Denial had blinded her. Deep in the bottom of her heart, where the earthquakes of panic started, she'd always known the truth, but she'd turned away time and again. She'd chosen inaction as if making plans created the need for them.

Wallowing in regret wouldn't fix things. "I need to do a lot," she admitted. "I have a will, and there's a trust for Maggie and Lauren. Other things. They all need to be changed."

"Changes are more complicated but doable." Valerie's smile wobbled, but it was genuine, as if complicated papers were a nice surprise. "I can't build the right forms or file amended records without the originals. You have to stay on site, but someone can collect them for you. Are they in a safe deposit box? With a lawyer?"

"I keep it here." Banks and lawyers were necessary, but she did not trust them with anything precious.

Valerie's composure wavered again. "Oh. Well. Then we can get it done now, and I'll do the filings first thing in the morning."

She pulled a laptop computer from her shoulder bag and attached her little radiophone to it with a cord. Grace brought the lockbox from its hidey-hole under her bed and went through the contents; powers of attorney for the trusts she'd set up here with money she'd taken from the church, a form will with instructions for paying off the improvement loans, insurance policies, and their new identity papers. And a hefty envelope of cash, in case they had to run again.

Valerie didn't comment on any of it, not even the name change documents for Grace and the girls. She asked questions for clarification and typed information into her computer. Documents appeared like magic one after another—thanks to a specialized courier service, according to Valerie—and stacks of paper built up.

"That wasn't too bad," Valerie said when they came to the end. "You fill in the highlighted parts and sign—or mark anything I need to change—I initial changes, witness and notarize, and it's ready to go. You won't have to worry about a thing."

Nothing made Grace worry more than people telling her

not to worry. Valerie seemed committed to offering expert help and providing comfort, as Elena had promised. But Elena wasn't here *now*. Her friends had sent her away.

Her misgivings grew, a bitter taste at the back of her throat. "Why hadn't I heard of Camp Liberty before today?" she asked. "Who pays for all this? It has to be expensive."

"It's a pilot partner program. We're two years into a five-year DPS exploratory grant." Valerie made a vague gesture. "It's in the brochures. Someday we hope it will be a standard option between full internment and full release."

She'd known there must be a catch. Being courted always led to being used. Tension clamped down on her skull. "So I'm an experiment? A lab rat?"

A blush stained Valerie's cheeks with color. "No. We've jumpstarted the process for you, but it has a proven track record. I can print you testimonials if Elena didn't leave any."

"She did. I read them." Grace fidgeted with the pen she'd used to sign her contract. Her hands shook. It was paranoia to worry about a ploy by the Assembly elders. The decision was made. And yet—this thorny buyer's remorse was growing from the seeds of past betrayal.

She plucked one fear off the vine. "This feels too easy. Like a con. Nothing surprised you. You were ready for this—for me—before you got here."

Valerie blinked at her, hesitant and embarrassed. "Easy? I suppose from your side—the DPS partnership gives us top-level Registry access to the pre-rollovers in our approved operations zone. That includes sealed and confidential files, if we apply for them, and I do. We have to vet potential applicants to make sure they'll be a good match for the program."

"Elena didn't recruit me specifically?"

"Yes and no. We have been filtering for high-level applicants, but Elena has been recruiting every poz she can get to sit still for a presentation since the day Camp Liberty went live. Her idea of client vetting is purely enthusiasm-based."

That wry comment rang true. It didn't help.

Valerie said meekly, "I can see I've made a horrible impression. I'm sorry. Everything is so rushed and confusing. I know this is hard. I promise you can depend on us."

Grace abruptly resented everything about the woman, from her too-reasonable reassurances and easy sympathy to her pretty clothes and pretentious job title. Maybe Valerie was sincere, but what did she know? Trust wasn't hard. Trust *hurt*.

The old pain bubbled up into words. "Don't pretend you know what this is like for me. All you do is *see* things. How hard could it be to roll into a talent like that?"

The pink in Valerie's cheeks flushed to a hectic red, and tears welled up in her eyes. "It was so easy I was done before I knew I'd rolled," she said, "but I found out the same way you did, by surprise from strangers. I was a wreck until I got my certification. And the first time I saw true, I had no control over it. That was terrifying."

Her tone warned Grace to pay attention, but contempt still had her tongue. "Oh, no, was it something ugly? It couldn't have been that bad."

"I saw my husband for what he was." Valerie no longer looked timid or tentative. Her eyes were a hot green as vivid as leaves against the sun, and her voice shook with angry pain. "I saw that the man I loved was a sadistic drug addict who believed the words 'until death do us part' gave him the right to beat me to death. And I saw he'd convinced me he was right."

Grace's heart sank as Valerie continued in a shaky voice, "When I left him, I had no friends, no skills, no savings—nothing but two hungry toddlers, their diaper bag, and a pile of debts. Don't you dare talk to me about easy, sitting here in this big, fancy house with more money than—"

She stopped, pressed her palms together in front of her lips. Whispered, "No. Sorry. That isn't fair. I'm sorry."

Shame washed over Grace. That quick pivot from rage to submission—oh, she knew the strain of it in her very bones. She'd made that same last-ditch effort to avert attack a thousand times, and it meant she had wronged Valerie deeply, mistaking empathy for manipulation.

She got up without a word and returned the lockbox to her room. The fault was hers, but attempting an apology too soon would be throwing water on a grease fire. A delay would give the unpleasantness time to cool.

All the way upstairs and back, she unsuccessfully tried to picture her home as fancy.

It was half the size of the rebuilds on the next block, and as for fancy—no. The woodwork was painted, patchy linoleum still covered half the hall, and grime hid in the corners. Maggie and Lauren had scrubbed the gold-flocked wallpaper in the stairwell so hard the pattern was a bare memory, but the memory remained hideous.

And then there was the clutter. When Jack had done his first walkthrough, he'd relocated lumber and tile to the basement so he would have enough room to turn around in the living room.

He had been able to stand without ducking, though. His happiness about that small comfort had been educational. His relief after Grace did some weight-bearing calculations to prove he could walk safely anywhere on any floor made her sad.

She'd never imagined how hard it must be to navigate a world so ill-suited to one's body. Would she end up like him? Worse? If she did, would she face those obstacles with half the composure he did?

With that sobering thought in mind, she returned to the kitchen.

Valerie pretended great interest in something under her fingernails. Her computer and phone were packed away, and her bag was on her shoulder. Ready to flee if Grace lashed out again.

Trust was still unfamiliar and uncomfortable, like a new shirt with a sharp tag, but she could endure it. Pain was no excuse for creating more pain.

Grace tidied up the documents she needed to complete and gathered her courage. "Ms. Wade—Valerie—I'm sorry for what I said earlier. I'm not usually like that."

When she finished straightening edges, she looked up to find Valerie staring at her.

"Am I turning green?" she asked, and it was only partly a joke.

"No." Valerie's gaze slid away into one of those diffident half-glances, but her lips curved up. "But you are flickering again. It's pretty. The aura stays longer each time it shows up, too. You still don't feel or see it yet?"

"Nothing yet." That situation could change without warning. Driving away good people was as much a mistake as embracing unworthy ones. "Please say you'll forgive my angry words. I'm not myself today. I suppose it's because I'm turning into someone else."

That was another weak joke, but she had to find something funny in this situation or she would fall apart.

Valerie made a muffled gurgling sound that turned into a giggle. The strangled noise tickled Grace's funny bone, and a laugh burst free. They snorted and chuckled together like a couple of children until shared mirth washed away the last of the toxic bitterness.

"I'm so glad you have a sense of humor," Valerie said once they got themselves under control. "I wasn't expecting that. I lost my temper too. Let's call it even?"

"Yes, let's. May I ask a favor? I'd like to do the read-through on my own. Alone."

"Are you sure?" Valerie squinted at her, then brightened. "You are. You want breathing room."

Footsteps on the patio made the cabinets rattle. Jack bent to look indoors, looming huge in the dusk. He was shirtless, and the ridges of muscle on his body stood out like lines on a shadowy anatomy chart. "Val, Amy says you're fine in there, but —you are okay, right?"

Despite the gloom, he still wore sunglasses, and he used his ball cap to wave off mosquitos. He looked harassed and grumpy, a colossus brought low by insects.

Grace pressed her lips tight to keep from laughing at him. She glanced at Valerie and saw her lips were pressed the same way. They both went off again.

Jack crossed his arms over his chest and waited until they sputtered to a halt. "Glad someone's having fun. You got time for a sit-rep, Val?"

"I have time, and Grace would like privacy." Valerie dabbed at her eyes with her blazer cuff. "Grace, call for me if you need anything, and I'll be back to witness signatures."

And off she went, into the night-dark yard, leaving Grace alone here with her thoughts and the precious illusion of solitude.

She sat stiffly upright in her chair at the breakfast bar and stared at her folded hands. This quiet respite was a gift beyond price. New concrete pours needed time to cure, new lumber needed time to dry. She needed time to sit with herself and—*be*.

One touch of her hand had staggered a giant and made an angel's wings glow with heavenly light. She didn't know how harsh her test would be or when the worst of it would come upon her, but it had begun.

She rested in inner stillness, letting her soul grow firmer in its new shape.

In due time, she noticed the dirt under her thumbnail. The thought *I should do something about that* brought her back to the world.

She was in rollover. There was much to be done. Her gaze slid from her hands to the household legal papers on the countertop beside her. The enormity of their significance made it hard to breathe, but breathe she must, for she had to deal with it, though it bowed her spine and made her head ache. Nothing happened in the modern world without reams of red tape, not even emergencies.

Especially not this *emergency.* She closed her eyes again and prayed for strength.

Thumps, pops, and other noises drifted through the open screen door to the back patio, testifying to the arrival of things with wheels. Low voices conversed, but the participants stayed out of view. Ice shifted and clinked in the glass beside her right hand, melting into the dregs of the tea she'd poured earlier.

I should put away the dishes. She stood, and a wave of dizziness struck.

The voices outside paused, and Valerie popped into view at the screen, cheeks and nose bright under the porch light, the rest of her lost in the evening shadows. "Are you all right?"

"Head rush. I'm fine, but—I'm sorry, I haven't started on the papers yet."

"Take as long as you need. Your team is arriving and getting briefed. I am told to pass along Jack's gratitude for opening the house to them."

"It was no trouble." If she allowed them into her life, how could she begrudge them a few sparse comforts?

Valerie rubbed her hands together as if she was unsure what to say but unwilling to leave unless she'd been helpful.

Everyone's watchful hovering reminded Grace of the way her pregnancy with the twins had ended, lying exposed in a hospital room with nurses maintaining a respectful pretense of propriety and the midwife repeating the same questions over and over: how was she doing, was she comfortable, did she have this or need that?

The loss of privacy and the obsession with her feelings weren't the only childbirth parallels. All these years later, she was once again praying for a blessed result amidst the busy commotion. So far, rollover hurt a whole lot less.

She gave thanks that Maggie and Lauren had missed this initial invasion of strangers. The sleepover couldn't have come at a better time. The girls would have to be told, they would have *opinions*, but those difficult conversations could wait until the house was calmer. They wouldn't be torn from her arms. They could adjust to anything less. They were young and resilient.

That thought provided her with a question to make Valerie feel useful. "How is Elena? She wasn't happy about leaving."

The blonde woman brightened up. "She'll be back tomorrow if all goes well. I spoke to her a little while ago. She's a little shaken, your onset affected Heather too, but they're fine."

"That's good. I'm good here for a while, I think."

"I'll leave you in peace then." Valerie ducked away.

Things had gotten off to a rocky start, but they were improving.

She rinsed out Valerie's empty glass, refilled her own, and wiped the counter dry. The simple, physical tasks soothed her nerves and further settled her mind.

God helped those who helped themselves.

She picked up her fresh tea, pressed the cool glass to her cheek, and reached for the waiting papers.

16: NO ONE KNOWS WHEN THEIR HOUR WILL COME

414 Elm Drive, Elgin, IL

GRACE FINISHED the documents before her ice melted. Evidently, turning her life upside down was easier than signing up two teenagers for school team sports.

It was also a huge burden lifted from her heart. No matter what else happened, Lauren and Maggie would be protected. They might never forgive her new choice of guardians, but she had to think of their lives first.

A hollow sensation remained where the fear had been. Other emotions tumbled into the gap, filling it to overflowing. Was that normal? How would she know? Did it matter?

No. She stood naked and alone amidst the shredded remnants of her past, and she felt—what? How *was* she feeling?

Exposed. Exhausted. Exalted.

She had questioned the church's teachings when she'd seen monsters save innocents from humanity's evil, but pride had hardened her heart. She had turned aside. Later, fear and the scars of past betrayal had blinded her to the true message of Josh's survival and return.

She could not deny God this third time, not when she'd seen awe in Heather's inhuman eyes and respect in Jack's careful retreat, not after recognizing a sister's suffering in Valerie's tears. There was no evil here, only God's whisper against the roar of the storm.

Here she was.

All her life, she had gorged on lies, Now the truth lay before her like a feast of celebration. What she'd been raised to call the mark of sin was nothing less than the kiss of God's blessing. Nothing was certain or predictable about rollover, but one truth was clear; it was not what she had been trained to fear.

I am not cursed. I am not tainted. If I die, it means only that I was not strong enough to contain the gift I've been given, and God forgives weakness.

She cradled her newborn surety close and resolved to protect and nurture it.

God also expected His children to atone and make amends. In those categories, she had barely made a start. She had more work ahead of her than behind.

Her hands shook as she gathered notepaper from the junk drawer and took up her pen. One page after another filled up with words scribbled in a haze of apprehension and remorse. Her lettering was ungainly and crude, her spelling was atrocious, but writing the message by hand would be the best possible proof it came from her.

When the feverish purge was done, her conscience quieted. She folded her penance in thirds, labeled it, and sealed it with one of the butterfly stickers Maggie used on her chores calendar. Now, to find someone who could see the letter to its recipient as fast as possible.

Her spine popped when she stretched her arms, and her

knees throbbed a complaint about the way she'd hooked her ankles around the legs of the bar stool. Her chest felt tight, and her eyes were gritty. Standing left her lightheaded.

Normally, she would ignore those discomforts as the predicable effect of sitting still too long after an active day. Tonight she had to wonder if they were symptoms.

The sky was pitch black past the patio now, and a cloud of excited moths surrounded the light sconce outside the door. That explained the dizziness. She should've eaten supper long ago.

Lights bobbed near the side gate, marking a cluster of shadowy figures. Grace called into the darkness, "Valerie, do you mind if I grab a snack? And would you or—um, anyone else —like something to eat? It's getting late."

"Nothing for us, thank you," came the answer from the darkness. "How are you feeling?"

I'm tired of being asked that. "Besides hungry? Tired, achy. And I'm ready." Ready to sign things. Ready to move forward.

"I'll be right there," Valerie replied.

Metal rattled out front, and upstairs, heavy footsteps thudded along the hall. The basement door slammed. Dishes in the cabinets rattled again, the way they did when big garbage trucks passed.

Grace speculated about the source of the noises as she sliced cheese, tomatoes, and leaf lettuce. Was her *transition team* setting up an office? Putting up cameras? Signs? Fences?

The squeaking and thumping continued while she ate her sandwich and salad. Would they treat this like an epidemic quarantine? What would the neighbors think?

It didn't matter. She would not have to leave home, her children would not be sent away. Being here together would remind her why it was so important she come through this trial whole.

The squeal of the patio screen door dragging over its track startled her out of her contemplations. She dropped her fork, and her elbow knocked against the bottle of dressing. It skittered across the countertop, right to the edge.

"Look out!" Valerie darted forward, grabbing for the container just as Grace snatched it up with reflexes honed by years of juggling tools and fasteners. Their fingers didn't quite touch, and Valerie recoiled as fast as she'd reached out.

"I'm sorry." Grace couldn't blame Valerie for looking spooked. Given how her onset had affected two others, she was happy to stay at arm's length until her power was identified.

"No harm done." The door screeched again as Valerie closed it, and she flapped her hands at it helplessly. "Sorry. It didn't make that noise before."

"Old houses complain about changes."

"Ha. My old body does the same." Valerie wiped her hands down the front of her skirt before taking a seat. "I'm afraid you'll be off-limits for a few days. Non-Emergency Diagnostics is always backed up, so your assessment may take a while. Unless you flare up hot, which we're hoping you won't."

You can't be hoping it half as hard as I am. Grace swallowed the comment when she recognized fear trying to masquerade as sarcasm again.

She and Valerie swapped stories about their children while they went through the signing and stamping. Then Valerie made a call that resulted in the paperwork duplicating itself right on the counter. She slid one set to Grace and put the others in her bag. "That's tied up with a bow, and Jack is almost done with set-up. You are now free to do what you like. Call family? Meet the team? Have dessert?"

"Go to bed?" She smiled to make sure Valerie knew her suggestion for a joke, then cleared away the salad bowl and put the documents on the hall table where she'd left the CLP information folder. "I should bring Maggie and Lauren home. I don't know if I have the energy or patience for anything else. Is that rude?"

Weariness was a heavy cloak across her shoulders, weighing down her limbs and muffling the fears she couldn't overcome with determination alone.

"Introductions can wait until morning," Valerie assured her. "The team is here to make things easier, not add to your work. You said the girls are at a friend's house tonight? Do they need a ride home? It's safe as long as they can be trusted not to touch you."

Fear escaped its containment in a bleak and drowning tide. *I might never hug them again if this all goes wrong.* The chance of disaster was tiny, but the knowledge was scant consolation.

She struggled to focus. "I'll ask if they can get a ride." They would have so many questions. Could she trust them to be discreet in front of their friends? "I don't think they're going to take this well."

Valerie said gently, "Would you like me to call for you? I don't mind."

"No. It should be me." She punched the number into the kitchen phone. Valerie discreetly stepped outside.

Joan, the host mother at the sleepover, rushed to offer condolences when she heard the words *rollover* and *home quarantine*. She assured Grace that driving the twins back would be no trouble at all, then turned over the phone to Lauren and Maggie.

Breaking the news was both easier and harder than Grace had feared. Persuading her children to accept her decision about DPS assistance was the hardest part. After the tenth chorus of *But why? Are you sure?* she pulled out the ultimatum "because I'm your mother, and I know best." That argument never worked for long, but she backed it up with the promise of a family discussion once they came home.

The call ended with Maggie's complaints still ringing in her ear. Dealing with them left her drained, but there was one more task she dared not put off. Just in case.

She fidgeted with the letter she'd written and asked Valerie, "When do you get to go home to your little ones?"

"My official duties are done, but my personal answer is, whenever things are settled for the night."

That was kindness above and beyond, for a mother with two young sons waiting. It washed away Grace's remaining doubts. "Can I ask a personal favor, then?"

"Of course!"

She pushed the letter across the counter. "I need this to go to the girls' father. You said he'll get copies of the new documents. I'll reach him another way if you can't add anything private."

"I—yes. I can do that." Valerie pulled off her hairband and smoothed her hair back with it. Seconds ticked by while she looked at the letter and chewed on her lip. "Can I ask you something odd and personal?"

"Go ahead." Dignity and privacy were clearly the first casualties of rollover. "Why not?"

"Because you've already been angry at me, and I don't want you to hate me." Valerie squirmed on the bar stool, and her eyes held concern and hurt. "It's important, Grace."

"Ask. If I don't want to answer, I'll say so. I won't hate you." Grace was confident on that point. "I'm prickly because I've been burned too many times, but I am very bad at hating."

That made Valerie's eyes twinkle, but she didn't smile. "Why do you call him their father and not your ex-husband?"

The penetrating question caught Grace off-guard and slid straight into her heart. Her pulse thudded in her ears. She dug her nails into her palms and dug deep within herself for the hard piece of truth she'd let fester for too long. "Because he broke what we had between us, not what he was to them. Two years on, I still panic when I remember leaving him, but when I think of him as a father, the memories are good."

She saw no judgment in Valerie's somber face, only concentration. That made her brave enough to say, "And I believe in redemption. I'm not excusing what he did. I'm not. But things are different, and if he could promise to do better, I would let him try again with them. I need to reach out so we can meet and discuss it when my crisis is over."

Valerie rested her clasped hands on the counter. Her fingers were trembling. "What if I could make that happen sooner? Given this—" one hand moved to rest on the letter, "I have to offer. If it would ease your mind, I can put you in contact whenever you want."

The weight of Grace's fatigue lifted on a numb, floating sense of unreality. What were the odds? God did work in mysterious ways. "You know Joshua. I can hear it in your voice."

"I do. I know him as Sal. It's a long story. He does not know who or where you are, and no one will tell him without permission. I swear that. But if you want to talk to him, when you're ready—"

"Now." It came out hard and loud, all emotion, no thought. She had to face down this one fear, face *him* before she lost her nerve, in case she lost any future chances. "As soon as I can, face to face. That's what I want."

Seeing him on a screen or hearing his voice would be better than nothing, but if she stood before him, she would *know*. And if she got the answers she needed, then the girls would have someone to hold them when she could not.

They would hate the whole idea, but it would be for the best. If this worked out. *If.*

Music and conversation drifted up from the basement, a

murmur of sound beneath the quiet rattle of the refrigerator. Outside, one of the neighbors was having a backyard party with fireworks. In the kitchen, all was silence.

They both jumped in their seats when Jack's voice came at them from the night-dark back yard. "Hey, Val, Are we doing met and greet before family drama, or should I send the off-shift to the hotel for the night?"

Grace struggled to shift herself back to present necessities. Valerie recovered first. She looked over her shoulder and back, then swept the letter into her bag and laid a hand on the counter, palm up. Entreating. "Tell me you're sure, and I'll make it happen," she said, low and urgent.

No, fear whispered, but she didn't have to listen. "I'm sure."

A flashlight bobbed into view as Jack approached. "Val? Did you hear me? We're loaded in, billeting is sorted out, and get this, the property is fully secured. You gotta come see it before Shells boosts you home to your chaos monsters."

He leaned an arm on the wall over the door and peered inside, looking more civilized now in a shirt and reflective vest. A tool belt was slung over one shoulder.

He made a face, and his fangs flashed. "I'd ask who died, but I got yelled at last time I made that joke. Something wrong?"

His expression was terrifying, but he sounded amused. Was that his version of a grin? *It is.* How many of his other frightening aspects were simply differences?

Not all of them: he could break a concrete block in one hand.

Valerie said, "It's nothing, Jack. I'll tell you later. I thought we were stuck at provisional status until a secondary containment unit arrived."

"We have a primary unit. Adapted bomb shelter, looks like. Sal tipped us off." Jack bared his teeth again and adjusted the brim of his baseball cap. "First nice surprise of the day. He called it a retreat stronghold, but Amy took measurements, says it's a proper bunker."

"I told you he'd be useful."

"He is an expert." That sharp-toothed grimace was not a smile. "He also chatters like a nervous monkey, and half of what he says is pure hundred-proof crazy. If Amy could punch him through the phone, he'd be missing teeth."

Bomb shelter. Grace sat up straighter as comprehension hit. They were talking about her rollover refuge. Sal was Joshua. "The shelter should be up to spec," she said. "I used the plans the DPS published for rural communities back in the Fifties."

Of course the stronghold had been a surprise to them. These people were ignorant of her faith, wouldn't know what measures it demanded. "I should have said something myself," she said. With everything else going on, it had slipped her mind. "We use it as a retreat for prayer."

"The big cross on the wall gave that away," Jack said dryly.

It was the first renovation she'd made to the property, more of her denial at work, to prepare for rollover the way she'd been brought up, despite doubting those lessons and fearing she would never be allowed to use it. Its existence had been a comfort.

Jack told her, "It's a good resource, especially since we're down one teleporter for the foreseeable."

Valerie said, "You're not keeping Heather on the team roster?"

"I'll put her in a watch slot, but she's offline until someone looks into that range fluctuation. Tees ramping up and down is normal. 'Porters, not so much. Now, which is it? Meet and greet, or release for the night?"

Valerie had her phone out and was flipping through a notebook. "Grace, it's up to you. I could use the time to make those calls we discussed."

She had time. The girls wouldn't be home for at least twenty more minutes. "Saying hello is the least I can do," she decided. "They dropped everything to come here."

She was exhausted, hot, sweaty, and wrung out, but that wasn't likely to improve any time soon. Best to get this out of the way. "Let me make a cup of coffee, first."

17: DO NOT LET YOUR MOUTH LEAD YOU INTO SIN

Outside 414 Elm Drive, Elgin, IL

JACK SMOOTHED one hand down the back of his head while he watched Grace pour herself coffee. His skin prickled as if he stood too close to a generator. The woman was throwing off power again. She looked tired and bedraggled, and she stank of fear sweat, but that sensation—it was damned intimidating.

Valerie had picked a hell of a time to go make phone calls.

Grace set down the mug to smooth back her hair. The energy ripple ebbed away, leaving her looking as null as anything. She adjusted her ponytail and twitched at her dress the way women always did. "Ready when you are," she said, speaking to her grubby bare feet instead of him.

"You'll need to come outside." He didn't say, *because cleanup will be easier if anything bad happens.* Stress and rollover were not a safe combination, and Grace was already wound up tight. He went with, "Some of us aren't comfortable indoors."

She blew across the surface of the coffee, then slanted a look up at him sidelong. Her lips twitched into a smile. "Lead on then. I'd like someone to be comfortable tonight."

Jack wished he knew if he should smile back or not. Half the time, she flinched, but only half. Nothing about her added up.

He had been ready for hostility since reading her DPS file. He'd spent much of his military career cleaning up after fanatics who fucked up other peoples' lives. *Idiotic* and *delusional* were the nicer words in his vocabulary for assholes who insisted everyone had to obey the rules of their religion.

Grace had been a little flaky at first, but she seemed moderately sane, smart, and down to earth around Valerie. How someone like that would belong to the same bugnuts church as Joshua call-me-Sal Moretti was a mystery for the ages.

Good thing Jack didn't have to understand her to work with her.

Grace paused at the patio door, frowning at her mug instead of opening the screen. "Now I feel selfish. I should offer some to your friends."

"No, ma'am, we have a coffee maker downstairs." And a thing that made hot water on command because Shells detested coffee. Grace's machine was nicer, though. One cup at a time, ready in under a minute—Gabe would be jealous. "We aren't guests. We're here to work."

"Still. What will they think?"

Valerie came in from the hall where she'd retreated to make her call. "No one expects you to be a hostess tonight. Don't stress over it. Jack, can I have a moment?"

That meant she was about to dump something on him. He sighed. "Sure. Grace, you can head outside if you want."

"I'll put away these dishes first. It won't take a minute."

That was a familiar maneuver. Jack's foster mother handled fear the same way, by fussing around the house. He could always tell how she felt by the condition of the floors when he visited. When they were spotless and sparkling, she was fretting over him.

Valerie came onto the patio and moved in close, saying softly, "I swear I didn't push. She flat-out asked me, and I couldn't refuse. Sal will be here in a few minutes."

"*Now*?" It came out too loud. By the sink, Grace hunched her shoulders as if she'd been struck. *Dammit*. "Couldn't your kiss-and-make-up daydream wait a day or two, for fuck's sake?"

"No, I don't think so." The mommy-frown came out. "This was never about warm fuzzies. It's about continuity of care. She's giving him sole *in case of* guardianship after they *hid* from him—and she is so serious about putting her affairs in order, I have to wonder if she's going precog. I get a major *do it now* vibe when I look at her."

Jack swallowed the rest of his annoyance. Valerie could be aggravating, but her instincts were good on squishy things. The way Grace had hit onset, her rollover would likely move quickly, and the chances of a hot abort were still high. If this worked, it would make the whole transition easier.

But that was still an *if*, and Valerie wasn't going to be happy about getting what she wanted. "Okay, but if he's coming, you have to leave ASAP."

"No!"

"Yes."

She wrinkled her eyebrows at him. "Jack, be nice."

"I am being nice. Shells can juggle fifty live tokens, but she can only *move* a max of seven at once. You can count as well as I can. If he's in, you're out."

The bunker made this neighborhood as secure as any camp-adjacent town in the lower forty-eight, but that was no reason to take unnecessary risks. "I'm not punishing you. It's a serious issue."

Doing rollover intervention on the fly was like crossing a

minefield; it could be done easily enough with a proper map and careful navigation, but easy and safe were not the same thing. This reunion was the opposite of careful. Grace might want it, Valerie might think it was important, but it was still was like lobbing a hand grenade into the minefield. And he was in charge of damage control.

Valerie got a worried-rabbit expression, which meant he'd pushed too far the other way. "It's only a precaution. Between the bunker and the team, we have countermeasures for every series, including E's and F's. Which also means if things go badly between the lovebirds, Sal's ass gets ported right back out."

"I would certainly hope so." Valerie glanced at Grace, who was now sucking down her coffee as efficiently as any Marine. "I hate leaving with so much uncertainty. Let me hold her hand through the meet and greet."

That was a fair compromise. "Deal."

At the next Camp Liberty board meeting, he would be outlining improvements to their *if-rollover-hits-early* contingency plans. He'd gotten lucky with the available crew this time. They couldn't count on having the right mix of personnel ready on zero notice—or on clients being paranoid enough to build their own containment.

First, they had to get through this job. He keyed his radio mike as he led the way toward the bomb shelter hatch beside the garden shed. "RP-one, everybody."

He pondered operational changes while he walked. Valerie herded Grace along next to him, following behind as if blocking her escape route. She explained why she would have to leave too, so at least he wasn't stuck with that chore.

Once he was in the clear patch between wooden edging and a bunch of weeds, he said to Grace, "There were thirty people in the volunteer pool, and usually we do interviews to match you with personalities you'd be most comfortable having around full time, but—well."

"But you're improvising for me." Her smile still looked pained, but she did raise her eyes as far as his face. "I hope you picked people *you* liked."

"I did. Four of them, in fact." Jack liked her better for trying, so he kept his mouth closed when he smiled, then focused on his crew as they trooped into view. "Guys, this is Grace Reed. Grace, meet your transition team."

Grace's mouth dropped open and stayed that way while Jack went down the line with a bare-bones briefing on each: name, hometowns, and day job; power rating and years of experience; and a brief explanation of how their talents and skills might come in handy.

They made a tidy presentation set, faces illuminated by down-tipped headlamps, bodies backlit by the lantern stationed at the bomb shelter hatch. The reflective stripes on their night duty vests and work pants outlined them gleaming silver lines.

Michelle Burris—or Shells, or Shelly, or Burt, Jack had never met anyone with so many nicknames—had wrinkled brown skin and a frizzy cloud of graying black hair, and she was their transport section. She worked as a commercial teleporter, shipping items and people to beacons all over the continent and above it. She wouldn't have been Jack's first choice since she required those personalized targeting tokens, but her W5 rating met their distance needs, and she didn't require physical contact.

And she'd been available.

Gabriel Fiori had a big white beard, maintained a big round belly, and practiced a jolly laugh on his seven grandchildren. He inflicted his huge repertoire of awful knock-knock jokes on everyone. Before rollover he'd walked an urban police beat for twenty-five years, and after it, he'd stayed in Mercury Battalion long enough to master an H3-N talent that made him a living deep freezer. He had an uncanny knack for detecting invisible powers which would be useful if Sal got out of line, but Jack played up his people skills rather than his powers.

Yasu Tanaka had twinkly eyes, an untidy shock of gray hair, and a bedside manner that made crying babies smile and coo instead. His minor D8-X talent for accelerating or decelerating biological processes wasn't nearly as useful as the rare variance that gave him full immunity to E- and F-type mental powers. Jack hoped they never had to make use of that talent or the man's medical training, but *better safe than sorry* was the cliché of the day.

Jack left Amy for last. Her size was literally the biggest reason. Grace still flinched at him, and at twelve feet-plus, Amy made him look petite. Her non-retracting claws were long enough to put his to shame, and she was standing so they were on full display, painted with multicolored glitter polish to match the eight-inch tall cranial crest and down-curved horns. Her face was a magnificent parade ground blank.

She was on the team as much for her experience as for her physique, not that Jack objected to having backup who could survive a nuclear missile strike. Amy was Gateway's DPS liaison. Jack had carried that title before her, so he knew it came with a whole raft of extra-legal powers. He'd never had to exercise them, and he hoped Amy never had to, either—but if a life-or-death snap decision had to be made, they would have the authority on site to justify it.

Grace's mouth was finally shut because her hands were clasped together right under her chin. Her eyes darted from all twelve feet of Amy to the other three team members and back.

Jack wrapped up by saying, "Between us, we can handle any problem that comes up. We'll do right by you, Grace. Any questions?"

"She—Amy. She's—the rest look so—uh." Grace gestured vaguely as she mumbled to a halt.

"They look so what?" Amy asked. "So short? So fashion-challenged? So old? No, wait. I've got it. The word you're looking for is *normal*. They look normal. I don't. You got a problem with that?"

The scent of her anger slithered through the air. She was definitely still on edge after spending the evening listening to Moretti's endless talk of the Devil, curses, tests, and sin. Jack worked to ignore the scent of fear and the iron taste of anger, but his muscles itched and shifted.

Seconds passed. Leaves rustled. No one moved. Jack gritted his teeth.

Grace swallowed audibly. "No problem unless you need to use the bathroom in the house. I'm entirely sure you won't fit."

The world didn't stop holding its breath. It only felt that way. Gabe chuckled a soft *ho-ho-ho*, Shelly racked up a tally mark in the air, and Yasu snickered. So did Amy.

"That's a fair burn," she said. "Call me if you ever want to rent out that containment bunker of yours. Studio apartments sized for a T1 don't grow on trees, and the water pressure in that shower is sweet."

"I thought the scale on the plans was off, a typo that got embedded in the public record or something." Grace's laugh sounded strained. "Obviously not. I was staring because you look familiar, which is odd. Until today I'd only seen—Tees—on the news or from a distance. A long distance."

"People say it's hard to tell us apart," Jack said. It was rude, but they did say it.

He didn't need telepathy to know Grace's hesitation had replaced the word troll, He knew what she was thinking now. The bad part about being around pre-rollover poz was seeing the question in their eyes when they looked at you: *could I live with becoming that?*

The answer written across Grace's face was *yes,* which surprised Jack as much as it relieved him. And Amy was beaming like a big, toothy dragon child with a big hoard of candy. She liked people who had enough guts to sass her.

Grace said, "Not alike. Familiar." She looked from Amy to him and back. "It was the Atkinson intervention. You were there. There weren't many Tees, and I watched the videos over and over."

Amy spoke up. "You might get to meet one of the others if I get called away on Battalion business. Kris Stanislav is on CLP's reserve roster. We recruited heavily from the hundred or so Marines on that op."

"It made that much of an impression on them?" Grace asked. "Oh, that's encouraging."

Great. They were bonding. They would chat forever if Jack let them. "Grace, it sounds like you're comfortable with this team. That's good. Any idea how your kids will react?"

Grace dug one bare heel into the grass. "We'll work through it. I have questions. How can a hotel be remotely economical? And what about your regular lives? You'll be stuck here for as long as this takes. What if it's weeks? Months, even?"

Valerie said, "Don't worry about those bridges unless we get to them. Take it one day at a time, and leave tomorrow's worries for tomorrow."

"I can't." Grace pulled at her dress with her hands, flapping it back and forth. "It's hard to stop worrying when everyone is tiptoeing around me like I'm about to explode."

"We all know that feeling." Valerie's eyes glimmered. "Just do your best. Sal—your Joshua—will be here any minute. Do you want to talk to Maggie and Lauren before meeting with him?"

They couldn't give her true privacy. Jack was ready to warn

her about that when Grace said firmly, "No. I have to deal with him first. And I want witnesses."

Valerie's phone beeped. She checked the screen and typed a quick note. "He's at the Transit pad." She sent an unhappy look in Jack's direction. "Do we have to do this your way?"

18: FOLLOW THE WAYS OF YOUR HEART

Outside 414 Elm Drive, Elgin, IL

THE TENSION between Jack and Valerie filled the yard. Grace moved to put a planting bed between them and her, acting on intuition learned from a childhood full of conflict. She knew a fight brewing when she saw one.

The non-verbal argument went on for several long breaths before Valerie sighed. "Fine. I'm ready when you are."

"Now is good," Jack replied evenly. "Gabe, walk Sal here from Transit. Shells, he'll need a token." Jack didn't watch their short exchange or the bearded man's departure. He kept his attention on Valerie, nodding approval as she put both hands on her shoulder bag. "Shells, send her to the Riverside office."

"You got it, bossman."

"Wait, I forgot—" Valerie was gone before she finished the sentence.

Dust twinkled, the air pressure equalized with a sharp pop, and a sharp tang of ozone hung in the darkness. Shelly swayed, then braced herself against Amy's leg. "Whoa, long ones always give me a head rush."

Grace jumped back from the empty space. Her pulse raced so hard her skin throbbed in time with her heartbeat. That was twice now Jack had spirited someone away in the middle of a conversation.

No one else seemed surprised. Maybe people coming and going without warning was an everyday occurrence for them. She should warn him to not do it in front of Maggie and Lauren. They would either be thrilled or terrified, and either way, they would be loud about it.

Dizziness washed over her. She was contemplating her family's reaction to *teleportation*. Nothing would ever be normal again.

Her knees gave up their fight with gravity. She sat down in the damp, cool grass and clutched at it. Every blade felt crisp against her palms.

"Safe delivery confirmed," Shells said in the distance.

"Good. Yasu, wait out front for the kids while—" Jack regarded Grace with a frown. "Or maybe not. Amy, tag in for Gabe as escort and tell him to play welcome wagon. Yasu, check her out, please?"

Amy strode away, and Yasu came closer to peer at Grace, eyes dark and intent, face shadowed under the bright headlamp. "How are you feeling, my dear?"

Of course he asked that. She concentrated on her lungs. *In. Out. In.* "It's—" *Breathe.* "—too much."

Jack took a step back, which was hardly reassuring, but Yasu knelt down, glancing over his shoulder. "Don't freak, Jackass," he said. "It's only shock. Completely understandable."

He had a kind smile, and his bushy gray hair made him look like an absentminded professor. He bent closer. "He's a retired Marine, and Mercury soldiers get yanked all over the map on the regular. They forget how mere mortals react to other people going *poof*. Try not to hold it against him. You're doing great. Keep breathing slow like that and put your head down."

He pressed a hand to her shoulder to push her forward.

Life screeched to a halt. Grace blinked and felt it in slow motion, caught in a pause between breaths. The yard blurred and brightened with blue-tinted light, the insects around the patio light dazzled her, like sparks moving impossibly fast, and the whole world spun in a stately dance with the moon, the sun—

Yasu lurched back to land on his backside next to her. "Yow," he said.

Grace sighed as the amazing perception faded. The brightness dimmed last and slowest, highlighting the open-mouthed amazement on Shelly's face.

Jack wore a murderous scowl, but to be fair, that was his default expression. "There's a reason for the 'don't touch' reminder in the briefing," he told Yasu.

"Hard habit for a doctor to break. I won't forget twice." Yasu wobbled to his feet and turned to get a fix on Jack's face. "Vitals are normal, no physical changes. But that power surge was something."

"Yeah. Dammit." Jack's jaw worked, and his teeth flashed. "Grace, I'm not sure you're up to the stress—"

"I have to see him." Urgency swelled like a bubble in Grace's chest. "Don't say I can't. Please don't."

She lost track of Jack's reply because lights were bobbing at the corner of the house. Amy appeared first, and a shadowed figure came out of the darkness of the side yard beside her. She reached out, claws enveloped the man's shoulders and arms, and her headlamp illuminated him like a spotlight.

"Joshua," Grace whispered. *No. They call him Sal.* She should do the same, leaving the name and the pain in the past.

His hair had gone gray at the sides, and he'd gained weight. There were new wrinkles at the corners of his eyes, across his forehead. The changes made him less imposing than Grace remembered. His lips were still kissable and perfect.

I missed you, her heart whispered. Betrayal, bitterness, and fear had shattered the bedrock of their love into fragments, but time hadn't washed away the shifting sands.

Or was he making her feel this way? Would she know?

Doubt smothered her yearning, and cold sweat prickled over her skin. A few hours ago, the thought of him had frightened her to the point of panic, and that dread didn't care how much she had changed in a short time.

"Are you deaf?" Amy asked him. "I said wait *behind* me. If you can't follow directions, I'm telling Shelly to 'port you somewhere minus your skin."

Grace's fear relaxed its grip enough. Amy was much closer to him, and she didn't sound bewitched. Knowledge was the first shield Grace had constructed against fear after she'd escaped The Ranch. She knew how Joshua's particular curse—no, say it, his *power*—worked. He couldn't affect one and not affect all.

Sal didn't move an inch. "I am waiting," he said. "But I had to see her."

A sob stuck in Grace's throat. He sounded the same as ever, his voice thick with emotions she didn't dare interpret. Her heart felt ripped in two, unable to forgive, unable to hate.

She scrambled to her feet. "Let him come."

Amy followed at Sal's heels down the strip of turf beside the patio. Yasu and Jack moved up behind Grace, which made her feel like a duelist in one of the period dramas the girls watched, coming onto the field with seconds at her back.

Shelly retreated into the house, and the screen door screeched along its track.

"Hi," Sal said when he was no more than an arm's length away.

"Hi," Grace whispered.

Two years' worth of tears broke through the barriers she'd built to hold them back. "I had a letter for you, but it's gone."

"Sarah—no, *Grace*—no, don't cry. I am so sorry." He leaned forward with the apology. "I thought I would have to wait until we stood before God to say that. I never meant to hurt you. I was stupid and lonely, and I didn't understand. I can do better. Thank you for letting me try."

His relief and joy brushed at her, like soft fur inside her skull, and this time she *knew* the feeling came from him. The strangeness of it was terrifying but not as paralyzing as she remembered.

"Hey, none of that," Yasu snapped. He waved them apart, stepping between. "Put a lid on it, son, or I will."

Sal made a pained noise and shoved his hands under his arms. "I'm trying. This is a lot, you know? Hard to balance. Put me in cuffs if you want. I don't care."

Off to the side, Jack growled like stone grinding. "No cuffs. If you can't control yourself, you have no business here. Suck it up or ship out."

"That isn't helping, Jack," Yasu remarked. "Son, would you like help? I can put your nervous system on slowdown for an hour or so. It isn't pleasant, you'll pass out if you try to move too fast, but it will mute your ability. If what you need is a breather—"

"Yes, do it. Do anything, but don't send me away."

"You'll feel weak, then numb. Don't fight it." Yasu put a hand on his shoulder, patted him twice, and then caught him around the waist as his knees buckled. "Whoops, that was easier than I expected. Jack, a hand here?"

Jack carried Sal to the table, where Yasu arranged him on

the bench sitting upright, arms braced at his sides. After giving him one last assessing look, he stepped back. "Grace, how's this? He can't touch you. Not physically or with his powers."

"I'm fine." She slid onto the opposite bench and tucked her hands under her thighs, fighting a petty, horrible satisfaction. *You would have bent me to the will of others, if I had let you. How do you like being powerless?* It was unworthy of her to enjoy this reversal, but she couldn't help it.

Yasu pursed his lips. "Why don't we give you two a little space? We can be witnesses from out of earshot, can't we, Jack?"

Jack frowned at the ground until Amy gave him a push. "Fine, but make it quick. There are kids on the way, remember."

"Don't worry," Shelly called from indoors. "Gabe and I will keep them distracted."

Everyone retreated inside except Amy, who went out through the side gate. Shelly slid the glass door shut. Night noises filled the yard, choirs of crickets and frogs competing for supremacy.

Grace's chest ached, but that wasn't Sal's power—it was the knowledge that there was no going back. He was smiling a little. She could not let that tentative, wistful hope grow. "You're here for the girls," she said. "Nothing else."

The light in his eyes dimmed, and his expression smoothed —slowly—to a sober stare. He blinked. "That's enough," he said. "Your trust was the most precious gift you had to give, and I spat on it. I'll take whatever you dish out and call it fair."

"Oh, Josh—Sal." He had never been the brightest light in the heavens, but he was as earnest and faithful as a man could be. She'd sworn to herself she wouldn't ask, but the question tore itself free of its bindings. "Why did you do it?"

"I wanted to make you see the church had gone wrong. When they said, *come home*, I didn't think." He paused, breathing hard. "They reported me, did you know that? Drove me straight to the sheriff. I didn't realize they meant to use me to control you. I swear on my life, I didn't understand. Not until later."

She steeled herself. "Too little, too late. I can make myself believe you're still a good father, but I can't forget you failed me that one particular way. God forgives all, but I can't."

Saying it aloud felt like breathing on a ripe dandelion head. The heart of the pain remained close but the rest floated loose, leaving her light and empty.

"I knew there'd be no fixing it." His frown arrived in a slow-motion display of sadness. "I screwed up when I went off to the DPS camp, I screwed up explaining it when I came back, I screwed up everything."

Why do you always make everything about you? Grace pressed her lips tight on those bitter words. "I can't blame you for leaving the church. Look at me, here and now. And I was always glad you didn't make me—that you left the church for your rollover."

"I'm glad, too." After a short silence full of the lost, broken future they would never have, he said, "Please tell me what you want. I don't know how to make this better."

You never know. You always make me do the thinking and deciding.

Unfair to hold that against him. He hadn't courted her with cleverness or strength of will. She had been drawn to his kindness, charity, and generosity. He had been a warm and welcoming hearth when she was wounded, cold, and lost.

That didn't make the vices of his virtues any less maddening. Grace's temper leaked into her voice. "You can start by apologizing to your daughters for giving them a year's worth of nightmares. Leah and Ruth are going by Lauren and Margaret —Maggie, actually. I let them choose, and they called it getting real names. And you know I'm Grace now."

"They told me. Why that name?" Josh swallowed hard. "Was it for the sacrament? The one I refused to perform?"

"Not everything is about you." No one could annoy her like this man. "I named myself after the woman who buried her enemies in lava and hellfire when they tried to take her children away. The one who lost control of her curse—her power. Remember?"

"I remember we argued over the news." Sal's chin twitched up. "You wouldn't stop talking about how she died. I was already losing faith by then. I said it didn't make sense for the Devil's servants to sacrifice themselves for other demons. You called me a blasphemer. I can't believe you're going to allow yourself to roll. You were always so—firm—when you talked about your grandfather's teachings."

"I didn't want to face my own doubts." It hurt to face that truth. "I was harsh. And wrong." An uncomfortable realization struck. "You've been sharing church secrets. Have you told them about the rituals? About the knife and the needle?"

"No!" His chin dropped to his chest. His neck quivered with the effort of lifting it. "I only answer questions or explain points they bring up. I would never talk about the Choice of Endings unless—do you want me to?"

"No, we've both left those ways behind. Let the past stay buried."

How could non-believers react to learning she'd built the bunker expecting it to become her tomb if she was damned with one of the greater curses? They didn't need to know what sacrifices she might have asked her own children to make. "Maybe I chose the right name for the wrong reasons," she said, thinking of it. "I was granted grace today in a whole different way."

"And thank God for that." Josh listed to the side, then straightened. "I can't do this much longer."

"Does it hurt?" She didn't want to care, but she couldn't stop.

"No. I'm only tired. Bone-tired. Where do we go from here?"

"Forward." Grace shifted on the bench, scratched an itchy spot on her arm. She hadn't thought to put on bug repellant. Both her ankles itched too. She might have picked up chiggers wandering around the lawn barefoot.

What a thing to worry about at a time like this.

So much more needed saying, but they'd made a start. "You stay here and answer religious questions for your friends and get to know Lauren and Maggie again. Valerie arranged paid family leave. You'll learn their routines, and if this is still going on when school starts, you help with that. And custody will go to you if anything goes wrong."

"Nothing will go wrong. Don't say that. I can't lose you again."

"You don't *have* me. I can't let you in my bed or my life—no, that's harsh again. I'm sorry." Her hands went out of their own accord, reaching for him the way flowers turned to the sun. She forced herself to pull back. "You have a place. I've left the girls this house and all the money I—" she fumbled for the best word, "—inherited from Father. If I die, you'll be their guardian and their trustee. I want you here until this is done and in their lives for always."

Sal sat motionless for several deep, shaky breaths. "They aren't my friends," he said at last. "These people helping you. They think I'm an ignorant hick. I don't have friends. You know what I do for a living now? I stock warehouse shelves for a boss who leaves notes so she won't have to see me, and I live in a closet of an apartment because no one will share a space with me."

"I don't care—"

"I care!" Sal's eyebrows twitched, the only outward sign of the passion in his voice. "Don't you get it? How can you trust our girls to me again? I was never strong, or smart, or brave. You were the only one who ever thought I could be. And I failed you too. Why would you give me this gift?"

Another long silence passed, marked by the hum of insects singing to one another before Grace found the words for her heart's truth. "Because you were brave enough to love me once. Because you were strong enough to let me lead. Follow me again. Be a father to our children again. Or convince me you don't want it."

His breathing slowed and steadied. He sniffed. That was the familiar sign that his frustration had ebbed, that he had worked through the thorny tangle of words to find ideas he could grasp. "I want it to the center of my soul," he said, "but I don't know how to smile and play nice with them. How do I convince them I'm not a demon and pretend we're still a family?"

He would do what she asked. He almost always did. "We *are* a family, and for now, you will be a part of the household. I never called you devil to them, only warned them against weakness. Keep yourself busy, and they'll adjust to you being around. There's plenty of work."

"I saw. This place is a big project. A lot for one person."

"The girls do what they can. They've grown up so much. You'll be proud of them."

His smile held a wry sadness. "I'm sure I will, but that won't help if they hate me. Do you know I wake myself up nights hearing them scream as you ran away?"

"That's something we have in common, then." Grace clutched at her patience. "Stop wallowing, Joshua, and work on repentance. If I can accept you, they can, and I—" She couldn't lie. "I want this for them."

"But not for you."

"No. They're the only thing still binding us." That would be enough to graft together a new household. It had to be. "You will always be their father. Hold onto that."

"I will. I promise—" The sound of car doors slamming and loud, high-pitched voices bounced over the house from the front yard. Josh exhaled hard. "Here they come. I will do my best for them. For you."

"I don't care who you do it for, as long as you do it."

That was all Grace had time to say before the girls burst through the side gate. They ran together across the lawn, leggy in matching shorts and sandals, with their hair loose, dark and wavy. Bearded, affable Gabe strolled into the yard behind them, stopping at a discreet distance to take up a watchful stance, legs braced, arms crossed.

The girls spoke over each other as they approached, voices bright and excited, like a pair of birds weaving a single nest of questions. "Mom, they said you're rolling and not being religious, is it true? Is Dad here for real? The old man out front can make snowflakes! Why aren't we running away? What's going to happen to us? Why can't we touch you? For how long? What kind of power are you getting?"

Their frantic exuberance proved they'd wheedled the basics out of someone—they'd been told enough to inform, but not enough to understand the gravity of the situation.

"I don't have any powers yet," Grace told them. "Slow down. Calm down. A lot has happened, and I can't explain if you're shouting at us."

The girls fell silent as they scuffed to a halt at the edge of the patio. They went stone-faced as they looked over Sal. Their eyes were fever-bright, their faces blotchy red from crying. Maggie flapped both hands at a passing moth and squeaked.

Lauren took the lead. "Are you okay, Mom?" she asked. "I don't get it. *He's* here, but we're not running? I don't want to go, but are you sure this is okay? What if he's done—you know—to you again? How are you feeling?"

Grace stifled a laugh at hearing that question again. "I'm fine, and yes, I'm sure. We've come to an—understanding. He's left the church too, and—"

Lauren interrupted. "But what if he's lying?" She came to the end of the table, glancing from one parent to the other. "You're really going to *roll,* Mom? Really?"

"I am. I won't have to leave you, and we will have help. You've met some of them already. Your father will be accountable to them as well as me."

Maggie shouldered up next to her sister, planting her hands on her hips and tossing her hair. "Well, I don't like it. We can take care of each other. He should go away and leave us alone."

"That decision is up to your mother," Sal said.

"You shut up! Don't talk to us, you—you!" Lauren jabbed a finger at him. "You did a bad thing. You aren't supposed to ever crawl into people's heads and make them happy or sad. We learned about it in real school."

"I don't want him here!" Maggie flounced backward a half-step. "If he makes my brain wormy again, I will hit him, I *will*."

This was getting out of hand faster than Grace had imagined possible. "Margaret Rose Reed, you lower your voice this instant. Shame on you."

"No, Grace, they're right." Sal nodded. "I don't deny it. If you've never sinned, pick up the first stone and cast it."

"You don't get to quote Bible verses at us!" Lauren stuck her nose in the air, supporting her sister's rebellion. "We don't do stupid church stuff now. We don't have to listen to you, and if you try anything weird, we'll scream and call the DPS, and I hope they put you in jail for*ever* this time."

Grace snapped, "Shame on you too, Lauren Marie. Those are horrible things to say!"

Lauren flapped both hands in a wide, aggravated gesture. "Mom, you had breakdowns if we said the word *Dad* for, like, three months. And now he's here and you're rolling? What is going on? You're scaring us! How do you expect us to act?"

Sal's gasp of dismay was a harsh noise. Grace reached for a calm, level tone. "I expect you to behave like young women, not rude children. I expect you to think before opening your mouths and spewing angry threats in front of guests. I'm disappointed in you."

Both the girls regarded her with identically disgusted expressions. Gabe gave her a thumbs-up from behind them. He was grinning broadly, teeth square and white in his bushy beard.

"But I don't *want* you to roll," Maggie said in a tear-soaked whine.

"God did not ask your opinion, and neither did I," Grace said, which made Maggie huff and Lauren roll her eyes. "Sweeties, you cannot be any more scared than I am, but this is not up for a vote. I will explain and listen to your concerns after you apologize for the disrespect. And we're not moving an inch from this spot until I'm satisfied. "

Her daughters were the kind of strong-willed, intelligent, independent young women she'd raised them to be. Issuing an ultimatum was a gamble, but she was their mother, and she knew their weaknesses. "I don't mind a few mosquito bites," she said as they tried and failed to glare her into submission.

"I'm sorry," Maggie said, and Lauren edged closer, clasping hands with her sister before echoing the apology. Then she said hesitantly, "Should there be popcorn now?"

That was the moment Grace knew her plan would work.

She exchanged a look with Sal, saw her memories of a hundred other nights reflected in his gentle blue eyes. Every serious family meeting happened around a bowl of popcorn.

Originally a way to reward two small girls for sitting still and listening, the tradition became a material promise that any conflict could be resolved as long as they faced it together.

It wouldn't be easy, but they would find a new way to be a family.

"Yes," Grace said. "Let's start with popcorn."

19: WHAT IS LACKING CANNOT BE COUNTED

August 17, 2019, Ironwood Ave, Moreno Valley, California

THE DIGITAL CLOCK on the kitchen wall read 21:55 by the time Valerie got home. She set her bag of Indian takeout and the bottle of wine on the breakfast bar and slipped out of her shoes. The house was quiet, which was a good sign. The boys must have gone to bed more or less on time.

Anna was watching television in the darkened living room. Light from the screen flickered over the strong lines of her profile.

Anna Garcia Fuentes was a tiny, handsome woman letting her black wavy hair go gray without pretense, and the bright, tailored dresses she sewed for herself always flattered her generous curves. She usually radiated competence and calm. Tonight she was wrapped in a jagged haze of suppressed anger.

When she turned, Valerie waved for her to stay put. The woman was hooked on a popular historical drama about life in Britain in the Forties after First Night. Tearing her away from the last few minutes of an episode would be cruel.

Anna turned to the screen with anger smoldering behind a smile. Valerie looked away before the dissonance could overwhelm her. Everyone was entitled to privacy, and she wasn't up to dealing with anyone else's unhappiness.

Her head throbbed from teleport hangover, and her muscles ached from the stress of traveling across half a continent twice in twelve hours by two different modes. Her empty stomach was gnawing at her spine, and her emotions were a muddled mess.

She rubbed at the transport tag above her collarbone. Its presence left her feeling vulnerable, but she couldn't ask Shelly to remove it just because she didn't like knowing she could be yanked around like a package. She couldn't admit cowardice when she was already feeling weak and stupid.

Jack had been right to push her aside. Recruiting Grace had been her idea. The transition plan might be stable now, but it might come apart at any second. Then everyone would see what a horrible person she was. What kind of idiot forgot to give back a letter that wouldn't be needed?

No. She raised her defenses against the acid drip of self-doubt. Those whispers were the ghosts of her ex-husband's toxic lies, a sneakier, more dangerous legacy than her need for quiet, controlled environments.

She had *not* failed. Jack had been right to send her away, but he had listened to her, first. That was a victory. And she'd flash-couriered Grace's letter back as soon as she remembered it. No harm done—except to Camp Liberty's financials, and she would repay the fee from her stipend if necessary.

She needed to relax and let it go. Grace's family was in capable hands. The day-to-day operational details rested on the transition team's shoulders, not hers. Shelly had sent a message reassuring her that the family reconciliation was going well.

Managing Camp Liberty's records and client processing was

her responsibility. She could only do that if she took care of herself. First, she had to send Anna home, get her food into the oven to reheat, and say goodnight to the boys. Then she could shed her suit and pour one precious glass of wine before tackling Grace's paperwork.

A dedicated person would have stayed at the office until the work was done, but she just *couldn't*. She felt guiltier with every extra hour she kept Anna on the clock. She wanted to hug her boys and rest in the comforts of her nest even if she didn't get a wink of sleep tonight.

Life was easier at home.

She focused on the television dialogue while she unpacked half the takeout containers onto the counter. When music began playing over the show credits, she walked the bag containing the rest to Anna. "Tandoori chicken, sides, and an apology for the long day," she said. "How was *Brighton Tales*? I hear the season finale covers the end of the war and the Pacific Wall going up."

"I heard the same rumor. I can't wait." Anna rose from the couch and shut off the television before taking the bag. "You don't have to feed me when you work late, Ms. Wade. It's my choice to wait rather than eat with the boys."

"I know, but Indian reheats well, and I know you love it."

Anna peeked into the bag and sniffed appreciatively. "I do, thank you. David won't eat it, and he fed my kids pizza tonight. I'll get this all to myself."

The words were cheerful, as was her smile, but Valerie could not ignore that thickening haze of aggravation. She used the excuse of opening the wine to avoid eye contact, but her fears grew teeth.

Anna had a tween girl and boy waiting at home with her husband. *What if she wants to quit to spend more time with them?* "How did things go today?"

Anna's smile shone true this time. "Johnny did the dishes without being asked and helped Gary with brushing his teeth. He also mentioned his birthday a dozen times. And he wanted my opinion on bicycles. We made a list of possibilities with prices as a math project."

"That's wonderful." Valerie couldn't find the courage to look up. If she saw a truth at odds with the amused pride she was hearing, she would cry. Her stomach tied itself in knots, and the smell of the food made her nauseous. "I don't know what I would do without you, Anna. Thank you again."

"It's nothing." Anna collected her purse and her knitting bag. "I'll be back at eight for you. I can't stay late tomorrow, so I'll line up a sitter in case you need one again. Good night, ma'am."

"Good night." Valerie sagged against the counter and put her aching head in her hands as soon as she heard the door close. Her palms were cold and damp against her cheeks.

Not every bad thing in the world is my fault: she repeated that thought until it outweighed the idea of running after Anna to beg forgiveness for the unknown insult. Then she left her food on the counter and headed for the boys' room.

The door squeaked softly when she pushed it open. She tiptoed to the matching beds by the dim illumination of the night light, picking up three socks, an action figure, and two plastic blocks on the way.

The toys went on the nightstand for Johnny to put away in the morning, and the socks went into the hamper next to the rocking chair in the corner. Valerie tugged up the bunny-patterned comforter Gary had kicked off before falling asleep.

He was curled on his side with both hands under his cheek. She smoothed back his pale hair and fully opened her eyes to soak in his sweet intensity. Her younger son rarely sat still long enough for peaceful moments like this when he was awake.

A forehead kiss, a whispered, "sleep tight, baby, I love you," and the bedtime ritual was done. A fretful, waking murmur was silenced by retrieving a plush octopus from the floor.

Johnny lay spread-eagled on his belly on top of his Batman bedspread with the flashlight he thought was a secret clutched in one hand and his latest adventure book in the other.

Valerie's breath hitched in her throat. She glimpsed many of her own frailties in Johnny, and he displayed his father's volatile impulsiveness too.

She tucked the book and flashlight under the mattress, then eased him onto his back and under his covers. Johnny's energy and aggressiveness needn't lead to abusiveness or addiction. Nor did his need for approval doom him to being used. Her vision was not foresight any more than it was mind-reading. She saw present truths, not an inescapable future.

Johnny's eyes opened when she kissed his nose. "M'mmy? Y'rome f'reals?"

"Hi, sweetling. Yes, I'm home for real. Annie says you were the best ever tonight. I'm so proud. Sleep tight. I love you."

"Mm'kay. Luffoodoo." He rolled over to hug his pillow.

Valerie's heart overflowed. Her older son was a miser with emotions other than anger. He might not remember any of this in the morning, but hearing the word *love* from him was an enormous gift just the same.

Back in the hallway, she pulled gently on the door until the latch clicked, then let herself relax against it. Her head was pounding harder than ever, and she was terribly tempted to curl up in the corner rocker with Gary's baby quilt on her lap and sleep with them until morning.

Tears stung her eyes. Once she would have finished this nightly circuit by lifting her mother from that rocker and helping her walk to the second bedroom they'd shared. The grief had scabbed over, but pain still broke through and flowed fresh when she least expected it.

She fought back sniffles and tears with her practiced list of gratitudes. The boys were her sun and moon. She no longer worried about them growing up without a roof overhead, going hungry, or being killed by their father.

Maybe money couldn't buy happiness, but it could purchase peace of mind. They lived in a house with two whole bedrooms and a swing set in the little fenced yard. The boys got new clothes when they outgrew or wore out the old ones. They no longer had peanut butter sandwiches for breakfast, lunch, and dinner for the last four days of the month.

This was a good life. And if she wanted to keep her gains, she had to keep pretending she was competent and in control. That meant fueling up, sitting down, and facilitating Grace Reed's smooth, legal transition through rollover.

The scent of hot garlic and blended spices reached the hall. Her stomach growled.

When she returned to the kitchen, a juice glass of pale wine sat waiting on the breakfast bar beside a place setting, her laptop, and her attaché case. Another plate and silverware had been placed farther along the countertop, where the laptop screen wouldn't be visible.

Anna was at the stove pushing samosas around a skillet. A saucepan steamed on the back burner. Her natural steadiness was still cloaked in ill-temper like a statue smothered by soot, but she was there. Working.

"Anna, why—?" was as far as Valerie got before her throat closed on a lump of impossible questions. If she asked, *Am I supposed to pay you for this*? it would sound like a complaint, but *Why did you come back*? and *What do you want?* were worse. "Are you all right?"

Anna didn't look up. "Go change into your comfy clothes, ma'am."

"But—"

"Go to your room." She pointed down the hall with a slotted spoon without turning. "Change. Shower if you have the energy. Take your time. I'll keep everything nice and hot. I called David, and he agrees I should stay tonight. He'll drop by with my makeup kit and a change of clothes for tomorrow. I have sheets on the couch."

"Anna, I can't impose on you like this." For one thing, she couldn't afford it. Not if she wanted to get Johnny the bicycle he wanted for his birthday.

"You are impossible!" Anna rapped the spoon on the skillet several times. "Can't I do you a favor? Will you be sensible, or must I throw a tantrum, break plates, and threaten to quit?"

The noise made Valerie jump. Her whole body clenched. "Please don't quit."

"Oh, are you listening now?" Anna finally turned, and her rocky sense of humor surfaced through the annoyance like a gleam of polished marble. "Wash up. Now. Before you say another word, keep in mind I win arguments against your stubborn children every single day of the week."

Valerie surrendered to the inevitable. "I'll be right back."

She returned after a quick shower, refreshed and comfortable in her bed-shirt and fleece pants. An overnight bag leaned against the arm of the couch: David must have come and gone.

Anna sat at the bar eating her chicken and salad. Steam rose from a teapot at her elbow and a cup in front of her. She poured a second cup of tea and placed it beside the wine. "It's decaf," she said. "Sit. Eat."

Obedience seemed the wise course. Valerie sat and let herself be served.

Her appetite had returned with a vengeance. She finished her butter chicken and dal masala before attempting conversation again.

"Would you really have broken my plates?" she asked as she pushed aside the bowl and pulled her computer close.

"Only the chipped ones you've said you hate." Anna collected plates and loaded them into the dishwasher. "And I would've pitched them at the sink to cut down on the mess. But yes, I would've done whatever it took to get your attention. You *have* to slow down, ma'am. Every time you start one of these Camp Liberty projects, you work night and day for weeks. You'll work yourself to death."

"I can't stop." Valerie took a long sip of wine, savoring the smooth, dry flavor. "This startup is incredibly important. Possibly historic. I'm not exaggerating. Besides, if I don't work, you don't get paid."

Anna crossed her arms over her chest and glared. "Back when I started, I was twice-a-week help. Light cleaning and taking your mother to appointments. Then it was three days, adding sports practices, groceries, sorting mail. Now it's Monday through Friday, two evenings, and household errands. Each time, I was the one who had to say, 'Ms. Wade, let me do this or that.'"

"I hate asking—" Valerie stopped when Anna raised an imperious hand.

"That's what annoys me so. Listen." She ticked off items on her fingers. "You pay well, you pay on schedule, and you stick to the contract. If there's extra work, I get extra time. You never call me *Annie* or *girl*. When you ask how my family is doing, you sound like you mean it. You make my work feel important."

Valerie blinked at the intensity rolling off Anna. "It is important."

Anna's hands went up, came down to clap against her thighs. "*I* know that. Why don't *you*? Don't you get it? If you kill yourself with stress, I'll never find another job this good. Do you know how many employers say please and thank you?"

"No?" She was missing something important. "Not enough?"

"Hardly any." Anna turned away to fill the tea kettle and start it heating again. "My title is family assistant, yes? This new rollover business you're doing will be incredible if it works, yes?" She waited with raised eyebrows until Valerie nodded, then nodded back. "Fine. Make it work. I'll pick up the slack. Rely on me and stop *apologizing*."

Valerie gathered her courage. "But Anna, my budget—I'm sor—I can't afford more."

Anna waved off the objection. "I am not working tonight. I'm having dinner with a friend. And if your boys sleep at my place once in a while when you're swamped or called away now and then? Pfft. Who charges for sleepovers? That would be less hardship for everyone, wouldn't it?"

"I—guess?" Valerie couldn't breathe properly. Anna considered her a friend? Blurring definitions, crossing boundaries, changing plans—those things made her uncomfortable, another legacy of years spent tied in knots and choked by uncertainty. Life was easier when topics—and people—stayed in their proper places.

Starting up her computer and arranging files soothed her nerves. She kept her eyes on the screen. "Can we talk about this tomorrow? I have a ton of work to do before morning."

Anna sighed. "I am cluttering up your emotional boxes, aren't I? Here's what I'll do. I'll hunt up a salary contract tomorrow and fill in new duties with fair fees, nice and tidy the way you like everything."

"That would be amazing. Thank you." Valerie opened the case file and sighed at the number of items remaining on the Day One checklist. She'd handed in Grace's Intake forms, but that was only the first step into the bureaucratic labyrinth of rollover. There were many more turns to navigate before she could rest tonight.

Their grant funding depended on meeting safety and developmental targets from the DPS rollover handbook. And proving they had upheld those standards meant producing every piece of documentation their clients would have generated during a normal internment or mentorship.

The Department of Public Safety was over fifty years old, and Valerie was fairly sure they'd never gotten rid of a single process in all that time. Deadlines and goals overlapped and occasionally conflicted. Each regional unit had multiple staff members to handle the required regulatory filings and progress reports.

Camp Liberty had her.

She couldn't do this alone forever, not if they wanted to expand.

She had a workable system in place, given enough lead time to personalize form templates, double-check file codes and confirm the proper recipients. That approach had gone out the window this time. If they ever had two clients at once, she wouldn't be able to manage both.

But that was a problem for another day. She had a dozen deadlines to hit in the next twenty-four hours, and she didn't like to think about the consequences if she missed any of them.

So don't think about it. Do the work.

The tea kettle whistled, Anna bustled about the kitchen and set a steaming cup of peppermint tea next to Valerie's hand. She murmured a distracted thank you before immersing herself in paperwork.

The lights in the living room went off. The glow from the hanging lamp over the breakfast bar was cool, and the darkness had a peaceful gentleness to it. Quiet breathing came from the couch where Anna had bedded down.

By the time Valerie ticked off the last box on the Day One list, her eyes were gritty, and her back muscles were threatening to spasm. She hit send on the final round of data entry with a sense of accomplishment. Once she received the completed Form 42 with the appointment date for Grace's power evaluation, she could go to bed.

The DPS network chewed on the information for several seconds longer than usual, then spat up an unexpected message:

Expedited Initial Evaluation Y/N? Select Form DPS73-IID459131 or Form DPS73-IID459142

Surprise jolted Valerie wide-awake. Grace had qualified for a fast-tracked power analysis.

Well, rats. She gnawed on a cuticle. This was a tricky one. None of their previous clients had met the mysterious criteria for early evaluation, not even the potential primes.

The priority algorithms were a tightly held secret, but everyone knew they favored hot rollovers who needed specialty training—elementals, and the E, F, and W series. Grace hadn't rolled hot. That put her in the standard queue. Average wait times there were in the two- to three-*week* range. Diagnostics was chronically understaffed. The analytical talents were rare, and the evaluator training process was grueling.

Form 42 was the easy out. It was the default. No one else would ever know she had faced this choice. Grace's ID would go into the queue, and in due time the agents who regularly served Elgin on their circuit would drop by to offer a trained estimate of her emerging power series and rating.

But why did Grace qualify? What secrets were Diagnostics keeping? Valerie was confident Jack and Amy could contain Grace if her developing power escaped her control, but that wouldn't keep it from hurting or killing *Grace*. Some rollovers were fatal. Not many, statistically speaking, but the cold truth was, people died.

Losing a client would be a huge setback for Camp Liberty. And one preventable death was one too many.

If Valerie filed Form 31, Grace would know her likely series and ranking before supper time tomorrow. That was tempting for several reasons. Reducing uncertainty was a proven way to ease the physical stress of rollover, and that would increase Grace's chances of survival. She could get a jump start on her training, too.

The danger with Form 31 lay in the possibility of catching the wrong evaluation team on a bad day. There was no appealing a Diagnostics decision. They could override Camp Liberty's operating exceptions.

The regular circuit evaluators knew and trusted Jack and Heather. The specialists who got dispatched for priority tests weren't known for trusting anyone. They didn't like change, and they didn't like risk.

Evaluators were supposed to be impartial, but a specialist team might yank Grace into a camp just because they could. It was unlikely, but possible. *That* would set back the program too.

And there was no telling how Grace would react to that outcome.

Valerie turned the puzzle over and over in her mind, but there were too many unknowns. The risk depended on the nature of Grace's talent, which was the whole point of getting an evaluation.

She could call for a consult, but it would still be her decision. The others were three hours ahead, and no one liked being woken up in the middle of the night. They would think she couldn't do her job. And they would be right.

She could consult in the morning, but short delays at the front end could mean extra *days* of waiting for a Form 42 appointment. Which might be too late for Grace.

Why, oh, *why* was she so stupid and indecisive and weak? She stared at the two buttons on her screen and wished desperately that she was someone else, someone confident and clever.

Hazy flashes of color wavered the edges of her sight, and sharp lines of pain curved around the backs of her eyeballs to gnaw at the inside of her skull.

The pain was a welcome one: it meant she was missing something.

Similar headaches had plagued her through the long months of her rollover while her new vision was developing. Whenever she refused to consciously accept what her talent was trying to tell her, the impressions bled into her peripheral vision as painful, haunting distractions. Most of her training had consisted of learning how to allow herself to see things she didn't like

But she'd never seen truths in an image. Why now?

She closed her eyes and took slow, deep breaths, pushing out her personal concerns. Her mentor had compared rollover to going through a second puberty. There was an identifiable point called onset, with obvious growth spurts, but other changes happened invisibly.

The answer to *why* might be Grace.

She had enhanced Heather's power and Jack's, too. If she was coming into a W-series power like energy boosting or probability manipulation, that would also explain the way events had converged favorably around her onset.

Luck-bending was a poorly-understood and highly problematic talent, thankfully rare. Pure energy manipulators were rarer yet. Both were critically dangerous to their wielders and required specialized early intervention.

If Grace was interned, it would set back Camp Liberty, maybe derail it, but their progress wasn't worth her life.

Valerie opened her eyes. Cool air from the overhead vents sifted down over her. The longer she looked, the more one button sharpened into focus. The truth was literally there on her screen.

She requested the expedited evaluation form. A warning screen popped up. She confirmed her choice. Another box splashed across the screen: *misuse of federal assets could result in civil and criminal penalties.*

Her fingers curled away from the keyboard. She forced them to dismiss that warning too. One automated information prompt after another came onscreen. She clicked them one by one until her cursor quivered over the *file* button. Then it was done. Her responsibility was discharged.

She put her head in her hands and hoped she hadn't ruined everything.

20: WHEN TIMES ARE GOOD, BE HAPPY

August 18, 414 Elm Drive, Elgin, IL

WHEN JACK ARRIVED to take charge of the day watch, Yasu was perched at the breakfast bar with coffee and a syrupy plate of pancakes in front of him. Jack slid the patio door closed and immediately ramped up his energy usage to compensate for his rising body temperature. The house wasn't sweltering yet, but it was getting there. He was overheating in shorts and a tank top. How Yasu kept from melting in a dress shirt and slacks was a mystery for the ages.

The man saluted him with his coffee mug and launched into a report without wasting time on greetings. Jack admired his ability to deliver a concise briefing while chewing.

The day was starting well. Everyone in the family had slept soundly and separately. The out-of-towners were settled on-site. Gabe was up and showering for his day shift. Shelly had taken swing shift and was watching the house monitors in the basement office. Amy was crashed in the bunker, happy to avoid commuting from Gateway for the duration. Heather might not join them until tomorrow. She was stuck at the DPS offices with paperwork to complete.

Grace was flaring power while she slept, but its form remained amorphous. Yasu was a running a pool on where and when she would settle. Jack put twenty on both the P and H series, those being the most common high-ranking powers.

He refused to bet on a date or time. Nature would take its course in days or months. All they could do was wait and guess until she showed obvious abilities or got to the front of the non-emergency evaluation queue.

Camp schedules were built around daily Diagnostic checks. If Grace had been interned, she'd have started today with a walk past the resident specialist. The rest of her waking hours would have been spent on work assignments. Interns were responsible for cleaning, cooking, and maintenance duties as well as attending general classes in power control techniques.

Here, she'd risen early to cook pancakes and sausage. She'd insisted on feeding Yasu too.

The doctor wrapped up his report by saying, "So here I am, overloaded with carbs and more than ready to hit the sack. They're having a second family discussion at the table."

"Discussing or arguing?"

"Deciding what to call each other. It's been an interesting conversation. Good luck."

Yasu went yawning out the back door toward the outside basement entrance, leaving Jack to debate with himself over his next move. Should he interrupt the family to reach the living room or go around to the front and use his key?

He was *not* ringing the bell like a visitor. The sooner the family adjusted to the team being independent as well as underfoot, the better.

He couldn't stay here. The barstools were uncomfortably

small, and once the meal was done, he would be in the way of clean-up.

Gales of laughter arose for the other room. Jack advanced as far as the entryway. Thanks to a wall mirror, he could see everyone at the table, while only Grace was face-on to him. She was too busy watching her family to notice him, so he paused to do a little recon.

Everyone was dressed for the heat: the twins and their mother in sleeveless dresses that looked hand-sewn from the same floral cloth, Moretti in patched cargo shorts and a thin blue tee shirt that fit tight across the shoulders.

Since everyone else, including Grace, was calling him "Sal," they must have reached a consensus on first names. Sal sat stiff and attentive across from his ex-wife, with his back to Jack and his chair pushed into the aisle. The daughters were on either end of the table.

There was zero room to move past them. Jack stood listening, waiting for a pause in discussion before asking to squeeze by. Forks were being waved in favor of which surname everyone should take. For some reason they thought they all had to have the same one.

The girls had swapped out their colored teleport tokens. That had to be the oldest twin trick in the book. Maggie wore the yellow one now, Lauren the green, and their father was calling them by the wrong names. Grace wasn't correcting him, which probably meant something, but it was none of his business.

Reed won the surname contest three-to-one. On a follow-up motion, Grace vetoed a motion by Maggie to dub her Garden Queen Mom. Protests and more laughter ensued.

Everything looked peaceful and loving on the surface, but they smelled tense. Their voices were a little too cheerful, a little too sharp. The whole scene was full of brittleness and sour emotional notes that told Jack how hard they were all acting. They were trying to persuade themselves everything was fine.

Sensing there wouldn't be a break unless he made one, Jack cleared his throat and moved into the room as far as he could. The scent of syrup and seared meat intensified, making his mouth water. "How are you all today? We're at shift change. I figured I'd lurk in the front room if I can scoot through."

Conversation stopped. The tension was out in the open now, increasing by the second. Both girls gaped open-mouthed. Sal leaped up as if his seat was on fire, hastily moving it aside. His face was an ugly shade of greenish-pale.

And Jack's stomach growled. Loudly.

"I'm so sorry." Grace also rose. She clasped her hands in front of her breasts. "It's rude to be eating right in front of you. Let me fix you a plate."

Tempting as that was, it would lead to the complication of handling the plate and the silverware, and that way lay chaos. "Don't trouble yourself, ma'am," he said. "It smells great, but I ate breakfast before I came in. Maybe another time. I do love pancakes."

Grace sank back into her chair, scratching her left arm hard enough to leave red marks from her nails. "If you're sure."

"I'm sure." The itching might be nothing, but it might be something. She'd been scratching herself last night before everyone bunked down. If she kept at it, Jack would wake Yasu for a consult. *Later. One problem at a time.* He edged past Sal into the short hall on the other side.

"I love pancakes too," Maggie volunteered to his back. "I ate four today. How many can you eat at once, *Mis*ter Coby?"

She gave his name a mocking lilt. It got under his skin. He turned. "More than you would believe, Maggie."

"I'm Lauren," she said, smirking.

"No, you aren't."

"It's rude to contradict people," she said like correcting manners was a winning strategy.

This was going nowhere. "Then we're even. Lying is rude too."

"Mo-o-om!" Lauren flounced in her seat. "Is he allowed to be mean? He's being mean to us. And he's wrong!"

"Is he, though?" Sal asked with admirable restraint. "I didn't mind you taking a little revenge on your mean old father, but now you're just lying."

Maggie blushed bright red, and Lauren said fiercely, "You don't know that."

Grace looked between her daughters and sighed. "He does, and so do I. Don't multiply your sins, girls. Actions have consequences. You're fairly caught, although I'm not sure how."

Jack explained, "They're gonna want to think twice about playing that trick on people who can smell the difference."

Tears welled up in Maggie's eyes, and Lauren said, "We *smell?*"

"Not so a null could tell." It was past time for a strategic retreat. "Look, one of us has to hang close 24-7, but I'll try to stay out of sight. Ignore me. Pretend I'm part of the wall."

"You're as big as the wall," said Lauren, and it wasn't a compliment the way she said it.

Grace gave the girl a look. Lauren hastily bent over her meal again. So did Maggie and their father.

Jack settled gratefully onto a couch that creaked under his weight. He'd been assured its destruction wouldn't be a problem. Looking at the condition of its upholstery, he felt no guilt about abusing the springs.

The breakfast discussion turned to boundaries and household rules. The girls occasionally complained. Sal occasionally objected. Grace settled most of the disagreements with a quiet statement or two.

Jack had known the woman less than eighteen hours—and she'd spent over four of those hours asleep—but he'd already catalogued five distinct phrases that inspired instant obedience from her family. Like Valerie, she had elevated disapproval to an art form. Unlike Valerie, she was good at it.

Jack idly wondered if it was a talent that came with motherhood, and if so, where Heather fell on the scale. He hadn't seen her with her little girl Talia much, and when she was with her husband, Donyel, she let him do most of the speaking.

Shelly came in the front door. Her curly, graying hair was wilting from the heat, and she was sweating through her cotton camp shirt and hiking shorts.

"Problem, boss," she said under her breath.

Jack's nerves went on high alert. Shelly could have called from her post in the cool basement where the portable air conditioner lived with the surveillance log and the secure DPS radiophone base unit. This was either personal, urgent, or both.

He nodded to show he was listening.

Shelly came closer, pausing to glance at the family. No—Jack leaned sideways to get the angle—she was eyeballing Grace.

"Spill it," he said.

"You didn't get Val's news, did you?"

Shit. "I saw she sorted out the routine paperwork like usual." He'd only glanced at the message header, but he'd been impressed. She'd been fighting mad about being sent home, but she'd still gotten everything filed on schedule. She must've worked her ass off. "I was going to read through it on office time later. What's the problem?"

"Grace's eval." Shelly tipped her head toward the dining room. "Val got it expedited, and we're scheduled to receive a Diagnostics duo from DC at ten-oh-three local."

"We're *what?*" Shelly shushed him with a glare. He lowered

his voice. "That's just fucking fantastic. She couldn't have called with that news?"

If Diagnostics said *intern her,* that would be that. And he couldn't count on anyone in this family reacting rationally to that news.

10:03. It was nine now. He had less than an hour to think of a way to make this project sound reasonable to a couple of power-drunk bureaucrats who would hate it on principle. Less than an hour to think of a way to handle Grace without causing a domestic meltdown if the worse happened.

Playing it cool and professional ruled out screaming or breaking anything. It also ruled out asking for a teleport into Valerie's living room so he could shake her until her bones rattled. *What was she thinking?*

It wasn't a fair thought. But didn't a major change in the timeline deserve more than an electronic note? At least a more alarming header? There was non-confrontational, and then there was timid.

Hell, Shelly could've told him before now. Yasu could've said something.

"Why am I finding this out *now*?" he asked.

Shelly crossed her arms and stepped back to improve the angle on her glare. "Don't you take that tone with me, young man. When the original appointment was for noon, Yasu and I thought, why ruin anyone's breakfast? Then it got bumped again, so here I am, covering your big email-ignoring ass. What's your plan, *boss*? I already know the first step will be *all hands on deck*. Gabe's waking up Amy, and Yasu's making tea."

"Good, and good," Jack said. Crisis first, complain about the disrespect later. If there was a later. "Amy should be our face for this one."

Her military background and power rating would emphasize their commitment to cautious preparation, and she could flash her liaison status if necessary. "I'll tell Grace what's up. Keep your fingers crossed and your 'port tags hot. Bunker her if you have to."

There was no proof that stress caused rollover spikes, but Jack had run too many interventions in his Mercury Battalion days to bet against it. And rollover was nothing if not unpredictable. Grace had handled last night's tensions better than he'd expected, but this meeting might dump a whole new kind of stress on her.

She stood when he and Shelly approached, a jerky motion that reminded him of Heather again. Both women had bird mannerisms when startled. Grace was sturdy and drab like a sparrow, though. Maybe her faded clothes and dull, mousy hair were a kind of camouflage. That was an interesting possibility.

"Let me guess," she said. "Bad news."

"Not necessarily." Jack looked to Sal. The daughters did not need to hear this, but if Jack said so, they would argue with him. He didn't have time or patience to deal with them. Grace's power tickled against his skin, rippling over it in waves stronger than ever.

He willed Sal to understand without having it spelled out. *Come on, idiot, grasp the obvious.*

And Sal proved he did have a crumb of common sense. "Come on, girls. Let's take a walk around the block."

He shooed them toward the front door. The girls protested and whined, but they went. Shelly called after them, "Take your time!"

Grace tipped her head to one side and rubbed her wrists as if they ached. "You want to talk out back again? In case I go into a crisis bad enough to bring the house down?"

And here he'd thought he'd been subtle last night when he made that suggestion. "Out back would be best," he admitted.

Grace nodded silently and took the lead.

She really did have a lot more going on inside than she showed the world. Jack was glad to know it. Facing Diagnostics with composure was going to take a lot of guts. The results of this process was often disappointing, occasionally terrifying, and always nerve-wracking.

And this confrontation would be worse than most.

Jack crossed his fingers. Hoping for the best was Elena's thing, but he could try it.

21: THEIR WORK IS GRIEF AND PAIN

414 Elm Drive, Elgin, IL

GRACE SLIPPED OFF her sandals and dug her bare feet into the dirt at the edge of the patio. The sun was hot already, a burning weight against her head and shoulders. She could have waited in the shade with Jack at the picnic table, but she couldn't sit still, not when her evaluators would be arriving any moment now.

The touch of living soil on her skin had always been a solace in times of struggle. The gritty warmth of it pressed between her toes, dry and soft, giving her something real to distract her from her rioting emotions and her itching hands.

She was glad for the warning Jack had given her. She was grateful for his care in answering her questions after he'd delivered his bad news. She was thankful Sal was keeping the girls clear. But mostly, she felt angry and resentful and lost.

To be granted hope for only a few hours seemed a cruel joke for God to pull. For a while after last night's revelations, she'd thought she could face anything. Instead, each new worry assaulted her frail new faith like the ocean swallowing up a beach one crashing breaker at a time.

And yet—every wave receded. She closed her eyes, anchored herself to the stillness deep inside, and let the fearful tide flow around her.

This was like being fourteen again, awaiting the church council's ruling on her scholarship appeal. They had looked at her and seen only someone—some*thing*—to be feared and controlled. Once again her fate rested in the hands of people who would see her shackled to their own purposes.

The elders had allowed her off the Ranch for trade school, but they'd driven a hard bargain. That experience had been a harsh lesson about the limits of power without authority.

Now, she inhaled the warm, rich summer air and let it out, opened her eyes to green leaves and colorful flowers. The garden was busy with humming insects. Sparrows chirped in the branches of her apple tree. Life surrounded and comforted her.

This was not the same. These evaluators didn't fear her. They feared real dangers. They were weighing her desires against the safety of others, not safeguarding their profits and personal power. She was no longer fourteen, ignorant and passionate, being manipulated by hypocritical liars.

The chigger bites on her left ankle grew too intense to ignore. She rubbed them with her right foot. Her life was hers to spend, and she would not regret exchanging it for her daughters' freedom.

"What are the odds of them ruling against me?" she asked.

"It isn't a trial, ma'am," Jack said from his perch on the picnic table. "You are what you are. I'd rather the Elgin circuit regulars made the call, but the ruling comes down to your series. I didn't want you getting blindsided, but it'll be fine unless we get a couple of conservative pri—ah, jerks. Might be fine. Maybe."

"You are not good at being reassuring." Grace turned and caught a very particular look of concern on his outsized features. It tickled her sense of the absurd. "Don't worry, I won't start crying."

He hid his relief behind a frown. "You're calmer than I expected after yesterday," he admitted, adding hastily, "I'm not complaining."

"I'm not calm. I've reached the point where I'm shaking so hard from nerves that it looks like I'm calm. But I would be panicking if you hadn't warned me, so thank you."

"No problem. I don't like surprises either." He hunched forward, massive shoulder muscles flexing under his yellow nylon tank top. "So don't surprise me with any harebrained escape attempts or any religious bull—objections, okay?"

"Okay."

No more running for her. No more hiding or fighting. If she was growing in power, then only horrors could grow from rage and despair. In her mind's eye, she saw lava flowing in bright, red searing rivers, heard the wailing of children with sooty, tear-streaked faces.

She had taken the name of a lost soul as a warning and a reminder.

If she was ordered to leave her haven, she would go. She would do all she could to keep her smoldering faith alive in the wilderness, feeding it with the breath of her memories and the fuel of her heart.

You will die, came that still, small whisper from inside. *You need to be here, in the close embrace of family and allies, or you will fail.*

She faced that possibility and found herself strangely unmoved. All good lives ended with plans unfinished. God was not always kind. Life was rarely fair. Those were truths she had accepted long and long ago.

"I can do this as long as you don't leave me to face them alone," she said.

"Deal." Jack tilted his head in a listening pose, then slid off the table and ducked under the edge of the awning to stand up straight in the sunlight. "They're here."

Amy arrived first, walking half-crouched beneath the green arching viburnums in the side yard, stopping at the corner of the house. Her short khaki skirt and tank top were designed to hold her rank insignia and pistol holster while leaving her dorsal spines exposed, and she looked grand and colorful against the shrubs.

She rubbed at one of her down-curved horns, then shook her head in response to a hand signal from Jack. Shelly came into the yard next, looking like a frazzled, gray-haired camp counselor in her shorts and shirt. She took a position opposite Amy and stood with arms folded, radiating disapproval.

Two DPS officials in suits and dress shoes strode briskly into the yard between them, looked around, then picked their way across the lawn to the patio. They loosened their ties and scowled at everything as they came.

Here, at last, were the hard-faced bureaucratic drones Grace had pictured in her nightmares. This stiff-shouldered, unhappy pair, rumpled and tense in gray blazers, crisp white shirts, lined frowning faces, looked *exactly* like the kind of merciless authorities she had feared the DPS would send to drag her away.

She had been wrong about so many other things. Maybe she would be wrong again.

One of them carried a black briefcase, the other a metal clipboard. Round pink disks decorated their left hands. Grace touched the matching blue tag above her collarbone.

Both men looked everywhere in the yard except at Grace.

She smiled while quivering panic built up under her ribs. "Hello, I'm—"

The one with the briefcase raised his free hand, palm out. "Do not speak. We've been delayed enough." He glared in Amy's general direction.

Clipboard pulled out a pen to make a note. "Three twenty-eight UTC. Begin."

They proceeded to peer at her as intently as a pair of cats at a mouse hole. Clipboard had chicory-flower blue eyes. Briefcase's were the shade of dead oak leaves on a cloudy midwinter day. Neither man blinked. Grace half-expected their noses to twitch.

She counted off by tens to keep from hyperventilating. The itching in her hands and feet grew to a maddening prickle. She rubbed her hands up and down her arms and fidgeted her feet, but she refused to look away. These men would pass judgment on her. She would never show them weakness.

Neither man had shaved in a while, and their eyes were bloodshot as well as hostile. Maybe their unpleasantness came from being tired, hungry, and uncomfortable. Maybe she should offer them pancakes and orange juice.

Uncertainty crept into Clipboard's tense expression. Briefcase's tight frown smoothed to a blank stare. They glanced at each other. Briefcase's shoulders raised and dropped in an expansive shrug, and he said, "Not an E prime."

"No," said Clipboard. "That's a relief. Prime, though." He looked at his notes, then returned to watching Grace. "Not B. Not N or H. Not D. Are you thinking what I'm thinking? Is she another G?"

"Like up in Camp Gruening last spring?" His partner set down the briefcase, scrubbed his hands over his face, and resumed staring. "I think so. Looks right, but what are the odds of catching two G's in a year?"

Grace had helped her daughters with their health class homework enough times to be up to date on the major designations. She would not have empathic powers like her ex-husband's. They had also dismissed any chance of sensory talents, water, animal or plant-based affinities, or medically-related powers. But what was G? She couldn't place it.

And why weren't her judges certain?

Amy came up behind them, silent despite her size. Both men flinched when she said, "What's the holdup, boys? You B1-R's can log assessments in five seconds. Spill the beans. I have ten bucks riding on an R main series designator, rank three or higher. Do I win?"

"Not R." They spoke as one and shook their heads in unison. Silence fell. Amy tapped her claws together with aggressive impatience.

Clipboard said, "It's your call, Fitch. You're lead on this."

"Fine." Briefcase looked Grace from top to toes once more, this time with a glimmer of pity in his eyes. "I'm calling it G1-C. Tanner, do you concur?"

"I concur," Clipboard said.

Grace's heart raced. She remembered the C. In the variant position, it meant her body would transform physically and dramatically, regardless of her primary talent. Would that tip the scales toward internment? *Unfair,* her heart screamed, but she stood firm. God gave with one hand and took with the other.

Amy said. "As site liaison, I confirm diagnosis received. G1C it is." Her tone of voice gave Grace no hint of what that mysterious G meant. "That means we're within regs to handle her—unless you insist on hauling her off. What's it gonna be, boys?"

Briefcase—Fitch—craned his neck to look up at Amy. "You're setting a horrible precedent here. This type of operation isn't scalable. The costs would be prohibitive."

"I didn't ask your opinion." Amy leaned down to bare her

teeth at him. "I asked, 'Are you taking personal responsibility for interning her?'"

He quailed. "No. It isn't worth the paperwork. Between you, the other personnel, and the certified containment unit, she's as safe here as anywhere in the country."

"Safer than Garfield," Tanner said quietly.

Fitch glanced at him, eyes narrowed, then backed away from Amy. "She'll peak within a week or two at the rate she's developing. Do what's necessary and keep the local office informed. We're done here, Tanner. Log it."

Tanner made another note. "Intake Evaluation complete, three-thirty-three UTC. We're five minutes behind schedule. Rebound to origin at local transport's discretion."

Shelly snorted. "My discretion? My pleasure. Grab your garters, guys."

The DPS evaluators disappeared. Cold air flowed around Grace, raising goose bumps all over. The chill aggravated her itching skin.

She rubbed her arms. Her palms scraped over raised bumps. *What now? Hives?*

No. The back of her arms rippled from fingertips to elbows, lifting into hard ridges like an alligator's hide. As she watched in fascination, the same change flowed up her legs before ebbing above her knees. Her stomach roiled, and a wave of vertigo hit.

When her sight cleared, Jack had crossed the yard to speak with Amy in a voice too low to overhear, and Shelly was nowhere in sight.

"Um," Grace said, to get their attention. "You know how you keep asking me how I feel?"

They both looked back, and Grace wanted to cry at the alarm in their expressions. They were afraid *for* her, not *of* her.

She could tell the difference, although she couldn't have said how.

"I feel strange." She held out her arms. The skin was turning darker now, and another ripple of change twisted her bones along with the flesh. A prickling pressure like electricity balled itself up under her breastbone, pushing outward as it grew until she could no longer breathe.

"Now might be a good time to move into the bunker," Jack said.

The sensation in Grace's chest crackled outward, up and down, and she fell with it, staring at a hazy sky while her body twitched and trembled in wild abandon.

Her muscles knotted around bones that bent and shook and *shifted.* Her mind floated loose above the broken creature thrashing against torn sod, so loosely connected to it that she did not know herself or the others who stood by.

Words were spoken, as meaningless as wind blowing. Shapes made nonsense noises, pulsed and glittered, and the earth glowed, alive with a light so intense it had weight and made a roar like floodwaters.

The heavy brightness pulled her down into her body again and pulled her deeper, into an immensity of silence and darkness.

22: STRENGTH IS NEEDED, BUT SKILL WILL BRING SUCCESS

August 20, 2019, DPS CA Region 20 Offices, Riverside CA

"ANY CHANGE IN GRACE'S CONDITION?" Valerie kept her voice flat as she asked the most important question on the morning briefing sheet first.

"Nope," Gabe said.

Feedback crackled loud in Valerie's ear as Gabe's beard rubbed over his microphone. She adjusted the volume on her headphones, feeling selfishly glad Gabe didn't like doing video calls with anyone but his grandchildren.

Honoring his preference meant she could hide her expressions. She swallowed a lump of guilt and grief and requested more information. "Sorry, none of these questions are yes or no. They sound that way, but they aren't."

He sighed. "Grace has been immobile and unresponsive since Yasu hooked her up to the monitors in the bunker day before yesterday. Except for her vitals and the energy fluctuations, she might as well be a—a—a rock."

Valerie sympathized with his difficulty finding a good

description. Grace's slide into full rollover had been extreme even by the dramatic standards of C-variant transformations. Yasu had used the word *unsustainable* in his initial medical assessment, two days past.

Over the course of a few minutes, Grace's skin had shifted and hardened until she was fully encased in a stiff, chitinous shell.

The smooth, rounded carapace held only faint outlines of limbs and the barest shapes of eyelids, lips, and fingernails. A scalpel designed for use on armored patients didn't score its surface. She breathed through nostril openings, and her heart beat once or twice a minute, but she was effectively entombed within her own flesh.

Unconsciousness was a small mercy. Better for her to sleep through a slow death by dehydration than suffer through it fully aware but unable to move.

Valerie shoved aside that thought and concentrated on the view through her open office door, watching the staff in the outer office go about their daily tasks. The fluctuating truths of the collective soothed her eyes. Nothing relieved the inner gloom.

Calm, she told herself. *Be calm.* Where there was life, there was hope.

"No news isn't bad news," she said to keep the conversation going. "This might be normal for a G1-C. The combination isn't on the mortality table."

Grace was rolling into one of the rarest power designations in the DPS master index. Gaias didn't rate a box on census checklists. The G series was routinely lumped together with Z and J. The series rollover table showed fatal outcomes for ratings from seven up to one.

But the sample size was too small to be valid.

Valerie aimed her thin hopes at the next question. "Any sign of her power peaking or leveling out?"

C-variant physical changes could occur at any point, but they were most common at the midpoint and the end of a rollover. The few Gaia events on record had been faster than average, which meant Grace might shift again and literally come out of her shell.

"She's not even close," Gabe replied. "Sorry, I've been hoping for that too. She's still in surge mode. We're on three-hour shifts to avoid overloading from the energy spillage."

"That's a lot of ambient power." She moved her cursor along to the follow-up questions, grateful for practical details to concentrate on. "Have there been any environmental effects? Do I need to file for variance permits?"

Gabe said patiently, "No, and no. She's deep enough the ground's soaking it up. I promise we'll call if anything changes before the next scheduled call at nine tonight. Do we have to go through the entire list every time?"

Valerie could hear the humor-the-nagging-lady tone in his voice loud and clear. "Yes, night and morning. I can change the order, but I need open-ended answers for all of them. Voice check-ins are on the audits. Jack usually does them."

"Yeah. About that." Gabe sucked air between his teeth. "I'm going to regret asking this, but—do you know why he dumped the chore on me?"

"I'm not sure." She had her suspicions. Jack hadn't spoken to her since sending her back to Riverside the night Grace signed her contract. "It isn't like him, is it?"

His latest leadership summary had read, in full, "No significant events."

That was wildly out of character. He always said he'd rather save everyone else from *bureaucratic bullshit* like these calls. Valerie said, "I think he's mad at me."

"You? What for?" Gabe's surprise sounded genuine.

"Everything? This is all my fault."

Jack had a right to be furious. She should've consulted him about expediting the evaluation. She should've called instead of sending an email. She should've known he wouldn't read the email in time. Maybe she should've picked the slower evaluation. Maybe the family reconciliation had been the mistake. If she'd done something different, Grace wouldn't be dying.

Gabe's sigh oozed with exasperation. "I didn't sign up for management, and I am not good at pep talks."

"Excuse me?"

"Look, Val, you did nothing wrong. This is a crappy situation, but it's no one's fault. It sounds like Jack's taking out his mopes on you. I'll talk to him, but first, I want you to stop kicking yourself."

"But I should have—"

"But *nothing*." Gabe's voice rose. "The when and how she's rolling—the parts *maybe* affected by stress—that's frosting on a shit cake. Didn't you read that information packet you sent? Gaia primes do not survive. All we can do is push the cake around our plate until the party's over."

"We don't know that." Valerie clung to her last little shred of hope. "Of the four G-Cs on record, three were rank nine. No one knows for sure."

Most power summaries in the DPS master index were over a page long and linked to multiple pages of variant listings, case call-ups, demographic studies, and related journal articles. The single paragraph description for Gaias had connected to a bare handful of individual case numbers from the Department's comprehensive database.

She had placed requests with the archives, just in case older cases were overlooked when the Department went digital. There might be some critical piece of information missing, a clue that could help.

Or they might be looking in the wrong files. "And Diagnostics might be wrong. Jack's report said they argued. Gaias are rare. Maybe she's a C prime shifter, and this is something temporary."

"No, Val. B-ones always bicker, but they're never wrong." Gabe cleared his throat, and his voice gentled. "Look. Just say 'I'll stop blaming myself' and pick another question, and I'll give you a nice, detailed answer."

Valerie wondered if he wheedled his grandchildren into doing their chores by striking little bargains like that. It was effective.

Saying something didn't mean she had to believe it, and the sooner she finished this call, the sooner she could put the sadness and stress aside for a time. She was taking a half-day for a school conference where she would meet the boys' new teachers.

Time away from the office and away from this case wouldn't keep her from worrying, but playing with Johnny and Gary all afternoon would distract her and refill her hope reserves. And if they exhausted her, maybe she would sleep tonight. Maybe.

She dutifully repeated, "I will stop blaming myself. Next items. Any concerns about the team or objections from team members to report?"

"No," he said.

"Gabe, please." Valerie bit her lip. "You promised."

"Kidding!" The phone picked up ambient noises. Was he laughing at her? "Team report. Shelly is being a total diva, but that's her usual M.O. Heather feels guilty she can't 'port anyone else until she's re-assessed, but she's dealing. Yasu is an arrogant SOB, but he and Amy both have a way with the kids. And Jack is getting better about delegating."

"No one's getting cold feet?"

"Not unless I turn their shoes into ice blocks." He continued before Valerie could do more than groan. "We're committed to seeing this through to the end and the aftermath. There is a silver lining to this, you know? Tragic story, humble, photogenic family—this will be good PR for the program in the long run."

"Gabe!"

"I told you I was bad at pep talks. I'm better at chewing people out. Leave Jack to me."

When was the last time someone had teased her like this? She couldn't recall. "Please don't say anything to him."

"I won't bring you into it. Death watches mess with people, even Mercury vets. I'll talk with Amy, and we'll help him get his head back on straight. That's how teams work."

"When it's a good team." Valerie bit her lip. "I'm glad you're my liaison right now, Gabe. Thank you."

"Liaison, is it?" He chuckled. "Now I feel fancy."

"You are fancy. Next, any issues with the family?"

"Moretti is so freaking wholesome you want to squish him like a loaf of fresh bread. I would swear he was messing with my head, but I don't sense it, and Yasu swears it isn't mind games either."

"It isn't. He is a human teddy bear."

"Good description. It's also an issue. No, that isn't fair. The issues are named Maggie and Lauren. They are freaky-submissive to his face, but they're fourteen, which means they're adorable one second and raging hormone monsters the next. This situation is hard on them too, I'm sure, but if you ask me, they're thieving, sneaky liars by nature."

That was the assessment of a detective with twenty-plus years of police work behind him, not the attitude of a doting grandfather. Valerie wondered how the teens had gotten on Gabe's bad side. "What have they done?"

"So far? Stayed up all night on their phones, whined their

way out of helping with dinner, ate candy for breakfast, and weaseled out of chores. Sal is way out of his league. It's a train wreck waiting to happen. Shelly and I both want to ground the brats for a year, but we're steering clear because we don't want to set a precedent. You want to change that?"

"No, you're right to stay out of it."

They couldn't let rollover monitoring cross the line into anything that could be deemed social assistance. The Family Services division would file objections first. A long line of other agencies would queue up behind them. Bureaucracies were territorial, and Camp Liberty might need broader support from those agencies in the future.

There was an easy solution to this problem. Valerie said, "Elena will lend a hand if you ask her. She's our recruiter, not a transition assistant, she's local, and the girls know her."

"It'll keep her out from underfoot, too," Gabe said, sounding pleased. "And if Jack puts Heather on backup babysitter duty, everyone will be happy. Excellent plan."

"I'll give her a call. How is Sal holding up, other than getting walked on by teenagers?"

"He's tragic, stoic, and way too pretty. And busy. He's throwing himself into the house renovation to keep his mind off things. Would it be a violation if I lend him a hand in my off-hours?"

"Your time is your own when you're off duty or only on call. Why so eager?"

"I want him to teach me some tricks before I tackle my own plumbing. And if I help, we'll have central AC in a couple of days."

Valerie smiled at the phone. "And you call his children devious?"

"They are," Gabe said. "I'm telling you, Val, family friction will be your biggest problem recruiting for these home-based rollover teams. My kids flew the nest ten years ago, and I can't say I'm enjoying the refresher course in teen angst."

At least you still think Camp Liberty has a future. Valerie hoped she would get the chance to have problems recruiting more teams. If they lost Grace, they might have a hard time attracting new clients for a long time. Superstition was a powerful force.

"Let's get through this case before you start borrowing trouble for the next one," she said. The information Gabe had volunteered was enough to fill in her last few boxes. "And that's it for the morning list."

"Hooray for us," Gabe said. "Speaking of trouble, there is a small thing bugging me. I suppose it falls under the 'not our problem' heading, but I can't let it go. It's a cop thing."

"Wait a second." Valerie went to close her office door and pressed at a sudden tight ache under her ribs as she sat down again. She could not handle any more stress. Just couldn't. "Should I switch phones so we can stay off the record? Nothing said over this line is private."

"It isn't sensitive. Well, it is, but it's only—her name is familiar, Val." The phone crackled again, and Valerie pictured Gabe tugging his beard. "Her old one. Sarah Moretti. I did background checks and got zip, but something's off."

"Her reassignment file is private, Gabe. Don't you dare get us caught up in a lawsuit. You signed nondisclosure agreements, including Sal."

"Relax, I know what I'm doing. I'm a professional." He hummed under his breath. "Sal doesn't fit. His clothes and habits shout dirt-poor, but his daughters have top-shelf electronics, and this *house*—reassignment stipends don't cover bus fare, much less real estate."

"Oh, that." The knot in Valerie's chest eased. "The money's from an inheritance. She asked for ID reassignment because she thought Sal was pressuring her into giving it up. I got the impression he wasn't the only one, but she didn't go into details."

"Old money in dispute, California, religious cult…agh. It's buried. Getting old sucks. What do we do if the ex re-connects with someone from their old life?"

"He won't." Valerie couldn't be more certain about that. "They're making a fresh start." *Assuming Grace survives to enjoy it.* She couldn't say that out loud, but the thought was never far from her mind.

Gabe said, "I won't stir any pots." He let silence stretch uncomfortably before asking, "But the confidentiality dies with her, right? Family Safety files revert to public record after death. The Homicide and Fraud units broke cases that way all the time."

"Homicide? Fraud?" Now he was making her nervous. "Gabe, what is going on?"

"I don't know. That's the problem. I can't help wondering, so I want to keep digging."

He was going to do what he wanted regardless of what she said. "It's your time to waste, but please don't go around interrogating people."

"Please! I'm the soul of discretion."

He probably wanted to help with the renovations so he could grill Sal about his background. And Sal loved being helpful. A headache gnawed at Valerie's temples. She ended the call and shut down her workstation. There was nothing to be done about the complication now, and it was past time to head to the school.

She made one more call on the way to her car. Elena answered on the first ring. "Hi, Val. What's up?"

Valerie navigated the stairs down to the first floor of the Public Safety wing of the building and walked into the warm, dry afternoon. "You always say you would do anything to help Camp Liberty succeed."

"I do, and I'm absolutely serious. Let me guess. You need a babysitter. Teen sitter. Supervisor. Whatever."

Valerie stopped in the shade of the facility's parking garage so she wouldn't lose the signal inside the concrete structure. "How did you know?"

"I talk to Heather every day. I won't say I know what Lauren or Maggie are going through, but I'm sure they could use a friendly shoulder right now. I have ideas for activities."

"Perfect. Thank you."

"Wait, don't hang up yet!" Elena said in a rush, then paused for a deep breath. "This isn't your fault. I keep having to tell myself that, so I wanted to say it to you in case you need to hear it too. And if you need a hug, Shelly offered to 'port me there and back for free. Or you here and back. That costs like, a zillion dollars, normally, so we should take her up on it. "

A rush of gratitude brought tears to Valerie's eyes. "The verbal hug is good for now, sweetie. Let's save the teleport idea for an emergency. Knowing she offered means a lot. And knowing you care means even more."

She wiped her eyes dry as she hurried toward her car. "I have to go. Don't forget to call Jack before you head over to the Reed's place."

"I'll get Lauren's number from Heather first. Jack can't say no if the site's cleared for the family, and I have an invitation. It'll be more fun to make it a surprise."

The thought of Jack's reaction to Elena's arrival kept Valerie smiling through afternoon traffic across town to the school.

Sometimes situations worked out for the best. Maybe Grace's situation would be one of them.

23: IT COMES WITHOUT MEANING, IT DEPARTS IN DARKNESS

August 22, Saint Francis of the Fields, Elgin, IL

ELENA TOUCHED her lit taper to one of the unlit candles below the gilded painting of Mary and baby Jesus, then extinguished the taper's flame with a puff of breath. Smoke curled up toward heaven, rippling in the still, cool air of the church nave. She let her prayer rise with the smoke before dropping the taper into the receptacle with its fellows.

Last, she turned to her companions. "Any questions?"

A buzz answered her. Heather's crest flattened in embarrassment, and she put a hand to her hip bag. "Sorry," she murmured. "Phone." She pointed at the door to the church before striding off to take the call outside. That left Elena with Maggie and Lauren.

The Reed twins looked ridiculously pretty like always, their pale eyes wide and solemn, their dark curly hair pulled sensibly back in ponytails against the humid heat of the day outside. They looked as unruffled by worldly troubles as any of the saints in the stained-glass windows high on the walls as they shook their heads.

No one looking at them would guess that their mother lay unconscious and dying in a bomb shelter under their backyard. Elena had to admire their poise. They'd been waiting patiently for four days since Grace's collapse. Last night, Lauren had asked what Elena's church was like, so this morning here they were, in time to look around before the first daily prayer service.

Elena considered it her good deed for the week. The twins were always whispering that Heather and Jack gave them the creeps. And their mother would be a C-variant. Elena was committed to giving them more exposure to people who didn't look like them.

Each night when she prayed for Grace's survival, she also gave thanks that the woman's daughters hadn't seen her yet. Elena had. She'd sneaked a good. long peek at one of the bunker monitors before Jack caught her.

The hard, black lump nestled on the cushioned sleeping platform had made her think of beetles and chrysalises—and also of coffins. And if it bothered *her*, she couldn't imagine how Maggie and Lauren would react.

She hoped they could learn tolerance. She hoped even harder that they would need to learn it for Grace's sake.

Lauren nudged her sister, who asked in hushed tones, "All those lit candles are prayers?"

"Every one." Elena regarded the dozen-odd flickering votive candles on the stand before raising her eyes to the stained-glass window above. "People pray for lots of reasons."

"Now what?" Lauren's chin came up. "I mean usually. What comes next?"

"I'm usually here on my way to somewhere else, so I light and leave. Some people kneel to watch the flames and pray. Others walk the stations of the cross, recite rosary prayers, or sit in the pews and think. There's no one right way to be here as long as you're respectful and quiet and don't go into the altar area without permission. Do you want to stay for the morning prayer service?"

"Not this time. This is so different." Lauren peered around the nave at the regulars gathering for the service. The congregation ran heavily to feathers, fur, scales, and tails. This was a newer building designed to accommodate their needs. "It isn't like our old church."

From what Elena had learned about the sect Maggie had been raised in, that was a compliment. She said, "It isn't like all Catholic churches either. There was a big split back in sixty-three when the Pope rolled. I think we're up to four daughter churches now."

"Why do religions always fight?" Maggie asked no one in particular.

"Maybe we can talk about that later? Somewhere not *in* the church," Elena said. "Do you want to light candles for your mom?"

Maggie wrinkled her nose, but Lauren nodded. "Yes, please." She picked up a match and hesitated. "Do you have to be here?"

"No. I'll wait with Heather by the door."

She was halfway there when she heard footsteps hurrying toward her. Maggie gave her a pained smile. "It isn't my thing. No offense."

"None taken. Catholicism isn't for most people."

"I meant religion. It's nothing but bogus lies." Maggie's chin rose defiantly, but she blushed too. "Sorry. I pretend for Lauren and Mom, but I will scream if I have to keep pretending to everyone. Please don't tell on me."

"Of course not." Elena had no idea why people blurted out secrets to her, but they did. Valerie said it was a gift, but if so, it was an uncomfortable one. She never knew what to say. "If you ever need to vent, Amy feels the same way you do."

Maggie might not be up for the challenge of talking religion with a twelve-foot-tall armored atheist, but it was the best Elena had to offer. Maggie crossed her arms, looking suspicious.

Heather approached down the aisle, wings slightly spread and crest up. "Something wrong, girls?"

"No," Elena said in chorus with Maggie.

Heather's eyes narrowed, and she said, "Uh-*huh*," in that annoying voice older people used when they thought you were lying. "Never mind."

She caught Lauren's attention with a beckoning gesture, saying, "You girls are wanted back home. Come outside, and Shelly will 'port you there."

"Is it Mom?" Lauren asked as she hurried over.

"No, it's a staffing issue." Heather's wings flexed. So did her fingers. Both were signs of inner agitation made physical. "Nothing to worry about. Shells will explain."

Elena knew evasion when she heard it, but she also knew when pushing wouldn't help. Heather would tell her what the crisis was as soon as she could

Heather shooed them outdoors with arms and wings. Maggie and Lauren kept moving fast to avoid any contact. That didn't bode well for Grace if she emerged from her shell looking inhuman—although maybe it.

Elena waited on the church steps until Shelly whisked the girls home in a double pop of cold floral-scented air—Maggie and Lauren both loved that exciting little exercise of power—before she pounced on Heather. "Staffing issue? We drove here. I could've driven them home. What's really going on?"

"Hush, child. Let's go to your car."

A wing curved around her shoulders and shaded her across

the hot, sunny asphalt parking lot to the cheap old car she'd gotten as a graduation present. The interior was like an oven, and it had no air conditioning. She opened the doors and waited for the temperature to drop to bearable levels. "What happened?"

Heather stretched her wings and fanned them, adding a breeze to the cooling effort. "Tornado swarm downstate. Morning tornados are bad. It's a mess. Gateway Company's been activated for disaster relief—the *whole* company, including detached duty personnel. Shells 'ported Amy to the forward base, and Jack figures you'll be called in soon too. The DPS and the Red Cross are bussing in crews like last year with the floods."

Elena powered on her phone to see if either organization had sent her an alert. Sure enough, she had a long queue of missed calls from her Red Cross youth group and the Elgin DPS office. That was what she got for shutting off her ringer in church. "Yikes."

"Got a few messages, huh? Jack said the office called him asking after their pretty PR poster child. They do love putting you where news crews can get pictures of you in a safety vest, don't they?"

"Yeah. I don't mind, I guess, but I hope I can go down with my RC club this time."

"And ride in a crammed bus for hours instead of catching a free 'port?"

Put that way, it did sound silly, but—"It would be nice to help people without cameras following me around like I'm a circus act."

If the DPS really wanted her, they would track her down. She'd signed a media release, not a contract. They didn't own her.

She called her Red Cross youth group leader to confirm

they were participating in the clean-up and arranged to meet them at the mustering point. Heather waited, watchful and wilting in the August heat.

Elena slid gingerly into the hot driver's seat once she finished the call. "My club's going someplace called Carlinsville," she told Heather. "Maybe I'll see you there? Where is the office sending you?"

"I'm going nowhere." Heather's voice was calm, but the feathers on her head and neck puffed out, betraying the strength of her annoyance.

"What? But they'll need 'porters." The need to move people and goods swiftly was always critical in emergencies like this.

"Not me." Heather flipped her wings back and shook herself into order. "My supervisor says the mandatory leave makes me ineligible. Probation is the pits. I could be helping. I could be pulling overtime, but no. I'm stuck in limbo. I've gotten bumped a dozen times for new low-level rollovers."

Guilt prodded at Elena. Heather's situation wasn't her fault exactly, but she still felt responsible. "I wish there was a way around it."

"Me, too."

An idea sparked from Elena's memories of all the legislation she'd studied while helping Valerie prep the Camp Liberty regulatory filings. "Maybe there is a way. If they called in Marines, that means it's a federal emergency declaration. And *that* triggers a bunch of immunities and provisions."

"You and your book talk. Can you translate that into regular-people words?"

"I think your boss is wrong. National stuff overrides local safety regs, which makes sense. Every pair of powered hands helps, and if a 'port of wreckage goes wrong, who cares?"

"The person it lands on?" Heather flicked her fingers, talons gleaming. "But my aim is fine. I'm stable within my new range. I know I am. I can *feel* it. That's why this is so frustrating."

"Where's the site? Can you get there on your own?"

"Easily. It's down by Alton, and I'm cleared for self-ports."

"Then go. Show up. Volunteer as a private citizen." Elena's excitement grew. "I bet you'd get put to work, no questions asked. The military has guidelines for field certifications. It's called brevet something or other. If you prove you're stable to someone who can sign the right papers, I bet you can get cleared. No more waiting for an appointment. Call Val, have her check with Legal first, then call Amy so you can find her? Please say you'll try."

"I will, I will!" Heather danced in place. "As soon as you go. If it works, I'll see you there."

24: WHEN CALAMITY OVERTAKES THE LAND

August 22, From Elgin to Carlinsville, IL & Beyond

ELENA DID NOT GET to travel to Carlinsville with her Red Cross group. The agent in charge of Elgin's DPS office collected her from the mustering area. Priority authorizations were presented, Elena was hugged and waved on her way, and that was that.

Agent-in-Chief Genevieve Falwell escorted her to the teleport station that was transporting Chicago-area news crews and high-demand rollover volunteers to the disaster area. Their arrival raised the usual stir of journalist recognition. Elena smiled for them, and Agent-in-Chief Falwell told her more about the situation while they awaited their turn for transit.

Seventeen tornadoes. Five counties. One town literally wiped off the face of the earth. The rush was on to get shelters up, power restored, and preventative measures in place before more rain came through and complicated the situation with flooding.

And those rains *would* fall. Meteorologists and precognitives predicted more storms in the next day or two. Preventing a local disaster was not worth disrupting the world's larger weather systems. That lesson had been learned the hard way during the winter of 1951.

Joint Operations was set up in Centralia. Relief workers were already mustering in Carlinsville, near the center of the damage zone, and journalists were eager to get involved.

Reporter-wrangling was where Elena came in. Journalists flocked to her like ants at a picnic, drawn by an unshakable belief that she was a headline generator. Working with them helped the DPS in two important ways. First, human interest coverage helped poz citizens. Second, every reporter following her was one not pestering a rescuer, intruding on a family's grief, or needing rescue after blundering into danger.

Sometimes she thought she might as well wear a reflective vest with *Juicy Distraction* printed on it.

The military team wasted no time on courtesies. One second, Elena was sweating on hot, sticky asphalt in a retail parking lot, squished up between Agent-in-Chief Falwell and a crowd of others in the marked go-zone. The next moment, without warning, the whole group was standing on hot, wet asphalt somewhere else.

Elena pulled up her raincoat hood against a steady drizzle and swallowed queasiness. Not all teleports were created equal. She would take a thousand of Heather's weird flights into nothingness over this shuddery sensation of coming apart and being put back together.

Exclamations and unhappy muttering came from the perimeter of the group. Another shiver ran though her. Jack was always calling her fearless and foolhardy, but it wasn't true. She was afraid of lots of things, horribly so.

Fear wasn't *helpful*, though, and someone had to help.

"Quiet down and spread out for a confirmation count!"

someone shouted. Everyone did their best to give each other space.

Agent Falwell murmured, "Oh, my," at Elena's shoulder as the crowd thinned enough to see their surroundings.

The low, gray clouds made a dramatic backdrop for a classic courthouse with a gap in its rotunda and a church missing half its steeple. Debris and downed trees clogged the nearby roadway, and smashed storefronts lined the street. Threads of black smoke rose across the horizon, and sirens warbled nearby.

The damp air was strangely still, untouched by any hint of a breeze, and the dark, empty buildings gave the scene a haunted air. Elena swallowed heartache. How many people had died, how many had lost everything or everyone they knew?

Her eyes stung—but no one here needed her tears. They needed caring hearts to lift spirits and strong backs to assist with the rebuilding.

"If I can, I should," she whispered to herself. "If not me, then who?"

Agent Falwell patted her cheek. "That's my girl. Keep busy, be interesting, and remember to smile. You're a love for helping out."

Elena endured the cheek-patting because Agent Falwell had four grandchildren. There was no stopping a grandma in doting mode. Her abuela was living proof of that. Besides, the closest camera crew was eating it up.

She pushed down the unhelpful frustration and put on a smile. "I know the drill."

They were efficiently herded down the block to a once-picturesque town square now cluttered with storm debris, supply pallets, and metal shipping containers. A huddle of canvas work tents occupied the grassy park in the center. A harried woman in a firefighter's uniform emerged from one tent with a clipboard. "Quiet down so I can get you sorted," she said. "Talent first."

She easily made herself heard without a bullhorn—and without shouting. Her voice carried, soft but with a physical force that vibrated Elena's bones. The woman had to be a rollover with sonic talent. That must be useful for communicating over the roar of a fire. It certainly helped establish her authority as the director of the marshalling area.

Teleporters were sent one way, telekinetics another Heavy lifters went here, pyros and water callers, there. Soon, all the powered volunteers were headed where they could do the most good. Agent Falwell trotted off to a supervisory job with a wave and a thumbs-up to Elena. The news crews recorded short takes and took background shots of aerial talents who zipped back and forth overhead carrying nets full of rubble and heavy equipment.

When Elena's name was called, a security ID was wrapped around her wrist, and the marshalling director treated her to a tight-lipped scowl. "Celebrity is a talent now? You here to show off what a good, tolerant null you are? Forget it. Go home, little Miss Famous."

Elena's cheeks went hot, but she might feel the same way if she didn't know better. She leaned in close. "You bet I'm a talent. Last year after Hurricane Humphrey, the press chasing me got poz fire and rescue onto the national news. Those poz got credit for saving lives, and that helped squash rumors about the storm being poz-caused. Think of it this way: where do you want cameras? Put me there."

The woman's frown turned thoughtful. "I'll see if any of the recovery crews will take you on. Sit tight."

She spoke briefly and quietly into her radio, then turned her attention to the mob of journalists. Once credentials were presented and liability forms signed, they were released into the wild. Some departed in company with local contacts, others started making calls.

Several hovered possessively near Elena while they broadcast first-on-scene reports. Soon, she was fielding all the usual questions—who did she know in the area, did she have an opinion about the storm. She learned their names and wheedled them into sharing scoops from their compatriots elsewhere.

Making people feel smart made them friendlier. Elena didn't know why the simple trick worked, but it did, so she took shameless advantage. Her new friends presented her with images and sought sound-bites from her.

She stuck with stock phrases of hope and support for the first responders because bawling on live television wouldn't make the right impression.

The F3 tornado here in Carlinsville had taken out dozens of homes and then cut through the high school and a strip of businesses after touching down near the courthouse. Many people had been sleeping peacefully despite sirens and radio warnings. The death toll was over ten here, with more severely injured and dozens missing.

An F5 tornado with a path over a half-mile wide had plowed through the tiny hamlet of Benld and left complete destruction in its wake. Alton had been strafed by three separate funnels, and the confirmed death toll was over fifty. The other twelve touchdowns had mostly struck cropland. Mostly.

Not all the news was awful. She was treated to great video of Mercury soldiers and civilian volunteers clearing roadways, rebuilding bridges, and removing debris. Teams of telekinetics and elementals could accomplish more in hours than heavy equipment could match in weeks, especially with teleporters leap-frogging them from site to site. They were few in number and limited by normal human endurance, but they were literally paving the way for others. Emergency workers and construction crews would replace them once their strength was spent.

They looked amazing in action. Elena made the most of that. She commented on the positive images that would stick with people longest: deep, raw gashes in the earth rippling smooth and coming alive with new green grass behind a pair of gray-haired women in camouflage fatigues; mountains of brick, metal, and wood sorting themselves into neat piles at the direction of a scowling old man wearing a fedora and suspenders; furred and tailed medical personnel striding up and down ranks of stretchers.

Generosity and nobility didn't often make headlines, so Elena did her best to make the bright stories stand out. Rare natural events always prompted speculation, and when tragedy struck, people wanted villains. The poz made easy scapegoats, but here they were, volunteering time and effort for victims who might shrink from them in disgust or spit at them on a normal day. Highlighting their heroism didn't prevent harassment or wipe out discrimination, but it sure didn't hurt.

After the excitement and upheaval of Grace's rollover, talking about anything else—*thinking* about anything else—felt wrong. Elena pushed back her growing discomfort by reminding herself that her location didn't matter to Grace right now.

One of the camera operators excitedly invited everyone in earshot to watch newly-uploaded helicopter footage of nearby Edwardsville. His audience grew quickly, drawn by the oohs and ahs.

The overhead view laid bare a wide path of destruction before zooming in. At the center of the damage, the earth had been scoured bare. Scattered buildings stood untouched in the long lines of rubble and bare foundations, saved by flukes of luck—or the talents of their owners. More homes stood roofless, guarded by splinter-limbed tree trunks stripped of bark.

Crews of Marines were moving house-to-house. Each squad boasted at least one giant Tee along with pyrokinetics and other elemental manipulators whose physical alterations ranged from minimal to extreme.

She was surprised to recognize one stocky, balding figure in Marine fatigues when the camera operator briefly zoomed in.

She'd known Perry Franklin had been drafted into Mercury Battalion for additional training after his DPS graduation, but last she'd heard, he was based up in Maine. The emergency declaration must have cast a very wide net.

It was nice to see him doing so well. He looked competent and confident, cleanly incinerating mixed piles of unsalvageable debris with the help of a telekinetic and an air elemental who converted the smoke to clear air. Construction equipment rolled down the cleared roadways in their wake.

The squads in the lead checked each property front to back, top to bottom. Utilities were sealed to prevent further damage, debris collected and sorted, and the properties marked so evacuees could return once travel bans were lifted. In the worst cases, bodies were exhumed from the rubble. Local fire and ambulance crews followed down the cleared streets, made safety assessments, and handled final arrangements.

The aerial viewpoint and the eerie lack of standing buildings or foliage meant multiple teams were visible performing the same grueling job. Their methodical progress looked inevitable and deceptively effortless, as obstructions melted away before their combined might.

Someone behind Elena said, "How do they know they aren't killing people?"

"This is the second round," the cameraman replied. "They did the search-and-rescue sweep before sun-up with receptives

—telepaths and empaths—up front. Nothing but shitty amateur local video of that. This'll screen better. It's unbelievable how fast they move. The heavy equipment crews you see moving in will take days and weeks to finish up."

Another of the watching reporters said, "You can see why there hasn't been a real shooting war in over fifty years. No human fighting force could stand against that."

There was one in every group.

"Those forces are human," Elena said promptly and firmly. "They're poz men and women who rolled active and got drafted, and they're soldiers, not monsters."

The pause grew tense before the man said, "It was only a figure of speech. I should've said regular troops, not human. I didn't mean anything by it."

"But other people do." She wasn't making any friends by saying that, but silence allowed intolerance to put down deep roots. Horrific violence grew from tiny seeds of *them* and *us*. "Words have power. You have power. You know that, right?"

The marshalling director returned, breaking the awkward silence. "Honey, I've got five Mercury teams and two fire departments requesting you for support duties. What is your magic?"

"I don't know. I follow orders and stay out of the way?"

"Ha! Now *that* is a talent." The woman added a second ID band to Elena's wrist. This one was yellow. "I'm giving you to a team in Edwardsville. Head back to where you arrived. Transit will lift you there."

The remaining press headed off in search of private transportation or other stories. Elena waited her turn behind two dozen wounded people on gurneys and stretchers being evacuated to distant medical centers. The sight of them made her heart ache harder than ever.

She smiled and said things like, "you're in good hands," and "you're going to be fine" to anyone who recognized her until it was her turn to go.

The 'porter in charge of her transit was either exhausted or not used to throwing people. Or both.

Elena arrived at her destination horizontal and so high off the ground the buildings looked like models. Falling.

She screamed. It didn't help.

Wings spread below her, gold-brown wings attached to a human figure who soared upward as fast as Elena was falling. They met in a breathless slam of limbs and a flutter of down, and a familiar gliding-through-nowhere sensation washed over Elena. Then she was on the ground in Heather's arms with her heart pounding and her stomach doing loops.

They were standing in yet another parking lot near a short, white-haired man who had lieutenant's bars and a telekinetic's insignia on his fatigues. His expression was thunderous with anger, and he was snarling into a radio headset. "That's your third foul ball, Pickett. Pitch 'em where I can catch them or tap out."

Elena said the first thing that came to mind. "Wow, Heather, I didn't know you could fly for real."

Heather laughed and squeezed her tight. "Neither did I! A couple of hours ago, I had to dodge a truck, and up I went. The corpsman from Gateway Company says it's a secondary power development, part of the same boost from Grace's onset that put us in Iowa."

Elena rubbed her cheek against the woman's arm. Her feathers were soft and comforting. "So I was right? They officially got you off probation?"

"Yup. Their guy said they see weird side effects on the regular, something about having so many primes in close quarters long term. Get this—" Heather pushed Elena out to arm's length. Her lips twitched, and the pupils of her eyes pulsed slightly. "They have a registration form and everything."

Elena felt a giggle trying to get out. "Val will love that," she said.

"HA. Val will feel guilty she didn't already know about it. Anyway, with all the energy Grace throws off, we might need to file a few more before this is over." Heather glanced past Elena's shoulder. "Hi, sir. Sorry to butt in on your catch."

The transit lieutenant was approaching. "No, I'm sorry for the bobble. Thanks for the assist. You've got another outbound waiting."

Heather curved a wing around Elena's back. Her eyes dilated and contracted as she frowned in concern. "You *are* okay, aren't you? I can't stick around. Dispatch has me taking medevacs all over the Midwest."

"I'm fine," Elena lied. She would not mess up Heather's opportunity. "I'm so amazed and happy for you. You can fly!"

Heather flexed her wings, looking self-conscious. "It's only TK, not true muscle flight, and the Marine corpsman said I'm not to overdo it, but when I saw you, I couldn't help myself. You be safe. I'll see you later."

The transit lieutenant frowned at Elena after Heather left. "I would've caught you in time, you know. I wasn't looking high enough at first. What're you doing here? You're just a little girl."

Torn between bursting into tears or hitting the man, Elena said, "Please, where is there a bathroom?" She desperately needed one.

He pointed to a portable toilet half-hidden behind a nearby building. Elena wobbled to it on shaky legs and avoided embarrassing herself with seconds to spare. When she came out, still shaky and weak-kneed, another familiar face was waiting for her.

Amy was at her flamboyant best today. She wore only

camouflage trousers and a packed equipment harness, and her giant clawed feet were bare and muddy. She was dressed to impress from the gaudily-painted radio headpiece clipped to her horn to the loosely attached accessories on her belt. Everything from signal flares and over-sized hand tools to a green-stained machete hung on loops and buckles, ready to hand.

She held out the backpack Elena had dropped on her way to the porta-potty. "You need to sit down a sec? You look funny."

The lieutenant was fielding another airborne arrival—a pallet this time—and he shouted a curse before it crashed down with a splintering boom of disintegrating wood.

The noise shredded Elena's composure. She wrapped both arms around Amy's big leg, buried her face in the tough uniform fabric and bawled her eyes out.

It was like leaning on a tree, except Amy put one big warm hand over her head and shoulders and patted her. "It's okay, kid. . It was just a rough landing. You're tough."

Amy was trying to be gentle, but the thumping rattled Elena's teeth. "I am not tough," she said through sniffles. "I'm not brave. I'm not. Why am I here? I don't want to be treated like I'm special or a problem. I don't want to prance around like some kind of—of—of—*mascot.*"

"You should've thought of that before you walked into the spotlight and posed for the pictures that made you famous. You want to run home to mommy?"

Maybe Amy wasn't trying to be gentle. Elena wiped away new tears and leaned away to glare up at the Marine's stiff, stony face. "I *never* asked to be famous. I thought we were going to *die*. And I didn't say I wanted to quit now. Don't patronize me."

"Then stop acting like a baby."

"I'm not!" But she was. She could hear the snotty tone in her voice. Mortified, she closed her eyes against new tears. "Crap. I'm stopping now. I'm done. I'm sorry. I won't let you down."

She hiccuped. Amy sighed, a gust of breath that ruffled Elena's scarf. Then she touched the tip of Elena's nose with the curved part of her pinky claw. "Listen up, kiddo. You're brave if I say you are, and I do. I called in favors to get you for my team because smiles and hugs from a famous, pretty, brave mascot are exactly what my guys need. So climb up."

"Do what?"

"I'm your ride. My squads are going block-to-block a mile away, and the twister dumped one half of this town on the other half. You've practiced piggyback runs with Jack, right?"

"For emergencies." She didn't want to be that high off the ground again, not so soon.

"What does this look like?" Amy slid one arm around Elena's waist and lifted her up so she could settle her boots in harness loops and grip tight higher up. "Ready?"

"Ready," Elena said, and it wasn't totally a lie.

Her stomach lurched whenever Amy hopped on, over, and around obstacles without slowing down. All around them, clusters of people worked to sort through the wreckage and restore order to the places the tornado had dumped things it had picked up elsewhere.

Amy's progress disturbed a flock of cheeping sparrows. Their flight made Elena flash on the sensation of falling and the relief of being saved. She leaned close to Amy's ear. "Thank you for helping Heather."

"She's pretty when she flies, isn't she? Hang on. Here we are." Amy maneuvered between a downed tree and a line of parked cars. "Hey, good timing. We're on a chow break."

The cafeteria line sat beneath a canopy marked with a big red cross. The sharp line between wind-damaged and wiped-out territory was eerie. Beyond the tent, nothing higher than her knees remained intact for blocks and blocks. Bricks, branches, furniture, clothing, and housewares lay everywhere in sodden piles.

People in various uniforms milled around a cluster of military vehicles and fire trucks and perched on curbs or chunks of rubble to eat their meals. Their voices carried over the background rattle of portable generators and the tearing sound of chainsaws in action. The scent of coffee wafted through the hot, wet air, mixing oddly with the garbage odors and exhaust fumes.

Elena's stomach growled. Amy laughed. "You're weepy with starvation, is it? Let's get you fed. No one starves on my watch."

Introductions were made over peanut butter sandwiches and apples on the way back to the work area. Elena gave thanks for name patches on uniforms as she said grace.

Amy was coordinating three units for her lieutenant, so she had a second heavy lifter on her own team. Corporal Jari Natha was a mid-sized T-series. A pyro and two powerful kinetics rounded out the crew. They were on the older side, the two men were bald, and both kinetics were named Smith. They went by Private One and Two and made the expected jokes about it. Private Georgia Sulaiman, the pyro in charge of the team's map, was subjected to repeated reminders not to accidentally burn it up.

They laid on the humor because the work was backbreaking and heartbreaking. They secured shattered buildings. They stacked up broken lives. And they moved on.

Elena rode in the cab of an Edwardsville pumper truck serving as a mobile cooling station. The crew members were fit young men and women, which made a nice change from working with people her parents' age.

Within two hours, she'd met thirty-five Mercury Marines

and poz volunteers working Amy's zone. They all acted as pleased to meet her as she was humbled to meet them.

They also looked old, overheated, and exhausted. Even the Tees were drooping. Elena wanted to bundle most of them up and take them home to drink iced tea and complain about achy joints with her abuela.

Instead, she gave out bottled water and snacks, laughed at their jokes, and asked about their families and their powers. And when two news crews showed up, she wheedled them into allowing workers to take breaks in their trucks too. Putting them together got them talking, which often meant personal stories making it to a media outlet. And since every reporter asked about the "unnatural" storm and pushed for tips about who might be at fault, it gave local poz a chance to blast that idea out of the water.

Which they did, much to Elena's relief. They dismissed the idea with delightfully condescending patience for the city folk who didn't understand weather. It was a marvel to witness.

Some firefighters told astonishing stories about destructive storms from their childhoods. Some shared their parents' tales from the turn of the last century, long before anyone rolled into powers. Those efforts wouldn't be enough to quell conspiracy theories, Elena knew, but they were better than nothing.

That progress didn't make up for the reporter who called her a spic monkey under his breath or the ones who talked about poz freaks when they didn't know Elena could hear them. The tiny pinpricks of disrespect bled away the last of her optimism as the gloomy morning slid into a hazy, hot afternoon.

More civilian rollovers showed up to help with the cleanup, and more residents returned to survey what was left. Elena kept herself busy and let the press fend for themselves.

The ground dried out, but the humidity rose, making the air

a sticky misery. Elena's odd, floating sense of detachment grew more pronounced. Attending church with Maggie and Lauren felt as if it had happened ages ago instead of a few hours. She wondered how they were doing and whether Grace's condition had changed, but those concerns felt distant and dilute.

Getting new water bottles into the chiller so they would be cold when someone needed them—that was important. So was insisting people eat a bite or two of food to keep up their strength. Greeting people by name and saying cheerful things made a real difference in their energy levels and moods.

They finished up where the twister had lifted at the end of a residential block. Out its way out, it had gouged its way through a hilly, wooded cemetery that looked old enough to have been there since the town's founding.

The shade trees had lost limbs, and their remaining branches were so wind-stripped the branches reached bare to the gray skies as if autumn had come early. Headstones leaned at drunken angles, and larger monuments had toppled.

Heather popped in just as Amy's team reached the limit of the touchdown path and converged with the other three squads. The teleporter joined Elena at the pumper truck instead of talking to them.

Her crest was flat, and her feathers were matted from the humidity. She absently groomed her crest with one clawed hand. "How's it going? I hit the legal 'port limit for civilians, but I can stick around until you're done if you want a ride home. Minors can only pull eight-hour shifts, right?"

"Yes. And I would love a ride, thank you." Elena blinked back tears. She'd been dreading the problem of getting home because she would not be trusting a stranger's teleport any time soon. And maybe she was spoiled, but she didn't want to spend all night on a bus either. "If it won't be a strain."

"Nah. Safety regs are conservative. I have four or five good hops left in me. Oh, hey!" Heather spread her wings to keep from staggering when Elena impulsively embraced her. "Okay, then. You're welcome."

Elena helped the teleporter comb her feathers back into order.

Amy ambled over. "Yo, Heather. You poaching my one-woman morale party?"

"Taking care of my second-favorite girl. Looks like you're wrapping up."

Most of the other Marines and volunteers were piling onto assorted fire and rescue vehicles. Most, but not all. Amy said, "Official pullback orders. National Guard and state services are stepping in. Not a moment too soon. We're running on fumes."

The trucks headed out. The Smiths, Corporal Natha, and one of the news trucks stayed behind. Elena said, "Your squad isn't leaving?"

"Not quite yet." Amy waved at the cemetery. "I never thought much about graveyards until you roped me into helping with your church things, but now it seems disrespectful to leave that mess."

"I thought you hated it." Every year on All Saint's Day, her parish youth guild picked a local cemetery to give a little extra care, providing cash-strapped maintenance crews free assistance with fall cleanup and laying flowers on the graves of those whose families had moved away or passed on. "You made lame excuses not to help the last two years."

"I was busy. Anyway. We're waiting on clearance to work around the graves, and then we'll tidy up. Shouldn't take much beyond a little muscle."

Elena flexed her arms. "I have muscles."

"Yes, you do. I knew you would want to help."

The local firefighters called in an arborist to evaluate which trees could be salvaged. Heather and Elena stacked up smaller branches. The Marines collected larger pieces of lumber, carefully righted tilting monuments, and moved broken or wholly misplaced headstones under the watchful direction of the cemetery caretaker.

It was somber work that encouraged a respectful quiet. Distance muffled the noise from construction and salvage efforts elsewhere. The loudest noise came from a flock of crows that came and went in their curious way. They behaved as if they supervising the clean-up of their territory.

One bird landed near the peak of a wind-blasted tree so big its trunk was wider than Elena's spread arms. It cawed loudly and insistently until more crows joined it. They bobbed on their narrow perches and yelled as if they were spectators at a sports event.

Heather cocked her head to the side, squinting at them. "They must have something trapped up there." She flipped back her wings and marched over to the tree, bending low when she arrived. "What's this?"

A bedraggled black and white cat huddled between two exposed roots at the foot of the tree. Its tail lashed from side to side, and it gazed fixedly into the wind-stripped branches overhead.

"Oh, you poor thing." Elena stroked it carefully, wary of claws and leery of fleas. It purred under her hand but kept staring into the sky. Heather looked up too. "What is she watching?"

The cat mewed. A tiny answering squeak came from a dark bump on a branch high above. A second bump squeaked, and a third.

Elena's heart sank. "Kittens? How did they get way up there?"

"Storm blew them, maybe?" Heather guessed. "Or they

climbed from a nest lower down. The mother looks feral. All skin and bones."

A crow rattled and cawed, hopping closer to its quarry. Bits of bark pattered down, and the kittens cried again. Their mother moaned. The grieving sound that brought tears to Elena's eyes.

There was no good reason this small tragedy should rip at her heart worse than all the others she'd seen today, but it did. "We have to help them."

Heather flapped her wings, making the air whoosh, and pitched a stick as high as she could. "Shoo, you nasty creatures. Shoo!"

The crows ignored her, but the commotion attracted the Smiths and Corporal Natha, "They bothering you?" asked Smith One. He squinted, and the whole tree shook. The crows took off in a flurry of angry calls, but the kittens screeched in distress. The branches immediately stilled.

"Oops," Smith said.

"Can we rescue them?" Elena asked. "I know they're only cats, but—" But she needed to do something good and right for its own sake. "Please?"

Corporal Natha paced around the tree and called over Amy, but they were both too short. Amy said, "The branches up there are too thin to take anyone's weight. Smiths, can you guys lift them down?"

The answer was *not now, not without squishing them*. Precision took as much energy as brute force, and both the kinetics were nearly out of juice.

The firefighters got involved next, but the ladder from the pumper was too short. They discussed calling a ladder truck, but decided it would sink to its hubs in the soft earth yards away—if they could get one to answer a treed-cat call.

"I could fly that high," Heather offered, "but I can't hover to grab them." She darted a look at Elena. "And if I fly, I won't have enough juice left to 'port myself home, much less take you. We'll have to take one of the motor transports."

"We can hover you if we don't have to *lift* you," Smith One said. "No problem."

"And Nari and I can play safety net," Amy said. "To catch anyone who falls."

Heather said, "Elena, honey? I'll do it if you want, but it's up to you."

Why was it up to her? She wasn't in charge of anything. Why did people always make her decide things? She caught herself before she said any of those whiny questions aloud. What did she want?

A camera whirred. Elena turned, and the photographer stepped back, eyes wide, a nervous smile on her lips.

Elena said fiercely, "You aren't helping."

Amy's scowl was menacing. "Why are you still here? This isn't news. Buzz off."

The woman snorted. "Seriously? Animal rescue is syndication gold. C'mon. Let me teach those blow-dried teleprompter jockeys a lesson about bailing early."

"Whatever." Elena considered her soggy, stinky clothes, her empty stomach, and her weary muscles, and the temptation of an early return home pulled strongly at her conscience.

But when she weighed her discomfort against the lives of stranded babies? That decision was easy.

The photographer was right about syndication. One of her photos made a big splash on the four big media outlets before the evening was out.

She caught Heather in the act of handing down a kitten to Corporal Natha. In the background of the shot, Smith Two fielded its falling littermate mid-air. Beside him, Elena lifted the frantic mother cat to rejoin the babies already cradled in Amy's arms.

It was an immediate hit.

That picture was priceless poz coverage, but it wasn't Elena's favorite one from the trip. Her favorite was the snapshot Amy took during their long ride home in the back of a Mercury special transport. Down on the metal flooring, braced between two seated, sleeping Marines, Heather sat cross-legged with the reunited feline family on a gray Red Cross blanket in her lap. Her bedraggled wings curved inward, perfectly framing the tabby kitten suckling at her thumb.

That was the photo Elena wanted to frame as a reminder to herself: little moments of love made up for almost everything else. That was the picture she printed for Lauren and Maggie before she went to bed, so it could be a good reminder for them that mothers came in all shapes and forms

She refused to give up hope their mother would come back to them.

.

25. CONSIDER WISDOM, AND ALSO MADNESS AND FOLLY

August 24, beneath 414 Elm Drive, Elgin IL

GRACE DRIFTED awake from visions of light and peace into a thick and bewildering darkness. She had dreamed of the taste of strawberries and the tug of a baby's mouth at her breast, but now she was awake in the dark like Jonah in the belly of the whale.

Her thoughts drifted, seeking a firmer anchorage. *Where am I? What happened? Why am I awake?* She stretched one hand over the mattress beside her, seeking comfort the way she had every night for decades, but the sheets were empty and cold.

Sharper thoughts cut through the sleepy confusion and poked her toward consciousness. This could not be her marriage bed. She had left Josh—no, Sal, now—ages ago. It wasn't the creaky secondhand bed in the new house. The surface squished like foam over stone, and the air was stuffy but cool, with a damp touch of mildew.

Recognition stirred. This was the hugely-oversized sleeping platform in the bunker. This was the tomb she had built to bury her cursed body, the place where she should have died by her own hand instead of accepting a bodily transformation.

She lay on soft sheets scented with lavender and prayed for the strength to live with the consequences of choosing survival. What had she become?

Reality would not wait on her fear. Curiosity stirred. She touched her fingertips to her face and found thick, knotty hardness where soft skin should have been. Her hands flexed oddly, jointed in ways that felt bizarre but natural at the same time. Tears pricked at the corners of her eyes.

Her eyes were open. Were the lights off? She'd installed night lights near the exit ladder and bathroom nook. Was she blind? She turned onto her side and curled around the fading remnants of the sweet dreams, unwilling to face that possibility.

God, give me the will to accept whatever you ask of me.

Her nerves prickled with a warmth like the touch of rough leaves. The sensation flowed through her and grew to a tingling promise of joy. Rapture dissolved fear and washed it away, leaving behind a quiet filled by the steady rhythm of her heartbeat and a vast symphony of melodic, wordless voices.

She rested, listening to that soothing music until one bass line rumbled and rolled up over the others, rising clear and pulling her back to full consciousness again.

The voice said, "Oh, Shells, wait 'til you see her fly. She went straight up, scooped Elena out of the air like a hawk, and 'ported out right at ground level—all on pure instinct. It was beautiful."

A higher-pitched line wove itself around the deeper one. "That geo-location sense would be nice. She'll have new job options now that she has range too. Lucky break."

Grace lifted her arms overhead and spread her gnarled toes wide, reaching for a prize hovering just beyond her reach.

"Grace?" someone said. "Did she move? She did! Grace,

you're awake? Take it easy, your body's changed, um, a lot. How are you feeling—whoa! Flare!"

The world flashed bright around Grace, prism colors against the black, sound rasping like scales against her skin. The air scraped her throat as she drew in a gasping breath, and she felt motes of oxygen seep into her lungs and course through her body. The sensation lasted for several weird, wonderful heartbeats before ebbing.

If this was power flaring, she could understand now why everyone had been so overwhelmed. Hysteria bubbled up. *How am I feeling? With every nerve ending, and I have a billion nerves, but I still can't see.*

"Am I blind?" she asked, and her voice burst like a visible liquid from her lips, a spray of golden dust against the black. She put her hands over her mouth, then her ears, then her eyes, trying to filter the turbulence one sense at a time.

And—just like that—she could see again. First, lines of light between her fingers, and then as she lowered her hands, the fingers themselves. Her hands looked and moved as they always had, smoothing down the thin cotton of her sundress, then moving to the blanket that covered her legs.

She set her palms against the quilted blue cotton Maggie had decorated with her first attempts at embroidery, focusing on a wobbly cross-stitched line of letters and flowers.

Her un-gnarly toes stuck out the far end of the blanket.

Had it all been a nightmare? Her dirty, grass-stained dress hinted otherwise. Her tongue was so dry it stuck to the roof of her mouth, and she felt as lightheaded as if she'd been fasting before a holy service.

She picked at the embroidery with a fingernail. Had she slept away a whole day? *No point in wondering when I can ask.*

She gathered her wits and looked up.

Her rollover refuge had changed since last she saw it.

Wooden crates were stacked like stairs to her sleeping platform's four-foot height, a fancier solution than the plank ladder she'd nailed into the side. And her go-bag was no longer the only piece of luggage on the floor. An open rucksack the size of a small couch leaned against a new metal workbench on one wall.

The bench held boxy electronics and a video screen with flickering images of the house interior, front and back yards, and this room. The technology looked incongruous below the red serpent cross painted on the white wall behind it.

The blocky church symbol glowered accusations at Grace: *Traitor. Sinner. Monster. Damned.* She sent up a silent prayer for continued faith and turned away from the bloody reminder of her past.

Amy and Shelly sat near the shaft for the entry ladder—on the floor and in a lumpy green armchair from Grace's living room, respectively. Shelly's white hair stood out from her head in a fluffy cloud, and her eyebrows were raised in surprised arcs. She wore a kaftan boldly patterned in reds and browns with gold fringe. Amy was in black stretchy leggings and a rainbow-dyed halter top.

The folding table between them held a complicated arrangement of cards and counters. A stick with a card gummed to the end dangled in Amy's claws like a forgotten toothpick. Both women sat stiff and unnaturally still.

Grace said, "Never mind, I can see now. I feel fine, except I'm starving. How long was I asleep? Why are you both looking at me like that?"

Amy reached up to stroke her left horn in a nervous tell Grace had noticed the night they'd met. The Marine said, "You gave us a shock. You've been down six days, Grace."

Six days? No wonder she was so hungry. "Is that normal for a —what am I? I tried to re-learn the codes with the girls when they took Health, but I couldn't make myself care what kind of dev—"

She forced her lips together to stop the nervous babbling. Tried again. "I remember the evaluators saying I would be G prime, but I don't know that series."

"It's rare." Shelly busied herself gathering the cards into a deck. "And there was nothing normal about what you turned into."

Grace remembered her legs going hard and scaly—but a glance under the covers reassured her they, too, looked as they always had. The DPS evaluator's remarks weighed heavy on her mind. He had said interning her wasn't worth the paperwork. "What happened? Am I done rolling now?"

Shelly rapped the card deck against the table. The sound hit Grace's senses like a slap and a flashbulb going off at the same time. She covered her ears with her hands. "Ow."

"Sorry," Shelly said in a whisper.

Little colored bubbles rose from the woman's lips to the ceiling and painted it in confetti colors. Grace watched them rise. Were they real? She stared at her dirty, cracked fingernails. "I don't look different, but—something is different." *I'm seeing visions and hearing things.*

Amy rubbed both horns and puffed out her cheeks. "Your power sig tells me you are not done. You turned into something hard-shelled, black, and bumpy six days ago and stayed that way until just now when you changed back in a huge gush of power."

Shelly stood, brushing at her hips to smooth her outfit. "We need Yasu. I volunteer to get him. Get her a drink and a nosh and try to be kind, will you?"

She disappeared in an explosion of dazzling ribbons and a clatter of noise. Grace shrank back as the glittering lines of power jumped toward her. They twined around her arms in dancing, sparkly ribbons that tingled everywhere they touched.

They tinted her skin blue and painted her fingernails lilac purple, then evaporated, leaving her chilled. And as soon as she thought, *But I don't want to be that color,* her skin reverted to its normal freckled, sun-kissed shade.

"Am I hallucinating?" she asked, unsure if she wanted the answer to be yes or no.

Amy squinted at her. "You were blue for a minute, if that's what you mean. You're probably seeing and hearing a lot of weird things. Roll with it, if you can. Ignore it if you can't."

"Roll with it. Ha." Grace swung her legs down off the platform and leaned forward. The blanket felt oddly silky against her palms, but fear coiled inside her belly like barbed wire. "I can see energy now, but it seems to come and go however it wants."

"That part is normal." Amy stood up, ducking reflexively before straightening and bustling around the space she made feel small by being so large. "We call this process rollover, but it's more like power rolling *in*. For a rank-one in any series, it's like filling a bucket with a fire hose. There's a lot of spillage and sloshing. That's the main reason the DPS isolates people into camps for safety."

The image was a vivid one. "What about the C part? C is for physical change, right? I'm back to normal. Will that last, or will I—change—again?"

Amy ducked away into the privacy-shielded cubicle in the back corner that held a floor drain, shower head, sprayer, and a spigot. She came out with a full glass of water that looked like a doll's cup in her hands.

While Grace drank the water, Amy delicately peeled open a ration bar from the survival kit. "Good choice, these," she said as she handed it over. "Best-tasting brand on the market."

Glitter and buzzing sounds accompanied her words, and her body threw off silver motes that smelled of fresh rain. Pain tightened around Grace's skull when she tried to focus on one sense at a time, so she stopped trying.

The food snickered at her when she chewed it and bounced going down her throat, gleeful about its imminent disintegration. She ignored the bizarre sensations as much as she could, and strength flooded back into her body faster than digestion would explain.

Worry voiced was worry lessened, so she spoke her concern out loud. "I'm going to die, aren't I? That's why the DPS evaluator didn't think interning me was worth the trouble."

"That's what he thinks." Amy took Grace's cup. "You might want to wait for Yasu or Shelly for this talk. They know how to say things gently."

"I don't need gentle. Tell me what G stands for. Exactly."

"G stands for Gaia, like T is for troll." Amy turned away. She didn't continue until she was in the bathroom alcove again, where Grace couldn't see her. "Gaia's don't get one power. They get all of them on call, more or less. The problem is, no Gaia ranked higher than eight has survived rollover since World War Two. They burn up, or melt, or transform like you did. You had no mouth, Grace. No veins for an IV. Nothing. We couldn't chip that shell with a diamond drill. If you hadn't changed back, dehydration would've killed you. Or starvation."

She worked the tap in the bathroom.

No wonder I surprised them. Grace swallowed a new and jagged thought. "Did—did my girls see me like that?"

"They did not." Amy was frowning when she came out of the alcove. "We briefed your ex. He told them you needed to be alone. Every morning they ask us to tell you they're praying for you, but otherwise they're so calm it's creepy."

Grace's cheeks warmed. "Poz in the Salvation Church either

didn't survive rollover or were exiled. Lauren and Maggie grew up knowing they might never see me again if I sealed myself into a stronghold like this."

Amy handed back the refilled cup. "Forgive me, but that's seriously screwed up."

Careful to avoid the Marine's fingers, Grace accepted the water and took a small sip. The throbbing red glow of the cross on the wall whispered accusations. Each one fell like a drop of acid into her ears—*heretic, blasphemer, sinner*.

How ugly her past looked, hanging there. She couldn't ignore it, so she threw out words to fend off the pain. "There's nothing to forgive. You're right. Looking back, I suppose I'd been doubting for years, but I couldn't stop going through the motions."

Amy sniffed. "Huh. I know what that's like."

She ran a hand over the spikes atop her skull, flattening them and letting them spring up again. "Your church is the reason you have this fantastic little hideaway, I know, but the God stuff puts me on edge. I'm an atheist. No offense meant."

"None taken." Grace hadn't realized the Marine's spines could bend like that. They looked so solid. She dragged her thoughts back to the original point. "Do you really believe I have a chance or are you trying to be kind?"

"I'm glad you're awake, and I'm betting you beat the odds. I can't say I know what's going to happen to you next. No one does."

"There aren't any living Gaias to ask?"

"None powerful enough to be helpful. Val pulled records back to First Night. Things were pretty chaotic then, but it looks like there were two survivors presumed G3 or better. So survival is possible. And according to data I liberated from Gateway's company archives, G is the only power series without a single field retrieval on record. All the G-series rollovers went start to finish in a camp."

"Mine started here."

"And you're still at home. Don't give up."

Hope rang in Amy's voice like bells, but the stinging whispers from the wall made a dissonant counterpoint. *Worthless,* muttered the cross. *Faithless, shameful. Coward. Disgrace.*

Grace's new and tender faith was little defense against doubts rooted in human frailty. She thought of her namesake, spreading destruction and death as she walked down a path paved with good intentions. Only tragedy could come of power harnessed to weakness.

"What if I can't—" The question filled her mouth, sour and heavy, but she couldn't bear to finish it. What if she was wrong? What if power inevitably corrupted?

"I won't let you go bad, Grace. I promise." Amy turned to the workbench and flipped several switches with one claw.

The monitors went dark, and a low sound pulsed through Grace's bones. Amy continued, "In fact, that's the real reason I'm on this transition team. Military liaisons like me answer to the Judicial Branch of the DPS. We're authorized to use deadly force in the line of duty, just like DPS agents from the Special Directives Unit. I'll take you out if you become a threat and there's no other choice."

That answered Grace's *what if,* but it raised a host of other questions. The most pressing one was, "How did you know what I was worried about?"

Amy leaned back against the bench and crossed her arms. "One, speaking as a giant who can crush car engines with her bare hands, every prime with a conscience worries. Two, you projected the question hard enough to make my eyes cross."

"Oh. Oh, no! I'm so sorry." If she knew how to control what was happening, she would.

"I know you would," Amy said, nodding. "And yes, you did it again. Don't sweat it. We'll get you an F series mentor. We have a military-grade EF damper, too, but it gives everyone splitting headaches. I'll take my chances with you until Yasu gets here to play watchdog. Nothing you do can hurt me, remember? Perk of my series. And the team won't let me hurt anyone else."

"Did you get this job because you're invulnerable?"

The big Marine's sharp teeth showed briefly. "No. I *took* the job because every DPS camp has to have a Judicial Branch rep on staff, and no one on Camp Liberty's board wanted the SDU making the life or death calls for our clients."

"That's a relief."

Amy cocked her head to one side. "Most people think Special Directive agents are heroes."

"I'm not most people," Grace pointed out. "Growing up, I knew them as the Devil's lapdogs."

Officially the SDU investigated and captured criminals whose abilities made them impossible for nulls to safely approach, arrest, or imprison. Unofficially they were real-life action heroes who blasted through legal roadblocks to save their fellow citizens from murder and mayhem.

They had ranked high in the Assembly Church's hierarchy of government evils. Her grandfather, in particular, had found them worthy of many wrathful, cautionary sermons.

She said, "And if they do the same job you do, then I guess the rumors about death squads were true."

Amy winced. "Not squads. And there are reasons it never gets beyond rumors."

Visions flickered around the room, wraiths of emotion and imagery that tickled Grace's eyes and tongue. Which part of her newborn power was bringing those to life, she wondered, watching them and listening hard to the stillness at her center.

"This is secret," she said. "You could get in trouble."

Amy smiled widely, all teeth, no humor. "I could get executed. Don't rat on me."

Her easy trust was breathtaking. "Why did you tell me?"

"Because you deserve to know. Because you're afraid. Because I'm tired of black ops and lies. Because I don't *want* to kill you and I don't trust the DPS."

A weariness spread over the room with those words, like a pall of mist, coloring her words, making the air thick. Grace struggled to inhale. "Does anyone else know?"

"Jack. He was Gateway's liaison before me. And I don't want to believe any of our volunteers are SDU moles, but it's possible. I wouldn't put anything past them."

"Have you killed people? Has Jack?"

Amy looked her square in the eyes and said nothing.

When righteousness and regret carried on a war inside the same soul, the bloody battles left their mark. The cost the Marine had paid for standing in defense of others showed up like shadows across her broad, harsh features.

Grace's heart broke for her.

Scorn her, cried the thorny, stinging voice of her abandoned beliefs. The Assembly cross on the wall glowed brighter by the second, clawing at her ability to think. *They commit sacrilege. Unbelievers dabbling in matters they don't understand, turning sacred rites into profanity, stealing souls from heaven.*

"How awful for you both," she said firmly, to drown out the clamor. "No one should have to bear that burden in secret."

If anyone knew that, it was her.

"Now see, that is why I believe in you," Amy said with a more genuine smile, but sadness and regret tasted bitter in the air. "You've got guts, and you've got heart. Oh—and don't sweat the C-variant part. Shapeshifting is a W-series ability. Remember that, if your final form ends up being, um, extreme."

Grace took another sip from her cup and considered the

implications of Amy's words. At the end of this metamorphosis, she wouldn't have *a* power. She wouldn't have *a* form. She wouldn't have *an* ability. God was giving her a basket of talents. She had best not to bury them in the ground and waste them.

If she lived. If she was strong enough to survive.

She spilled the rest of the water over herself when a rainbow explosion of crashing cymbals deposited Yasu out of nowhere just behind Amy's right elbow.

The old man shook his head, and the room felt brighter, smoother, and warmer for his presence. "Sorry to startle you, sunshine," he said. "You spooked Shells pretty good, so she sent me directly."

He lifted a gym bag onto the platform bed. "Lauren told us you kept this bag ready with clothes and sundries for your rollover or other emergencies. Let's start with a shower, shall we?"

Before long Grace was clean and back on the bed, feeling a little befuddled by the sensory overload of her soap and shampoo. The soft, yellow-checked flannel pajamas she wore now had started pink, then changed color twice before settling on the current pattern.

Yasu remained unfazed by the manifestations, walking her through procedures for obtaining a finger-prick blood sample and measuring various vital signs so he didn't have to touch her. She was declared in fine fettle, whatever that meant, then given more water and fed another cheerful ration bar. This one tasted like rose petals and snickered inside her belly until the tickling gave her hiccups.

Yasu smiled thoughtfully when Grace admitted why she was staring at her stomach. "That's a new one. I suggest you ignore the food unless it starts objecting. If it does that, let me know. We're in uncharted waters, dear. I appreciate your honesty in reporting."

"Why would I lie?" What would be the point?

"Patients lie for any number of reasons." Yasu walked up the crates onto the mattress and sat down cross-legged beside Grace—just out of arm's reach. He folded his hands in his lap. Energy rippled the covers near him, invisible except for the way it moved the cloth. Something hummed in a low register no one else seemed to hear. Grace edged away from him for safety's sake and wished she knew if the noise was a purr or a growl.

Yasu said, "Since we're talking about truth, perhaps you'll tell me—honestly—what emergency you planned to face with a scalpel, a loaded pistol, and syringes preloaded with enough pentobarbital to kill elephants."

They'd found the grace kit in the go-bag.

The sympathy in Yasu's eyes left Grace feeling infinitely regretful. *This emergency,* she wanted to say, but the words wouldn't come out.

Memories bubbled up like poison, stilling her tongue and drowning her in a flood of shameful secrets.

26: FOR WITH KNOWLEDGE COMES SORROW

414 Elm Drive, Elgin, IL

A CHUNK of melting ice escaped the towel around Jack's neck and slid down his spine to the waistband of his shorts. He fished it out and dropped it onto the brick patio, where it melted fast. Despite the muggy heat, this was a comfortable watch post. The awning kept the patio shady, the raised flower beds around it were effective heat sinks, and the metal table was both high enough to sit on and sturdy enough to hold him.

Best of all, after days of banging, drilling, and omnipresent dust clouds, the old house had new central air conditioning. The draft from the open sliding doors was keeping the damp cloth on his back nice and cold.

Jack squinted over the lawn and bumped up the polarization on his sunglasses so he could focus on the other big problem in his life. The woman who owned this house was dying, and an operation whose success could have improved the lives of millions might die with her.

"Why don't you go home and play in your own garden?" he

asked Elena. "Better yet, pack your bags and get off to college where you're supposed to be."

Elena straightened up from whatever the hell she was doing with a basket and a long stick. When she pushed sweat-dampened dark hair back over her shoulders with one gloved hand, she left a smear of dirt on her cheek and neck. Heat shimmered above the outlined areas full of green things between them.

Her eyes narrowed. "I can skip orientation," she said. "I don't want to leave Lauren and Maggie until we see this through to the end. You agreed to it."

"You played dirty." Jack bared his teeth at her. He had no damned defenses against an opponent who countered his arguments with a simple sad-eyed *please*. Now she stood frowning at him with those dark eyes all squinty and angry, chewing on a length of hair that had escaped her ponytail.

"I am pretending I didn't hear that." She bent over the plants again and poked things with the stick. *Jab. Jab. Jab.* "Otherwise, I would have to mention dirty tricks like getting thrown at Heather and ending up in Iowa."

"She's forgiven me for it." He wasn't sure if Valerie had, but he wasn't sure of anything where Val was concerned. He might never forgive her for calling Evaluation and adding to the pressure on Grace at that critical time. "I made the right call. You're a null, and you had no business in the middle of an unstable rollover kickoff. Heather ended up with a permanent power shift. You could've been killed."

"Oh, are we doing the safety talk again?" Elena jammed the stick down. It stayed put when she put her hands on her hips. "The situation here is stable, plus there's Lauren and Maggie, and the yard needs work, and everyone else approved it too, and—and you *promised*."

She stamped her foot. Jack retreated to his fallback position.

"Hang around as much as you want. I'm only saying you're wasting your time."

He knew how this would end. He had seen the reports and videos. One day soon, the pod-like thing that had been Grace Reed would go up in flames, dissolve into thin air, turn to stone, or quietly stop living, and that would be that.

Elena's whole idealistic plan for the future was about to crash and burn, and there wasn't a thing Jack could do to stop it. The injustice of it made him want to howl with frustration. He repositioned his ice-filled towel and sighed instead.

He should have found a way to fix things, but he'd failed. "This isn't going to have a happy ending," he said.

He'd so wanted to give her one.

"Oh, Jack." Elena picked up her basket and came back to the patio with it. There were orange and red things in the greenery. Carrots, Jack guessed, and tomatoes, maybe? They smelled like musky dirt.

The table creaked when Elena sat down next to him, and she stripped off one glove to wrap her grubby hand around his pinkie finger. "I won't shrivel up and die if this—okay, don't curl your lip—*when* the worst happens. You watch. Val and me, we'll find a way to move forward. Sal will step up and be a voice for us—I know you don't like him, but he'll be great on camera. I have ideas."

The earth should tremble in fear when Elena got ideas. Her particular talent was making wild ideas feel reasonable.

Jack turned his hand so her palm rested on his: tiny, dark, and delicate against his hard skin. "Okay, tiger. As long as you understand."

"I do. Keep your big shoulder handy for me to cry on. It's so unfair. Grace was—is—*interesting*." She hopped off the table and patted his knee. "We're good then? You'll stop brooding, and I can go back to the garden?"

"We're good." He didn't dare pat her on the head. She would bite his arm and break teeth. "You seriously enjoy grubbing in the dirt?"

"I do, but I don't need an audience. Why don't you go inside?"

"Because it's noisy and dirty, and I'm tired of being asked to move heavy things."

The staccato noise of a nail gun in action punctuated his explanation. The girls were back in school as of today, and Sal was installing new flooring in the front parlor with Gabe's help.

The retired police officer apparently saw something in Sal no one else did. Since someone had to watch over him until his permanent E-series residence permit came through, that was working out well. With power tools in hand, the pair of them were as happy as pigs in clover.

Jack had refused Sal's first offer to keep working on the renovations "while Grace is busy," because the man annoyed him on principle. Leave it to professionals, he'd suggested. Sal had promptly produced various union certifications and went on and on about the detailed project outlines, building plans, and permits ready and waiting.

And then he started moaning about remorse and making things better for his children.

Jack had given him permission to shut him up.

Sal's competence wasn't affected by his social awkwardness. If nothing else, the improvements would make the house easier to sell, and the air conditioning was heavenly.

Elena gestured at the open door. "You're cooling the whole neighborhood."

"Why yes, I am." He considered it a fringe benefit. Not only was it a waste of money, the strain was also taking years off the lifespan of the new unit. Jack had gotten a whole lecture on the topic from Sal. Luckily for everyone involved, Gabe had intervened before blood spilled. "Are you going to complain about every light in the house being on, too? Maintenance costs are covered. Stop fussing and go play with your stick."

Elena stalked off, leaving the basket behind. She shook the stick at him again after she pulled it loose. "It's a hoe, you big doofus. I am weeding and harvesting. You could help."

"No, I—" Jack sat up straight as the unmistakable scent of Shelly's teleport trace wafted out of the house. She was supposed to be in the bunker. "Uh-oh."

Elena leaned on the hoe, looking worried. Jack lifted a finger, *wait*, and Shelly's voice blasted into his ear. "Sitrep, boss. Amy and me were playing cards and swapping war stories when there was this huge power surge and—bam—she's up and talking and looking like herself again."

Jack cranked down the volume while Shelly kept on babbling. "It is too weird. She didn't look a bit starved, and her eyes! Right when she sat up, it was like looking into—I don't know. I'm shaking. My skin is crawling. I popped out as soon as I could think of an excuse."

Jack jumped in when she finally took a breath. "Okay, Shells, you did good. Better to leave than to scare Grace." He needed Shelly steady, and she needed reassurance, not a critique. "Find Yasu and pop him down to look her over. The ladder is hell on his knees."

Shelly took another audible breath and let it out on a shaky laugh. "Already done. When I showed up in his room, he said sit down, send him in, and report to you, which is what I'm doing. I feel awful for panicking, but bless it, I need a drink."

"I'll buy you one when this is all over. Deal?"

She laughed, as Jack had hoped she would. "Deal."

"Seriously, Shells, do you need to tap out?" He watched Elena abandon the gardening again to rejoin him. "If you're shaken, you can stand down. We have Heather."

"Oh, you think she's enough, do you?" His ears popped, cold floral air puffed over him, and Shells was right in front of him, handset at her ear. Her eyes were red-rimmed and puffy, and her lip trembled. She lowered the phone. "What if there's an emergency, huh? I don't need to be in the same room with Grace to move her. Are you trying to get rid of me?"

Elena slipped an arm around the older woman's waist. "He's being overprotective. It's his *thing*. We don't have to let him get away with it. Listen. Do you think I could see Grace? Is she up to it? I wanted a chance to talk."

Shelly gave the girl a hug. "Sure, sweetie, if you want. She won't make your skin crawl since you're null."

"Not a good idea. Not yet," Jack said. He wasn't overprotective, dammit. He was cautious. "Did anything feel weird about your teleports after the power surge?"

"No," Shelly said after a hesitation long enough to tell Jack she hadn't stopped to consider the one known side-effect of Grace throwing off stray power. "Her surge felt like being near an elemental doing a calling: energy but not mine. That means she's pretty far along, yes? She's starting to channel unconsciously."

And they both knew what that meant. When the other Gaias on record had reached that stage, they'd destabilized. It wouldn't be long now. A day or two, maybe.

Jack said, "Okay, nothing changes for us topside. Share the news with Gabe and Sal, will you? Then take a break. And remember, it's always time for a drink somewhere."

Shelly promised to keep her phone on and went inside on her own two feet, leaving the door wide open behind her. Jack resisted the urge to check on Amy with a phone call or head down himself. If she or Yasu needed a hand, they would call—unless they couldn't call for extraction fast enough, in which case there wouldn't be a damned thing he or anyone else could do to help.

Elena wrapped her arms around herself and looked out over the hot, bright yard. "I'm not in the mood to weed anymore," she said in a small voice.

She'd read the same histories Jack had skimmed. She was smart. For Gaias, the ability to channel power came right before the final stages of overload and fatal collapse.

She was trying so hard to not cry it broke Jack's heart.

He said, "Climb up here and teach me about what you're doing. It's all plant shit to me. Why do you ignore the yellow ones? I swear the things you pull up look exactly like ones you leave alone other places."

"That's because plants are only weeds when they're where they don't belong." She wiped her face with the back of one hand and re-did her ponytail before she joined him on the picnic table.

"So are the yellow things weeds or not?"

"Which yellow things?" she asked in her cranky-old-lady voice. She spent the next few minutes explaining vegetables and herbs, and Jack pretended he was interested.

A clatter and crash of falling lumber inside the house interrupted a lesson on the difference between cilantro and parsley. The sound of Gabe swearing followed the racket. Then Sal was at the open patio door, crossing the threshold at a dead run.

Jack had no idea where he was going and didn't care. He came off the table and moved to block the man.

Sal came to a skidding halt. His eyelids fluttered rapidly behind his dusty safety goggles, his plaid work shirt hung askew, and he smelled of sawdust, blood, and rank fear.

He raised his hands, fingers spread, and crimson dripped from the right one, front and back. He'd put a nail straight through it.

"She's calling me." His voice warbled high. "I have to go to her. Please. I *felt* her calling. She needs me. I know I shouldn't be able to—but I did. I felt her. I feel you."

There was no question who he meant by *her*. Either he'd snapped, or things were getting strange in that bunker. The safe solution to both problems was obvious. Jack stepped aside. "Go ahead."

Sal bolted for the bunker trapdoor. Jack realized his mistake a second later when Elena said, "Hey, no fair. If he can visit, I can too," and sprinted after Sal.

27: THE EYE NEVER HAS ENOUGH OF SEEING, NOR THE EAR ITS FILL

August 24, DPS CA Region 20 Offices, Riverside CA

VALERIE CHECKED her Camp Liberty phone log as soon as she got to her desk. Jack had called twice while she was driving into work, and again between the parking lot and her door, but he'd left no message beyond, "Call me ASAP."

She wrestled with the urge to ignore him the way he'd been shunning her. If there were a real crisis or a serious bureaucratic tangle, he would have either left a message or ordered Gabe to call. Jack might be petty, but he was too professional to let his feelings get in the way of the job. That meant he either wanted to bitch at her, or the worst had happened.

If he had questions about filing a death report, that could wait until she was settled behind a closed door so she could cry while she filled out paperwork.

But if Grace was gone, then surely Elena would've called too, looking for consolation. No, this had to be Jack wanting to yell at her. No need to hurry into that.

She tucked the phone into her briefcase and unpacked

everything else, organizing her morning by slapping files loudly onto the desk. The noise worked off some of the aggravation, but her bra strap caught on the teleportation tag near her shoulder as she stretched to tidy up the papers.

Shelly said that was the best location for tags, but it snagged no matter how Valerie adjusted it. It was another irritating reminder of the pointless friction between her and Jack.

Delaying evaluation wouldn't have helped Grace, and if she had been rolling into an obscure W talent or an E series one, there would have been real risks to the team.

Jack had no right to hold a grudge over Valerie putting safety first, not when he'd used that exact excuse to send her home. A new understanding struck with that thought: she and Jack were both stewing in the same toxic swamp of resentment, guilt, and frustration. And if she didn't return his message, it would make her as childish as he was being. That was unacceptable.

She sighed and retrieved the Camp Liberty radiophone from the briefcase.

Jack answered so fast he must have had his hand on the button. "Valerie. Shit. Listen. Things are fucked up, and I don't know how to fix it."

"Do you have to swear every third word?" She regretted the question as soon as she asked. Annoyance was running interference for worry again. Grief tried to elbow its way into the emotional mix. "Grace is dead?"

"No. It's—shit. There's no explaining. We need your eyes. Come look. And bring your magic briefcase of paperwork in case you decide interning is the best we can do."

"Me decide? Why?" Valerie didn't realize she'd stood up until her knees went weak, and she landed back in her seat. A hundred horrible possibilities galloped through her mind. "Did she come out of her shell? Did she hurt someone—is she losing

—no. You would've aborted if there was danger." She found calm certainty within the whirl of her anxiety. "What do you need me to see?"

Chirps and blebs of noise broke through the connection, washing out his answer. "Fuck—long—explain. Energy's—high —oping you—we're missing. Please. Don't—nt—to abort."

"All right, I'll be right there." He'd said please, and they needed her talent. Valerie caught herself picking at Shelly's transport tag with one finger. "Give me a few minutes to tie things up, and I'll call for a port."

"—nk you—ll Shells. Not—ow long my—one—ast." Static pulsed through Jack's voice. "Out."

Three minutes and two phone conversations later, Valerie was thankful for Anna's foresight a week past and full of guilt for being a bad mother. Then she called Shelly. A long, dizzy blink later, she was on Grace Reed's pretty, shaded patio, breathing humid Illinois summer air.

Her hair went frizzy and stuck to her neck, and her eyeballs ached, adjusting to the change in light. Shelly paced along the far edge of the patio in a tailored shirt and shorts. Gold earrings glinted beneath her gray curls, and her complexion was too pale for her make-up.

The wrinkles between her eyebrows softened when she smiled. "Welcome to the madhouse. Sorry about the heat, but it's too crowded downstairs to port you in there direct."

That was not reassuring. "What is going on? Where is everyone else?"

"In the bunker. Except for Heather. She took a personal day to deal with her reinstatement paperwork. And Gabe. He has twin duty until further notice. He took them shopping. And me. Because I got the hell out. I'll walk you over there. C'mon." Shelly grabbed Valerie by the wrist. "No time to waste."

Valerie was hurried toward the grassy corner of lawn where

a metal hatch yawned wide open behind a shed. Shelly said, "No hard feelings about the other night? For what it's worth, I didn't like being part of that. Jack was right to send you off-site, but— I'm still sorry."

"I'll get over it." Holding a grudge was impossible in the face of such visible remorse.

Threads of energy pulsed in Valerie's peripheral vision. Bright lines like strands of sunlight trailed behind Shelly as she moved. They came from everywhere, high and low but never crossing, an ever-shifting web centered on the teleporter.

Spotting such subtle connections usually required intense concentration. Here it was effortless. Iridescent shimmers surrounded everything like soap bubbles spun gossamer-thin. "The whole yard is saturated in stray power," she said. "Does it bother you?"

"You bet it does." Shelly shivered. "I'm jumping out of my skin so bad I'm getting nauseous. I think Jack's overreacting, too. This is still well under the legal limit. None of the alarms have gone off."

"It's like being inside a kaleidoscope." She'd read about this phenomenon, but the dry incident reports hadn't done justice to the visual wonder of it. "Why Jack is freaking out? This is a known side-effect. Energy build-up is normal toward the end."

"There are other—um. Complications." Worry and amusement both danced their way across Shelly's face. She kept her hand on Valerie's arm as they arrived at the bunker. "I can't begin to describe it. You'll see. I'll stand rescue-ready in case anything goes wrong, and there's a Mercury team on standby, too. I'm sure it'll blow over once—well, you know."

She shrugged, looking old and sad.

Once Grace's rollover finishes killing her, she meant. Valerie covered Shelly's hand with her own, squeezed gently. "I know."

She shut her eyes halfway through the long climb down the

bunker ladder. The rungs felt solid but visibly quivered, and the concrete walls flickered with disorienting rainbow sparkles. When she reached the bottom of the shaft, she stumbled blind into an obstacle and bounced off.

Her eyes opened, and she recoiled as every instinct screamed out *danger!*

The enormous creature sitting in the archway to the main bunker blinked at Valerie, then swiveled its head with unnatural ease to look over its shoulder through the arch. "I don't look bad, huh? You are such a liar."

Valerie blinked and recognized Amy. She cleared her throat to swallow the lump in it. *Just to be sure*—"Amy?"

"In the flesh." The Marine's voice was almost recognizable: dry, amused, and only slightly deeper than usual. A dramatic growth spurt had lengthened her torso more than her limbs, while subtle changes to her facial bones and extensions to her dorsal spines made her resemble a fantastic cross between a cat and a lizard.

People with T-series abilities were known for undergoing radical growth when charged up on power, but this was more extreme than anything Valerie had ever seen. Her next irreverent thought was: *now I see why she wears super-stretchy halters and skirts.*

Despite all the changes, Amy looked indefinably *right* surrounded by the haze of power in the air. The Marine's yellow-eyed reptilian gaze still held her intelligence and humor.

She grinned, displaying needle-sharp teeth. "I'm going to need a lot of new spine lacquer if this doesn't wear off. What do you think of purple?"

A basso growl rolled over the end of her question from somewhere in the room beyond her. "This isn't funny, dammit."

The hair on the back of Valerie's neck stood up, and the chill ran down her spine. *Is Jack affected the same way? Why is that so much more frightening?*

Elena's voice echoed slightly when she spoke from inside the bunker. "I am not a liar. I said you were beautiful, and it's true. Hi, Val. I got caught up in the middle of things again."

Jack said, "It's my fault. I should've had you 'ported to fucking Australia."

Valerie reached for patience. "And I will send you both to your rooms if you don't stop bickering. Amy, I refuse to talk through you, and you don't look comfortable. Can you climb outside to the yard?"

The Marine's eyelids closed halfway. "You tell me. Should I? Is it safe? I'm riding a rampage pulse a thousand times bigger than anything I've ever handled. If I lose my grip and go into full combat rage, the neighborhood is toast. Think I can hold it?"

That question stabbed straight to Valerie's heart. She gave it the serious consideration it deserved. "I don't see anything twisted, unstable, or unhealthy in you. How do you feel?"

"I feel amazing."

"And you look fine to me. As harmless as an indestructible giant can get. That's assuming you trust my talent, of course."

"Hush, now. Of course I trust you. Jackass is the paranoid one." Amy's skin rasped along the floor. "I'll squeeze up and out as soon as you scoot past me. Keep your eyes open. Something is rotten in there. Jack is right about that."

Yes, but what does rotten *look like?* Valerie squeezed around Amy to see the room for herself.

The space was both larger and brighter than she'd expected from the photos in the daily reports. She knew the dimensions by heart: a floor forty feet square split into two levels, ceilings twelve to sixteen feet high over it. The walls were painted a vivid white, and fixtures near the matte-gray ceiling bathed the room in cool diffused light.

A scarlet glow against the white drew her attention to a mural above the recording station. The image burned into Valerie's mind and squeezed a whimper from her. Symbols had power. Symbols carried meaning. The serpent-draped cross pulsed with hatred, blasting out a message of deception, suffering, and death.

She'd seen that cross in all the daily briefing snapshots. Reality was the difference between admiring a picture of a tiger and being mauled by one. Sal's earnest descriptions of the Salvation Assembly Church had portrayed a refuge from the outside world, no different from a dozen other splinter sects.

The cross—once mere paint, now saturated with energy like an emotional sponge and dripping hatred everywhere—told a different story. It was pure malevolence grown from deep, bloody roots and shot through with murderous rot.

Valerie's heart contracted into a hard, painful knot. The last time she had felt so repulsed by a visual revelation, she'd gathered up her babies and fled for her life.

Sunlight lit up the room as Amy reached the top of the entry shaft. The warm glow disappeared when the Marine slammed the hatch down.

The idea of being trapped in here with that *thing* on the wall made Valerie's soul shrivel. Tears blurred her vision. Her shoulders hunched, her stomach rolled, and her knees went watery.

No. The painting was only an echo of evil, not a true and present threat. Its potency was a side effect of the ambient energy, nothing more. She looked straight up at the safe gray of the ceiling and held her breath until the nausea and fear ebbed.

"Do you need to sit down?" Elena asked. "You look dizzy."

"I'm fine," Valerie said, determined to make it true. The ceiling was smooth and blank. Blank was safe.

She got her sight under control and lowered her gaze. The next thing she saw was Elena, sitting on the edge of the tall bed platform. Sleeping platform. The top was padded, and Elena was kicking her heels against the paneled side. Her unwavering constancy of spirit was a glowing balm to Valerie's nerves.

Elena's hair was tied back in a sleek, black tail, and sunburn added a rosy glow to her nose and ears.

Jack was off to one side, below Elena only because he was seated on the floor, wedged tight against the closed door to the bathroom cubicle. Valerie forced herself to glance past him instead of staring. It took a supreme effort, because there was a lot more of Jack to see than usual. The changes were superficial compared to Amy's shape-shift, but the result was far more dramatic.

He was *huge*. His clothes hadn't survived the power-induced increase in mass and height the way Amy's had, and he'd lost the cap and glasses that normally hid his face. His limbs had stretched, becoming too big and long for his body, and the blankets kilted around his waist barely covered the essentials. His skin was dark gray and pebbled, and his tufted ears and under-slung tusks would have looked at home on any gargoyle perched on a Gothic cathedral roof.

He had both arms wrapped up tight around his bent legs in an awkward hunch, and his face—in that moment, Valerie realized how rarely she saw Jack's eyes.

His irises were a deep, liquid brown, the spirit in his gaze was as gentle as his body was fearsome, and his fear was as vivid as his embarrassment. He was terrified he would be stuck in his present form.

Telling him to stop panicking would not be helpful. Valerie said, "You'll be fine. It's not a true shapeshift. The changes are energy-driven. But if you want me to stay, that cross on that wall has to go. It's an offense against nature."

Elena said, "Wait—what? Destroy Grace's religious icon? Without asking?"

Jack replied, "Stay out of this, tiger. Yasu, can we risk waking her to ask permission?"

His voice rumbled so low it thrummed in Valerie's sternum and long bones. She wondered *how is he enunciating around those teeth?* but would never ask.

"No. I'm barely stabilizing her now," Yasu said in a hoarse, tight voice.

Valerie stood on tiptoes, searching for the source of his voice. The doctor knelt far back on the platform, arms outstretched, hands resting below Valerie's view. His gray hair waved around his face like tendrils of seaweed in moving water.

He lifted his chin to her. "Hello, Val. You've jumped right to a conclusion I was approaching the long way. Do it, Jack. She's right. That infection has to be drained."

"Done," Jack said.

When he stood, Valerie gave up on discretion and let herself stare. He looked so much like a statue come to life she expected to hear stone grinding. The most stunning aspect was how well his outward form still reflected the essence she always saw.

He rubbed his bare hand across the image, one-two-three, leaving behind swathes of gray, roughened concrete. Dust and gravel pattered to the floor.

To Valerie, the air perceptibly brightened, and an invisible weight lifted off her shoulders. She inhaled deeply and let out a long, relieved sigh.

Jack dropped to a crouch and braced his arms on his bent knees. His gusty exhalation stopped short of a growl. "That was why I felt like rats were gnawing on my bones? *That*? How? Why?"

Valerie had some guesses. Gaias could transfer power. Grace had soaked that cross with enough energy to make it an emotional broadcast focus. She had been right to worry about Grace influencing people, back before the diagnostic evaluation.

For once, being right didn't feel like a victory. Valerie climbed the boxes to the platform and stepped carefully onto the soft surface.

Elena followed her, shuffling along on her knees—oh, to have young knees again—radiating a glow of anxious concern.

"Are you going to get mad at me? I know I shouldn't be here," she said, "I only wanted to talk to Grace, but then everything got out of control."

"Later, Elena." Valerie struggled to make sense of the tableau before her on the platform. Grace lay on her side atop the rumpled sheets with her hands tucked together beneath her chin. She wore what looked like a lacy white wedding gown, which made as little sense as the sight of Sal—wearing denim and work boots—holding her tight from behind in a spooning embrace.

Yasu had one hand on Grace's shoulder. The other rested on Sal's wavy salt-and-pepper hair. The doctor's talent looked like a bubble of clear water to Valerie's power-soaked senses. Oily threads of Grace's energy coiled in slow-motion through it, drifting past Sal to change in color and brighten before they circled back to her.

Blood seeped from Sal's nose, ears, and the corners of his tightly closed eyes. A bared-teeth grimace contorted his face. His hands were also covered in blood, although Grace's dress was clean.

Valerie said, "Someone fill me in, please. How did they get like that? What is Sal doing to her power output? And what is she *wearing*?"

"This?" Yasu stroked white satin with his thumb. His voice remained calm and precise despite having a dreamlike slowness. "It was flannel pajamas until I stirred up some old trauma, and she went into a power implosion. The spillover bumped my talent up high enough to slow her down, and Sal started doing his thing and put us in a holding pattern. Erasing that cross helped, but we're not improving. Sal, what do you say?"

"S'better." Sal stirred, licked blood off his lips. "We're still stuck dancing. I won't let her down. She won't give up, not if I keep giving her these hugs."

That made no sense. Valerie asked. "Is he delirious? Hallucinating?"

Elena spoke up, "I think he's showing her living memories. Happy ones." She leaned her head against Valerie. "Like the First Night presentations we got to experience in Senior History class. Retro-something or other. We could all see them at first. Even me."

"Retrocognition," Valerie supplied absently. "That isn't in Sal's profile."

And she couldn't think of any way visions of the past could be helping Grace.

Jack shifted his weight. The entire room vibrated. "It's *her* talent, not his. Her memories, too. He's only, I don't know, steering her."

Yasu said, "It might've been a latent ability of Sal's. Most of what Grace is doing seems to be unconscious, like the dress."

"And that damned cross." Jack rubbed the back of his neck. It sounded like tires on gravel. "And boosting us. She's in a bad place, Val. We all caught what she was re-living before Yasu damped her down. We need to snap her out of it."

Valerie bit her tongue on *And you think I know how?* "Let's see if I understand this. Sal is giving her happy memories?"

Jack's ears drooped. "Maybe? Memories definitely do something for her. She woke up when Amy and Shelly were down here swapping war stories about power accidents."

Elena said, "Maybe hearing about other people's powers damps hers down? Does that make any sense, or is it one of my ignorant null ideas?"

Her voice rose to a squeak, hopeful and doubtful at once. Valerie slipped an arm around the girl's shoulders and brought her in close for a quick hug. "It's a good idea. Move back, and I'll take a long, close look."

The energy flowing between Sal and Grace defied close examination, flickering at the edges of her vision. She bent closer, and one of the wavering strands rose to meet her. Energy tingled over her skin, and she no longer saw Sal lying on the bloodied sheets.

He was below her on a blue-striped blanket over sere yellow grass, but he wasn't the Sal she knew. She looked straight down into a smooth face untouched by age or pain, into sparkling eyes free from doubt. She felt him bare and scrawny against her bare flesh—*oh, no, not mine*—and he beamed up at her like he'd won the lottery.

"I love you," he said, passionate, beautiful, and so very young. "I will never hurt you. I'm not him. I'll take whatever broken crumbs you have to give me and sing hallelujahs."

Happiness—*not mine, no*—squeezed Valerie's heart.

The scene melted into another. She watched Sal spin in a circle with a giggling toddler held overhead like a trophy. The little girl shrieked her excitement while her twin raced around them, clapping her hands and laughing. Joy fizzed through Valerie and infused every cell of her being.

For an instant, it was as if Grace watched at her shoulder, then turned away. Anguish tore through the moment as other memories poured over Valerie—not like Sal's visions, nothing so concrete. These were more like dreams: brief sensations, deep emotions, and associations that made no logical sense.

The distinctive pull of a blade through meat; the sticky heat and odor of blood pouring over her skin; a crinkle of white taffeta, a whiff of cologne, twists of sharp pain, bruising impacts of fist on flesh, the brutal knowledge that she deserved pain, she was sinful, dirty, worthless, alone—

—And sunshine flooded over her again. Kisses and promises and laughter drove back the darkness, and *something* shoved Valerie hard, knocking her into herself again.

She had covered her eyes with her hands. She lowered them and stared at clean, soft fingers she felt certain should be calloused and shaped differently. Smaller. Younger.

Valerie had her own nightmares. She recognized the kind of wounds Sal was trying to staunch with his love, and her heart filled to overflowing. *Oh, Grace. How strong you are, to carry such scars and still fight so fiercely.*

She considered the details of what she had inadvertently shared, and insight lit up her mind like a starburst.

Sal's efforts to steer Grace away from her painful past hadn't failed. Grace was getting lost in other memories when she tried to imitate Sal's projecting technique. She was using his talent as a template in her struggle to wield a similar one.

Hope lifted Valerie's spirits. Clumsy as Grace's efforts were, they meant she was gaining some control. Before Yasu and Sal had contained her, she had amplified everyone here in a reflexive attempt to push away the power coming in.

That natural instinct was the deadly one. At the higher power rankings, uncontrolled release led to self-destruction. Discipline was the cornerstone of management.

Sharing Sal's memories was not distracting Grace, it was giving her *direction*. Learning power control by shared experience might be the key to her survival.

Logistical questions tumbled through Valerie's mind. Could Grace learn new skills faster than her rollover overwhelmed her with additional power? How much training would transfer from series to series? Could they risk bringing people here to work with her when she had so little control? Would anyone else trust her observe them so intimately?

First things first. Right now Grace's clairvoyance was undermining her ability to learn anything. If she couldn't tell the difference between reality and memory, despair and disorientation would defeat her before she started. But if she could *see* the difference—

Of course. Valerie took Grace's hand before doubt and fear could tarnish her idea. "Listen to me, Grace. I know you feel lost, but I can show you the way home."

The air sparkled with the hopes of everyone in it. Valerie closed her eyes. "Concentrate on my voice. Focus on me. Sal will help you. Look for the memory of the night I learned I was rolling. That should show you how my sight works, and then you're going to learn to use it for yourself."

28: THE WISE HEART WILL KNOW THE PROPER TIME

August 30, 414 Elm Drive, Elgin, Illinois

THERE WAS TOO much to learn. Grace regarded her week's worth of achievements and compared it to the huge DPS binder of rollover abilities with a growing sense of dismay. The list took up a whole ream of paper. She hadn't filled a single page yet.

How could she ever master every different talent that existed?

The hatch to the bunker creaked open, and a familiar mind tickled at hers like a cat stropping her ankles. Gabe's deep, cheerful voice came echoing down the ladder shaft. "Hello, the house! Ready for your bedtime story?"

"Can't wait," she called back, then yawned because the mere mention of bedtime was enough to make her want to sleep forever. *Everything* tired her out.

She did a quick centering exercise she'd picked up from Valerie and took her place at the little card table currently serving as her desk. The small decorative lamp on it threw soft light upward in a calming mosaic of colors, and the beaded shade made a happy chiming sound when she bumped the table.

The gaudiness and noise gave her a focus, helped her keep herself inside her skull. The tickle of Gabe's thoughts quieted. Picking them up again would be easy enough, once he gave permission. Courtesy mattered.

She had Valerie to thank for knowing how to block unwanted insights into people's minds—Valerie, and Sal, and a nice woman from Georgia who had spent a whole day chatting with Grace about her job as a telepathic patient advocate but never had told Grace her name.

The three of them had saved her from getting permanently lost in her past and dragging everyone around her into the mess. Valerie had shown her how to *see* what was happening, Sal had taught her how he kept emotions locked inside himself most of the time, and the medical advocate had provided the last important element: how to recognize and protect the concept of *self* while reaching outside that boundary into the chaos of *other*.

The woman's non-verbal communication techniques had translated well into filtering a wide variety of extrasensory inputs. Grace hadn't fully mastered the trick of blocking visions of the past when they pounced on her, but she was willing to believe she *would* figure it out. She only needed more practice.

So much practice.

She'd been at this for days now. All day. Every day. Volunteers came, assured her she didn't need to know their names, and left after teaching her new tricks. Some powers were harder than others. She still couldn't 'port despite Heather and Shelly's best demonstrations, despite an afternoon spent with a Marine of Amy's acquaintance who told the best stories and left her a recipe for borscht. She could give energy to Amy and Jack, but she couldn't figure out how she'd reshaped them.

That failure was a major frustration. She'd already developed inhuman traits once by accident. It was bound to happen again. The C variant in her designation stood for Carnie, as in carnival freak. Shapeshifting was high on her want-to-learn list.

Gabe was helping her with a different palette of abilities. For the last two nights he'd been telling her about a riot he helped de-escalate into a snowball fight. By concentrating on the memories connected to his words, Grace was training herself to imitate his particular brand of energy manipulation.

Last night he'd digressed into explaining how he'd moved out of the city to keep his ex-boss from asking for favors. It had been a good lesson, but not the original one. She wanted to master the trick of his ability by the time tonight's session ended.

Which still left her with an infinite number of others to learn.

How could she possibly master them all? If energy flowed down a new and unmapped channel when it crashed over her next time, she would burn herself up, or drown herself, or freeze herself to death.

No. I will not. She resolutely shoved the worry into a mental box and locked it tight. She would collect Gabe's ability tonight. She had to succeed.

Gabe walked into the room like he owned it, as usual, turned the other folding chair around backward and swung a leg over the seat. He was limber for a man of his years and girth, and he grinned across the table at Grace as he set out two plastic bags full of candy.

"I have visual aids for this part," he said. "Or rewards. Tasty either way."

The lamplight gave his smile a menacing edge. Or maybe

Grace was reading into the visuals what she sensed of his essence. Despite his easy chortles and twinkly smiles, the big old man felt fundamentally dangerous. He dressed more formally than most of the team, with his collared button-up shirts and pressed denims, and inside he was as twitchy as a barn cat watching a mouse hole tonight.

He had secrets. They tasted like Amy's secrets, without the clean, sharp flavor of the Marine's centered honesty. Grace had so far successfully avoided seeing what those secrets were. Courtesy mattered. *Consent* mattered. But she knew they were there. They sat salty on her tongue and made her nose itch.

Gabriel lined up a row of gummy bears facing a row of candy fish. The plastic bags crinkled as he picked out the colors he wanted. His big Santa Claus beard bristled as he pursed his lips. "Where did I leave off yesterday?"

"The two gangs were—" Grace had to stop to yawn. *Why did plastic have to be so noisy?* "Sorry. They'd put down their knives and guns to pick up snowballs. You said that would be a good breakpoint."

"I said that because you were falling asleep on me. We're wearing you out with all this work. You're a trooper." He moved a yellow fish forward, into a patch of golden lamplight, and shook the bag of candies. "Okay, I was standing here, next to Big Bobby Johnson, the snot-nosed little rabble-rouser."

He spun a tale of two groups of adolescents who didn't want to fight but had boasted themselves into a corner. Grace concentrated on his descriptions of building ice blocks and spinning snow piles. The scents of sugar and artificial fruit wafted across the table. Energy swirled around her, chill and hot, running through her mental fingers, defying control.

The candy smell intensified, and the rustling grew louder, drowning out Gabe's voice.

She was elsewhere—else*when*—standing in a dark room,

licking her lips and tasting raspberry gloss. She hugged the crinkly taffeta dress tight to stop the noise.

Her heart thudded hard, feeling like it was about to jump out of her chest. The chapel looked strange and terrifying at night. In the daytime, the skylights were bright with colored glass and made the big room fresh and airy. Now they were dim rectangles far overhead. Starshine touched the backs of pews with silver and shone into the Blessing Room, casting dim rectangles of light across the quilted spread on the big, four-poster bed.

The doors only opened for this solemn ritual in the hours of night. It was meant to be private, intimate, but the unfamiliar sounds and shadows were terrifying. She tiptoed to her place and settled against the headboard, smoothing her skirts to silence.

It was not a comfortable way to sit in a dress, but hiding under the covers was forbidden. The women had told her that when they helped her to dress and coached her in her role.

Her part was to be silent, patient, and humble. She was to be exalted.

All she felt was fear. That was wrong. That was failure. She should be thankful to be here, grateful she was worthy of this honor despite the taint in her blood. Instead, she was so scared she wanted to throw up and cry.

Fear was proof of her sinful nature, her father would say, and he would shake his head at her. What a disappointment she was, smarter than any girl needed to be, too flawed to live up to ideals of piety and gratitude he tried so hard to teach her.

A stronger woman would put her faith in God and fear not.

She bit the inside of her cheek, distracting herself with the little pain, and blinked back tears. She would make him proud. She *would*.

Nervousness was normal, she had been assured. *Remember*

it's an honor, the women whispered, with warning squeezes of their hands. Once this ritual was done, she would be a woman in the eyes of God. With this most personal of blessings from the head of the church, she could take her place at another man's side and be a good wife and mother.

Terrified butterflies fluttered inside her stomach. Nothing else remained in there, not after all the times she had vomited since morning. She breathed deep, smoothed her hands over her hair, and ran her tongue across her teeth. Every part of her had been bathed and purified, scrubbed and scraped bare inside and out, all to make her ready for her father's touch.

She closed her eyes and wondered how much it would hurt.

Warm air caressed her face, and a rumbly, *friendly* voice said, "I can't believe you fell into a backflash right in the middle of my story. Was I that boring? Can you hear me yet, or do I have to freeze your eyebrows to wake you up?"

Freeze my what?

Grace opened her eyes. A flood of colors, textures, sounds, odors, and flavors dissolved the sterile past. Sensation anchored her to her body again, rooting her in time and place.

The beaded lampshade swung back and forth. Rainbows danced over the tabletop where the small army of candy fish had routed most of the gummy bears.

"Oh, dear," she said.

Gabe popped a green fish into his mouth. "You're back already? Good. That was quick."

It hadn't felt quick from her side, but time was one of many things that behaved oddly for her now. "I'm glad. It was a bad one."

"I only caught a tiny hint, which is progress. You are getting the sensory and mental stuff locked down."

Gabe had been watching his props before Grace had gone

wandering into the dark valleys of memory. Now he was staring at her chest.

Of course he is. Grace glared down at the awful dress, which made a reappearance whenever the horror show of her past rose up to literally haunt her. A quick thought transformed the confection of taffeta and lace back into her favorite fleecy loungewear.

Why can't I transform my body that easily? She'd done so several times without consciously willing it but never by choice. Her flesh might be malleable, but the talent did not respond to her will.

No one had asked her to explain the significance of the dress, a mercy for which she gave thanks every time she ended up wearing it. "I'm sorry. I was paying attention, but the memories ambush me. It's so frustrating."

"They're called backflashes," Gabe said. "Trust me on the lingo. When a memory is backed by R-factor energy, it's a backflash. I worked with my share of clairvoyants, back when I wore a detective's badge. I saw enough surprise furniture appearances and dancing corpses for a lifetime. Don't stress over perfection. Even the best retro specialists get blindsided."

"So a dress is nothing shocking? Good." Grace picked up a red candy fish. She could be grateful for small blessings. "Lauren and Maggie both adore these. You're lucky you have any Latin Dukes to show me."

Gabriel's teeth showed in a grin. "So you did catch some of the story. Good."

"Better than good." She bit into the candy and concentrated on the details she'd absorbed before the past sucker-punched her.

The decapitated fish grew a coating of hoarfrost. A whisper of a breeze carried the scent of winter through the room, and her whole body relaxed into the streams of power that were trying to fill her up.

Manipulating the temperature of water was ridiculously simple and used up a lot of energy. Other water sources burbled happy welcomes to her from the pipes in the walls, whispered greetings from the soil beneath the concrete floor, called to her in yearning, distant voices large and low like whale song.

It could accept any energy she needed to divert—although not without consequences. It was nice to know she could dump power into water for short respites from the overload, but she would have to be careful. Accidentally freezing Lake Michigan would be an awkward side effect.

She looked up to see Gabe's white eyebrows risen halfway up his forehead to his receding hairline. She said, "You got a fun power. I like this."

He replied, "I don't know whether to clap or cry. It took me weeks of practice in camp to get that kind of fine control."

"I have good teachers, and I'm a motivated student." Grace popped the frozen candy into her mouth and melted it on her tongue. Gabe didn't need to know she could freeze him solid as easily as she had the candy. "I need to learn fast if I want to live."

"That's a good goal." Gabe rubbed a hand over his beard. "Look, Grace. Someone needs to be honest with you, so I'm going to say what no one else wants to tell you. If I don't, you'll probably catch it from my thoughts."

She raised a hand to stop him before he embarrassed them both. "No one has to tell me. I came into E and F primes first, remember? Everyone is thinking *wanting isn't enough*. You think I'm a lost cause, that this is delaying the inevitable."

She also felt the denial most of them used to hide that belief from themselves, knew how hard they struggled to show encouragement. She only heard the despair as a whisper in her head when that particular talent pushed itself to the forefront: *she can't last much longer.*

Storm surge could batter the strongest stone to gravel. She learned fast, but power kept flooding into new talents before she was ready to handle the last one. "I understand why everyone worries," she said, "but you're wrong. If we keep working, I will overcome this."

The words had the sugar taste of truth. God's plan still included survival. She felt that truth as a thrum in her bones, a quiet promise that buoyed her up like a chorus of a joyous song.

"I hope so," Gabe said. "If anyone can get through this, it'll be you."

He packed away the remaining candies into their bags. "Sal says you're the stubbornest person he's ever met. And the smartest. You know he's still head over heels for you, right? I can't decide if it's pathetic or admirable."

The sweetness on Grace's tongue went sour.

Poor Sal. She could give him respect, affection in abundance, and love of a new and different kind, but that was all. Her heart would never again open to him in the same way it once had. The scars ran too deep. "Admire him," she said. "I do. I'm bad at hating but worse at forgiving, and he loves me anyway. That makes him the bravest, strongest man I have ever known." *So there.* "Part of me will never stop loving him, and I give thanks every day that he's here. I owe him everything."

"You owe him." Gabe shook his head. *Twitch* went the cat's tail he didn't physically have, and intangible claws flexed. "He likes to talk, your man does, and I was a detective. I've found out a few things I'd better tell you before you pull it out of my head and flip out."

Too late. Bits and pieces of knowledge surrounded her in a choking, stinking cloud.

He knew her secrets.

Grace closed her eyes and clenched her fists against a roaring tangle of emotions that left her unable to breathe and turned her blood to ice and fire. *Guilty. Trapped.*

Power tugged at her, promising escape. In her panic, she grabbed it and let it yank her *elsewhere*. Then her connection to it broke with a sharp pain like a rubber band snapping against her whole skin.

Her eyes were tear-filled, but she knew she was in her garden before her vision cleared. A lingering pinch at her collar bone had her rubbing at the withered remains of Shelly's transport tag. The flexible bit of plastic had stuck tight through all her other changes. Now it came loose and fluttered to the ground.

Crickets chirped, and the moist, still air smelled of compost and jasmine. Moonlight showed Grace pale blades of grass under her bare feet. The patio light was off. The house was dark but for the kitchen night-light.

How late is it? she wondered and knew the answer as surely and easily as she had known where she was without seeing it. The night was more than half over, she'd felt weary a short time ago, but now she felt as fresh as if she'd slept away a lazy Saturday afternoon.

The effortless sense of time and the absence of exhaustion combined to horrify her.

How much more strangeness would be visited upon her? Would she still be herself if she was changed beyond recognition?

God performs wonders that cannot be fathomed, she sternly told herself, *and miracles beyond counting.*

The Book of Job had been a particular comfort of late. She must follow this path wherever it took her. *Whatever comes, accept and embrace it.*

The advice was much easier to give than to follow.

A square of light brightened the lawn, and the unmistakable sound of a window opening came from above and behind her. “Holy crap, Grace, are you okay?” Shelly asked. “You scared the daylights out of me, and I killed the tag on reflex. Sorry. I bet it stung like crazy.”

“I’m fine.” More than that, she understood why her power had unnerved Shelly so much from the start. Their talents were remarkably similar. How odd that Shelly only used it for moving things when she might do more.

She collected her wandering thoughts. “Um. I didn’t mean to ‘port like that. What should I do now?”

Shelly smoothed her hands over her hair. “Heck if I know, honey. I’ll wake Yasu.”

An unspoken thought came across loud and clear: *if she can teleport herself, how will we contain her if she goes nova on us?* And with that thought came images of explosions and tidal waves and crowds of people falling as one, dissolving into screams—*we’ll have to act fast and go orbital, no other choice—*

Grace wrenched her mind clear of the marching progression of thoughts. Choices grew like trees sprouting branches made of death, and they came from Amy, who was coming around the house from the front porch. Other sleeping minds woke, leaving Grace adrift on a sea of confusion, alarm—and betrayal.

She had entrusted her life to these people, and they were plotting to kill her.

Wait—did she deserve death? She’d left that judgment in Amy’s hands for a good reason. Was she out of control? Would she know?

Panic threatened again.

Her ears rang with the sound of Gabe calling to her, voice sharp with authority. “Grace Reed, you get your butt back down here this instant!”

If he had been angry, if Grace had felt *anything* from him other than exasperation, she might have done something stupid. But his emotions felt exactly like hers when the girls were being aggravating. The familiarity was a lifeline.

She followed his feelings back to him on reflex—*pop*—and only wondered if it was a good idea after she was back in the bunker standing behind her chair at the table.

A second after that, she realized she hadn't *heard* Gabe—and more, he hadn't expected his summons to work. His fear-tainted surprise hit her like a slap across the face, and blue-white energy flared around him as the shock turned defensive.

Power called to power, and Grace lost her precarious control on the energy pouring into her. *Accept, accept, accept,* she chanted as shudders wracked her body. Her clothes wriggled around and audibly protested being clothes instead of fusing to her skin in the shape of feathers or fur or leathery armor. Red light pulsed through her vision.

Fire rose, called to life by Gabe's ice, and the floor shook as stone woke inside her heart. Metal shrieked, chains rattled, and a strident alarm went off, adding to the chaos—and she recognized the mundane source of the flashing red light.

Gabe had hit the crash switch to seal the bunker.

No—she would have cried out if she could have drawn breath to scream. His action would cost him his life if Grace could not contain herself, and she could not.

She didn't want any more deaths on her conscience, but she could not contain herself.

Couldn't.

I'm sorry. I tried.

The world poured over her in drowning torrents and carried her into chaos.

29: CAST OFF THE TROUBLES OF YOUR BODY

Beneath 414 Elm Drive, Elgin, IL

IMMEASURABLE ENERGIES SATURATED Grace's body. It didn't hurt. It was intoxicating. She wanted to laugh and weep at once, to run and dance and shout, but most of all, she wanted to wield that power like a hammer or a whip or a sword.

Oh, it was so tempting to let the *allness* flow free, to rage, to sweep the face of the earth with cleansing fire. It would feel *good* to let it loose.

No.

Good did not mean right.

Thou shalt not commit murder, that was the commandment, and she would not err the same way twice. She cast her soul away from the dizzying tumult in her body and mind, threw herself into the thrashing cords and coils of power, and gave everything she was into God's mercy. If this immensity must destroy anyone, let it be her alone.

She hung in eternity. Peace came on delicate glittering

wings, in a soft embrace of warmth, a sweet stillness like the slow unfurling of new leaves in spring sunlight.

And for the first time Grace could ever remember, she was not afraid.

The truth was so simple. Not easy, never that, but pure, singular, and wondrous. She had been right to think this power impossible to contain or master, but it need not destroy her. No mortal was ever meant to *hold* this might, but it could be wielded *through* her, in trust.

There would be sacrifices. She would have to surrender all she had, all that she was.

Could she accept that? Would she?

Maybe it should have been harder to let go. She'd fought so much to get this far, worked so hard, loved her children so fiercely.

Letting go was the easiest thing in the world.

I will, she whispered into the silence and the dark, blew softly on the husk of her old life and let it drift free, and the covenant was made.

The raging flood quieted to the glassy stillness of a pond after a storm, and the scent of new-turned earth rose around her as she remembered having a nose and lungs again.

Her body recalled a familiar shape, one that felt not *right,* but manageable, and she was whole once more.

"Oh, my goodness," she whispered. *No wonder this experience breaks people.*

Everything she had struggled to attain was hers now. Reality was hers for the taking, for the sensing, for the shaping. Tapping into the currents of life around her and diverting them was as secure as breathing: effortless and automatic to a certain point, fully within her control beyond that.

Foreboding rippled through her awareness. This was only a trough between waves, a pause between birthing pangs, a chance to recruit herself and absorb an abundance of riches before more was added. The next, last inrushing of her rollover would be indescribable.

What a terrifying, glorious prospect. *Of such miracles are galaxies made.*

The bunker was a mess. Debris from broken furniture and tumbled crates spilled across concrete now marred by yawning cracks and bulging heaves. Weak illumination from battery-powered emergency lights made everything look flat and yellow. Haze hung in the still air, thick with a stench of burned plastic and hot metal.

Her eyes were watering.

Gabe stood motionless before her, across the shattered remnants of the table. Energy flickered icy blue in his eyes, glowed frigid white around his body, made a frosty lacework of his beard. Every hair was standing on end, staticky and wispy and covered in ice, including his eyebrows.

Grace wanted to giggle, but she didn't dare. If she laughed, Gabe would startle, and the resulting confrontation would turn deadly.

Possible futures wove themselves around the room in a tapestry of threads, most of them frayed and scarlet with Gabe's blood. Grace stood quiet, hands open, and waited.

This was not the time to let her light shine. Fear hardened hearts and birthed atrocity, and she held fearful power now. For a few fragile days yet, until her rollover was complete, it was imperative she not be seen as a threat.

It would take the wrath of Armageddon to kill her, but the deed could yet be done. Her conscience demanded she avoid those futures at any cost.

Gabe's frigid power pulsed, squeezing snow from the still air, squeezing Grace's lungs with its arctic touch. His determination was colder yet. "Don't move," he said. "If you've got yourself under control, nod and say yes."

"Yes." Grace turned aside a thousand ugly futures with that word. "Thank you for sealing us in. That was brave of you."

"Not brave. Desperate." *Just doing my job,* he didn't say aloud. His satisfaction and relief were ringing hallelujahs of emotion, impossible to ignore. "I thought we were both goners, but you damped that flare like a pro."

"It was different than the rest. I think—I think it was the last surge. No—" she paused to savor a revelation. There would be no more weird flares of energy on any level mortals could sense. She knew that the way she knew the sun would rise and the planet would continue to turn. "I *know* it was the last."

Gabe's eyes were glacially cold. "Got a gut feeling, huh? You just know you're done."

"Yes." It was a lie and the truth at once. "It's hard to describe. Is that normal?"

"Common enough." Gabe smoothed down his hair and beard, then wiped ice-melt from his brows. "Safety tests are a formality for most primes. I'm glad for you. And for me. Your certification will be a cakewalk compared to tonight."

Grace let his thoughts flow around her, bitter and cool, emphatically not her own. It was so easy to interpret them now. Too easy.

He was prowling and twitchy inside, stalking around his many secrets, and the sensation was intimidating. The things Gabe knew about her past were like mice compared to the collection of Leviathans that lurked deeper in his memories.

Rather than meet those monsters by accident, Grace put him at a mental distance and asked a question to focus his thoughts on something practical and grounded. "How long are we stuck down here like this?"

They weren't stuck, exactly. She could 'port herself and

Gabe out any time she wanted. The question was, would that be wise? The power she carried was enough to save or destroy multitudes, but it didn't come with an instruction manual. She was much closer to omnipotence than omniscience and a long way from either.

Gabe kicked at splinters of wood and bits of concrete rubble, began stacking it up. Prowling and twitchy. "Lockdown triggered the anti-port barriers, and you blew the telecom, so they'll be on a seventy-two-hour hands-off protocol up top. Jack being a cautious S.O.B, there's likely a Mercury intervention team on-site too."

The unbalanced pile of debris collapsed under its own weight. He abandoned it and settled onto one of the remaining crates near the exit doorway. The conduit leading to the uncovered lockdown switch rose at his shoulder like a vine with one red, dangerous fruit at its tip.

He said, "Short answer, three days—long after I've suffocated—or whenever we unlock the hatch. I'm too shaky to go up that ladder, and I'm sure as heck not letting a trigger-happy Marine catapult you into orbit before you know what hit you."

Grace put her back to the sleeping platform and sat down with her legs crossed like a child at a campfire. *Look at me, innocent and harmless.* "I'm in no rush."

Unsaid things folded in pattern after pattern, more like a kaleidoscope than a tapestry now.

Jack had decided against calling in Mercury on Amy's recommendation—but sharing that news with Gabe would set off a cascade that ended in countless deaths. Confessing she could open the hatch from where she was sitting would also end in bloodshed. Delivering reassurances to anyone up top by telepathy set off the most destructive event chain of all.

The tumbling designs of rejection, conflict, and carnage mesmerized her. Choices glowed like gems in the shifting composition, their arrangement changing by the second, rippling with decision points missed and actions taken elsewhere.

The act of watching the future shaped it. She concentrated on the present, lest she be lured into madness.

And Gabe said, "Grace? Can you hear me? Your eyes have stars in them."

Stars? "Sorry, I was distracted. If you want to wait the full seventy-two hours, I can keep the air fresh. Or 'port us past the lockdown barriers."

Gabe frowned, rumpling up his beard. "Gaia, right. You're prime in every power."

He was wondering if Grace was strong enough to manipulate his mind and if his defensive talent would warn him in time.

Was this God's joke on her, that she had been gifted a heaping share of the persuasive abilities she'd once feared? "I have more choices than other primes," she told him gently, "but I'm no more powerful." *Not yet.* "The difference between *can* and *will* is all that stands between any of us and damnation."

Gabe thought long and hard over his next move, and the impression of a hunting cat intensified. He was back to nosing and pawing at secrets. "My gut says you're safely rolled—stable and in full control. My senses agree. I want to believe you—but I would hate to be wrong."

That declaration brought his biggest secret rolling to the surface, and what a whopping behemoth it was. Gabe was the failsafe whose existence Amy had suspected, the agent embedded by the Special Directives in case a dangerous Camp Liberty client lost control and had to be lethally contained.

No, his mandate was broader than Amy's. He had been sent here specifically to kill Grace if her rollover didn't do the job for him.

Her first, stunned reaction was, *That explains a lot about Gaia survival rates*. She wrinkled her nose as other ugly details landed in her awareness.

Gabe's rollover talent was *much* more powerful than he let on, and there was a tiny hole deep inside him where remorse should have lived. He had killed, again and again, on the orders of others—fire elementals, seismic talents, telepaths—and regretted not a single murder.

A day ago, this situation would have terrified Grace to frozen immobility. A decade ago, she would have *cowered* before a man armed with deadly authority and armored in self-righteousness.

Now he was only a baffling surprise. The void in his heart had smooth edges as if it had been cut out and cauterized. She could hardly ask how or when he'd lost his conscience, or if he'd removed it himself, but she did wonder, and she grieved for his loss.

And the question remained. *Why he hadn't acted?* He'd had many an opportunity to eliminate her before tonight, and yet, she lived.

Maybe he had been waiting for the right moment, the way some predators felt compelled to play with their prey? If so, he had waited too long.

She couldn't hate him for being the way he was, no more than she could hate a barn cat for its lack of manners. But just as she wouldn't keep a feral cat in her house, she wanted him out of her life.

"You aren't wrong," she said, watching for any sign he was about to pounce. *I'm done as far as anyone will be able to feel or see.* "But I'm fine with waiting here as long as you are."

"Long enough to recoup the energy I dumped into defense, then. And don't you dare offer to pump any into me, thank you." He shifted, cleared his throat. "It's weird to sit here and do nothing, though."

The complaint trailed away into a shrug. Chill thoughts like lines of frost filled the room. Grace inspected the designs they made on the cold window of Gabe's soul.

He's tired and afraid of something other than me. And he doesn't like being afraid. She offered him a shiny distraction, the way she would dangle a bit of yarn for the icy cat he so resembled. "What were you about to tell me before things got so exciting?"

Gabe laughed, short and sharp. "When you panicked, you mean? Are you sure you can handle it now? If we're both wrong about your rollover status, you might pull the roof down."

"The past can never hurt me again." Grace was thrilled to realize that was true. "And I'd like to hear what you think about my secrets, rather than catch you thinking too loud."

The world held its breath with her while Gabe looked around the room. "That's valid. And it would kill time."

He left his crate to tug at a tangle of beads and wire and came up with a dusty bag of candies. He sat down right in front of Grace, mirroring her—a gesture of trust if ever she'd seen one—and rummaged in the bag for a gummy bear.

"It started when I dug into the mystery of where you got your money," he said. "I found out you were hiding from more than your husband. Felt like finding a treasure chest in a muck heap. A lot of people have been looking for you for a long time, Sarah Carter."

Carter. Her maiden name, soiled beyond redemption, buried for more than a decade. Grace waited for fear to jolt through her like electricity, waited for her lungs to collapse and squeeze her heart into a useless lump.

Nothing happened. A tingle of nervousness was as close as she could get to the knotted mix of terrors that had driven her from her home into the wide world. "I ran from a lot of things," she admitted. "Including myself."

"And I found you." Gabe sounded terribly smug. His beard bristled around his grin. "I'm sitting with the woman accused of embezzling millions of dollars from the Salvation Assembly Church, killing the High Elder, and then disappearing. There are no official photos—that is one seriously weird religious quirk, by the way—but I mentioned the name to Sal, and he should never, ever play poker. You really are her."

"I was." Grace's breath caught in her throat. The fear had died to ash, but guilt still had the power to sting. *Coward. Thief. Monster. Murderer.*

"What did you do with the rest of the money?"

Anger chipped an edge onto her shame, and energy flickered to life along her skin. She squeezed her hands and let it seep through her into the earth, where it would only surprise earthworms and nourish bacteria. *Grounding.* She took a deep breath, tasted vengeance in the air, exhaled it again. *Centering.*

"There were never millions. It was a trust, around a quarter million. The things the church did with money—the dirty accounting would've come out when Father's estate was settled. They blamed it all on me. My disappearance washed it away."

Gabe snorted. "Bank fraud. Why am I not shocked? How much of it was real?"

"My mother's family was rich. They tied her money up tight when she joined the church. She tithed her trust income. When she rolled and went to God, the income came to me, not Father. She had a safe deposit box of little gold bars too. Whenever Father took me to town to make a quarterly withdrawal for the church, he bought more bars for the box. He called it my dowry and warned me that the other Elders didn't need to know."

"Oh-ho! So there was embezzling! Wait—no." Gabe

frowned, working his way through it. "Your father might've been skimming, but it was your money either way."

"In the eyes of the church, it was all his." The elders had betrayed her in so many ways. "After Father was dead, the other Elders came to me and told me I had to make a sacrifice to protect his legacy and wash the Devil's taint from my blood."

"And then they smeared your name."

"After I signed papers releasing the trust to them." They had laid their trap well. The memories burned like acid. The threat of exposure and prosecution had put her right where they wanted her, safely under their thumbs. "It didn't matter. I had Josh—Sal—and my babies, my friends."

She had found happiness in her prison, but she had lost work she loved, the planning and building the elders had hated because it put her too much in the world. Her freedom was the real sin they'd punished, and she had accepted that penance.

But after years of truce, the elders had gone to Sal and lied, telling him *she* had asked *them* for the boon of his return.

They had feared she would become unruly again without a man to tame her the way her father had done for so long. And they'd believed they could control him.

They never had understood Sal's strengths or her weakness. If they'd left well enough alone, she would have stayed on the Ranch forever, doubting but obedient—and she would have died there in rollover, under their watch.

God did work in mysterious ways.

"What happens now?" she said. "We've been living off the gold Father set aside. Are you going to turn me in to the authorities?"

Would he try to kill her? Would he pounce now that he'd played with her long enough?

"Nah." Gabe sounded as pleased as any cat who'd ever dropped a dead mouse at his owner's feet. "It was a puzzle. I solved it, and I wanted you to know that I knew. That's the end of it."

"But I'm a wanted criminal."

"No, you aren't." His predatory glee was joined by another emotion. Not condemnation. His satisfaction was a cool, refreshing breeze. "First, your father's death was registered as a fatal rollover. That ruling is not open to change. He had a religious exemption in place at the time of that rollover. Second, you were an *alleged* thief two legal name changes back. Charges aren't a conviction. Third—do you want to hear some delicious irony?"

Gabe's words went chasing after bitter, metallic-tasting thoughts now. Grace held her breath and nodded. Better to hear the irony than be clobbered over the head with it.

He tossed a gummy bear into his mouth and gestured with the next one. "Those open Sarah Carter warrants grew into a long, quiet Federal investigation of the Salvation Assembly Ranch. Property access surveillance, comm taps, and records searches, the works. The FBI had decades of cold cases that dead-ended at the Ranch's gates—murder, rape, blackmail, bigamy, you name it. Because of you, they were able to start building cases."

That was a glorious revelation. "Why haven't I heard about it?" She had obsessively searched for news about the Ranch every day without fail.

"It's ongoing. They're nowhere near ready to wrap, but I have friends in low places. Warrants *will* go out eventually. Count on it. And once those weasels start turning on each other, everything will wash clean."

He cleared his throat. "And fourth, if that didn't clear you, you'd still be safe from prosecution. Applying for a Family Safety relo was pure genius. *All* past identities cease to exist legally unless you sign away the seal or die. When

Sarah Moretti was archived, Sarah Carter went into the vault too."

"I always thought if the elders found me—never mind." Ignorance had brought her misery, not bliss.

Her eyes went to the rough, bare patch of concrete where she had invested a simple painting with the tortured, twisted emotions she had hidden from herself. So much pain inflicted with the best of intentions. She imagined the whole wall clean and white, cleansed of the past, and it became so.

Gabe glanced at it, then back to her. "Clean slate. Exactly."

"Should I tell the girls any of this?"

"I wouldn't trust them with the time of day. They're teenagers. Maybe when they're older. Maybe never. Some things never need to see the light of day."

That was as close as he would come to revealing his secret.

He put a hand on her knee. If his tail had been real, he would have been lashing it back and forth. "Here's my main point, Grace. I know real evil when I see it, and that's what I saw when I dug into your past. Jail is too good for the men you escaped. My hat's off to you for getting away clean."

This was why he had rejected his duty: respect, or something akin to it. Boredom played an odd role too. This abdication would turn him from hunter to prey, but he was eager for the challenge: could he disappear as well as she had?

Grace couldn't grasp his reasoning in its entirety. His heart was hollow and savage, and that made his world view a chilly, alien thing.

She laid her hand over his and said, "Thank you," because that covered everything spoken and unspoken.

"You're welcome," he replied. "I would gladly shake the hand of whoever slit your father's throat."

She looked him straight in the eyes. "You know you already have."

“Sassy woman.” He stood up. “Go ahead and take us up? I’ve said my piece, and I’ve zero doubt you’re through your rollover safe and sound. Time for me to go on about my business, and for you get on with being Grace Reed, mother, homeowner, licensed general contractor, and the first living Gaia prime rollover in half a century.”

She couldn’t be all those things, but the idea made Gabe happy, so she patted his hand again. “I will do my best. That’s a promise.”

He gifted her with a twinkly, merry smile. “And from you, that means something. ”

30: THROUGH WISDOM A HOUSE IS ESTABLISHED

Early hours of August 31, 414 Elm Drive, Elgin, IL

SHE 'PORTED Gabe up and outside with her to the green, moonlit warmth of her garden near her apple tree. Its gnarled branches were bowed under the weight of their fruit, and the cider-sharp scent of windfalls rose from underfoot.

A chiming alarm went off inside the garden shed in the far corner of the yard, near the bunker. The yard and house lights were already on, casting blocks of brightness over the patio and vegetable beds. Jack, Amy, and another Tee-series woman stood at the back wall of the house.

The newcomer was halfway between Jack and Amy in height and bulk, and she had a spinal crest like Amy, although hers was low and bumpy. She had on leggings and a yellow, flowery, kaftan-like top that belted at her waist. Amy and Jack wore webbed harnesses over stout canvas trousers. Jack had swapped out his ever-present tinted glasses for a helmet with a clear visor.

All three wore bracers that would send an alarm to others if

Grace used any influential powers on them, and energy glittered around them as they moved to block her and Gabe in the corner. Their tense alertness and the ambient energy made her nerves sing. The night tasted of bitterness, and violence tumbled through the patterns of the world.

If she had to flee, the fence behind her would be no obstacle, and she had the choice of up or down as well. But no—she lost herself in the awful possibilities of each choice.

Gabe took her by the elbow and hauled her forward to a conversational distance. "Hail fellows, well met," he said, which was apparently some kind of code because the others relaxed.

The blood-colored pieces of future tipped and fell into new patterns, ones filled with spots where hope shone through. And Gabe said, "It was a textbook high-tide surge. She feels solid to me now but judge for yourselves."

They did just that, for the longest ten seconds in Grace's life. Their suspicion prickled at her gently, like a baby hedgehog's spines. Jack spoke first. "Impressive baseline aura, but it's smooth as glass."

He lifted the visor on his helmet and tapped a button on the side. "We're clear. Shelly. Stand by."

The new Tee said, "If you hadn't told me she was rolling, I'd never know. Congrats, Ms. Reed. It won't be official until you're certified, but you are looking great. Well done."

"Thank you," Grace said, and "sorry for the fuss," and "Nice to meet you," because she couldn't think of anything better to add.

"Same," the new Tee replied with a fang-flashing grin. "I'm Kris, by the way. With a K, for Kristiana. Mister Fiori, I'm here to sub for you, although it looks like I won't be needed for long."

"Do we have to chat here? This stinky apple muck is ruining my shoes." Gabe stalked past the Tees toward the house. "My back aches, and I think my blood sugar's low, but why do I need a sub?"

"Your grandson is in the hospital." Jack caught up with him, stopped him with a gentle touch on his shoulder. "Your daughter called maybe a half-hour after you hit the lockdown switch. As if things weren't complicated enough already."

"Dammit. Billy has a heart condition." Gabe ran his hands through his hair. "I need to be there. I need to go."

Gabe sounded distraught—he *felt* worried—but Grace could see into that tiny, desolate emptiness where he made the emotions happen now. He had no grandson. He had no *daughter*. One thing was true: he wanted urgently to leave. This was his chance to escape the poisoned cage of his life and run free.

Jack said, "We've got you covered. Yasu packed your kit, and Shells has your home co-ords cued up. Will that work?"

"That's great, man. One sec."

He tromped back to give Grace a quick hug and spoke softly at her ear. "Trust your trolls. I know you can because I was told not to." Then he put her to arm's length and gave her one last jolly smile. "Good luck with the rest of your life, Grace Reed. Don't expect Christmas cards or plan any reunions. Not my style."

Then he nodded to Jack, who muttered, "He's ready, Shells."

The universe spun itself into a bright web around Gabe, and he was gone.

"Godspeed," Grace whispered after him.

His advice clung to her thoughts like a hopeful vine tendril, exerting relentless, patient pressure. She didn't *want* to build her life on an ugly framework of deceit and silence. Not again.

The Tees escorted her back to the house, enveloping her in their powerful auras and looming over her like trees. As they reached the patio, Amy said, "I'm glad you beat the odds, Grace. Unbelievably glad."

"I'm glad too." The Marine's warm, vivid happiness was a benediction, and trust bloomed in its wake. "And I need your help now more than ever."

Jack frowned down at her. "Relax. We aren't going anywhere until you're certified."

Grace opened her mouth to explain the threat she faced.

Words poured out in a stream she could not control, could not stop, could not comprehend. *Bloody footprints of murder, hope in a cloak of silence, sand spilling out, mountains of death*—signs and portents spilled from her lips in a cascade like the roar of a waterfall or the howl of a storm.

When the message was done with her, she covered her mouth with both hands. "What *was* that?" she whispered between her fingers. Her raw throat healed itself on a swallow. "I don't know what I said."

"That's okay. Everyone else does." Amy rubbed at the down-curved horns guarding her cheekbones. They were larger and more pronounced than they'd been a few moments earlier. "Guess that answers the question no one was asking. Gaias get stuck with sybil episodes like regular precogs."

"Zip it," Jack snapped. "Wait one while I button us up."

He turned in place to inspect the yard as if the blameless plants might now hide threats. "You caught that?" he asked Yasu over his radio connection, nodding when he got confirmation. "Good. Wipe the log and give us a bubble. We are now an oracle detail."

Then he said to Grace, "Precogs get messy, so comms erasure is SOP for a hot hunch that hinges on secrecy." And then, inevitably, he asked, "How are you feeling?"

Grace shook her head. "Confused."

He chuckled, a sound like boulders grinding. "That's

normal. The words are nonsense, but it hits your audience like a data dump. My takeaways: Gaias don't die in rollover, they're murdered, you're on a hit list, and the sky's the limit on body count if we don't keep you under wraps for—a while?"

He looked to Kris with that last. She said in a newly basso voice, "That's about what I got. Timeframe felt real mushy."

"A week or two," Grace said. The future wheeled and tipped, bright and dark by turns. Honesty compelled her to add, "And most Gaias do die in rollover, for what it's worth."

She wanted to be reassured the Tees were taking this so calmly, but it felt too easy. And they were distracting. They had pulled in power on reflex, making themselves bigger, stronger, tougher. The earth hummed with energy, eager to offer them more.

"You're willing to help me, just like that?" she asked.

"Short answer, yes." Jack ushered her to the picnic table, hovering over her until she sat down, then retreating to a guard position at one corner of the patio. "Mercury veterans will never disrespect a precog. But don't try to help us analyze. That makes things messier. Amy, you're the liaison. DPS is opposition now. You need to step out?"

"Hell, no. The DPS doesn't hold my oath." Amy went to the patio's far corner and bared fangs at Jack. "I'm solidly on Team Prevent Doomsday. What about you, Kris?"

"Count me in." Kris went down on her knees in the grass in front of Grace, bringing her face down to the same level. She had big, brown eyes and a serious demeanor. "I failed someone named Grace once, and she died," she said gravely. "I won't fail you."

The universe wheeled again. Heat shimmered down the length of Grace's spine, searing this solemn moment into her life. "No, you won't."

Jack shifted his weight. Sighed. "Do you have to be so dramatic, Kris?"

Kris rose smoothly to her feet, looked down her nose at him. "Yes, I do."

Grace smoothed her wrinkled dress. Her hands didn't shake. Her heart was full of gratitude and fear, and her head was jammed with revelations. A wonderfully calm energy flowed through her. She wasn't tired.

But, oh, she wanted a hug. "Where are Lauren and Maggie?" she asked. "And Sal?"

"The kids are safe with Elena, across town," said Jack. "And your ex is off-site with Yasu, Heather, and Shells. You want everybody back, I suppose."

"It's important." She considered as many factors as she dared. "I need to act as normal as possible as long as I can, too. How fast can I be certified?"

"Whoa, now. Getting certified isn't keeping a low profile," Kris pointed out. "Can't we carry on like you're still in rollover until—whenever?"

Grace shook her head. That would be honest—after all, she *was* still rolling—but the perils along that path multiplied by the second.

Amy said, "Not after the size of that last flare, Kris. Prime completion is the least-scary way to explain it away. If we don't ask for certification ASAP, that would raise other red flags. Hide in plain sight is our best option."

Jack asked, "Safety certification or full, Grace? If you want employment stamps in every ability you're prime in, it's going to take forever."

He was trying to make Grace smile, so she obliged him. "Safety certification will be fine."

"That's still gonna take you hours, but the camp-release tests are standardized, and the local office can run them. I'll try to get you a priority appointment. It's as quiet as we can hope to get. That work?"

Grace allowed herself the tiniest glimpse of starry eternity. "It doesn't not-work."

Jack nodded. "Then I'll wake up Agent Falwell and call in a few favors. Amy, give Heather a ring about the family, will you?"

"On it." She stepped aside and tapped at her ear.

Once she was preoccupied with her call, Jack asked, "Grace, are you sure about her?"

That was the easiest question yet. "I'm sure of you three. And Sal. No one else. Not yet."

"Okay, that's our inner circle, then."

Moments later, a patch of utter blackness yawned wide in the air over the garden beds, cold air popped, and Heather winged to a landing on the lawn with Sal held tight against her side.

He stepped away and stood there, shoulders back, staring. Tears and power made his eyes glow in Grace's sight.

She held out her hands, and he walked into her embrace without hesitation, without fear. This was what she needed most.

One day at a time, one breath at a time, surrounded by trust and faith: that was the path she would walk as long as her enemies allowed it.

31: A CORD NOT EASILY BROKEN

Night into morning, August 30-31, 239 Louis Street, Elgin IL

THE LONGER LAUREN stood arguing with her mother on the phone in Elena's basement rec room, the more Elena's fingers itched to snatch the receiver away from her. Instead of focusing on the wonderful news that Grace was alive and safely through rollover, Lauren was having a tantrum about having to stay here until morning.

And since noise that bounced up the basement stairs to the main floor went straight up to the second-floor bedrooms by way of the vaulted great room ceiling, she was going to disturb Marco as well as Papa if her protests got much louder.

Elena closed the door to the basement and came back downstairs hissing, "Shh, Lauren. The last thing we need is my nosy little brother waking up."

Lauren ignored her, but when Elena reached the console table behind the couch, where Lauren was saying "But—Moooooom—" for the third time, Maggie came up and wrapped both her hands around Elena's left arm.

It was halfway to a hug, clingy and needy, and Maggie's hands were sweaty. "Arguing with Mom never works," she whispered to Elena. "Never. Why isn't she happy Mom's all right?"

Elena gave her a proper hug, resting her chin against Maggie's bony shoulder. "She is, Mags, but she was worried, and people worry differently."

The twins were perfectly matched in their curly dark hair, fair skin, and brilliant blue eyes. They were equally full of bouncy energy, too, but their personalities were as different as a rock and a pitcher of water.

Sweet Maggie was an expert at avoiding confrontation and more comfortable with evasion than Elena ever would be. Lauren's brand of angry rebellion was far more familiar territory.

When Elena's mother had been interned, the weekly phone calls from Camp Belvidere had felt like punishments. Looking back, Elena could admit she had been a resentful little beast. But Mama kept calling, and Papa kept putting the phone in Elena's hands over and over despite the sulks and shouting matches. He let them scream and rant and argue their way into a new relationship.

Eventually.

She turned Maggie slightly and glanced into the dark part of the basement, beyond the seating area with their sleeping bags and the big television. As she'd suspected, the noise had brought her father out of his office.

Poor papa. When he'd moved his home business into the basement to avoid disturbing everyone else with his nocturnal habits, he hadn't taken slumber parties into account. With Teresa in middle school now, he was talking about better soundproofing.

He stood in the dark rectangle of the open door, with his

fuzzy, foxlike ears laid back and his big, sensitive eyes flashing reflections from the ceiling lights. He said nothing to draw Lauren or Maggie's attention, but one ear swiveled forward.

That was the same as a raised eyebrow: he was wondering if Elena wanted him to intervene. She shook her head, mouthing, "No, thank you, Papa."

He blew her a kiss before retreating. Which proved once more he was the best papa in the world. Mama was the parent who'd urged Elena to offer the house as an emergency teleport destination for the Reeds. But Papa was the one at home most times Elena had them over for short visits. He was the one who had answered their shy questions about rollover and his ears and night vision like an Outreach pro.

And since Mama and Teresa were away on their traditional mother-daughter birthday camping trip this week, Papa was the one who'd taken charge when the twins arrived on the literal doorstep earlier, weighed down with their go-bags and speechless with fear.

Elena should've been the one to greet them, but the red alert notification on her Camp Liberty phone had caught her in the middle of reading her college orientation packet. One second she was daydreaming about choosing classes and wondering how often she would get lost; the next, she was picturing her friends dead. It was too much. She froze.

Papa was the one who stepped up, dropping his workday—worknight—responsibilities to help the twins roll out their sleeping bags in front of the big television in the rec room. Papa was the one who got them set up with extra pillows, fluffy bath towels, and overnight sundries.

She'd been sitting on her bed with her silenced phone in her shaking hands, too stunned to think straight, when he came up to collect her. He'd even suggested she put on her comfiest tee-shirt and sleep shorts to encourage the twins into their pajamas.

Then he put them to work making popcorn and fresh lemonade in the kitchen while he told them bad jokes, and he got them settled with cartoons before returning to work. And not once did he make Elena feel like a failure for freezing and hiding like a frightened baby.

She'd kept their surprise visitors occupied for hours since then. They'd made snacks, played stupid card games, and shared school gossip.

But Papa was the one who'd given her back her courage. She would try to do things his way, with patience and tolerance, even though she really wanted to smack Lauren over the head.

She gave Maggie a quick, reassuring squeeze. "Let's try to let them work it out, okay?"

Maggie heaved a sigh. They let the argument continue until Lauren's face was blotchy red and streaked with tears, until she shouted, "But it isn't *fair*. *He* gets to be there!"

That was halfway past enough. Elena reached out.

Maggie got there first. She snatched the receiver from her sister and put it to her ear, holding Lauren back with her free hand. "Hi, Mom, sorry Lauren is being a jerk, give Sal-daddy a hug from both of us, can't wait to hug you again, love-you-see-you-tomorrow-bye."

She gently placed the phone receiver back in its cradle and glared at Lauren like an angry reflection. "How hard was that? Don't ever bring *him* into it. Not unless you want to be grounded forever."

Lauren sniffed and wiped her arm across her face. "You always think you're right."

"And you always ruin everything!" Maggie balled up her fists and stomped her foot, which wasn't as dramatic as it would've been upstairs. The basement carpet was cushy. "If you'd just hung up, we would've told Elena that Mom wanted us home, we would've gotten a ride or called a taxi. When we got there, it would've been too much trouble to send us back."

"Okay, no." Elena's temper pulled her voice up tight. "I'm not saying a phone fight at midnight is good, but that would've been worse."

Maggie crossed her arms over her chest. "If you say so."

On that huffy note, she marched across the room to the television corner. Lauren trailed after her, still sniffling and slump-shouldered. They flopped down onto their sleeping bags—matching, of course, bright pink and sequined, useless for anything serious—and heaved matching theatrical sighs before glaring at Elena.

She felt a tickle of amusement, watching them huddle shoulder to shoulder with their matching pillows—pink, like the sleeping bags, of course—in their laps. *Great. I've convinced them to stop fighting and ally against me.*

"I do say so," she said, fighting to keep any hint of laughter out of her voice. "First, everybody says this part of rollover is pretty intense. Your mom deserves some time for herself, don't you think? Second, her team will be busy with boring procedure stuff, and Jack would ship you off without thinking twice. Third, I am not an idiot. I would've called for confirmation. Fourth, lying is wrong, and you know it. Shame on you."

That brought a thoughtful frown to Maggie's face. She was probably working out how to work around the first three obstacles, but maybe she would remember the last point too.

Baby steps, Valerie would say.

Elena set the box of tissues in front of Lauren, then sat cross-legged on the sleeping bag Papa had put out for her—the one Mama had repaired with a cartoon animal sheet from Marco's everything-dinosaurs phase. Her fingers trembled from adrenaline overload as she collected the card game they'd discarded when Jack called on the house phone.

"Anyone else cold and wobbly? Because I am," she said. "Between the scare when the red-alert went off, and you popping in, then finally getting good news when we were waiting for bad—I don't know about you, but I feel like I'm made of noodles."

Maggie made a rude noise, and Lauren said, "Nu-uh. You're saying that to make us feel better."

"I'm not," Elena insisted. "This has been the longest night in my life. I was scared for you, for your mom, for everybody."

"Mom *will* be fine, right?" Maggie asked. "Now that she's done rolling? She isn't making us stay away for our own good?"

"We hate when she does that," Lauren said.

Now was not the time for Elena to voice her own doubts and questions. Now was the time to be confident and reassuring.

She set aside the card deck and lay down, propping her head up on her hand. "Jack wouldn't have called with the all-clear unless he was one-thousand-percent sure the danger was past, but they may not let you back 'til she's safety-certified. We might as well tuck in for the night."

Maggie and Lauren exchanged a long glance. Maggie hugged her pillow tighter. Lauren said very softly, "We're not sleepy. Can I ask a question? About your dad."

"What about him?" Elena was proud of herself for keeping her voice nice and steady. She'd shown them the family photos, and Papa hadn't said anything about them being rude, but he wouldn't.

"Mom's going to look different now, right? C-variant like your father. What if that's why she wants us to stay away? What if she's afraid we won't love her if she looks different?"

Elena sat up again. It was a legit question. "What if you don't?" she asked. "Could you love her if she had scales? Or fangs?"

"Yes!" both girls said without hesitation, which made Elena proud of them and ashamed of herself at their age.

"It might not be something that shows," she warned them. "And it's rude to ask, just like it's rude to ask people about sex or gender or R-status."

"I could never!" Maggie fell onto her back, laughing. "Can you imagine? Hi, mom, do you have big, furry feet now? I would die first. Lauren, you'll have to be the nosy one."

"No, never!" Lauren sputtered into giggles too. "Can you imagine? What are we going to say if we can see? Gosh, Mom, what big teeth you have, like Little Red Riding Hood with the wolf?"

The snickers and giggles shifted into sobs, and Lauren clapped her hands over her eyes, wailing, "Oh, no, why am I *crying* again? What is wrong with me?"

"There's nothing wrong with you." Elena wanted to hug them both, but they were in each other's arms a second later, bawling on each other's shoulders, so she let them weep out the rest of their fear and frustration together.

"Crying just means you're feeling a lot more than you can hold in," she said once they were reaching for fresh tissues. "Haven't you ever been to a wedding where everyone bawls? Didn't I just say how overwhelming tonight's been? Me, I'm a screamer. I want to *shriek* when I get worked up, even if it's because I'm happy. Or especially then."

Two sets of bloodshot blue eyes regarded her solemnly. Then Maggie said, "Bullshit. You do not."

"Maggie!" Lauren was on her feet in an instant, "Language!"

"Don't tell me what to do," Maggie said smugly. "No one put you in charge!"

"Oh, yeah?" Lauren snatched up her pillow to thwack her sister—and beaned Elena on the backswing.

Well. She couldn't let that go unanswered.

One intensely satisfying pillow fight later, they were lying on their backs, heads cushioned on each other's tummies, trying to catch their breath and making each other giggle by giggling.

Maggie was the first to sit up, leaving Lauren's head to thump on the carpet while she snatched up her pillow and screamed into it. Elena followed suit in the spirit of practicing what she preached. Lauren held out for a good five seconds before adding her voice to the muffled chorus.

And that's when Papa decided to show up again. "Everything all right?" he asked in that chipper voice Elena would swear he used to annoy people on purpose.

"Yes, Papa, we're fine." She got to her feet and smoothed her tangled hair into a new pony-tail. "Sorry for the noise."

"Mm." He slanted back one ear, and the wispy white fur on his head and neck lifted and settled again. "I have some good news, but I'm not sure my hearing will survive the reaction. Promise to keep the volume and the pillows down?"

"Yes, Mr. Moreno," the twins said. Elena crossed her arms and held her breath.

Papa said, "I just got off the phone with your father. Camp Liberty has provisionally cleared your mom, and they've scheduled a formal clearance from DPS Elgin in the morning. Since the few hours between now and then would be no longer than a typical camp visit, he got you approved to come home."

Elena beamed at her father. That was good news. Papa had called Sal and shared that tidbit about visit timing. She would bet her allowance on it. Sal wasn't people-smart and rules-smart like that. Papa was.

The twins were not impressed. Lauren frowned, suspicious. "But Mom said it wasn't allowed."

"Your father stepped up and spoke on your behalf." Papa

smiled mostly with ears and eyes these days. "Is that a bad thing?"

"No," Maggie said, long and slow. "No, that's a good thing. We can go home?"

"I'll drive you over as soon as you're ready," Papa said.

Later, Elena sat in the front passenger seat of their battered station wagon next to Papa and watched the girls run across their front lawn toward their waiting parents. The bright security lights on the front porch lit up the whole scene.

Grace didn't look any different except for the shining happiness in her smile. Sal looked rugged, weary, and proud, standing with his arm around Grace's waist. Lauren and Maggie stopped an arm's length away and edged sidelong against their father's side instead of hugging their mother.

Then Grace knelt and spoke, and Sal edged his brood of two closer until they were in a huddle with hands clasped and heads bent.

"That's nice," Papa said, sounding very pleased with himself. "All's well that ends well, eh?"

Nothing was ended. Any family with two active poz parents would face a long hard adjustment period in the coming weeks and months. But Papa knew that. And Grace was *alive*. That was a miracle.

Elena leaned over to kiss him on the cheek. "It couldn't be better. Thank you, Papa. I am so glad I don't have to babysit them through breakfast."

Papa turned the car for home, and exhaustion crashed down over Elena like an invisible avalanche. She slid down in the seat and yawned. "I should be happy, but I'm too tired," she said. And she wanted to scream into a pillow, but that could wait until she was alone. "Thank you for driving."

Papa drove in silence for a few blocks. "I'm proud of you.

You know that, don't you? Your mother and I are full to bursting with pride, but we're worried about your future."

Hearing things like that always made her want to squirm and hide. "I try to make you proud," she said. "I'm sorry about earlier tonight."

"I know." He put one thin hand on the console between them, then patted her leg. Giving her a chance to shrink back, just in case, and that made her heart ache. He went on, "But you shouldn't be sorry. That's what I wanted to say."

"I don't understand." She stifled another yawn.

"You don't need to be perfect." He pulled the car into their driveway next to her little blue rust bucket and parked. "You are so independent and almost grown up, but you don't have to solve all the world's problems alone. You can't. No one can. "

"I know." Elena swallowed the lump of emotion in her throat. The sky was full of stars here on their block, ever since Mama had appealed to have the street lights removed and everyone else had installed dark-sky porch lights. They had good neighbors.

The engine ticked quietly, loud against the muffled night noises.

"You know it with your head, but not your heart." Papa slid his hands along the steering wheel and didn't look at her, which was a relief. He also didn't unbuckle his seat belt, which meant he had more to say. Elena braced herself for more unhelpful parental wisdom.

He cleared his throat. "Your mother and I don't love you because you're brilliant, or brave, or unstoppable—although you are all those things, you get it from her—we love you, *period.* Hard as you try, you can't always win. Things won't always end well. But we will always love you. Promise me you'll remember us when you're rich and famous and running the country?"

The last part made Elena laugh, as he'd meant it to do, and that made the promise easy. "I will remember! I love you too, Papa."

"Good. Now, we will never speak of this again. Last one inside has to make waffles for Marco."

He let Elena win, and the waffles were delicious.

32: THE QUIET WORDS OF THE WISE

September 1, 414 Elm Drive, Elgin, IL

JACK ZIPPED his go-bag closed and rolled up his sleeping pad, leaning it against Shelly and Yasu's empty, folded cots in the corner. Crates stood ready for packing up equipment. Grace's exit interview was done, and the last of her paperwork was in Valerie's hands out in California. Camp Liberty's first successful prime session was coming to its end.

That left the packing, the good-byes, and the sense of impending doom.

He wanted to go home and sleep for a week. He probably wouldn't get that chance, but a man could dream. He went up the basement steps into the side yard and pushed aside overgrown shrubs to join Amy at the front corner of the house

Her gaze was locked on a confrontation unfolding on the front lawn.

"That isn't looking good," Jack observed.

"You think?"

Sal stood nose to nose with Agent-in-Chief Falwell from the

Elgin DPS office on the driveway, and the pair of them were carrying on a full-blown fight at a whisper.

Jack had often worked with the frail, white-haired Elgin unit director over the years, but he'd never seen the woman angry like this. That was worrying.

Agent Falwell's driver, a thin, wrinkled man Jack didn't know by name, looked no happier than his boss. He was pacing around the black sedan over which he had been standing guard since parking it in the driveway two hours earlier.

His vigilance was another bad sign.

Dark-bellied clouds scudded by overhead, lending an ominous greenish glow to the proceedings. Jack wondered if he should be worrying about the weather. After seeing the damage from the previous month's catastrophic natural tornadoes, he was taking nothing for granted. Natural didn't mean harmless.

"What's the drama?" he asked.

"Falwell wants extended supervision on Grace, but Sal is sticking to the script we gave him about precedents." Amy kept watching the discussion. "Probably because he only understands a third of it and doesn't want to admit it. He's doing better than I expected, given his normal spinelessness."

"He gets protective of Grace. She passed her exit exam with flying colors. Falwell stamped the release papers herself, Shelly and I witnessed, and Yasu signed off the physical. She's owed free release. Just like you and I were."

"Point, but under the circumstances, Gaias being so rare, I can't blame Falwell for wanting her kept under observation."

Jack thought back to the long morning of tests and challenges. "She did mention probation, but Shelly put a new tag on Grace as a final precaution, and they were all smiles and chatting about collaboration on new protocols when I went. What could go wrong in ten minutes?"

Amy flashed fangs at him. "With bureaucracy involved? I

shudder to guess. Once they stop hissing at each other, I'll let Falwell know I'll be here for the foreseeable. That should keep everyone happy."

"You're what?"

"I am renting out that bunker. I don't hate barracks life, but that bed and shower are worth coughing up a chunk of my pay. Grace remembered me joking about it, and she offered a fair price. . It's inside the housing perimeter. I checked."

"It's a hole in the ground."

"Says the judgy boy who lives in a thirty-by-thirty box on a slab and who has to shower at work." Amy showed her fangs. "It's a *nice* hole. And Sal has ideas for laying in an entry stairwell and a proper door."

She was *excited* about a dank hole in the ground. Sometimes Jack didn't understand people. "I came out so you could go say your good-byes before Shelly 'ports Kris and Yasu home. An hour or two of packing, and then I'm for home too. Everybody sleeps in their own beds tonight."

"We hope." Amy didn't need to say more than that.

"We hope," he agreed.

Precogs were messy. Hot hunches self-destructed more often than not. A prediction's existence could cause enough variables to shift that the foreseen future never came to pass.

A man could hope.

The garage door rattled up, and the family van backed onto the driveway. Elena was in the driver's seat, and she eased past the DPS sedan while Sal and Agent Falwell separated a step and schooled their faces to show smiles to Lauren and Maggie.

The girls blew kisses out the van windows and warbled silly exclamations at the world until they were halfway down the block. They had cheered Grace through her control demonstrations like a pep squad at a football game. Four solid hours of enthusiasm.

"I won't miss those squeals or all the praying," Jack said. "You're lucky you don't fit indoors, I swear. Night duty in the house sucked."

Amy body-checked him with staggering force: her version of a friendly slap on the back. "Don't be such a grump. Those two are angels compared to some of my old dance students. Let them have their happiness. Who knows how long it'll last?"

"As long as they have the happies far away from me."

It still wasn't safe to join the driveway discussion. Agent Falwell had gone back to hissing at Sal before the van reached the corner. "Can you hear what they're saying?"

"A bit. I caught privacy and overreach. You?"

"Nothing but mumbles."

"Be nice if you could call up that overload rampage form on command. The floppy ears looked hilarious, but sonar hearing would be useful."

"Screw you, Amy." The three hours Jack had waited before his body bled off the excess energy from Grace's mid-rollover crisis had been pure hell. *If I'd been stuck like that*—he made fists, dug claws into his palms to give himself something else to focus on. "I never want to pull that kind of power load again."

"I was going to ask Grace if we could collaborate on a controlled surge. One powerful enough to give me a bigger tail so I'd have a proper counterbalance."

Jack boggled over the word *bigger*. He hadn't seen any tail on Amy that day while she'd been overpowered, which meant it had been hidden by her skirt—he closed his eyes against the mental picture. "Don't say shit like that. My delicate nerves can't take it. And don't you dare talk Grace into experimentation. You'll get yourselves in trouble."

"Party pooper."

From behind them, Grace said, "No, he's right. It wouldn't be safe. We're coming to a crossroads."

She stood barefoot in the sun-browned grass at the back corner of the house. One hand held back the overgrown bushes so she could see down the side yard, and she held her other arm defensively across the front of today's faded floral sundress.

Brownish hair, sun-weathered skin, muddy-colored eyes, and broken, dirty fingernails—Jack couldn't point to what lifted her appearance from plain to riveting now. Part of it was the way she carried herself—not so much confident as steadfast. The rest came from the changes rollover had wrought. There was an intensity that threadbare clothes and a slouch couldn't hide.

She carried within her the power to literally change the world. The force of it pressed against Jack's senses like the unceasing drone of a blizzard wind.

And every flower in the yard glowed brighter when she smiled. She said, "I think of it more like an ocean tide, but wind works too." Then she winced. "Sorry. You didn't say that, did you? Sometimes you think very loudly."

"But never deeply," Amy said with a snicker.

Jack elbowed her. The EF alarms he and Amy still wore hadn't gone off, so Grace wasn't exerting any energy in that area, yet she'd picked up his thoughts.

"Only the ones you bonk me with," Grace told him. "Sal's vetoing the idea of a press release over there. Since you're wondering."

"News coverage?" A chill of unease traveled up his spine. He'd had enough experience fending off the press to know a horrible idea when he heard one. "Oh, hell, no."

Grace nodded. "Don't worry. It won't happen."

Her assurance had a depth that went beyond confidence. The energy behind her words made the air shimmer. Jack glanced Amy's way, saw a spark of answering worry in the Marine's eyes.

Grace's confidence implied that she had either persuaded someone against the idea, or she was indulging in precognition again. The first was criminal, and the second potentially worse. Fooling around with prophecies rarely ended well.

"You're sure about that." He kept his tone neutral and unquestioning, but if Grace could eavesdrop on his emotions, she already knew he was nervous.

This was the reality of what they had accomplished. There wasn't any damned way to stop Grace from doing whatever she wanted—nothing short of reducing her to component atoms.

Grace's eyes darkened as her pupils dilated. *Not even that would end me now,* came to Jack as a whisper inside his skull, and then Grace said, "I am so sorry. I'm juggling too many things. Please forgive the intrusion?"

Jack was struggling to make sense of that wistful, frustrated apology when Amy said, "Grace, I need you to tell me you didn't use empathic persuasion to talk them out of a press conference. Arresting you now would be ten kinds of impossible."

"I would never steal someone's free will. Never." Grace smoothed her hands down her sides, and a blush stained her cheeks. "And I try to stick to the now, but bits and pieces get through. They'll call a truce in a minute when the rain starts, Agent Falwell's boss will squash the publicity idea, and someone will call someone else, and Valerie—then it gets bad. Unless it gets bad earlier."

She ran her hands over her hair, pressing both palms against her scalp. "I held back enough during the certification tests to keep Agent Falwell from panicking, but I can't hide under a bushel forever."

That sense of foreboding pressed harder against Jack's skin, raising a prickle of rampage energy in its wake. He looked to Amy, who nodded. She'd felt it too. She shifted from side to side, crunching gravel underfoot, and muttered about damned prophecies.

Jack knelt to look up at Grace. "I can't believe I have to say this, but we can't defend you if you run around committing crimes. Evaluation fraud is a felony."

"I don't have any choice!" Grace closed her eyes and flapped her hands with increasing agitation. "No, that isn't true. I chose the least harm possible. If I'd shown Agent Falwell any more of myself, she would have wanted to run more tests. Those tests would have frightened someone, and then it—would end badly. Armageddon, Book of Revelations, hellfire and brimstone badly."

She paused, breathing deep and slow for ten breaths, before opening her eyes. Her muddy-brown gaze had an eerie depth to it. "That's also what happens if you do your duty and report me, Jack. So do it and get on with ending the world, or help me save it. Nothing has changed. All I need is more time."

The honorable option remained so obvious Jack wasn't sure he could trust it. Maybe he was being logical, or maybe his judgment had been compromised.

No. Mercury's motto was contain, protect, preserve. Grace wasn't containable. That left protecting her to preserve others. If he, Kris, or Amy ratted her out, they would share responsibility for a massacre they could have stopped with their silence.

The gray sky flashed with lightning, and thunder rumbled. Grace studied the clouds, and her lips thinned. "It's going to rain and make the garden muddy," she said irritably as if she didn't have the power to move the storm.

That tipped the scales for Jack. He heaved himself to his feet. "Nothing has changed."

Amy clicked her claws together. "How solid are these hunches of yours, Grace? Compared to that first vision, I mean."

"How should I know?" She grimaced. "I am a baby learning about the floor I crawl on. Some things are clear. Don't talk to Valerie. I know she's part of your team, but she *must not* know. Gabe is beyond reach. Shelly, Yasu? They might choose wisely. Elena, Heather—yes, but—yes?"

Her face had gone slack, eyes dropping shut. She flapped her hands. "I know I am babbling. There's too much in motion, and much of it pains my heart."

Amy said, "Don't be sorry. You're making more sense than some precogs. You do what you need to do, and we'll do what we think is best. Jack and Kris are as close as a phone call."

"We'll need a battle plan," Jack pointed out. "If it comes to any fighting."

"Plan without me." Grace slipped past him. She paused in the gap of the open gate between side and front yard, half-hidden by the wood panel. "The less I talk, the longer this truce with the future will last. This much is safe; I am not a fighter, but fighting can't be avoided."

"So cryptic," Amy said.

Grace's eyes went dark and sparkling like a starry sky, then warmed to brown again. "I wish I could say more, but it would get out of hand."

Fat, warm droplets of rain pattered down, harbingers of the coming deluge. The water spattered against air a foot above Grace's head and fell to either side. "I know you two aren't believers," she said, "but if you could wish me strength, I would appreciate it. Everything I turn my mind to doing now—has consequences."

Consequences sounded like something Jack would be happy to avoid. "How long do we have? Are we talking hours or days or months?"

"A week if I go say good-bye to Agent Falwell now, and I will do that. I am greedy and want more time with my girls and Sal."

The clouds opened up as she was hurrying to join Sal and Agent Falwell. Rain came down in torrents, steam rose from the pavement and sidewalks, and the DPS driver popped open an umbrella.

He could've saved the effort.

Water cascaded down around Jack and Amy without touching their skin, held back by matched, curving barriers of still, clear air. Out front, Falwell, Sal, and Grace stood dry within a similar dry half-sphere.

Amy stuck her claw tips into the rain, creating a series of waterfalls. "Cute. Multiple separate force-fields. And she was carrying on a conversation while she raised them. I think I'll light a candle to her and pray she gives me that permanent tail I want. Bodyguard to a goddess. That'll look nice on a resume when I get drummed out of the Corps, huh?"

"Stop it, Amy. Seriously." His skin crawled when he thought about having a tail.

Amy put a hand on his shoulder. "Seriously, Jackass? We're breaking the letter of our solemn oaths to defend their spirit. We'll be lucky if it doesn't get us killed before I get court-martialed and you get yourself exiled to an atoll somewhere cold and stormy. If I don't crack jokes, I'm going to break down and weep like an infant."

The wind rose higher, and curtains of water rippled across the yard. Agent Falwell ducked into the car while Grace and Sal walked arm and arm toward the front door, conferring quietly about who-knew-what.

"Yeah," Jack said. "Me, too."

Amy turned toward the back yard. Her rain shield moved with her. "C'mon, big guy. Let's pack up and tidy up the house for the family."

Family—a thought struck Jack as he followed Amy to the patio.

For all of Grace's talk about death and destruction, she spoke about her daughters and her ex-husband in tones warm with love. That reassured him more than anything else he had seen and heard.

"We really are going to need a battle plan," he said. "If she won't fight to defend herself, someone's going to have to do it for her."

"Let's talk to Kris," Amy replied. "She always has interesting ideas."

33: THE STARS GROW DARK

Night of September 1, 414 Elm Drive, Elgin IL

SAL CAME TAPPING SOFTLY at Grace's bedroom door in the deepest hour of the night, long after the girls went to sleep and their new tenant had retreated to her rest.

Grace was ready and waiting for him. She sat up in bed and brushed the world with a light caress of intent. Moving objects with threads of energy was child's play now.

The latch and hinges obeyed her will, the door swung wide open, and there he stood, big, broad, and hesitant, determined but uncertain.

The night light at the end of the hall made him a shadow of himself. Grace turned on the ceiling light with another flick of thought and took in the view.

He wasn't dressed for sleep. He still wore his puttering-around-the-house clothes: worn jeans with the left knee torn out and a white cotton tee the twins had decorated with pink glitter-glue flowers.

Grace smiled because he was beautiful inside and out. He

was soft grass by a dusty trail, a fresh breeze over cool water, a warm hearthstone on a cold night, beside a fire banked low. He was no longer *her* comfort and solace, but she could appreciate all he had to offer.

Sal did not smile back. He shoved his hands into his jeans pockets and sighed.

A muscle always knotted more on one side of his jaw than the other at times like this, when he knew words had to be said, but he couldn't find the right ones to frame a thought, or when his thoughts stumbled over themselves, tripped up by the idea of speech.

Grace no longer had to guess the meaning of his silences.

What now? he was asking with bright, somber eyes and tight, worried mouth, impatient hands, and tense curled, bare toes. *What happens with us now?*

Exasperating man, ever hopeful. His stubborn streak was strength and weakness both. Grace answered him with an outstretched hand. *Come sit with me, and we'll work it out together.*

He didn't hear the words, but he felt the invitation. His eyes went wide and wary as he approached. He sank onto the mattress, down at the end of the bed—neutral ground.

Sensing emotion had not been among his talents, not until he'd recklessly flung himself into Grace's mind to anchor her. To save her.

"Do you mind?" she asked softly. She hadn't meant to channel excess energy into the others that day. Did he see it as a violation? She might have, once upon a time.

"Nope," he replied, equally soft. "I *like* it, sweetheart. It's like the puzzle piece I was missing. If I'd been able to feel you then, things would be different now."

But he hadn't, and things weren't different. She let that small, sad truth grow cool between them.

Sal shivered. "No one you boosted is upset, so you can stop fretting. We all re-certified through Mercury, slick and simple."

"Good." Grace patted the bedspread at her side.

He edged closer. Grace touched the familiar tension bump at the corner of his jaw. Physical contact was a tiny, transcendent joy. "I missed touch," she told him. "That was the worst part, how careful everyone was about touching me."

But you didn't miss me, his downcast face accused, and he wasn't wrong.

"Not like that, no." Their love was a hearth gone cool, for all that the iron and stone of it remained whole and strong. "I would say I'm sorry, but—"

But she wasn't.

To create a livable future, she had to sever herself from her past.

"But you aren't," he said, speaking slowly, working it out. He took her hand, looked at their clasped fingers. "I don't know how to love you now."

He wasn't sure how to go on, what to *be* if he wasn't a sexual partner, a protector, or a provider. He could not believe Grace would want him for any other reasons.

The bed bounced under them as he shifted his weight. Then *everything* shifted.

The universe wheeled around her in a dazzling whirl of eternity. She gasped, overcome by the incomprehensible beauty of it—and it was gone, sunk deep into the pool of stillness at her center.

But it would return, and soon. *I hoped we would have more time.*

When she blinked her vision clear, Sal was staring at her, radiating—awe? She wanted to ask if she had frightened him, but she was afraid of the answer.

Sal didn't need the question. He ducked his head, shook it

gently. "Remember the spring I was courting you? We camped up by the Snake River. The river was flooding, roaring and powerful and—magnificent? Vast? That's you. You were always a lot, but now there's so much *everything* inside you, I don't have words."

He made a face, self-conscious and shy. "It sounds stupid."

"I think it sounds poetic," Grace said because hugging him would be too much for him to bear. But a small truth—that much would be a gift. "You see things clearly. You always have. That's what saved me, you know."

He stretched out alongside her, crooked his arm to prop his head on his hand. It was an act of courage as much as acceptance, and they both knew it. He frowned at her. "No, I don't. I've never known what you see in me, honestly."

She laid down to stare at the universe beyond the dark ceiling, then laced her fingers with Sal's. She placed their clasped hands on her belly, low down over the womb where she'd carried three babies and birthed two to life.

Once she settled the world inside her, she turned her head. Sal had wrinkles between his brows now. They smoothed away when she laid a finger on them. "I liked your memories better than mine," she told him. "Mine were poisonous and sharp as knives. I would have cut myself to pieces against them, but you wrapped me safe in the sunny, soft, happy times. Stop wishing you had a lion's courage or a warrior's heart. You're a builder of nests and a guardian of chicks, my handsome husband, and that is what I love in you."

He put his chin on her shoulder and snuggled up close. "You just called me a goose."

"Gander," she said solemnly. "You are not stupid. You are not weak. I love you."

The lines beside Sal's mouth deepened. "But was I ever what you *wanted*? Were you ever happy? Are all your memories sad?"

"Of course not." Of course he would ask that. Everything that happened in the world revolved around him. Exasperating man. Beloved man. Grace suppressed a sigh. "I was happier with you than without. Guilt steals from joy and makes chains of fear. You took the weight from me and carried it gladly."

Sal's chuckle was a sob in fancy dress. "You always say things in the most complicated ways. Tell me plain. Do you want me to stay? Not here in your house, I—couldn't ask that, but I can find work and an apartment nearby."

"You will stay in this house." She put her hand to the familiar curve of his cheek. "But I won't, not for long. We won't be a family much longer."

She closed her eyes on tears. *You will finish this house and make it a home, you and our daughters, but I won't be there to see it.* That was the single harsh thread connecting all her futures. She was lighter for confessing it despite the pain it caused.

"I'm sorry," she said because saying the words mattered. And Sal wept without shame because half the pain was his.

"You'll do what needs doing," he said. "So will I. I'll do right by our girls for you." His breath hitched in his chest when he spoke, but he meant it as a holy vow.

Grace felt the universe rearrange itself on his words. She clung to him and turned away from the wheeling patterns of hope, not wanting to see if those bright spots grew stronger or were swallowed up by hate.

34: WICKEDNESS WAS THERE, IN THE PLACE OF JUSTICE

September 6, DPS Administrative Offices, Riverside CA

ONE WEEKEND and three workdays after Valerie closed the book on Grace Reed's Camp Liberty experience, she walked into the office and saw something—wrong.

Someone is in trouble, the room declared. The usual fog of concentration hung over the office floor, but no smiles pierced it. None of the front-line case workers delivered their usual distantly-courteous greetings. They kept their heads down, and wariness rippled through their everyday impatience in bright, cautionary flashes.

What did I do? was Valerie's conditioned response, ingrained by years of punishment. Her conscience was clear, but the reflexive lurch of dismay left her nerves twanging. She hurried to her office, feeling like a mouse bolting for its hole.

Her door was open, and inside, a bored process server awaited her. He wore a crisp suit jacket and an annoyed expression. More importantly, he held a blue-and-white envelope embossed with the security seal identifying it as an *immediate* summons to stand before a Judicial Branch board.

Valerie groaned under her breath.

The court cases and evaluations that had once terrified her with their consequence were now commonplace, but that didn't make them fun. Now that Camp Liberty was between clients, she had been hoping for a few simple, satisfying employment assistance cases.

The summons explained the tension in the outer office, though. The scheduling assistant assigned to the desk nearest Valerie's door was new, got excited about everything, and liked to chat. Before lunch, everyone in the building would know Valerie had caught a new priority court case.

The process server verified Valerie's identity, handed over the envelope, and hurried off. Gabby came to hover and fidget just outside the door.

"Do you need a lawyer?" she asked in a breathless voice. "My cousin is a lawyer."

"No, thank you." Valerie exerted all her willpower to keep from rolling her eyes. "With five licensed assessors in this office, you'll see people getting these all the time. It's never exciting. I will need you to clear today for me, please."

Gabby looked disappointed, but she gave a determined nod and hurried off.

Thanks to various televised dramas, people associated the Judicial Branch with punishment for violent felonies, but those were the exceptions, not the norm. Most Boards were convened to address strictly DPS-related infractions, and most of those proceedings were bureaucratic and boring.

Valerie popped open the envelope with an impatient flick. The single page inside sliced her middle finger as she removed it. She sucked on the cut as she read the summons, and a hot flare of anger flickered to life at its tone.

This subpoena had been issued by a team of internal auditors. It ordered her to report immediately to the Judicial offices for deposition. Camp Liberty was being investigated for misuse of resources.

The accusations of malfeasance were baseless and would be easily countered, but it was still alarming. And insulting. And the short notice was a rude imposition.

The whole matter stank of political maneuvering. Someone might be clearing their way to a cabinet appointment by sweeping aside the work of pesky outsiders so they could take credit for developing an internal program.

She had paperwork validating every expense. The *immediate* part stopped looking inconvenient. The sooner she testified, the sooner she could set the record straight. She gathered up the relevant documents and passed along the court information to Gabby in case anyone needed to find her later.

The woman whispered, "What kind of trial is it?"

Valerie gave in to impulse and leaned close to whisper, "Don't ask. It's confidential."

The assistant's eyes widened. "Oh, wow."

Valerie solemnly nodded back. Confidential didn't mean interesting, but Gabby would learn that herself. Valerie could only fight so much ignorance per day.

She went across the campus to the Judicial building, up a tiny elevator and down a familiar dingy hall to the reception office. Frosted glass doors punctuated the windowless hall, The time-faded murals on the faded plaster walls did nothing to improve the ambiance. They portrayed historic victories and interventions in a style that reminded Valerie of wartime propaganda posters.

The usual reception clerk took her signature, and gave the usual legal recitation in a terminally bored voice. "When appearing before a Board, you are bound by Pritzger restrictions. All actions and communications under court supervision are legal record and can be used as evidence. No active power use except by request of an authorized court officer. Only a court officer can release you from these restrictions. Got it?"

"Yes, yes. You know I know the drill."

"I do." He smiled and directed her back the way she'd come. "Your party's in J27, the old hearing room. It was the only space available on short notice. Have fun."

The door to J27 opened into the hall as Valerie approached. An unsmiling brunette woman wearing a black suit, lawyer's badge, and high-heeled shoes stepped out. She courteously held the door for Valerie before moving on. Her heels clicked away down the hall.

Valerie paused to appreciate the view from the doorway.

J27 was a relic of a time when courtrooms were designed to impress. The room was paneled in dark woods and furnished with old brass fixtures. A mural spanned the far wall behind the raised judge's bench and witness box: two floating figures and a woman wreathed in flames held off a wildfire while beleaguered adults hurried a mob of children in school uniforms to safety beneath a frothing archway of water. Three chairs sat empty at each of the lawyer's tables past the gallery railing.

The whole room was empty, in fact, and a fog of danger hung in the clear air, so thick it was visible despite Valerie's best effort to avoid *looking*. Even as the sight registered, metal clicked behind her. Heart racing, she turned and shoved on the door bar. It didn't move.

"Hey! Open up!" At first, her fear was buffered by anger. Mysterious empty rooms and locked doors were the stuff of conspiracy thrillers. This had to be a prank or a mistake.

Minutes went by. No one responded when she knocked again. She rattled the door bars and pounded on the panels. Nothing.

Her anxiety was rocketing toward panic when the door to the judge's chambers opened.

The brunette from the hallway led an entourage of two black-suited men to the counsel table on the room's left side. Her high heels clicked on the floor here, too, and her pace made a brisk declaration: *why yes, I am the boss.*

Her hair was styled in a no-nonsense bob that likely cost more than a day's pay for Valerie, her face put her age somewhere between thirty and sixty, and her poise was intimidating. The older of the two men was jowly and graying, and he waited politely for the woman to pick her chair before sitting down himself.

The younger man flopped into the remaining seat and crossed his arms over his chest. He had a carrot-colored crew cut and freckled skin so pale the veins showed through. He carried himself like a soldier, and his eyes gave Valerie chills. They revealed a soul as dangerous and remorseless as a boulder poised to fall from a cliff.

The woman removed her ID badge and replaced it with a different one. That explained the theatrics at least in part. The logo was unmistakable, and it matched the ones the men were wearing.

The Special Directives Unit had a well-deserved reputation for eccentricity and paranoia. When SDU took an interest in any operation, they smothered it in secrecy. Valerie itched to give them all a closer examination but didn't dare. The Pritzger warning was fresh in her mind, and this meeting was official until she knew otherwise.

She didn't need to use her visual power to know she was in trouble.

The SDU agents sat there staring at her. Waiting. Valerie could play the silence game too. She walked through the gate from the audience gallery and set her files on the other empty table—as far from the cold-eyed redhead as she could get.

The trio at the plaintiff's desk turned their chairs so they could watch her. No one spoke. Valerie fidgeted with her files, unwilling to surrender the tiny advantage she held by remaining on her feet.

Her nerve deserted her after another full minute of silence. "If you're trying to intimidate me, it's working. Does the spy theater mean there was a security leak that led to the audit? If I'm in trouble, I have a right to know, don't I?"

"Clairvoyants," the redhead said in a tone most people saved for expletives. "You see everything and comprehend nothing."

The woman gave him a long disapproving look before turning to smile at Valerie. "There is no audit, Ms. Wade, and you're not in any trouble. Please, sit. You'll be more comfortable. This is complicated, and explaining will take some time."

One of the chairs at Valerie's table rose a foot off the floor and moved around the table to her side. The gesture delivered a subtle message: anyone who could maneuver furniture at a distance could also easily stop a fleeing witness.

Valerie repositioned the chair before sitting down. She could be subtle too: she would cooperate on her own terms. "Why pretend there's an audit?"

"To account for the time and provide cover," the older man said. His deep, resonant voice was a perfect match for his graying dignity. He could have made a grocery list sound profound. "We need to share highly-sensitive, compartmented material with you."

"Total deniability also applies," the redhead said. He sounded bored now. "The information you will learn does not exist, we were never here, and if anyone else learns of this meeting, they will be executed with prejudice. Forget Pritzger penalties. We will bury you."

The threat was pure hyperbole, but those cold eyes promised it was deadly serious. The way both his companions reacted told Valerie it wasn't an exaggeration.

They weren't pleased by his candor, but they accepted what he said as true. Her stomach tied itself in knots. "I've never worked on anything requiring a clearance in my life. Are you sure you have the right—" *Victim? Target?* "—person?"

"Quite sure. Oh, dear." The woman wrinkled her nose, like a hostess caught in a social gaffe. "Introductions would be polite. You can call me Adele, this is Adam—" the dignified older man nodded, "—and the unpleasant boy with the big mouth is Alex."

And I'm the Queen of Sheba. Valerie thought. How naïve did they think she was? If the reason for this meeting was a cover, so were the names.

Allowing herself to be aggravated helped stave off the rising panic. Forget the Pritzger restrictions, Alex had said. Did she dare look closer at them?

No. A shudder ran through her at the thought of knowing Alex's full nature. She said, "If we're on first-name terms, call me Valerie. Why are you here?"

Adele's smile took on a sorrowful edge. "Your little rollover experiment has been declared a failure. We would like your assistance arranging an orderly shutdown."

"Failure?" Valerie's head throbbed. "No! Camp Liberty is going to be a huge success. The program released its first prime case to local authorities a few days ago. We're planning to expand, not shut down."

"No, you aren't." Adam massaged his nose between his fingers and thumb. "If you try, Camp Liberty will lose its grant, and its board will be charged with—oh, we'll think of something. This is only a stopgap. Legislation is in the works to explicitly deny camp exemption of any kind to rank five or better."

"But why?" Valerie's outrage escaped into words before she could stop the impulse. "People want this, and we've proved it can be done safely. The DPS already allows exemptions. Some countries don't intern rollovers at all."

"No, they do worse." Alex sat back with a triumphant smile.

Adele turned to frown at him, then broke the sticky silence with a pained smile for Valerie. "We'll get to that in a moment. Ms. Wade, we know your intentions are good. What you want is a fantastic dream, and I wish it could happen too, but it can't. There's far more to internment than medical support and occupational training."

This was making less and less sense. "Yes, of course, but the system is overloaded and failing now. If internment doesn't meet the needs of the people it's designed to help, what's the point?"

"Public safety, of course," Adam said indulgently. "All other services are secondary. Internment is the only safe option for a number of reasons—"

Alex interrupted. "Show, don't tell, man. We aren't here to argue."

"He's right, Adam." Adele nodded. "The demonstration, please."

"Fine." Adam waved, and a glitter of power rained down from nowhere. He flicked his fingers, and it floated to Valerie, surrounding her in a fog.

Her view cleared, and the courtroom was gone, transformed into a scene of bloody slaughter against a distant backdrop of mountain peaks and bright, hazy sky.

Before her, people fell and died on tidy graveled roads, in front of white-painted wooden buildings, cowering beside antique vehicles. Noise and smells as intense and real as the visuals assaulted her senses.

The illusion swept her up, moving her past vignettes, and

dissolving them in her peripheral vision. Everywhere she turned, violent death followed: deafening, foul, and tasting of hot metal and smoke.

A huddled mob exploded in a spray of gore; people fled across a flower-dotted meadow and melted into heaving, shapeless mounds of flesh; a red brick building with an American flag outside evaporated into ash and boiling steam; a woman shrieked as her legs became stone and vines sprouted from her mouth.

One man was in every scene, untouched by the mayhem. His clothes were old-fashioned, his hair was worn in a graying crewcut, and his smile—Valerie shuddered, immensely glad her talent wasn't active. The visual of his glee was terrifying enough.

The illusion mercifully faded. Valerie's stomach churned, and her whole body shook and quivered. "What was that?" she whispered.

Adam said, "That was a re-enactment built from camera footage of the Camp Chafee Disaster back in 1948."

"I've never heard of it." Valerie clasped her hands together. They were damp and shaking. Her voice shook too. "How can that be?"

Adele sighed and waved a perfectly-manicured hand. "Officially, it never happened. Records of incidents like that one were revised to prevent public panics during and after the war. In 1949, policy shifted to prevention. Certain combinations of power designation and rating were declared non-viable."

Non-viable carried the stink of euphemism about it. Valerie's heart sank right down to her shoes. She'd been shocked to learn no G-series had survived rollover in over seventy years, but now—"He was a G prime?"

Alex answered sourly, "Oh, no. Forensic evidence suggests Martin Latham was no more than a G4 or possibly a G3."

Adam ran a hand through his silver hair and made a dramatic gesture. "And in the two hundred seconds before Latham was neutralized, he caused forty *separate* recorded incidents. The series is inherently unstable. Do you see why we need camps now? Immediate oversight is a critical element of the viability program."

"There's a *program*?" Her heart was pounding hard, and her head throbbed too. She couldn't stop seeing all those terrified, innocent victims, and it made rational thought impossible.

Adele nodded. "Of course there's a program."

Adam continued, "G is far from the only problematic series. We are also *very* conservative about releasing Ps and Rs down to rating 3, a wide range of W categories and—" he hesitated at a quelling look from Adele. "The important thing is, we need to fix the situation in Elgin before it goes any further. If Reed was in a camp, it would be easy to separate her from the general population without alarming her. But we can't reach her where she is, not without being noticed. And can you see imagine what will happen if Grace Reed is at large when she breaks down like all Gaias do?"

Common sense shrieked at Valerie to agree, but she couldn't. "I can understand your fears." She spoke slowly, trying to collect her thoughts. She hoped her face wasn't betraying her conflicted emotions.

The needs of the few must be balanced against the survival of all. She had heard that her whole life, but where was the balance point? Did these people realize they were admitting to genocide? Didn't they see the deaths they sanctioned were murders? At least two of them were active poz themselves. How could they rationalize away such violence?

Her shivers subsided, but the haunting images of violent death kept bubbling up. "Internment didn't help all those other people assigned to the same camp, did it?" she asked. "Or maybe they don't count because they were poz?"

Adam snorted. "Don't be absurd. We're all poz here, Ms. Wade. Bigotry doesn't come into it."

Valerie wasn't sure of that—self-hatred came in all shapes and sizes—but she *was* sure antagonizing these three would be a mistake. "How did they stop him?" she asked.

Adam told her, "The off-site teleporter watching those cameras lobbed him as far as the ionosphere and followed up with a five-kiloton atomic bomb. That containment option is thankfully obsolete."

"We nearly started World War Three," Alex said, "because we didn't have time to warn the Russians. Treaties were signed. We are in violation of international law right now, thanks to your idealistic bullshit."

"No, we are not," Adam snapped. "Dial back the bullshit, sonny."

"Gentlemen." The quiet word from Adele had both men sitting back in their seats. She stood and leaned forward on her hands, saying earnestly, "The United States sequesters more of its rollovers than other developed countries, but we also have the world's best viability numbers. You don't want to know how some other governments handle nonviables, Ms. Wade. You really don't."

"Maybe Adam should show her some examples." Alex turned his cold gaze and colder scowl on Valerie. "Why the *hell* didn't you abort to internment once you knew for certain you had a developing Gaia on your hands?"

She had an answer for that one. It burst out on a wave of fear-fueled resentment. "Did I know any of this?" she demanded. "Did any of us? I called for a priority evaluation, and they said, 'don't bother.' If you knew better, why didn't someone step in? Why did *you* let Grace complete her rollover if you knew it would be a disaster?"

"We didn't know." Adele's expression turned sorrowful. "Ms. Wade, we are not the villains here. If the SDU didn't desperately want your brave experiment to succeed, it never would've gotten a grant. We didn't act earlier for several reasons. First, Gaias rarely survive long enough for sustainability to matter. Second, the usual preventative measures were in place. They all failed. That has never happened."

Valerie bit her lip. Who were their agents? She did not dare ask. Which one of her friends or their friends was a secret assassin? Doubt was a weak, sick feeling in her gut and a sour taste in her mouth. "But Grace is fine," she whispered. "She earned her certification."

Her mind filled with visions of Grace's house painted in blood, the garden in flames, the neighborhood a shattered field of rubble. "How can you be so sure? What if she doesn't need to be—"

She couldn't say it. Couldn't bear to think it.

"Neutralized," Adele said gently. "It's our job to be sure, and our backup protections do not fail. We have to conclude she has subverted everyone around her. This is why rollover cannot ever be mainstreamed, and it's why this mistake must be cleaned up before chaos and destruction spread out of control. Time is short, and you're our best chance to regain the upper hand."

Valerie took one deep breath after another, stared at the mural, and clenched her hands until her nails bit into her palms. Nothing helped.

Adam rose, approached her, knelt beside her chair. "Believe me, Ms. Wade, I wish we didn't have to ask for your cooperation, but you're the only one with access who we *know* hasn't been compromised."

"You're wrong," she said. "Grace is a good person. She would never hurt anyone. I don't care what you call it. I can't hurt her."

"We wouldn't ask that." Adam's smile was sympathetic. "And we aren't passing judgment. Good people do horrible things without intending it. She is dangerous, Ms. Wade, she has to be contained, and we can't get close enough to protect innocents from harm. That's where you come in."

A single, bitter laugh escaped Valerie's lips before she got herself under control. "Do I get thirty pieces of silver?"

"Don't be ridiculous." Adele sat down at the table again, crossed her legs, and studied her manicured nails. "Think of all the people who will die if we leave her loose. Once she is neutralized, we can easily control the aftermath."

"You have children," said Alex. "Think of them. Do the right thing."

Valerie's heart turned to ice in her chest, and despair numbed her thoughts. She knew exactly what that was. That was a threat veiled as encouragement.

I'm sorry, Grace, she thought, and she asked, "What do I have to do?"

They told her.

It was a plan made of contingencies—if this, then that—but none of the acts would be personal save the least-likely one. She clutched that consolation tight to herself. Preserving the many at the expense of the few was not a comfortable duty, but it was *hers*.

This wasn't about betrayal. It was about doing the job of keeping people safe. That made the idea bearable, if barely.

When they were done going over details, they sent her from the room with everything she would need: travel clearances, security documents, and an envelope full of cash to cover expenses, a small metal box holding liquid death.

Inside her mind, chilly terror spread into a welcome numbness. The eerie sense of detachment was an invisible cushioning force, distancing her from the horror of what she was about to do.

She called home on the way to Transit, made arrangements with Anna, and asked her to give her love to Gary and Johnny. Her heart ached and bled inside its cold, protective shell, but she could not risk going home to say good-bye before she left.

Gary would ask *why* the way he always did, and Johnny would react with a sullen pout but dissolve into giggles when she hugged him—and if she held them and looked into their innocent, trusting eyes, she could never go through with this.

She had no choice. She was doing this for them.

Whatever happened, they would grow up knowing their mother had tried to do the right thing.

35: CLOUDS RETURN AFTER RAIN

Night of September 7. 414 Elm Drive, Elgin, IL & elsewhere

EVERY NIGHT, year after year, Grace had prayed for sleep without dreams.

She had prayed for relief from fear-filled nightmares, begged forgiveness for her many sins, and asked for guidance in days to come. Some nights she had laid awake for hours apologizing for her faults and worrying over her children's future.

During this last, precious week of her life, sleep had become a memory. Dreams stalked her waking hours, past and future whispering tales of hope and madness. Power gnawed at her skin and bones, and the whole wide world sang glorious, terrible songs no one else heard.

The mysteries she sheltered within her body grew more intense with each passing day. At night, she watched moonlight crawl across the restored tin ceiling of her bedroom, listened to the music of the universe, and prayed for wisdom.

Soon, the world sang.

One of its melodies tugged her from her bed and pulled her

downstairs, outside into the yard where she could sink her toes into the loam and press life against the soles of her feet.

The noise in her mind quieted, and she stretched out her arms to catch the breeze. Cool air filled her lungs, tasting of dying grasses and dew-touched herbs.

The close, commonplace rhythms of the season calmed her. Life murmured within the house, in the neighboring homes, and below in the bunker where her new tenant slept. The world hummed a tune of cycles and rest; for every leaf that withered, a new seed grew.

Grace pulled herself back inside her skin without disturbing Amy's sleep. If her visions were true, the Marine would be a pivotal player in the hours ahead. She would want to go into battle at her best.

And there *would* be a battle.

Her many futures were falling into ever-simpler patterns, delicate lines and gems of bleak, sharp colors she refused to observe too closely for fear of disturbing them.

She sensed Sal long before he reached her but let him approach unremarked, enjoying the sight of him without bothering to turn around.

Starshine picked out the silver in his hair and highlighted the tired slump of his broad shoulders. Shadows filled the lines around his eyes when he smiled at Grace's back.

Once she had loved him, once she had feared him. Now he slipped his arms around her from behind. "You always had trouble sleeping. How many nights did I find you curled up under a live oak in the pasture?"

"Too many." His touch stirred warmth beneath her skin, deep inside between her hip bones. There was no demand in his lustiness, no expectation, only a friendly welcome. *Familiar, intimate, comforting.* She wrapped her arms over his, hugging his essence to herself, felt his smile against her ear.

She said, "When I said I would never trust you again, that was anger talking—anger and hurt. You know that, don't you?"

"I do now." His joy reverberated through Grace, a chiming of notes that blended with the busy chirping of night insects. He said, "You're flowing faster tonight. Deeper."

His voice woke a new harmony in the earth underfoot. It rose through Grace's calves, up the length of her thighs into the cradle of her pelvis, shaking her bones and waking frosty prickles of fear with its reminder of the way her precarious flesh had shifted when it first absorbed its full wave of power.

C-variants forfeited their bodies to the power that coursed through them. Change was coming, and it would not be denied. *Maybe the evaluators were wrong,* whispered temptation. *You've come this far. Ignore this feeling.*

She pushed denial behind her, recognizing sinful pride beneath hope's disguise. New energies were building inside, a fretful hot-cold rush like water rising, eating away at the fragile shell of her flesh. The body could not serve her needs as well as the new shape she could sense was nearly ready to burst free.

God's glory was a tremendous burden. Its use would have effects far beyond her ability to comprehend. When should she act? Who should she help or curse? Why? How? Where? The questions piled one on the other, daunting in their complexity.

When was the most urgent one now. The compulsion to direct the immensity of her power kept growing. Muscle and blood, sinew and nerve, she was keeping herself gathered in, but the time would come to cast off those limits and see what became of her.

"I'm flowing too fast," she said. She had to be honest with someone, and who better than the man who knew her soul's every dark corner? "I'm out of time, Sal. I wish I could stay forever, but this is my last night."

Sal tucked her closer and laid a kiss against the skin beneath her ear. "I'll stand with you until you go, and you'll take our love with you when you leave."

God had given her unexpected gifts along with the terrifying, transformative ones. Her exasperating, boneheaded ex-husband was proving himself a rock as firm as her new faith, surprising no one more than himself in the process.

Grace was thankful for him and for the family he had made possible, the one she knew would continue—if they all came through the next little while without her triggering the end of days.

Glittering sparks of electricity popped and crackled around her at that thought.

Sal didn't flinch, and he didn't let go, but Grace barely dared think about Maggie or Lauren now for fear of what her thoughts might do. "You'll have to give them my last hug," she said. "Tell them I love them."

"I will." That simple. Peaceful. Trusting. "Be here, now. It's enough."

This was the man she'd married. Not a strong-willed one, or much for deep thinking, but one as pure as sunshine and generous as the sky was wide. She drank deep from the fresh well of his humanity, and he poured himself out without hesitation.

Love inhabited the very substance of the house behind her, everywhere Sal had anchored it with nails and sanded it smooth, everywhere he'd breathed it into new air ducts and brushed it over cracked old plaster, everywhere he'd painted it onto the walls themselves. He'd crept back into his daughters' hearts with the same lack of fuss or fanfare, turning the same patience he used in his handiwork to the repair of the family he'd broken.

Their lives flickered around Grace like happy fireflies, flashing memories of things learned, meals made and shared, projects begun and finished. The sparks burned where *forever* met *never again,* but she embraced those pinpricks of pain. Those, too, belonged in the pattern she would use to reshape herself.

Soon.

The world roused and howled. Broken wails of anger and grieving clawed at her heart. There was so much suffering and hatred. The ground itself cried out for relief. She could ease those pains. But should she?

Some part of her chortled *yes, yes, do as you wish, anything at all,* but that way lay madness. She knew that. She'd seen it. And yet, the need to act would not be denied. The power was seed in her hands, spilling through her cupped fingers and begging to be planted so it might sprout.

The answer to *when* overflowed her awareness and became an imperative: *now.*

Choice was all that remained in her control: *where* and *how* should she cast herself loose and be re-shaped as she fell? She listened harder than ever before, sifted through all the places and times and possibilities.

The right choice—the only choice—rose easily to mind. *So close. No wonder it calls so loudly.*

"Time for me to go." Grace stepped away from Sal before she burst out of her own skin and harmed him.

"Where?" The word stood in for a multitude of other questions.

"Not far." Grace pointed. "Six blocks that way, and then a mile over rough ground. They're going to come for me, and that's the best place for me to meet them."

Sal stared in that direction as if he could see Grace's destination. "And you don't want me with you." His throat worked as he swallowed shame. He was no warrior, but he still felt he should want to be there.

"No," Grace told him. "I want you here, drying our daughters' tears and showing them the bright goodness in the world you see. I *need* that. It's the best defense I have."

He might have argued, but that wasn't his way. He sniffled. "I wanted more time."

"Me, too." Power crawled along her arms, a rippling aurora of green and gold. "But it's almost too late."

Tears came up hot and spilled down her cheeks when she turned away from him, but she had to do it. She let her heart go and turned from past to future.

God, please help them, she prayed, *and hold them safe in the palm of your hand.*

She went to the back of the yard and knocked politely on the bunker's closed hatch before transmuting it to air. "It's time," she called down the ladder shaft. "I need you."

A minute later, Amy heaved a bathtub-sized clanking bag onto the lawn and swung herself after it, landing with a thump. Worms died, and the grass whimpered.

Energy leaped eagerly to Grace, wanting to fix the damage. She reined in the impulse and struggled for the focus of words. "I'm nearing the end of my beginning," she said. "The path forward is set with traps my conscience won't let me evade, and events converge best if I'm on the testing grounds when they come."

"You're getting the hang of the cryptic prophecy stuff." Amy unzipped the bag and clipped an elastic-banded radio earpiece to one horn. Then she efficiently donned a web harness and a heavy fabric kilt with sewn-on pouches. "Let me make sure I've got it: it's about to get ugly, and you only see a happy ending if we face it on Marine territory?"

"Yes." The house creaked as wind circled it with the sound of her voice. "Now, please."

"Lead on. Unless you're 'porting us both somewhere. Either way, I'm calling Jack and getting his plan in motion."

"I want to walk." She was clinging to every last, small part of her life for as long as she could.

Reaching the huge wall of grass-covered dirt at the edge of the base property didn't take long. The walk brought them to the high, rigid metal fence at the top. Amy made her calls as they walked, and Grace sent power here and there in streamers and trickles to keep from overflowing herself. Changing the world in small ways, leaving behind small gifts. That couldn't be so bad, could it?

"It's good ground." Amy surveyed the blasted landscape stretching all the way to the horizon. Not even moonlight could soften the harshness of the cratered, lifeless waste. "No bystanders, room to maneuver, and most of it is toxic and torn to shit already."

"I wanted to avoid violence. That's all I ever wanted."

Amy snorted, looking down at her. "Sweetie, the fight will be coming to you. You take care of Armageddon, and we'll take care of you. Are you sure you don't want Val looped in? She's all about finding legal, long-term solutions, and she'll be pissed about being left out."

"Maybe so." Grace resolutely refused to think about Valerie right now. So delicate, that decision. So much anguish. "But if she's meant to be here, she will be."

"It's your party. Let's get it started. Unless you want to do the honors?"

Amy would have ripped a hole in the fence with her bare hands. Grace made it disappear. All of it. The effort felt *good,* like stretching in the morning after sleeping too long. Amy waved a hand through the empty space, then stepped through.

"Did you turn it into air?" she asked. "Because I can think of a lot of things it would be fun to vanish. Nice, harmless ideas, before you start getting all pious."

"Like what?" Grace asked.

As they walked across the horrific wasteland to await the arrival of deadly enemies, Amy regaled her with suggestions for epic practical jokes. After a radio call from someone named Farley, whose angry questions became court-martial threats, Amy waxed more eloquent and got personal with her vaporization ideas. Most of them involved clothing, and they *were* funny.

For years Grace had prayed for dreamless sleep. Now she prayed for greater understanding, clung to her rocky faith in God's purpose, and gave thanks that she would not face the coming hours alone.

36: MORE BITTER THAN DEATH

September 7, Various points here and there

"ALL RIGHT, your payment cleared, and you're here. What's the big secret problem?"

Shelly Burris held the door to her posh suburban New Jersey home like a shield. Both hands gripped the edge hard while she peeked around it at Valerie. Her nails were freshly manicured, and evening cosmetics minimized her wrinkles. Her lips were painted in smoky plum. She wore a rose silk wrapper over a matching lace slip, and a loose scarf covered her gray hair.

"Sorry to interrupt your evening." Valerie held one hand over the transport tag tickling her skin. She hoped the desperation beneath her smile didn't show. "I need a favor. A whole series of favors, actually."

"Now is not a convenient time."

"I see that." Embarrassment warmed Valerie's cheeks. She had interrupted a romantic encounter. "I'm sorry."

"I don't do favors for anyone. Transport is my job. I get paid for it."

And Valerie would not qualify as a friend if she kept pushing. That much was clear to see. The sadness and regret radiating from Shelly didn't match her brash, bitter words.

Valerie wanted to apologize for causing that pain, but necessity drove her. "I understand that, too. That is why I wired the fee for getting me here before I called. Please, Shelly. It's important."

Shelly eyed her for a good long time before saying, "You'd better come inside. I'll start some coffee and talk to my man. You look like dog vomit, by the way."

That came as no surprise to Valerie. She'd done a lot of crying over the last few hours. She was directed to a floral-upholstered seating group in a huge room with a lofted ceiling and tall windows that overlooked a wooded lot. There, she wrestled with her conscience one more time.

Every time, she lost, and that led to dwelling on the one huge mistake she had already made. If she made another bad choice—her skin went hot and cold, and she shivered. This *had* to be the right choice.

"Here," Shelly said. "You could use this."

The cup of coffee was welcome warmth against her numbed fingers. "Thank you."

Shelly sat stiff-backed on the edge of the couch opposite and folded her arms under her breasts. "Let me guess. Miz Rules-and-Regs needs something or someone 'ported somewhere privately. Under the table. Off-schedule and unreported."

"Yes."

"No. I don't do unrecorded 'ports. Period. Don't worry, I won't hold it against you. If I stopped talking to everyone who asked once, I wouldn't have any friends at all."

"Let me explain."

"No. The answer is always no." Shelly sipped her coffee. She looked cool, collected, and dignified on the outside, but on the inside—

Hurt, Valerie's eyes told her. *Disappointed. Worried.* Porcelain clinked on glass when Shelly set her cup on the coffee table. "How else can I help? I can put you up for the night or as long as you want. I can give you money, call you a taxi. What do you need? Because honey, I can tell you need something."

"I need you to listen!" Valerie snapped her mouth shut on the exclamation, pressed her lips together, and inhaled. "I'm sorry, Shelly. You're right. I don't break laws. I can't believe I'm asking you, but the fate of the world might depend on it, and I'm scared I've already failed."

And then she burst into tears. The terror and helplessness came pouring down her cheeks in a blinding flood, and all she could do was hug herself and sob.

Heels clicked on wood and then tile as Shelly walked away. Despair overtook Valerie.

This was it. People were going to die, and every death would be her fault. Her throat closed tight around grief and self-loathing. Nothing she did ever went right. She screwed up everything she tried to do, no matter how hard she tried.

Beside her, the couch sank beneath a weight, and a handkerchief was pressed to her hand. A man's voice whispered, "It can't be as bad as that, can it? Problems never look impossible once you share them. Dry your eyes and tell us how we can help."

The voice was familiar, but it took Valerie a moment of shocked confusion to place it. She mopped at her face with the soft, cologne-scented cloth until she could see clearly again.

She had no idea where Yasu had come from, but he was beside her—slim and slump-shouldered—looking disheveled in formal slacks and a mauve dress shirt buttoned one hole off.

"What are you doing here?" Valerie blurted out.

He raised his bushy gray eyebrows very high and retreated to the other couch. "I hardly know where to begin. Two consenting, currently-unattached adults, mutual attraction—I'm sure you can fill in the rest."

Shelly came up behind him and poked his shoulder with one manicured nail. "Don't be mean, old man. Val, he's single, I'm divorced, we decided to spend some time together after we wrapped up Grace's contract. We were having a nice evening until you showed up to have hysterics all over my upholstery."

Yasu said, "Now who's being mean?"

"I'm an ice-cold bitch. Ask anybody." Shelly sighed and sat down beside him. "But I'm not made of stone. All right, Val. I'm listening. Convince me."

37: POWER WAS ON THE SIDE OF THEIR OPPRESSORS

September 7, Elgin IL, and neighboring areas

JACK ARRIVED outside Camp Butler's main gate in a steamy downpour that rendered him half-blind and completely drenched. He dropped his gear bag to the grass and yanked off his sunglasses. Water splashed up to his knees.

Heather squeaked in disgust and bashed him in the face with the top of one wing as she launched herself away, off to collect two more allies while he lurked here for a quick look at the opposition. She blinked out in a puff smelling of pepper and damp feathers, and lightning crackled overhead, lighting up the heavy clouds.

If all went well, Heather would be back for him after she 'ported the others straight to Amy's position. Jack couldn't decide if he should laugh or cry. They were about to put themselves between Mercury Battalion's heaviest unit and its chosen objective on its home field—in the middle of the night in the pouring rain.

If all went well? Better to ask, *what else could go wrong?*

He regretted the thought the instant it crossed his mind. Right now, this was a case of overwhelming force meeting indestructible target. If Grace exerted herself to fight back...*everything ends in fire and blood,* she had said more than once, and Jack knew in his bones she hadn't exaggerated. Things could get worse.

He growled, thinking of the message from Amy that had awakened him. "Sorry, Jack. She started talking about the end times and walked into Marine country. I guess that's the best we could've hoped for."

That was pure bullshit. Meeting an interdiction team on military property would be better than confronting one in a neighborhood full of non-combatants. It wasn't as optimal as a dozen other scenarios he would've chosen, though.

Grace had picked a hell of a way to start the party, too. *Trespassing onto restricted Federal land, for fuck's sake.*

Civilians who breached the defenses around the training range were presumed dangerous and treated accordingly. Camp Butler's security systems were discreet but comprehensive. No one wandered through them by mistake. Getting past multiple sensor arrays and through the elementally-reinforced fencing took a powerful and determined trespasser.

Powerful and stubborn perfectly described Grace. Now Gateway Company was on the move to subdue her.

Water sparkled in the headlight glare from trucks and flatbed equipment transports as they rumbled out the nearby gate. Red tail lights and orange hazard blinkers gleamed balefully as vehicles turned to follow their fellows up the access roads around the base. Fog rendered the buildings a hundred feet inside the fence invisible between lightning flashes. Shouted orders and thumps of boots on pavement carried through the mist.

The ground shivered underfoot, hinting at other preparations in progress. Aviation fuel, hot metal, and the distinctive smell of ammunition scented the wet breeze, and power pulsed through the air. Tee squads were pumping up for combat. Jack's muscles tensed and thrummed in response as their rampage called to the energy throbbing in his veins.

This was not a typical trespass interdiction. The camp was spinning up for an all-out assault. That was not a proportional response to a single intruder, especially not if they'd ID'd Grace. Gaias were officially listed as non-destructive and monitored more for their E-F abilities than anything else.

Amy hadn't heard a peep about Grace through the base grapevine, but someone obviously knew there was more to the picture. *Who tipped them off?*

For all Jack knew, Grace had told them. All conversations about de-escalating the potential for violence had stalled at, "When it's time, I'll think of something." Who knew what Grace might think was a good idea? She had retreated deeper into vagueness with every passing day.

Jack could not protect someone whose idea of strategy was painting a target on her own back and yelling, *come and get me*. And yet, what choice did he have?

He was tempted to walk through the gate, call in favors and get himself to the captain. He could explain the situation and make one last plea for sanity. Captain Jefferson might believe him.

Stopping all of this before someone did something irrevocably stupid might be that simple. But if he was wrong, he would be sitting in a cell when the world ended.

Displaced air washed over his back, dry and smelling of sugar and roses. Heather said, "Hold your breath," and it was too late for might-have-beens.

He landed halfway up a steep hillock of concrete and stone rubble. Thick veins of mud flowed between the larger chunks of debris, and he sank calf-deep in stinking muck. The mud glowed, casting a malevolent light upward to paint the low-bellied clouds in shades of sickly yellow.

The spot was a familiar central landmark on the range, built over the years on the bones of a demolished building. One remaining intact wall rose fifty feet straight up from the barren flats, and multiple paths led up the thirty-yard apron of debris at the rear. Its height made it a useful vantage point, although its exposure made defense interesting.

The storm was in retreat here, the rain a weary patter. Above and behind him, Heather said, "That's it for me. I can't take this energy turbulence. Good luck."

Her departure sent a splatter of cold water down Jack's bare back. At least she'd gotten them all here before bolting. He saw the dim forms of two other Tees down at the bottom of the hill. That would be Amy and the one friend whose total discretion and support they'd been willing to stake their lives on.

And perched on a boulder right beside him, Elena sat with her knees bent nearly to her chin to keep her pink rubber rain boots out of the mud. Her nose peeked from the hood of a bright pink rain slicker. Her face was tipped up, looking past him with wide-eyed wonder.

Grace stood barefoot on a low line of bricks at the top of the hill. The wind played fretfully around her damp, muddy sundress. Her wispy hair was dry and unmoved by the breeze She held both arms skyward, palms up. The ambient power level pulsed high enough to lift rampage to the quivering edge of Jack's self-control.

He whispered a heartfelt curse as aurorae burst into the visible spectrum.

"Wow." Elena fidgeted, making her boots squeak. Her shadowed face scrunched up into a wary scowl. "Hi, Jack."

He flashed teeth at her. "Hi, tiger. Nice outfit. Very perky."

It made her look like a child, innocent and guileless. She looked him up and down, radiating suspicion. "You're not going to tell me I'm a useless null and shouldn't be here?"

"Nope. When you're included in a vision, you get the choice."

One more reason to hate fucking precogs. Grace's remarks about Elena and Heather had been ambiguous but positive, so he and Amy had quietly brought them into the loop.

Being Elena, she probably would have ended up in the middle of things at the worst time possible if they'd tried to exclude her.

"I feel useless," she said, "but I couldn't hide at home once Amy told me. What about Heather? Are you going to growl about her running away?"

"Nope again. She's done her part. This is strictly a volunteer gig."

Null or not, Elena had as much right as anyone to be here. If this went sideways, here or home in bed wouldn't make a damned bit of difference. And Heather had a husband and child she could 'port halfway around the world. That still might not be safe, but Jack might have chosen that over duty if he were someone else.

"I'm not judging anyone tonight," he told her.

Elena kicked the toe of one boot against rocks. "Huh. I was so sure you'd be mad at me."

"Sometimes you are wrong," he said gravely, which made her snort.

He slogged away to greet Amy and Kris. They needed to discuss what he'd seen.

A pulse of turbulent energy caught him halfway. It swept downhill in a ghostly mist, accompanied by an unheard whisper: *"Brace yourselves. You'll need this."* Energy crashed over him a moment later. He lost his vision during a red-hazed, grinding adjustment period, and the ferocious urgency remained once he regained control. The familiar drumbeat of his ramped-up pulse—*ready, steady, ready, steady*—anchored him while the rampage peaked out and made itself at home.

He hadn't gone weirdly monstrous this time. Grace had lived up to her promise that she wouldn't press more power on him than he could handle, now that she had control over what she passed on.

A quick shake, top to toe, gave him the basics: he'd popped up a solid three feet and thrown on more armor mass than he'd ever carried, with extra muscle beneath. He flexed his jaw, confirming speech was still a practical option.

Then he noticed how much sharper his senses had become. Heartbeats, heat signatures, heady aromas—he tuned out what he didn't need and brought the rest into focus.

Grace was still on the hilltop communing with the sky. Stray tendrils of light and mist chased around her. The fog swirled away in the updraft, revealing his other two companions again.

Amy had been boosted into a rampage form like nothing Jack had ever seen. Huge and sinuous, she leaned forward on one hand like a runner at the starting line. The thick, muscular tail she'd wanted swung out behind her, and she bared a snoutful of teeth at him. "Smart man. You picked up a civvie kilt like I suggested."

"I did." He'd bought a lot more than that, anticipating the need to upsize everything, and he regretted not one dollar of the specialty tailor's exorbitant fees. There were times a man did not want his danglies hanging in the breeze. This was one of them.

He pulled his new gear harness from the duffle bag and greeted the last member of their ragged band of rebels. "Hey, Kris. Glad you could make it back."

"Hi, short stuff. Wish I could say I'm glad to be here."

She looked as steady and cool as always. Next to Amy's twenty-foot length, she was petite, but she still topped Jack by a foot. Bumpy ridges of armor rose along her back and sides, right up through most of her short black hair: a textbook example of a T-series at full rampage, only scaled up by a substantial percentage thanks to Grace's power assist.

She wore nothing but stretch leggings, and she swung a steel bar in one hand, spinning it like a cheerleader's baton. "I'm underdressed," she said, watching Jack load up baton, chain, and bracers from his duffel. "My old gear is in storage, and Grace said not to try for it."

"Got you covered, sister," Amy said. "My usual kit should stretch for you, give or take. In the other bag there."

Soon Kris was settling a loaded fight harness over her dorsal armor with a practiced thump of her heels and spinning the baton again. "Just like the bad old times, only this time I feel like we're on the right side."

She turned those sharp eyes of hers on Grace, and the spin of the baton slowed while her sharp mind worked faster. Then she grounded the weapon with a crunch of broken rock. "Okay, so we're technical advisors. Best case, we demonstrate confrontation isn't necessary, worst case we coach Grace on least-force countermeasures?"

Count on Kris to shoot straight to the point. "That covers it."

This was going to be a bloody mess. It was easier to swat a fly than to catch one alive. If it came to combat, Grace didn't have the training or experience to use her raw power wisely. She didn't know the mechanics of battle, didn't even know the vocabulary.

As if she'd heard him, Grace said, "No, I don't. Maybe ignoring what I didn't want to learn was a mistake, but it's far too late now. I think it was always too late. I trust you to tell me what to do."

She hadn't said those words aloud, hadn't moved a muscle from her statue-stance on the hilltop. Did she know she was projecting telepathically? Jack didn't want to ask and didn't trust himself to answer her ignorance without losing his temper.

Unfazed, Kris replied aloud, "Teamwork under fire takes practice. We can read the opposition and give you direction, but you need to understand that you *will* get overwhelmed and react on instinct. That means people will get hurt and die unless you let them overrun you without defending yourself. In that case, you die, we die, everybody dies—which is the scenario we're trying to avoid."

Amy said, "Way to look at the bright side, Kris. Grace, here are some practical tips. Don't reflect things. Deflection is better. If you haven't already put up a shield like the one you made for rain the other day, do it now. That's your foundation. Fight fire with earth, earth with water, air with fire. Absorb what you can, redirect the rest, preferably where people aren't. Some attacks are targeted, some cover whole areas, but they all come from individuals. Trust us to point you at the sources. Got it?"

"Got it," Grace replied, again without turning to speak. "I hope."

"I hope so too." Amy tugged at one of her horns. "Jack, which units caught the trespass call? How many squads are we looking at?"

"The whole damned company and then some." He relayed the preparations he'd seen. "I can't believe they're rolling out the kitchen sink over a fence breach."

"Maybe I wasn't clear," Amy said. "She vaporized the whole range fence, Jack. Instantly."

That changed the picture, but not by enough. "They're still too ready. I swear they've called in reinforcements. It's like they were waiting on high alert. They're going to drop the hammer hard. I would bet a couple of paychecks they're cleared for preemptive action."

Elena splashed up beside him as he finished speaking. Fear was an unmistakable odor—hot, sour, and warm—but it had a thousand subtle variations. He'd never smelled fear like this on Elena. For once in her life, she was scared out of her wits.

She grabbed his thumb and squeezed. "Maybe I should stand up to speak for her?" she said. "You know, beforehand. It wouldn't be the first time I've done it. That's mostly how I thought I might help."

Jack chewed over her suggestion, at a loss for words. The offer was brave, and Elena was right about being the best one to play negotiator, but it wouldn't work. How could he explain without frightening her worse?

Kris said, "Bad idea. They'll smear you all over the landscape and never even know you were there."

Elena whimpered.

So much for softening the blow. "Seriously, Kris?"

Kris shrugged expansively.

"It wasn't a bad idea." Amy's tail scraped back and forth, moving in counterpoint to her headshake. "Bad timing. Elena, you're the best peacemaker we've got when the time comes, but do not walk out in front of anything without our say-so."

"Right," Jack said. "Keep your head down. Promise me."

Her smoldering glare was framed in pink, shiny plastic. Jack refused to blink.

Elena made a rude noise. "Fine. I promise."

Kris lifted one finger. "Okay, then. The plan is, 'hunker down and ride out the first wave without racking up too many casualties, then—" she raised a second finger, "—pull out a white flag and form a protective wedge around the cute null?'"

"That'll do." Amy lifted her head in the direction of an

approaching roar. Her crest lifted, and stray energy spun loose from it in wispy tendrils. "Looks like time to hunker."

Grace lowered her hands and rubbed her bare arms as if warding off a chill. "Elena, come up here where I can shield you best," she said aloud in a shaky voice. "They're coming."

38: WHOEVER DIGS A PIT MAY FALL INTO IT

September 7, Camp Butler Training Range, Elgin, IL

ELENA COULDN'T FORCE herself to let go of Jack. Her legs trembled, fear boiled up in her stomach, and she could not move. Jack was so big now it was like holding hands with a warm, living fortress, and she wanted to say *can't I stay with you?* because she could face anything if she was next to him.

She didn't want to admit that, so she bit her tongue. Jack pulled his thumb free and nudged her with two fingers, pushing her gently uphill. "Stick to her like a burr, tiger." His voice was so deep it shook her bones and made her teeth ache. "I mean it."

How could he be sure that was the right choice? Elena wanted to weep and couldn't say whether it was fear or rage. She focused on her muddy boots and ran until she was up on the heights again, breathing hard and wondering how trying to save lives had gone so wrong.

She'd been wondering that ever since Amy called her over to have ice cream and told her how bad things might get for

Grace. Elena's reaction then—*why can't everyone just get along?* —echoed in her mind now.

She stumbled and fell twice in the short distance. All the Tees could see in the dark. Elena couldn't see much except Grace, who had her arms raised high again as if to hug the gusty wind. Her toes were at the edge of the bricks, hanging over nothingness. The air shimmered, flickering greenish-blue, then red and gold.

Elena wondered how much more the others saw. What images would a camera catch? So much at stake, and here she stood in the dark with her fragile null body, her dull, ordinary senses, and all of her noisy doubts. *What are you doing here?* she asked herself. *You're a stupid little girl who's going to get in the way. Who needs that?*

"I do," Grace said without looking down. "You remind me there is power in gentleness and kindness. Never tell yourself that's useless. Never let anyone else say it. Come closer. Everything will be fine for you."

Elena didn't want to start an argument now of all times, so she did as she was told. The air was fresher near Grace, the weedy rubble dry and free of the awful mud. One of the stones behind the wall was a good seat height. Elena dusted it off and sat. What else could she do?

Paired lights dotted the shadowy landscape, moving closer in lines from all sides. Lightning crackled from sky to ground without thunder, dueling with gouts of flame rising from below. The flashes revealed glimpses of figures hanging midair and more beside the approaching trucks. The ground shivered underfoot, and the air near some of the trucks shimmered.

The clouds were too close and much too bright. Jack loomed up black and huge against them, blocking the view from the rear. Elena clenched both hands into fists until her nails bit into her palms. She'd always thought that was a book thing, not a real-life thing, but the cuts all over her hands felt real enough.

Grace closed her hands into fists, too. She blew out a breath, low and slow, and stepped off the wall to stand beside Elena. "To everything there is a season," she said after looking all around, and she put a hand on Elena's shoulder, squeezing tight. "Pray for courage with me?"

Elena was already doing that with all her heart and soul. There was comfort in hearing someone else thought it might do some good.

Jack rumbled, "Dig in, everybody."

Below, Kris appeared at one corner of the demolished building. Amy moved into view on the other. When she stood up on tiptoes, her head rose halfway to the top. Her head tilted, bringing her elongated muzzle and sharp teeth into profile, and she yelled a wordless challenge into the night. The sound bounced off unseen surfaces and echoed back. Kris tipped back her head and howled along with her, a noise full of exhilaration and defiance. Then Jack added his voice to the din, a bass roar that shook the very ground.

And the darkness answered.

39: A TIME FOR HATE, A TIME FOR WAR

Near Elgin IL

A TREMENDOUS SHRIEK cut through the air, rising in pitch and then dropping again as it passed overhead. Elena clapped her hands over her ears. A vast curtain of red flame and arc-bright lightning blossomed mid-air, parting in two to sheet down on either side of the hill. Everywhere it touched the rocky, barren ground, bright walls of fire blazed up.

Thunder pulsed in a deafening *BOOM*. Rocks bounced on the ground near Elena's feet. More stones rained from the rubble-filled windows onto Amy and Kris's shoulders. The distant rumble of engines stopped, and the night fell quiet again except for the flames, which crackled and popped like the world's biggest campfires.

"What was that?" Elena asked. The flames lit up the hill, but they hadn't caused any damage and didn't surround it.

"I didn't deflect that," Grace said. "It never came close. Why did they miss?"

Jack said, "They didn't. Warning shot, possibly, telling you to sit tight. They've stopped a half-mile out. Might be sending out someone to talk after all."

Something pinged off the top of his shoulder, sparking bright as it bounced away. The crack of the gunshot arrived an instant later. Then, with a crackle like firecrackers, projectiles hammered into Amy and Kris and disintegrated against their armor.

Kris said dryly, "Or maybe they'll use the light for sniping. Talk about pointless, unless—hang on. Are they're running a power reconnaissance?"

"Might be," Amy said. "Would make sense. There isn't much of a record on what a Gaia can do. Grace, if we're right, they'll be testing standard weapons nex—yikes."

Blue-white light flared directly overhead, once, twice, and again, accompanied by muffled bangs. Elena's ears popped at changes in air pressure. Flaming fragments struck an invisible dome of air, trailing thick smoky tentacles as they slid down to sizzle against the rocks near Amy and Kris. More smoke and a rank stench rose wherever they hit.

Elena imagined what would have happened if that stuff had landed on her, and fear sent shivers all through her body. What if Grace couldn't defend them? What if she got distracted? *How can this be fine?*

"They are spooked," Amy said. "Straight to 'ported incendiaries, not machine guns or LAWs first. They'll come in with heavier shells next, Grace, and use that to distract you from a powered ground assault."

"Oh, no, they won't." Grace lifted one hand and pulled it back. In the distance, bubbles of light burst silently to life on the ground near one line of headlights. Smoke foamed up to meet the clouds before collapsing fast. Yellow-orange explosions lit within the fog, accompanied by a raucous clatter of noise as if someone had set off a thousand firecrackers and a whole fireworks show all at once. "There. No more bullets, bombs, or rockets."

A beat of silence later, Kris said, "Um. Did you just set off all their ordnance at once? From here? By waving at them?"

"I didn't have to wave." Grace released her grip on Elena to flap both hands. "It felt good. I made sure it didn't hurt anyone. I did what you said, deflected all the heat and bits into the ground. Did I do it wrong?"

"Eep," said Kris.

Jack said, "No, that's good. That'll make them think twice. If you can push out your shield perimeter as far as you can, that would be better. It's a little tight if we need to move."

Grace cast a worried look at his back. "As far as I can? But that's—"

"Can you do it or not?"

"I can, but—"

"Do it."

Grace bit her lip and wrung her hands together.

"Don't just stand there, Grace!" Amy snapped.

Elena wanted to shout at them to shut up. They were pushing too hard, badgering and flustering Grace instead of listening to her questions. She knew how that felt.

Inspired, she tugged on Grace's dress. "When people are confusing me, I do whatever makes sense," she whispered. "Maybe make a shield as big as your yard at home? And visible, so no one runs into it by accident?"

"Yes. Oh, yes. Thank you." Grace combed loose strands of hair behind her ears, and the night sky rippled with delicate soap-bubble rainbows. The dome rose higher and crept out fifty yards or more in all directions. Beneath it, the broken landscape lit with a foxfire glow. She rubbed her palms against her hips before resting one trembling hand atop Elena's head.

"That scared them too. Everything makes them afraid and angry. So much anger."

"Don't get distracted," Jack said. "I don't like the way those clouds are moving."

"Could be they're flying in melee specialists," said Amy. "We have close-in elementals in the rotation—"

Kris snapped, "Incoming, eleven o'clock ahead. Four. Crap. Sorry, Grace. In front, high and to your left."

"Got them," Grace replied, but she wasn't saying it. Her lips didn't move. She wasn't watching anyone, either. Her eyes were shut, and her forehead wrinkled with concentration.

Elena put her fingers in her ears and still heard Grace explain, "Don't worry about jargon. I'll understand what you mean. What do I do with a river of clay and dirt? It's rising, but it can't get underneath us. I have us in a sphere."

"They might pile it up to see if they can break your shield. Check your six." Jack crunched down the hill to get a better look. "I've got three squads of Tees on this approach carrying a crew who sheds heat."

"I know them. That's a close-range pyro and two kinetics," Amy said. "Haile scoops up raw sand and dirt, Grinnell heats it, Max throws the hot glass. I have two squads in my arc. Hey, that's my fire team. Watch them for a wicked ice-rock-'port combo, Grace. Kris, who do you have?"

"No one. Might be a crossfire issue. Or ranged attacks. Are there any line-of-sight hitters on base these days?"

"Not many. There's an N who turns air into nasty gasses, one prime flamethrower, and LOS 'porters who throw those melee pyros and strongmen—oh, shit." Amy jolted upright in her agitation, and her crest flared. "Grace, what if—"

The question came too late for five soldiers doing their duty. They appeared simultaneously in a star formation in midair and hit the shimmering barrier as one. None of them survived the transition.

One came through in parts—bones and metal first, then lacy nets of white, red, gray, and lastly yellowish flesh that collapsed like a deflated balloon. The clothes fell flat and slid earthward. Two hit like birds on a window and slid limp to the ground. Two simply dissolved, penetrating the shield in a spray of droplets to fall like black rain on the earth below.

Elena noted the horrifying differences that meant three different teleporters had launched the doomed group. She could not look away. Her body felt disconnected from her mind, and she was grateful for the odd sense of detachment.

Either she cataloged details, or she screamed hysterically until she passed out. She did not want to scream and draw attention to herself.

Grace was doing enough screaming for all of them. She dropped to her knees, hands against her ears, and she was hunched over with her face against her thighs, shrieking at the top of her lungs. The light of her defensive dome vanished. Soldiers charged across the now-dark ground, shadows flickering past patches of the nasty mud.

"I didn't mean it, I didn't mean to hurt anyone," Grace wailed. "Why couldn't they just leave me alone? Why?"

"They are doing their job," Jack said, calm and ferocious at once the way Elena remembered him being back on the day they'd met. "Dammit, Grace, put that shield back up."

Grace sobbed harder. "No. I'm a murderer already. What if I stop wanting to stop? What if I start to want it? What if all this is temptation? More of them will die if I do that, and now I can't even die to atone for my sin. No more. I can't do it."

Elena sniffled back tears. The under-lit clouds wavered in her vision. Resentment rose, wicked and hateful. *Maybe she can't die, but the rest of us can.* And Grace rocked back and forth on her knees, weeping.

Jack cursed low and helplessly. "Now what?"

Amy's voice came up from below. "Hang tight, Jack. Reinforcements are on the way. Ready, Kris?"

"Boost away."

Rock crunched, and Kris came vaulting up and over the wall with her baton in one hand and a green-glowing light stick in the other. She dropped both and shook mud off her bare feet with fastidious, cat-like flicks.

Her eyes glittered, and her black hair bristled with static. The joints where her armor shifted over her muscles lit up bright, and the excess energy she was shedding made the air crackle. She lifted Grace to her feet as easily as if the woman was a toddler.

"Listen up, woman," Kris said. "You think they'll stop because you're sorry? They won't. They have orders. They will roll right over us. Me, Amy, Jack, Elena. Red smears. You don't want blood on your hands? Too bad, mama bear. This isn't temptation. It's a test. You have claws and teeth. Protect us. You're the only one who can. Hear me?"

"I hear you." Grace gulped in a breath. "I hear. I'm sorry. I'm weak, I doubt, I'm afraid."

"Don't be sorry. Be stronger. *Defend us.*"

Grace wiped her face with her hands and met Kris's eyes. What passed between them, Elena didn't know, but Grace nodded.

New shimmers of color burst to life around her, coursing away over stone, crackling in the air. The glow illuminated the charging Tee squads. When the light stopped expanding, seven Tees were inside the safe zone. The rest of the advance crashed into it. Flames washed up, oddly soundless, liquid stone and water crashed down from above.

Grace made a low keening sound and closed her eyes, shuddering.

"Keep it up," said Kris. "That'll do." She put down Grace and bared her fangs at Jack, who was watching with a look of total bewilderment on his face. "You suck at touchy-feely shit, Jack-ass. Get down there and clean up stragglers with Amy. I've got this."

Jack growled and strode past them, right off the top of the hill. He landed with a whomp and raced toward the enemy. Amy followed him at a lope that ate up the ground.

"I do not miss that crap." Kris turned in place, taking in the view. Elena scrambled out of her way. Kris scooped her up and tucked her into the crook of one arm. "Do you mind? Jack will kill me if I step on you."

"No, it's fine." Elena slid her boots into the proper belt loops for a front-carry and stood up to grab hand grips without thinking. Kris's skin was warm against her back, the armor beneath it firm but yielding. Elena felt safe surrounded by all that protective strength. "Thank you."

"No problem," Kris bounced her up and down. "Reminds me of when I had boobs and hips and babies. All righty, then, Grace. Mean old Auntie Kris will walk you through this. Start with those Tees ganging up on Amy. You fed us power. Take theirs back. Then let them retreat, yeah? Adapt the barrier to let them through. You got that?"

Grace nodded. Her lips moved, and Elena knew it was the Shepherd's Prayer without hearing it. She whispered it herself to keep the vivid memories and grief from taking over.

It helped.

Before long, Jack was spinning in a circle to build up momentum before tossing his defeated opponents back through Grace's shield. He wasn't nice about where he sent them. The spot he sent them through was a standing wave of hot lava twelve feet high at the time. He was kinder to the few normal-sized human projectiles, lofting them into clear air where others could catch them.

Then he and Amy retreated to the base of the bluff and kept watch. If Kris missed opportunities, they spoke up, but Grace didn't leave them much to do. Wave after wave of assaults, both elemental and purely physical, failed to breach her defenses.

The onslaught eased at one point, but Elena's hopes were dashed when her vision snowed, and vertigo made her stomach heave. This was all so pointless. She was sick. She should surrender.

Kris lurched to the side and went to her knees. "They called in a brain bender," she said, slurring.

"I don't think so." Grace's eyes searched the horizon. Her face twisted with loathing. "She won't die," she said to the thin air, speaking to people far from where she stood without raising her voice. "I was merciful. Don't try again. The next one will get handled the way I handled the bullets."

And that was that for psychic attacks.

The Marines went back to looking for physical weak points. The drifting smoke thickened, and piles of steaming stone and mud rose ever higher. Kris had Grace pull in her defensive line, not because she was tiring, but to keep the opposing force in view.

When the attacks stopped, an eerie quiet fell.

Grace's shield was a shimmer above a laser-bright red line no more than fifty feet from the hill. The battle haze and ground fog quickly drifted away, and stars dotted a black sky above. The shield's pale glow illuminated the Marines maneuvering just beyond it.

There were too many. Elena knew from working with Jack that Gateway Company's complement fluctuated between one-fifty and two hundred. There were three times that many soldiers maneuvering between foxfire-glowing ridges of displaced earth, pools of steaming liquid, and lumps of cooling rock.

And beyond them, at the rear, black bags and stretchers were being loaded into trucks adorned with red crosses.

Jack sometimes called his fellow Mercury Battalion soldiers 'glass cannons,' and the description had stuck with Elena. The massive energies they handled took a heavy toll on their aging bodies. Bad decisions, slip-ups in communication, tiny lapses in discipline—even simple exhaustion could have lethal consequences. Tees were nearly invulnerable, but they were the exception.

The casualties were not Grace's fault, not directly, but Elena wept with anger. This was all so *pointless*.

Kris set her down and stretched. "Four straight hours of concentrated, coordinated assaults. That was an impressive display of mass stupidity."

Amy and Jack rejoined them on the heights. Amy crouched at the bluff's edge near Kris. "Think they'll parley soon."

"Let's hope so." Jack held up his radiophone to their audience, wiggled it. "Hint, hint, people. Grace, how are you feeling?"

Grace wrapped her arms around herself and shivered. Her eyes were red-rimmed from crying, sunken above tight, tense cheeks. She licked chapped lips. "I am sick of people asking me that. I feel everything, and everything hurts." Her voice cracked. "Heat so harsh the rocks scream. Cold that shatters the air. Stems drowned, leaves shredded, roots sucking up poison. Fur burned, muscle stripped, death soaked in foulness, scarred and twisted ugliness. We've torn open all the wounds, and they cry out. They scream. That's why I was called here. To stop this forever. To make it end."

"Easy on the crazy goddess talk," Amy said. "If you don't mind."

Grace's laugh held so much pain it made Elena's chest go tight. The woman picked up a brick. It crumbled to dust in her hand. "I am trying. It gets harder. So much begs to pour through me." She picked up another brick and frowned at it. It turned to water that steamed away. She wiped her hand against her dress, leaving a gray streak. "No. Not yet. Not here. I have to go through that fire alone."

The radio earpiece on Amy's left horn chirped. "Oh, perfect." She bent her head to Jack. "Here, maybe they're using my call code because they don't have yours. If it's Farley threatening me with court-martial again, tell him—"

Jack silenced her with a raised finger and pressed the earpiece to his cheek. "Jack Coby. Go ahead. What? Yes, clearly I'm with her since I'm answering her fucking pho—Grace? Again, do you have eyes? I'm standing right the fuck next to her."

He shook his head while listening until another chirp announced the end of the call. Then he shook himself all over. Amy prodded him with one finger. "Well?"

"That was Valerie. She says—it's too complicated. I'll let her explain. She'll be here in a minute."

"How does she know where to—" Amy swung her head around. "Grace? I thought you didn't want Val involved. What changed?"

Grace shrugged. "Everything and nothing. What will be, will be."

Amy and Kris exchanged a glance Elena couldn't interpret.

Next, Jack's phone buzzed. He looked at it, then at the Marines who were pulling back and dismantling things. A trio of civilians now waited in an empty space where soldiers had been, standing beneath a cluster of floodlights on a tall pole.

Two pale young men in black dress suits flanked a dark-haired older woman who wore an impractical gray skirt suit and sensible rain boots.

Elena recognized none of them, but they had a familiar, bureaucratic demeanor she distrusted on instinct. The men's smiles made her nervous. The woman had a handset at her ear. She lowered it with a shrug and spread an open hand at the shield. *We're here,* was the obvious message. *Let us in so we can talk.*

Jack growled curses and popped the speaker button on his handset so everyone could hear the conversation. "We're not dropping our defenses," he said. "We didn't start the shooting in the first place. The shield stays until we get cease-fire assurances. Can you give those, and on whose authority?"

"My name is Adele Banyan. My associates and I are from DPS Special Directives. We have authority to negotiate a peaceful end to this standoff, and we're willing to come in as a gesture of good faith."

Everyone looked at Grace. She shook her head.

Jack said, "We'll come to you. Give us a few minutes."

"We'll wait." the woman gave him a thumbs-up. "We're here to help."

40: FOR THE LIVING KNOW THAT THEY WILL DIE

Near Elgin IL

THE NEEDS of the world tugged at Grace's skin, yanked at her hair, made her bones throb and her teeth ache. Worse than a baby's hungry wail, worse than a toddler's unceasing whines, worse than the constant, eager questions of curious young minds, they competed for her whole attention and destroyed her ability to think about anything else.

She used skills she hadn't tapped in years to turn aside the raging tantrums of the violated land and soak up the desolated heartbreak of lives thrown away for nothing. One by one, she sorted the contents of her chaotic reality as if she was folding a basket of clean laundry. When that chore was done, she plucked *here and now* from the whirling cloud of possibilities that crowded her senses. What was the most important thing to remember right now?

Valerie.

She grabbed the woman off Shelly's silken line of reality before the present teleport intersected with future tragedy.

Instead of arriving piecemeal on the far side of Grace's defenses, Valerie landed healthy and whole inside the safe zone near Kris.

Shelly's transport tags did not react well to the change in course. The one on Grace's collarbone shriveled to a scrap and fluttered to the ground. Valerie slapped at her chest, frantically beating a flaming spot on her blazer.

Grace soothed away the burn beneath that charred hole with a thought. Valerie went still and raised her head. Grace looked back. *Betrayer. Betrayed. Neither. Both.* "Hello, Val. I'm glad you came."

Valerie's eyes flashed bright before settling to a green glow. Grace waited until her welcome was accepted as truth, then said, "You are sick with guilt. You'll feel worse when you look around. If it helps, I don't blame you. Not for all of it."

Valerie's shoulders tightened defensively when she looked over the devastation surrounding their oasis of peace. "Oh, my God."

Elena cried, "Val, it was awful," and launched herself at her mentor without giving Kris time to properly put her down. She landed stumbling and fell into Valerie's arms, which sent them both staggering until they bounced off Amy's hip.

Giving them time to sort themselves out was a matter of self-defense for Grace as much as a courtesy. The urgent clamor of their emotions battered her until she hurt all over. Val cradled the girl and made sympathetic noises while Jack exchanged nods with Kris. They both stepped away to keep an eye on the rest of the world.

Valerie rested her chin on Elena's dark hair. Grace waited, letting the other woman look her fill and regarding her in turn.

"They showed me horrible things," Valerie said. The agony of her choices was written across her face, and the air throbbed with her pain. "And they said you had to die for the rest of the world to live. I know you. I should have known better, but they said *think of your children,* and I was afraid. None of this would have happened if I'd been brave enough."

Grace blinked away a rush of futures that hadn't happened. "Spilled milk. I forgive you. That's what you need to hear, isn't it?"

Valerie blushed a fierce red and closed her eyes. "No, that doesn't help. Aren't you angry? Hurt?"

"Both. Deeply." Grace's heart bled from the wounds Valerie's deeds had inflicted. Anger seethed and boiled inside. She would not deny those emotions, but neither would she act as a child and lash out for resentment's sake.

Withholding forgiveness like a prize would only hurt them both. Grace was strong enough to absorb this blow, and *an eye for an eye* only made the world blind. "I'm furious and bitter, but I've made choices as bad or worse. I am not worthy to cast the first stone. None of us are."

Amy raised her hand like a child in a schoolroom. "Can somebody catch me up? Val, what did you do?"

Grace answered for her. "She trusted authority over her vision. She delivered secret orders and secret permissions to the base commander here. She personally warned him to take action immediately if I exercised my power in public."

Tears trickled down Valerie's cheeks. "He said to leave it to them, but I had second thoughts and then third and fourth ones, and I came to warn you as soon as my boys were safe. But —" she gestured at the horizon. "I left it too late."

Her pain cried out for easing. Grace told her, "There were worse choices. That matters. You didn't say enough to panic anyone into ambushing me at home. You didn't try to lure me away to be annihilated earlier. You did not smile to my face while stabbing me in the back with poison."

How did you know that was one of their backup plans? Valerie didn't ask the question aloud, but the awe and fear that accompanied the unspoken words sparkled around her.

"I see might-have-beens," Grace reminded her. "The hypocrites in your Special Unit tell themselves insanity is inevitable for Gaias, then make any other outcome impossible by pushing us past sane limits. I am *human*. I can be distracted, get angry, make mistakes."

She looked down on the three powerful, deluded people waiting to make a farce of negotiation, three of a secret group whose willful pride had killed thousands. It would be easy to send them to God's judgment with as little mercy as they would give her.

But no. She would *not* cast that first stone. "Maybe God can forgive them for breaking so many lives in their arrogance. I can't. I never wanted this. I was never a threat. You couldn't know that, though. You acted in doubt."

Valerie wiped away her tears. "I should have trusted my sight. I couldn't kill you in cold blood, but I doubted myself, and they were so sure I had to tell someone, and then—I am so sorry. I should've come straight to you."

"No. If you had abandoned their cause, they would have abandoned secrecy." Grace blinked away the future where Elgin was a smoking crater, Chicago another one beside it, and she was lost to a madness born of grief, a malevolent force without conscience. Valerie's conservative, careful cooperation had pruned away that rotten branch of tragedies. "This is better."

"Oh." Valerie squeezed Elena so tight the girl squeaked and squirmed.

Better was not good. Her enemies were plotting, discussing options, building up their determination for her destruction. They were pathetic, really.

They were still tempted to strike her with their doomsday weapons, but that whole bloody cascade of realities was safely dried up. The Marines had taught her how to avert attacks from above and below, how to snuff the life from explosives. Nothing would ever again cause that particular kind of harm near her unless she allowed it.

Perhaps she should allow them to try. Let them destroy themselves and this whole filthy situation. They would be easy to erase, and they deserved death a thousand times over.

The bedrock beneath her shivered, unhappy with the direction of her thoughts.

She calmed it. Anger was a temptation, but she would turn her cheek. Only one real threat to her remained, and he stood before her with his partners, held on an invisible leash

Other sufferings moaned at her attention, begging for ease from injuries near and far. *No,* she told herself sternly. *Focus. Here and now.* After this was sorted out, she would attend to all the other concerns.

If anything remained of them and her.

"I can't condemn you for being caught between a rock and a hard place," she told Valerie, "And you came to me to confess, as soon as you pried yourself free. All of it matters. If I'd rolled into this power in a strange place, surrounded by strangers churning up the world in their struggles—I would never have come this far. I owe my humanity to you and Elena, and my Sal, and—everyone."

"You were always a good person," Elena said, jutting out her chin.

"But I might not have stayed that way." She wanted to smile but held it in, knowing the girl would take it as mockery rather than affection. "You all gave me safe harbor when my storm rolled in. You sheltered me, clothed me, and raised me up."

"But how do we get you out of this mess?" Valerie gave up her hold on Elena so they faced Grace side by side.

"You don't." The world plucked at Grace's soul, again and

again, pouring itself into her body. She would break free of herself any moment now. "All you can do is bear witness and hope I can save us from the worst. The timing is so, *so* tight. Everything will be decided in the next few minutes."

"Where do you want your tactical backup?" Amy asked. "By which I mean us."

She wanted them wrapped in cotton, wreathed in smiles, safe and happy and far, far away. But if they left now, she would die, and their lives would still be forfeit soon after. "I'm too selfish to ask you to leave, but—" How much was it safe to say? Nothing. "You can't stop them. I'm not sure I can, but I will try."

"Grace, what kind of stupid stunt are you planning?" Jack's voice was a rocky growl of warning.

"I'm going to give them a glimpse of the monster they expect to see."

41: IN THE PLACE WHERE IT FALLS, THERE IT WILL LIE

Near Elgin IL

THE WIND KICKED UP, blowing grit into the tearstains on Valerie's cheeks. She squinted at the aura of untapped power dancing around Grace, and the revealing glimpse dried up her last remaining doubt. The woman was *good,* and that goodness was worth preserving.

Amy thumped her spiky tail against the stones—*She looks gloriously perfect like that,* was Valerie's distracted thought—and scratched her dorsal crest. "They want you dead, Grace. How is scaring them going to help?"

"I don't know," Grace said. "Let's find out together."

She picked her way through piles of debris, downhill past Jack. Pebbles gathered before her to make a smoother path, and as she passed, black loam rose to mix with sand and rich clay on either side. Kris and Amy took the direct route down, straight over the sheer side of the ex-building. Jack adjusted the straps on his harness and retreated after Grace.

His expression was hard with the righteous anger Grace

hadn't shown on her own behalf, and he didn't check to see if Valerie followed. He was huge now, knobby all over with armor and muscle. He had claws longer than Valerie's hands and fangs set in a jaw that could crush granite. But to her, he looked like the hurt and vulnerable young man he was.

Watching his silent, massive display of disappointment and rejection, Valerie's throat went tight around remorse. His forgiveness would be a long time coming, if it ever did. She followed hand-in-hand with Elena and kept her eyes on his back, hoping he would turn around and let her apologize once more.

They came around piled rubble to the base of the wall, and the wispy rollover energy she always saw around Jack flickered the way it did when he was shifting up or down a rampage cycle. Then it steadied to a vibrant glow.

Valerie's heart dropped right down to her feet. That unmistakable bright-burning signature was all-too-familiar. *Oh, no. Not him. Not now.*

"Val, what's wrong?" Elena tugged on her hand to pull her into motion again. "What do you see?"

"Nothing, sweetie." She swung Elena's hand back and forth, reaching deep for the appearance of hope. *Maybe I'm wrong.* Maybe it wouldn't matter. "Never mind."

"Oh, Val." Elena's sniffle was followed by an epic sigh. "Don't treat me like a baby."

"I don't. When was the last time I put you in a time-out like Johnny or Gary?"

"Ha. Never." Elena rubbed her nose against the back of her free hand. "They're okay, aren't they? When I snuck out tonight, past Teresa and Marco's rooms, I was thinking about how nice it was that you all would be safe in California."

"They are as safe as I could make them," was as much as Valerie had time to say before they caught up to the others.

The boys were on an adventure with Anna and her family in a place where retaliation from the DPS would cause a huge diplomatic incident. Courtesy of Shelly's unexpected generosity and a surprising network of unofficial international contacts, the children would be sleeping off jet lag and seeing kangaroos soon.

They'd had been so excited they'd wriggled like worms through their good-bye hugs. With luck, they would be back home in a week, transported by the same means, none the worse for the impromptu vacation.

With luck, and assuming we survive this. She glanced again at Jack, at the bleak shroud of his death wrapped close around him. Her eyes didn't lie. Jack had been living on borrowed time for years now—he broke the lifespan record for early-onset rollovers every day he woke up—but the loan was coming due. He might have weeks yet, even months, if he lived quietly. But if he pushed himself, he could burn out tonight.

He joined Amy, Kris, and Grace on a wide, flat spot of ground with a high, crumbling bluff behind them. Adele and her two new underlings waited with exaggerated patience outside the rippling curtain of Grace's shield. The portable lights on their humming generator stand cast watery shadows over the bare, muddy soil.

A little maneuvering put Grace in front of Amy, and she beckoned Valerie closer. Kris moved to Amy's left and gave Elena a hand up to curl protected against her side, high off the ground. Jack took up a position on the right and slightly back.

Adele's lips moved. Her voice came through Jack's radiophone speaker after a slight delay. "Why bother with the monsters, Grace? You don't need muscle for defense like I do."

Valerie gave the woman's escort a closer look. "You brought the only monsters here, Adele."

She couldn't identify the men's particular talents until they used them, but she could gauge their tremendous intensity—and they gave her the creeps, pure and simple. Whatever they did with their talents had soiled and twisted their essential natures.

Adele made a show of surprise. "Is she your mouthpiece now, Grace? Changing up from the trolls to a prettier puppet? That's unexpected. I didn't think you would let Ms. Wade survive if she failed the mission I gave her."

So this is a catfight, is it? Valerie snapped, "I'm no one's puppet," even as Grace said, "I need no mouthpiece."

After a taut silence, Grace continued, "These are friends, not puppets. Unlike you, they understand the stakes here. You're causing this crisis. Leave me to my fate. I don't want to harm anyone."

"So you say, but a crisis is inevitable. Power corrupts. Your position is unsustainable, but I'm authorized to make a deal with you. If you surrender peacefully, we will send you where you can't be a threat to others. I swear it."

You lie, Valerie thought, and Grace briefly glanced at her before saying, "What guarantees will you offer, Adele? Will you promise no one else here will be held accountable or face punishment? All my allies will go free?"

"I promise you'll regret refusing my offer," Adele said, avoiding the question the way she'd avoided introducing her partners earlier. "We came here protected against any persuasive powers, and we're prepared to die if that's what it takes to stop you. And believe me, we *can* stop you. Joey, Keith, get ready."

One of the two men bared his teeth in a pained grimace and shook two metal rods down from his sleeves. They melted to nothing in his hands, dripping flame to the ground. Fire seethed beneath his skin. The ability he held dammed behind his willpower would be as inexorable and relentless as an erupting volcano when he loosed it.

The other spread his arms wide and became a hole in the night. A searing white light flickered at the edges of the inky darkness of his form. The soap-shimmer of Grace's shield thinned and quivered near it.

Jack said, "Grace, that's looking like a breach. Can that guy hurt you?"

"No, but he will hurt the world when he breaks himself on me. And the three of them can hurt all of you. I'm sorry. I didn't want it to come to this."

"We always knew it might. Guess we'll just have to hold them off as long as we can."

Rock crunched, and Jack came past Valerie without looking down. The power he carried made his passage feel like a mountain walking by.

He held a baton in one hand and swung a wicked length of chain in the other. "Amy, can you cover the weak spot?"

"On it. Val, what do you see?"

Valerie couldn't *do* much to help, but she could share what her ability revealed about their opposition. "The one is a bottomless pit sucking in rollover energy, and the other—is he pulling lava up from the Earth's core? He is."

Valerie said bitterly, "You call those two sustainable, Adele? Their powers are more acceptable than Grace's? Really?"

The woman gestured vaguely. "Their ranges are limited to touch, for one thing. And someone has to save the world from people like Grace." Adele's cool façade frayed, tearing on sharp points of fear and rising anger. "Stop using your victims to speak to me, bitch. Why do Gaias all do that?"

After a fraught pause, Amy said, "Wow. And you think Grace is the crazy one?"

She placed herself to block the weakening shield. "Okay, I'm set. Kris, you're okay with nanny duty?"

"I am." Kris set down Elena and loomed over Valerie. "Get behind me, both of you."

Valerie gratefully took shelter behind one of the Tee's substantial legs. Elena snorted. "Get behind you so you can die first?"

She stomped right up to the shield at Jack's right side. Her pink rain boots squeaked and squished as she went, and she planted her hands on her hips as she glared at Adele. "Grace never attacked or hurt anyone until you came after her. Whatever happens here will be your fault. You aren't being fair."

"And you're a mindless puppet. Maybe I should pity you, but you caused this, you and your stupid celebrity influence and your naïve ideas."

Adele backed away, and stones lifted from the ground around her. Her companions moved in and forward, bracketing her. She flexed her fingers, and the stones hovering around her rose higher. "Last chance for leniency. If you make us fight you, we won't hold back."

"Fine. I surrender." Grace smoothed one hand down the front of her silky white dress and regarded her now-clean feet with a tiny, wistful frown.

Her shield vanished. Valerie's ears popped as the air on both sides of the dome equalized.

Adele waved her men forward. "Take them all out."

"You liar!" Elena took a step forward. "She surrendered. You promised!"

"Shut *up*." A cloud of Adele's orbiting stones zipped forward. Jack lunged to block them, and so did Amy, but they were both too late. Elena's head snapped back, her body jerked and shuddered, and she fell limp to the ground.

Part of Valerie's heart fell with her. A little voice in her head said, *this is all your fault,* and all she could see was the puzzled look on Elena's face, the small dark hole in her forehead. "No!" she cried out.

She took a step forward without thinking. Kris cursed and moved to shield her.

The air filled with stones again. The missiles made a clatter like Gary shaking his piggy bank, and for every one that bounced off Kris's armor, three more jinked and dove around her.

Tiny fists punched Valerie hard in the back and the gut. The shocks sent her to her knees without the breath to scream at the pain of it. Her hands went to her middle before her brain said—*no, don't touch*—and then she was floating above herself, above everyone, watching a nightmare unfold.

Below, her broken body lay sprawled, holed clean through, insides spilling out.

Grace knelt beside her, hands clasped together, rocking in place. Spreading blood stained the skirt of her dress black.

Amy roared, charging past Elena's motionless form. A graceful pivot took her beyond the darker-than-black adversary standing between her and Adele, while Jack brought his baton and chain to bear on the other man. Kris went sprinting after her friends.

Retribution was nearly in their grasp when it all fell apart.

Jack's adversary raised both glowing, heat-rippling arms and caught both of Jack's weapons in the parry. The batons sheared off and went flying, trailing molten droplets. Then Adele made a gripping motion and swung Jack aloft with her raw kinetic power. She held him aloft and smirked at him.

Amy sent the shadowy energy-sucker crashing to the ground with a powerful flick of her tail. A blaze of power erupted from her skin at the point of contact and streamed into the void. More and more energy poured from her into him. Her body shrank and changed shape, and she lost her balance as she lost mass.

She was naked and merely human when she staggered into the lava-caller's waiting arms. Her flesh lit up like a burning torch everywhere they touched. She dropped in a smoking, charred heap, and the lava-caller spun just in time to meet Kris's howling arrival.

Her staff jabbed forward and buried itself deep into his body, dripping slag as it impaled him. He screamed, high and thin, but he shoved himself forward, and Kris dropped her weapon an instant too late. His hands plunged into her abdomen.

Armored skin burst into flames, muscle and bone boiled away. Kris fought on, ravaging him with tooth and claw until the shadow walked up behind her and touched her leg with a single finger. Her ashes blew away on the heat of their combustion, rising above the eviscerated, smoldering corpse of her opponent.

Adele lowered Jack slowly, still smiling, and brought him within reach of her remaining ally. A small, bloody corpse dropped to the ground an instant later. She spat on it.

Then she directed the shadow to advance on Grace and followed at a judicious distance.

Grace lifted a tear-streaked face at their arrival. "For what it's worth, I'm sorry for what's to come," she said calmly into the face of the abyss. "I hope you find peace."

Adele's eyes narrowed. "Don't bother with mind games," she said. "You can't reach him. No one can."

"No. They took everything from him, even his name." She held out her hand. "Hello, Joey, Sternbach. I'll remember your name in my prayers."

Their fingers touched. Energy gushed free, but instead of draining Grace, it roared up between them like a firestorm, feeding on itself and growing, spinning outward in an ever-expanding circle.

The chaos swept up corpses and soil and shredded Adele to atoms. It scoured the earth down to bedrock as far as the horizon before it exploded up and out, carrying Valerie's perspective with it. Distance bestowed an eerie, terrible beauty on the destruction.

Intricate patterns of fire sprang to life, and sparkling lights of human habitation went dark. Clouds of debris roiled up, brilliantly lit from within. Daylight broke around the far curve of the Earth, and details sprang to life in the glow of the dawn's advance.

Grace's bright storm of destruction subsided and sank when it reached the rippled black lengths of the Ohio and the Mississippi rivers. It came to a standstill in whorls of turbulence over the Great Lakes to the north, and it piled up in a perfectly straight line short of the rounded Appalachian range.

The churning maelstrom took the only direction left to it and came shooting straight up. Chaos enveloped Valerie, and everything just—stopped.

42: IT PLEASES THE EYES TO SEE THE SUN

Near Elgin IL

VALERIE WAS LYING on the ground—embodied, whole, and thoroughly disoriented. Someone's dirty toes and a clump of muddy grass were the only things in her line of sight.

She scrambled upright to stand swaying beside Grace, who now wore a clean, white sleeveless dress. The woman's expression was distracted, as if she was listening to a distant conversation. A blush painted her cheeks rosy pink, and a pleased smile played around her lips.

She glowed from within.

Dawn kissed the horizon behind her, a line of pink-gold glimpsed between black silhouettes of trees. The brightening sky cast fairy highlights onto a of night-touched prairie landscape. Birds peeped and burbled in their hidden nests, and a cool breeze rustled through the sweetly scented leaves and grasses.

Leaves? Trees? *Birds?*

"What is going on?" Valerie asked.

Grace's blush deepened. "Everything and nothing."

Trees and grass were not the only mysteries to process. Nearby, Elena now lay on her side in a bed of soft grass. The dark hair spilling from the hood of her shiny raincoat framed a serene, sleeping face unblemished by any wound.

Jack made an even more unlikely Sleeping Beauty. He was flat on his back on a bier of stones surrounded by short green grass. His kilt was tangled in his legs, and his mouth hung open far enough to show off fangs and emit snores.

Kris wobbled to her feet from a patch of sunflowers near him, gaining height and armor before she paused and looked around. She lifted the edge of the clean, pastel-blue kaftan she was inexplicably wearing, then shook her head.

A naked man lay pinned beneath a thorny bush beside her. Kris made a face at him, then slogged through the wildflowers toward Amy's huge, dragon-like form. The Marine was all but hidden by blooming roses

Much closer was Adele—alive and without visible injury—fenced in by tall thistles at Grace's side. Burrs stuck to the bureaucrat's graying hair and clung to her suit jacket. The tall thorny plants had her neatly imprisoned.

Her face was ashy-white. "But you're—why aren't we all dead?"

Valerie pressed one palm to her belly and found it whole even as she remembered it torn open. The visions of what she had witnessed as she lay dying made her head spin.

She had died. Everyone had died. *Was it an illusion? Is this real?*

When the vertigo cleared, her sight finally came into proper focus.

The barren, shattered stones she had seen dissolving into fiery chaos were still there, below all the rich vegetation. They pulsed beneath the vibrant, complex web of living things above them. The bones of the land shimmered with power.

Grace's power.

Valerie stopped short of touching Grace's arm. "It wasn't a dream. All that destruction was real."

Grace nodded somberly. "Yes."

"How?" *How am I alive? How can any of us be alive?*

Grace shrugged. "I'm a conduit. I reached my full capacity in time to cleanse that poor boy's energy and add it to mine. Then I put it to better uses."

She walked up to Adele, and her expression turned harsh and tight. "Do you understand your error now? You could crack open the earth's crust from here to Pittsburgh and suck the life from every living thing between here and Saint Louis, but I would remain. You cannot end me. *Do you see?*"

"Yes," Adele mouthed without a sound.

"Good. I am not God to punish you for your sins, but if you and your masters do not change course, you will be obliterated. You have been warned. The murders must stop."

"But even if I wanted—I—we'll be in no position to do anything once we report we failed here." Adele glanced at her naked, sleeping minion, smoothed down her hair, plucked a thistle from it with a grimace. "I'm as good as dead."

"Not if you claim victory," Grace told her. "Tell the world you destroyed me. Who will argue the point? Not me. Once I'm out of sight, you may change your spots and work for change or suffer the consequences. That will be your choice."

"Wait—if you could disappear, why didn't you?" Adele's eyes went wide. "Before—" she fumbled for words, then waved broadly. "All this?"

Green fire flickered high around Grace. "Because I couldn't," she said, adding a punch of sadness to the words so powerful it carved a hole in Valerie's heart. "Not then. I've been stalling for time since the night I passed midpoint—the night your agent defected. I could have hidden before today, but innocents would have suffered. Now, I have the power to erase my tracks and protect those I leave behind."

A jet rumbled high overhead in the lightening sky. Adele frowned, eyes narrowed. Valerie could see she was confused, trapped in a tangle of clashing thoughts, but why?

Grace leaned closer to Valerie, a wry smile lifting her lips. "She can't get past the idea that I was still rolling when I passed my safety certification tests. It was easy to hide my light under a bushel, really."

Adele shook her head. "Don't joke about it. You're only proving Gaias are psychopathic monsters who can't be trusted."

"Says the woman so steeped in deceit she's lost her own name." It was a gentle rebuke Grace plucked a handful of rocks from the ground, set them spinning mid-air. "We both know your precious rules would have led to millions dying instead of dozens if I'd been honest while I was still vulnerable. None of this—" she flung both arms wide, and with a crack of sound, the stones became puffs of dust "—had to happen. Every death I could not prevent is on your head."

Adele cringed when the rocks exploded, but when nothing else happened, she raised her chin in defiance. "Take your revenge on me, then. You are an obscenity, and my only regret is that I failed to stop you."

The ugliness of Adele's unswerving devotion to procedures and policies made Valerie's eyes sting. Would she see the same ugliness in her mirror if she kept to the path she was on? She breathed in the damp, cool taste of dying grass and turned earth and rejected that future with all her might.

She would turn down a different path.

Grace told Adele, "Death was never my goal, only yours. You

did fail, and I am grown beyond your reach, bent and twisted, but whole."

"Bent?" Valerie echoed the word, and then understanding came on a sinking sense of shame. "The violence hurt you."

"How could it not?" Grace sighed. "Our experiences shape us. I will never be what I might have been if I'd been spared that battle."

"And I took the orders to Gateway." The enormity of her mistake turned Valerie's insides to water and turned her veins to ice. "I am so, so sorry."

"No." Grace took Valerie's face in her hands. "I told you, no more apologies."

Her brown gaze was a muddy, flooding river of bitterness, but it was not drowning deep. Her thumb brushed Valerie's cheek, wiping away a tear. "We are heart-sisters. You were forced to the breaking point and beyond, and you've paid your penance. Rest in God's love and grow stronger in the broken places."

Adele scoffed. "Please. Spare us the pious bullshit."

Grace turned on her, and Valerie raised a hand against the glory of her aura as she wrapped herself in raw power. The Special Directives agent went from sneering to groveling in a heartbeat. She lay face to the dirt, arms protecting her head, and Grace's voice made the ground shudder.

"There aren't enough apologies in the universe for you or the other smug hypocrites who hoard power and blame your victims for their starvation. You are so steeped in corruption you can't smell the rot. Clean your house and repair it before it falls down around you. Or don't. Your future is out of my hands. I'm done with you."

Thunder rumbled, and light crackled across the bowl of the sky. A flight of birds rose, whirled, and settled again in the nearby trees.

In the silence, Adele struggled up to her knees, wiped mud from her pale cheeks. "Where will you go when you disappear?"

"Nowhere you will ever find me." Grace smiled. "Nowhere at all, really."

Energy saturated the air again, an intangible leviathan whose passage shook Valerie's bones inside her skin as it circled round and round. The glowing force trailed fiery lines through the earth and squeezed sparks from the sky.

Grace captured one tiny speck between two fingers.

The air around her swelled with an unbearable majesty of power. The strength of it filled Valerie's mouth and throat until she was breathless with it. Her eyes filled with tears, but she could not move a muscle against the pressure. Groans came from the others as they struggled, and Elena whimpered, stirring in her sleep.

Grace lifted her chin. "Go in peace," she said, and she flicked the spark in her hand at Adele like a child snapping a rubber band.

The other woman flung herself facedown again, and the firefly-speck passed over her, arcing into the distance. It vanished, and the world heaved and whirled, turning itself inside out.

When Valerie's vision cleared, Grace was gone.

43: A TIME TO DIE, A TIME TO BE BORN

Near Elgin IL

THE AIR CLOAKED itself around Grace with giggles and whispers, bending itself this way and that to hide her from human senses and mechanical sensors. So easy to coax atoms to her bidding.

Now what? she asked the wide world.

Move, the stillness told her without words, and her power shook her until every cell strained to channel it. She would know the place when she came to it, and then she could rest and let go all her mortal concerns.

No sooner did she take a step than she was surprised again, this time by a most unexpected greeting.

Hello, sister. The words came as a sigh of air, a faint buzz of insect wings, a splash of clean, cool water—a distant presence sending echoes of itself to knock on the door of Grace's soul. She rubbed her hands over her skin, and her belief that she was unique crumbled to dust, leaving her heart free to swell with clean, new joys.

"I am not alone!" She gave words to her astonishment, and the heavy weight of solitude lifted from her spirit like a fog rising. She shivered in awe at the futures her new knowledge revealed. *"Not alone!"*

Her happy laugh startled a flock of starlings into the sky. "Hello, oh, hello!" she cried, and she spun in giddy circles until her dress caught around her legs and her hair whipped free.

Past friends and old enemies glanced up, startled anew by the birds' abrupt flight, but they didn't hear Grace's voice, nor would they ever again, unless she chose. She was beyond them now, beside and apart. *But not by myself, ah, thank you, God, for this wondrous gift!*

This was not the place to pursue revelations. Not while the temptation to meddle in other lives was still so sharp, and her own wants were so hard to separate from the world's needs. She took herself farther from fast-beating hearts and fragile bodies, dancing light over quicksilver grass, under the waking trees, through stone and water.

Each step brought her closer to the particular spot where the world waited ready to introduce her to her final, natural form. G1-C. The idea of inhuman variance was no longer a fearful thing. It felt right and proper.

Each breath she took lifted her heart higher.

Life rolled and purred, responding to her happiness with demanding thumps and tugs. *Me. Now. THIS.* The energy pushed at the inside of her skin, strained the center of her bones, eager to escape. She let its tendrils catch hold of blossom and twig as she walked on, hurrying because it felt so good to scatter herself wide like this.

The buzzing-crackling-splashing presence followed her. Its warm, amused sense of familiarity was a companionable resonance. *You are not the first to know this exaltation. With luck, you will not be the last.*

"This is a wonder," Grace replied. "I am glad beyond words to know you exist. I thought I was the only one."

You feared isolation, said another new voice, *and rightly so. Welcome.*

This presence carried darkness in its depths, a lowing of cattle and a furry sense of a jostling herd. Grace shivered at the stony reach of its strength, licked the taste of metal and dust off her lips. "Hello to you too, brother. Did I see truth when I saw a dead and cindered world, or was that madness?"

Until you survived to meet us, you could see only the worlds without us. Those futures—they came to be in other spheres of creation.

She bit her lip. And Amy had accused *her* of being cryptic. "How many of us are there?"

The bright glitter of dew on a distant mountainside chortled: *More than you knew.*

Dark, bitter surf roared in her ears, and thick, wet strands of weed rippled in grief: *Far fewer than should be.*

A chill reverberation finished with the boom of ice cracking into thaw: *We are enough.*

And into the silence that followed, eternity whispered: *NOW.*

Grace stopped where she stood, turning away from the sunrise breaking warm and bright, gazing over shadowed brambles and old trees busy with the business of leaf and acorn.

And she was afraid, but her heart answered, *I am here.*

Her body ached and twisted in the grip of the power coursing free now, between *elsewhere* and *everywhere.* It was ecstasy to surrender all she had gained, to let the world bend her to its will and accept its full and final embrace.

The rush slowed and spread into a wide, quiet flow, spreading in a million tiny capillaries that connected her to the universe, steadying it and her. When the change was done, she was heavy with exhaustion but light of heart. The clamoring in her mind was gone, and the peaceful quiet crooned a lullaby.

She settled and stretched with a sleepy yawn. Her sturdy new body rustled as she shifted.

They'd thought her trapped in a shell at the start of her rollover, but no. She had been a seed, then a fragile seedling blown on winds of change, and now she was rooted safe and deeply.

She raised knotted branches to the sky and wondered, *But am I human still?*

Oh, how they laughed, her new sisters and brothers.

She would be human so long as she remembered flesh, and how would she forget that when the teeming world would forever remind her? *Try,* the breeze urged. *Play.*

The way of it came to her like remembering someone's name, impossible until the knowledge was there. She remade herself, examined her hands and feet. The shape was too limited, too *small,* but it would suffice for short periods.

She pulled her hair forward to see its frizzy ends. She'd made it mousy brown and lank, the same as it ever was. When next she wished to walk clothed flesh, maybe she would play more. This was enough for now.

She hugged contentment to herself and watched the sun rise higher with human eyes until she chafed within the restraint of skin and bone. Then she flung her power wide and expanded into her fullness again. *Ah. Much better.*

Sleep beckoned. The pulse of the soil was a welcome melody, the morning sun was gentle and full of life, and she was so very tired.

"Rest," her brothers and sisters urged. *"Let time run without care. Grow, heal, learn the dance of seasons and the many songs of life. We will keep watch with you."*

Before she let herself drift off, she stretched into the world once more, itching to fix small details. She might regret those decisions later, but future consequences were no match for present guilt.

She couldn't rest easy until she had done all she could to repair the pain left in her wake.

Last, she reached out to kiss her sleeping daughters and breathe in the scent of their lives —a sweet memory to keep her company in dreams to come—and to caress her beloved with the merest touch of all the joy she had to give. He could not bear more.

"Come and visit me," was the whisper she left in their hearts. *"You'll know when."*

44: AND THEY WILL THRIVE LIKE GREEN LEAVES

Early November 2019, in and around Elgin IL

ELENA SHOWED up on Jack's doorstop on at 9 A.M. sharp with a gift-wrapped box in her hands, a wreath of orange flowers hanging over the arm of her stylish gray raincoat, and a determined smile on her face.

The raincoat and the smile both made him want to break things. First, he had only a few clear memories of the night Elena's previous raincoat had gotten riddled with holes—none of them recalled much—but he remembered seeing her dead. Thinking about it made him twitchy and angry. Second, he was tired of people smiling and pretending things were fine when they weren't.

"What do you want?" he asked.

Elena's eyebrows went up. The awful fake-happy expression vanished. "Wow, hello to you too. I'm okay, thanks for asking. Not good, but okay. How's the dying going?"

That was better. That was his Elena, the one who wasn't afraid to tackle him head-on.

"It's going okay." Jack opened the door wider to invite her inside, out of the soggy drizzle. "Sorry, tiger. I'm getting grumpy about people dropping by to check on me."

"You say it like caring is a bad thing." She marched over to the folding chair he kept for infrequent visitors, tripped on it, then sat down.

Jack bumped up the lighting level for her. For once, she didn't remark on the untidiness of his place. She also didn't comment on his appearance. He asked, "Shouldn't you be in a class somewhere? Are you ever going to college?"

"I took a deferral. I won't lose my scholarship if I wait a semester. After Grace, and then the hearings, and then you..." The haunted darkness in her eyes gave the lie to her casual shrug. "I need time to get my head together."

"But you aren't checking up on me."

"No, it's All Saints Day. I was wondering if you would come along on my field trip this year. Please?"

That was the problem with being on terminal leave. He'd lost track of the date. It was November. Every year on the day after Halloween, Elena did community service work in old cemeteries. Most of her friends, Jack included, made sure they had work obligations that day that would interfere with the fun of scrubbing some stranger's headstone.

He hated cemeteries, and he didn't see the appeal of working outside on a cold, wet autumn morning.

Declining invitations from friends meant coming up with legitimate excuses. He was running out of those. "I'm busy."

"Busy doing what? Sleeping all day? You aren't even dressed."

"It isn't like I get cold." He had only put on trousers in a concession to the likelihood of interruptions like this one. He gave a significant look at the recliner where he'd been settling in for another day of living vicariously through other peoples' fictional adventures. "I have plans."

"You are such a liar. Pretty-please? I'm prepared to bribe you."

She handed over the box. Jack grabbed his sunglasses before accepting it and sitting down. The wrapping paper might look good to someone who didn't see up and down the spectrum as far as he did, but the gaudy pattern made his eyes water. He slid a nail under the ribbon to slice it off and carefully unsealed the paper, handing both over to Elena for safekeeping.

"You're allowed to tear it open," she said. "That's half the fun."

"For you, maybe." The scents of sugar and cocoa wafted up from the open box. Jack burst out laughing at the contents: chocolate skulls decorated with flowers, white skulls wearing foil hats painted in dots and swirls, and frosting versions of the flowers Elena had draped on the chair back. "You are one of a kind, tiger. Everyone else is bending over backward to avoid talking about death. You're giving me candy corpses and inviting me on a graveyard trip."

Elena grinned, but she also got the wrinkle between her eyebrows that meant she was concerned. "You aren't offended, are you? Mama and Papa are going all the way with Day of the Dead this year, and sugar skulls are traditional gifts. Skeletons too, and little gravestones, but I had to draw the line somewhere."

"I'm touched, to be honest. I don't know what Day of the Dead is, but you win. I'll come wash graves and rake leaves with you."

While he put on more clothes, Elena delivered one of her meandering lectures about religious holidays and some kind of cultural-roots renewal. He let it run in one ear and out the other as usual. The cheerful trivia made a refreshing change from the awkward social chatter he'd been enduring for weeks now.

The way people treated him like an invalid was driving him wild. People wanted to visit, but they spent the whole time acting like he might fall apart if they said the wrong thing. Or they talked like he was already gone.

He might be dying faster now, but he wasn't dead yet, damn it. And he sure as hell wasn't fragile. The worst part was that none of them would admit they were visiting now in case he died before they got another chance.

Valerie couldn't even look at him. The last time he'd seen her, she'd gone all blotchy-faced and stared at the floor the whole time he was in the same room. That had been a month ago. They'd all been giving depositions about the night Grace officially died.

Not that Jack believed the public story for an instant.

The powers that be could swear up and down that the Gateway training range had been restored to the virgin prairie and oak savannah of a previous century by Grace's death energy, but that didn't explain why the land *kept* repairing itself —which it was doing.

During the same hearings, Amy had asked him if he'd heard about the range. He had, of course. Rumors traveled. The damages from every exercise the Marines ran on the property now disappeared overnight. It was an open secret, a bit of inexplicable good fortune none of the locals questioned for fear of losing it.

Amy had asked, he'd shrugged, and they'd avoided discussing the possibility that Grace was involved. Sal knew more than he was saying, too. The man had said all the right grieving things, but he wasn't a great liar, and his daughters were worse. Not one of them believed Grace was dead any more than Jack did.

"Who's included in *us*?" he asked as he locked his door. He'd had enough of the Reed family for ten lifetimes, but Elena liked everybody. "And which cemetery are you working?"

"I'll ride so I can give you directions. Take us to Camp Butler's front gate first. We're meeting Amy and some other people there." She pulled up her hood against the continuing rain and headed for her car. "I like the salt and pepper look, by the way. In case you wondered."

So she had noticed. His hair was more than half gray now. White strands outnumbered black ones, and new ones turned every day. Jack let the subject drop rather than get into a conversation that was sure to go wrong.

They spent the drive talking about how happy Elena was that the Corps hadn't sanctioned Amy for the whole Grace incident. Like most civilians, Elena equated the phrase court-martial with "found guilty" instead of "on trial." It had taken the board less than an hour of sequestered classified document review to clear Amy and close the file.

When they got to Camp Butler, Amy met them at the guard shack and waved them to the visitor's lot. Four other people stood waiting by a Tee-friendly off-road transport there: Gabe, Shelly, Yasu, and Kris.

Amy had reason to be here. She was off-duty, in her civvie skirt and halter, but she worked on base. The others, dressed in puffy layers and rain gear, did not. None of them even lived in the same state. Last Jack had heard, Gabe was down in Florida taking care of family, but there the man was, a good few pounds thinner, beardless and sun-tanned.

Jack tamped down on a nervous urge to power up. If there was danger here, it wasn't one his strength would solve. "What kind of game are you playing?" he asked Elena as they parked. "There's no cemetery on base, and that transport isn't street legal."

"It's a surprise party, obviously. Don't pester me. Amy said to get you here. I don't know any more than that. I suppose she persuaded everyone else like she asked me to persuade you."

Elena was looking smug and more than a little sad. Both emotions made Jack suspicious. "This isn't some kind of weird intervention thing, is it?"

"Nope. I asked that. Trust her, please? I do."

When she turned up the power on that pleading expression of hers, what else could he do? "Fine."

Everyone piled into the transport and attempted the kind of cheery conversations about nothing that made Jack's temper run short. He tuned out the excuse Gabe used when he said to call him *Mike*. It took shaking the man's hand to make him pay closer attention.

Prime level energy leaked from the old man like fog pouring off dry ice. His grip was cold, his eyes colder, and his tight smile wasn't jolly. It was a warning. *Don't ask.*

It didn't take a genius to recognize that *Gabe* must have been a fake identity. Mike was a lot more powerful than he'd let on. Jack accepted the warning at face value. He didn't have the patience left to worry about other people's dramas, and Mike's story was his business.

Unless he was a threat.

"How long are you in town?" Jack asked. If the man was staying, some hard questions would have to be asked and answered.

Mike's mouth relaxed into a more-familiar grin. "Just today. I got a call, and Amy arranged a lift from Shells. I believe I now owe her my firstborn or my soul. Relax. If I can enjoy a picnic, you can try."

That sounded like the man Jack had known. And Amy wouldn't have allowed the man on-base if she thought it would endanger anyone. Jack accepted Mike's joking reassurance and got through the rest of the pointless greet-and-chat with everyone as politely as possible.

When they loaded up, he took the front seat to get away from all the family talk. Elena didn't let him escape, scrunching herself into the space between the front bucket seats. And Amy remarked, "You're getting snowy up top, Jackass."

"I know. Don't tease me about it."

The glare she gave him in reply was pure staff sergeant and zero teasing. Her dorsal spines and horns were painted in swirly rainbow hues today, but that didn't detract from the force of the non-verbal warning: *Keep an eye on it.*

He nodded: *I will.*

Elena glanced between them, catching the tension but ignorant of the reason because it wasn't a thing they talked about. Not with nulls. "I think he looks very distinguished," she said.

Jack had never paid much attention to hair until recently. When Tees rolled, most kept some hair on top of their heads and lost all the rest, which was no more ridiculous than being able to eat bricks. He'd kept his trimmed short and ignored it as the pointless decorative accessory it was.

Now that it was going gray, he couldn't ignore it. The color change was the closest thing to an early-warning system an aging Tee got. By the time his hair went all white, his physical control would be waning. Before that happened, he would need to pick a final resting place far from anyone he could possibly harm in his final flareout.

A Tee without self-control was a destructive juggernaut. He didn't look distinguished, he looked old and dangerous.

Amy kept teasing him about taking a trek into the Andes or up Everest. Kris suggested a world cruise and a panic button to 'port someplace in the middle of the ocean. They'd both obviously done planning for their futures. Jack didn't like either option. He didn't like mountains or swimming. Mostly, he didn't like thinking about dying.

He couldn't ignore his hair, he couldn't ignore the constant joint aches, and he definitely couldn't ignore the nausea that floored him whenever he tried to rise into rampage. The signs were clear: his body was burning itself out. Death was tapping him on the shoulder.

It bothered him more than he'd expected, given he'd known for ages he wouldn't live to see thirty. He slumped down in his seat. "This ride had better not be an excuse for more help-Jack-deal-with-mortality bullshit."

The remark got him an eye roll from Elena, and Amy said, "It's a picnic, Jackass. Don't get paranoid. And don't flip out when I turn onto the test range. It's closed all week for a science research project, and we have clearance from ten to sunset."

The test range? His memory hiccupped, coughing up a sensory jumble of pain, rage, despair. The impressions slid from consciousness like oil off metal, and he let them go. "A picnic in the cold and rain?"

"Sit back and stop whining," Amy said.

The ride was quiet, the large space inside the vehicle full of things not said and feelings not expressed. Outside the windows, the late autumn scenery passed in a steady parade of browns and tans. An occasional flash of green marked undergrowth late to the fall party. Birds startled up in flocks and settled again in bare trees.

A graded gravel road took them through patches of meadow and trees. They went by clusters of trucks. Bustling crews in cold weather gear were sampling this and that.

According to Amy, so many academics wanted to study the renewed ecosystem that there was talk of turning the southwest portion of the rang into a nature preserve. That was the section they would be visiting today.

Elena chatted with Gabe-sorry-Mike and Shelly about native plants and the wildlife population, which was apparently high. The truck's passage flushed out squirrels, rabbits, a fox family, and two coyotes. A thick-necked buck deer challenged them for right of way for a few mad seconds.

Jack had been over every foot of this property hundreds of times. He'd memorized the map. It still took him most of the ride to see familiar bones beneath the new mantle of life.

Memories swelled and receded again. He had *died* here, weeks past. His body remembered. So did Kris, Elena, and Amy, judging from their somber expressions and the way conversation drifted into silence.

When the road ended, Amy parked and organized the distribution of several day packs, then led the way down a path of trampled undergrowth into the woods.

The clouds lifted, washing away to a hazy yellow sunlight that cast long slanting shadows. Colors sprang out bold and sharp everywhere as the day brightened and warmed. *I guess we'll have nice weather after all.*

They spread along the trail in singles and pairs. Amy swapped stories with Kris, Yasu and Shelly held hands like kids, and Elena skipped along after Mike-suits-you-better-than-Gabe like a small, bouncy shadow. Jack let them pull ahead while he placed their position on his mental map.

Soon they would be coming over a fold in the land to a curve of bluff overlooking the river. Low clumps of yellowed undergrowth and green brambles huddled against ranks of gnarled trees. Some were bare-branched in gray or brown, but more were clinging to their brown and russet leaves. Jack couldn't process it all. This whole zone had been a mess of burnt, bare limestone and pitted stony soil when he'd last seen it before his discharge.

A high sound like birds calling caught his attention. He

tensed up. The southern edge of the range wasn't near enough to be overhearing kids in playgrounds or dogs barking in yards.

The laughter and squeals came closer. Amy stopped near the top of a rise and put her hands on her hips. A fluffy brown animal charged over the crest of the hill, barking wildly as it dodged past Amy and continued down the trail. The dog was hotly pursued by two small fair-haired boys and a little girl with bouncing black braids who looked like Heather's daughter.

Sure enough, Heather herself popped into sight above and ahead of the hunt. She dropped down to grab the dog with the grace of a stooping hawk, then landed and flipped back her wings, holding the dog's collar tight while she listened to some loud and garbled explanation from the children.

Then she chivvied the whole gaggle back the way they'd come. Two older girls joined them on the trail near Amy and Elena. One of the teens had a larger, better-behaved dog on a leash. Jack's heart did a weird clutchy jump inside his rib cage when the girl waved to him. *That's Maggie Reed.*

She and Lauren bounced excitedly as they spoke to Elena. Valerie and Sal joined them a moment later, out of breath, carrying a cooler and a rolled-up blanket between them. Heather's husband Donyel brought up the rear, saying something to Amy that looked apologetic.

And that was when Jack realized the boys with Heather must be Valerie's sons. This wasn't an ambush. It was a reunion.

And Mike had said he didn't do reunions, the liar.

But why were they having a reunion *here*? As soon as Jack asked himself the question, he stepped off the trail and headed over the rise on his own. If he was wrong, he didn't want anyone watching his disappointment.

The noise of everyone else coming together in a big cluster of hellos and hugs rose behind him, pushing him on.

The west side of the hill displayed more of the woodsy

scenery he'd seen on the east side—brambles and dry weeds wending through a forest halfway to winter—but one difference stood out. At the edge of an open stretch of grass, one tree rose high above the rest, its spreading branches richly dressed in red-brown leaves. The foliage glowed in the hazy daylight, and the tree's higher branches stretched to embrace the sky.

Jack didn't know how long he stood there, soaking in the details. He jumped in surprise when Valerie spoke from behind him, saying, "She's magnificent, isn't she?"

"That is her, isn't it?" He turned. "I'm not imagining things. That's what happened to Grace. After."

"Yes." Today Valerie was looking at him. Like Elena, she had dark circles under her eyes, and her face was puffy and droopy around her chin. She blinked rapidly, tears welling up. But she didn't look away. "She's happy, you know. This is a better outcome than most of the other possibilities."

"She's a tree. How can you know what she's feeling?"

"I can see it, of course." Valerie gave him one of her down-the-nose up-at-him looks, and that made Jack feel better than he had in weeks.

Then Val said, "I am sorry. I've needed to say that to you. I have such horrible memories. And dreams. The dreams are better. She cushioned things for you, she told me in one of them, but I didn't want—I'm bearing witness, she calls it. I remember it all. If you ever need to ask about that night."

He grimaced to keep from snarling. He didn't want apologies. He didn't want anyone to suffer. "Let it go, Val. We all did what we thought was right. If you want to make it up to me, stop acting like I'm dead already. I like you better when you act like you have a backbone."

She laughed and wiped away tears. "All right. I'll try."

Amy and Elena joined them, Elena jogging along to keep up with Amy's long strides.

Jack asked Amy, “How long have you known she was here?”

“I came across her on an exercise weeks ago. It was like she said hello to me inside. You know, goddess shit.” Amy picked a flake of polish off a dorsal spine. “I went back to my place and mentioned it to Sal, and he says, *‘I know,’* in this smug asshole voice. After I stopped yelling at him, I offered to get him clearance to see her. Things kinda snowballed.”

“She looks happy,” Elena said, and she slid her hand into Jack’s and squeezed hard. “Beautiful and alive. I’m glad for that. And I’m glad you got to see her.”

“She’s a tree. It’s not like we’re hugging,” he said, but his heart knew better, and when Valerie pushed him, he approached Grace as softly as he could walk.

His boots still sank deep into the dark, wet soil, and he stopped. Would that hurt her?

Elena shoved him forward.

There was welcome under the shadows cast by those wide branches, and he inhaled peace with the spicy, cold scent of fallen leaves. He touched the rough, ragged lines of Grace’s trunk. A pulse of her power, slow as moving sunlight, rolled through him. He felt the earth sliding into quiet winter, busy with the work of life under the chill shell of decay. Rebirth.

Rage he hadn’t consciously recognized uncoiled and drained away, leaving him as empty and light inside as the cool air stirring around him. His eyes were no longer built to spill tears. He sniffled away the ache in his throat.

Elena patted his hand, and Valerie’s sad smile didn’t make him so angry now. Dying was no time to be alone.

He said, “Today—this took planning. The others weren’t leaving already, were they?”

Amy snorted. “You mean, did you scare them away by being your growly self? No chance. They’re setting out lunch. It’s warmer on that side of the ridge, and Sal thought you should get a chance to say hello to Grace without children screaming in your ears. I know we make you uncomfortable, but we want to be with you while we can."

"Thanks for that." He didn't know how to say he was afraid staying would make everyone else sad.

Amy aimed a thumb at the hillside. "So, anyway, I'm heading back before someone eats all the cupcakes. Are you bolting like a baby bunny, or will you hang out and make good memories for us to hold onto?"

That made the choice easy.

They made a lot of happy memories that day. The food was tasty, the scenery was beautiful in a bleak way, the weather was unseasonably warm, and everyone wanted to make it happy. The dogs were smart enough to leave Jack in peace, and the kids learned to do the same. The conversations got less awkward by the time they were packing up.

Everyone said their good-byes to Grace before leaving.

They were in the truck and halfway back to base when Amy said, "You know, if you really don't want to see the Andes before the end, there's a local place I can recommend."

She turned in the seat, all teeth and muscle mass and self-confidence. Jack bared fangs back at her. He didn't have the right words to say what he was feeling.

He couldn't imagine a better place to sit down and face eternity than leaning against Grace and watching the sun set.

But he wasn't ready yet.

"When the time comes," he said, "and not one minute sooner."

APPENDIX: POWERS & RANKINGS

The Department of Public Safety assigns a letter-number-letter classification to every R-factor positive citizen who rolls into an active power. The first letter designates a primary ability, the number gives an idea of its intensity relative to others with similar abilities, and the second letter indicates variations or secondary characteristics.

Additional letters—or doubled ones—are sometimes assigned for cataloging precision, but they are rarely noted outside official paperwork. (like the extra 4 digits in a zip code)

DPS staff with personal agendas or quotas to fill can bend definitions like pretzels to justify putting particular power manifestations into designations, and the whole set-up is vulnerable to misuse. Annual scientific conferences hold high-powered discussions about the need to revamp the whole system, but no one has come up with a better one.

This is an abbreviated list of common power classifications and a brief explanation of ratings and variant assignments.

I. Series Designations

A: not used
This letter is reserved for the secondary variant space. It indicates a "pure" specimen of a particular power. For example: someone classified P1A has pyrokinetic powers in the top power tier, but has no secondary powers such as telekinesis or air control, and no physical changes distinguish them from the non-powered population.

B: Perceptive
This covers powers like enhanced senses, or any inexplicable abilities to sense specific traits or conditions. The variant letters for this series narrow down the nature of the perception.

C: Carnie
This slang term(considered offensive) refers to any rollover who exhibits a radical change in physical appearance. Physically deviant individuals who exhibit other powers are assigned to that series, with a variant indicator.
Individuals assigned to a primary C-series designation are basically furry, scaled, or feathered people. (See also: S-series, T series.) This Hazardous Variant tables for C's runs several hundred pages long.

D: Doctor
Individuals who can cure—or cause—disease or injury by laying on of hands or by proximity or any number of other ways laid out in the variant listings for this series. Most of the higher power-class rollovers in this series can heal *and* harm at will.

E: Projective empaths and manipulative telepaths
Not as rare as the general public believes. Sequestered on discovery and treated as deadly threats until certified safe by specialized F-series psychics.

F: Fortuneteller.
Precognition, telepathy, receptive empathy and telepathy, and clairvoyance that isn't tied to a sensory element—most of the typical psychic powers. Why F? The first psychic identified was a precog, and by then someone had already assigned P, T, and E to more obvious, common, and dangerous powers.

G: Gaia
Second-rarest series. If something is alive, or organic, or…basically if a thing exists, a G-series can affect it in some way. Most G's do not survive the rollover transformation, falling prey to the overwhelming and distorting effects of their own powers.

H: Hydro. Water elementals.

I: not used. (yet)
Too easily confused with H or lowercase L

J: Jockey.
Animal and/or plant control and/or communication.

K: Kryptonite.
A rollover whose power negates other powers. Usually specific to another power series which would be indicated by the variant letter.

L: not used yet. *See I*

M: not used. W got assigned first.

N: Nature
All natural-world related powers that don't fall into any other designation, including some air-benders and weather-workers.

O: not used. Too hard to distinguish from zero or Q.

P: Pyro
Heat and flame elementals without a concurrent earth manifestation. Various manifestations of pyrokinesis.

Q: not used.

R: Earth-movers, magma-summoners and other stone or volcanic-based powers. R was chosen because the letter falls between P for pyrokinetic and S for seismic....and S had already been by the time the first R-series power was catalogued.

S: Superhuman
Enhanced strength, speed, senses, or any combination of the three. Also used as a variant letter for carnies who are also super-strong etc.

T: *see also carnie.* Troll.
Various manifestations of skin/ height/ muscle/ weight/ strength /hormonal changes. Most have enhanced senses, all can boot their strength, speed and regeneration to enhanced levels under stress.

U & V: not used.

W: Weird.
Telekinesis and teleportation in a variety of forms from personal and passenger movement or translocation to portal opening and summoning things/people from a distance.

Y: Like A, reserved for describing variants

Z: Elevated R-factor detected, but no power develops. The rarest of primary designations, only discovered/ added after the blood tests for rollover were invented.

II: Power ratings

A rating is only meaningful within a power series. There's no attempt to compare the "power" of, say, a B1 rollover who can see through foot-thick lead walls to the power of an R1 rollover who can measurably move a continent, or a W1 who can create a point-to-point teleportation gate big enough for a truck to drive through.

The number is assigned through a comprehensive set of objective tests. Results are compared to collected historical measurements, providing a consistent and impartial result.

A numeral one indicates the strongest manifestation if the designated ability series, a rating of zero means practically no sign of the ability indicated by the primary series letter can be detected.

The change in power between rating tiers is even, but the rollover population distributes unevenly into the space.

This, like primary series designations

III: Variant designation

Every power series has an alphabet's worth of variations, far too many combinations to detail in a simple work like this. Before databases, the catalogues required multiple bindings, like an old encyclopedia set or the Reader's Guide to Periodical Literature. The early inclusion of additional letters to define powers was a white flag of cataloging surrender by the system's creators. Here are some of the complexities:

Multiple abilities are more the norm than the exception, and some power series show more variation than others.

The variants are all series dependent—the same letter means different things connected to different primaries. J stands for "jump" attached to a W teleporter, meaning altitude control, but it means a medium weight restriction when applied to a W telekinetic, and something entirely different when attached to each of the assorted B sensory powers.

Each primary variant series has its own letter/number set of deviances, and some of *those* have variances.

Series and variant assignment still relies on subjective observation and human judgment as much as hard data.

All in all this a lousy cataloging system, but its limitations stem from its origins. The people who designed it never expected it to be *permanent*. Picture the poor doctors, police, doctors, firemen and air raid wardens tasked with organizing the thousands–even tens of thousands–of hysterical, confused rollovers on that first, dreadful night in the summer of 1943. Those first responders were working in total ignorance and facing a bewildering array of symptoms. An inspired few created quick-and-dirty rules of thumb to triage their charges as quickly as possible. Accuracy and precision were not priorities.

It worked well enough to be imitated and implemented on a

international scale before anyone with more sense could protest. The military and the scientific community adapted the flawed template to suit their needs and stamped it with their own flourishes, and the newborn Department of Public Safety chiseled it into the stone of bureaucracy.

It's unwieldy, and no one likes it, but unlike the Metric system (adopted by the US in 1969 and finalized in 1976 in this world) no one has come up with anything better yet. Or to be precise hundreds of excellent proposals have been offered up, but none have been effective enough to justify the upheaval and expense of changing now.

People being people, amateur cataloguers keep their eyes peeled for rare rollover types as diligently as any birdwatcher works on an Audubon life list. Trainspotters have nothing on monster buffs.

ABOUT THE AUTHOR

K. M. Herkes writes and publishes books that dance in the open spaces between science fiction and fantasy, specializing in stories about damaged souls, complicated lives, and triumphs of the spirit.

Professional development started with a Bachelor of Science degree in Biology and now includes experience in classroom teaching, animal training, aquaculture, horticulture, book-selling, and retail operations. Personal development is ongoing. Cats are involved.

When she isn't writing, she works at the Mount Prospect Public Library. She also digs holes in her backyard for fun, enjoys experimental baking, and wrangles butterflies.

Visit dawnrigger.com and check out extras like free short stories, story-inspired artwork, links to the author's social media, and blog rants on life, the universe, and writing. While you're there, sign up for rare Dawnrigger Publishing email alerts and get a subscriber-exclusive free short story .

MORE BOOKS BY K. M. HERKES

The Rough Passages Series:

Rough Passages

The Sharp Edge Of Yesterday

Stories of the Restoration:

(in recommended reading order)

Controlled Descent

Turning the Work*

Flight Plan

Joining In The Round*

Novices

*collected in paperback as *Weaving In the Ends*

CPSIA information can be obtained
at www.ICGtesting.com
Printed in the USA
LVHW020912170321
681674LV00004B/34

9 781945 745188